The story of Josephine C[...] in her novels. Born in [...] she was one of ten child[ren ...] out the worst in each o[...] without love and laughter. At the age of sixteen, Josephine met and married 'a caring and wonderful man', and had two sons. When the boys started school, she decided to go to college and eventually gained a place at Cambridge University, though was unable to take this up as it would have meant living away from home. However, she did go into teaching, while at the same time helping to renovate the derelict council house that was their home, coping with the problems caused by her mother's unhappy home life – and writing her first full-length novel. Not surprisingly, she then won the 'Superwoman of Great Britain' Award, for which her family had secretly entered her, and this coincided with the acceptance of her novel for publication.

Josephine gave up teaching in order to write full time. She says: 'I love writing, both recreating scenes and characters from my past, together with new storylines which mingle naturally with the old. I could never imagine a single day without writing, and it's been that way since as far back as I can remember.' Her previous novels of North Country life are all available from Headline and are immensely popular.

*Also by*
# JOSEPHINE COX

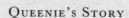

First published in 1998
by HEADLINE BOOK PUBLISHING

First published in paperback in 1998
by HEADLINE BOOK PUBLISHING

10 9 8 7 6 5 4 3 2 1

ISBN 0 7472 4959 8

Typeset by Palimpsest Book Production Limited,
Polmont, Stirlingshire
Printed and bound in Great Britain by
Clays Ltd, St Ives plc

HEADLINE BOOK PUBLISHING
A division of Hodder Headline PLC
338 Euston Road
London NW1 3BH

# JOSEPHINE COX

# *Love Me Or Leave Me*

HEADLINE

# DEDICATION

When I was signing in Leicester last year, two lovely sisters came to see me.

One of them brought something to show me, and we had a wonderful talk, and a good cry as well.

I know they read all my books so are bound to read this.

Please get in touch. I'm so anxious to know how you got on.

# CONTENTS

# PART ONE

---

# JULY 1954
# THE FARM

# Chapter One

BLIND WITH RAGE, he hit out. 'You're no bloody good!' The hook of his walking stick caught her hard on the temple, splitting the skin and sending dark blood down her shocked face. 'You're too much like your mother!' he screamed. 'Useless. The pair of you.'

Through her pain, Eva looked at him, her quiet green eyes betraying nothing of what she felt. She didn't speak. She knew from bitter experience that to utter even one word would only send him into a greater fury. So, her heart pounding, she stood, head high, unflinching. Silently defiant.

Father and daughter faced each other as they had done so many times over the past two years. Many emotions passed between them: anger, love, guilt, and a sorrow too deep to voice.

He was the first to shift his gaze. 'Where is she?'

She turned away.

His voice followed her, low and threatening, 'Answer me, you bugger.'

She swung round and stared at him, her silence like a painful physical presence.

Momentarily subdued, he could not draw his gaze from hers. The quiet pride in those beautiful green eyes touched his heart. In spite of what she might believe, he had always loved her; always believed she was special. There was a time when his whole world centred round this lovely creature. Now, with her eyes on him, he felt like a criminal. Once she had smiled on him, and he on her. Once there was a close and unique bond between them. Now, there was nothing.

He remembered the child she had been, filled with the joys of life, delighting in all around her; he recalled the sound of her girlish laughter, the way her young eyes sparkled whenever she saw something new – a bright flower peeping through the ground after a hard winter, a glowing sunset that lit the sky with a halo of dazzling colour. And he would never forget the look on her face when he had let her cradle a newlaid chick in the palm of her tiny hand. How gentle and caring she had been, and how desperately he had loved that darling child.

The memories unfolded and the tears were close, but he pushed them deep inside himself. All that was a lifetime ago. Before the accident. Before he ceased being a man. God Almighty! Why did it have to happen? Life was cruel. But then so was he. He had turned his resentment on his wife and only child, tormenting and hurting them as if they were to blame when it was no more their fault than it was his. Guilt overwhelmed him. He alone had destroyed the wonder that lit her eyes.

In a soft, repentant voice that took her by surprise, he asked, 'Do you love me, Eva?'

She hesitated.

'The truth, mind,' he urged. 'I need to know.'

She lowered her gaze. She never wanted to hurt him.

'You've never lied to me,' he persisted. 'Don't lie to me now.' He paused, fearing her answer, yet knowing what it must be. 'Eva, do you love me, like you used to?'

'No, Father.' She raised her eyes. They were immensely sad, the gaze profoundly honest. 'I don't love you the way I used to.' Admitting it broke her heart. 'I'm so sorry, Father.' Once, a lifetime ago, she had loved him like no other being on earth. Now, he was like a stranger.

He bowed his head. 'You hate me then?'

'No, I don't hate you.' Love and hate were powerful, draining emotions. Eva had learned to suppress them well. But the sadness, the regrets, were always with her.

He felt her sorrow, and it was more than he could bear. Pain returned, and with it the rage. 'Where the bloody hell is my breakfast?'

'I'll get it for you now.'

She half turned, only to be stopped by a vicious blow on the shoulder. 'I don't want you to get me anything!' he snarled. 'How do I know you won't poison it?'

Angry that he should have lashed out at her yet again, her response was swift and condemning. 'You're a nasty, spiteful devil. You don't deserve any breakfast.'

'Go and find your mother, damn your eyes.'

'Why should I?'

'Because if you don't, I might just smash everything she values more than she does me.' To make his point, he jabbed his walking stick at a small blue vase until it rocked back and forth on the mantelpiece. 'She wouldn't thank you for not fetching her then, would she, eh?'

Eva caught the vase before it fell to the floor. She gave him a withering glance. 'Hand me the stick and I'll fetch her.' Her voice was low, trembling with anger.

'I'll give you the stick all right, you bugger!' he growled. 'Across your bloody legs, that's where.' Falling back into the chair like an old sack, he began whimpering, 'I'm ill. Fetch her. Tell her she's needed. Go on! Get a move on, damn you.'

Aware that he had the ability to bring on his own crippling pain whenever it suited him, Eva carefully replaced the vase, gave him a glance that warned, 'Don't touch it', and then swiftly departed.

Quickening her steps through the old farmhouse with its damp walls and low wooden beams, she went into the yard, glad to breathe the fresh summer air. She ran down the crooked pathway and on across the field, heading for the long barn beyond the orchard.

Her mother would be there, she was sure of it.

⟐

ALONE IN THE barn, Colette Bereton swung the axe high in the air, her small, muscular body stiffening with effort before she brought it down again in one long, easy stroke. There was a satisfying thud as the razor-sharp blade sliced through the log in a shower of splinters.

Taking a moment to throw the kindling into the wicker basket, she stretched her aching back, groaning in a soft northern voice, 'God help us! Me bones feel like they've been stretched on the rack, so they do!'

She looked up as the sun disappeared behind dark clouds; the heavens suddenly threatened rain and the air, too, had taken on a cold mood. 'July is always unpredictable,' she muttered. 'One minute blazing sunshine, the next yer arse is freezing.' She shrugged. 'Seems to me we'll be needing more kindling than this little lot.' She glanced at the half-filled basket. 'It's hard work an' no mistake. What I need is a good strong feller to help me out.' She shook her head, thinking of her husband, Marcus, a man she still loved in spite of everything. 'I had the finest man alive,' she murmured, 'but that was a lifetime ago.'

She fell into a deep, brooding silence, not for the first time wishing with all her heart that things had not turned out the way they had. Now, that same 'fine' man was crippled inside and out, heart and soul smothered by pain and resentment. The burden was not only his; it was hers too, and Eva's. He had only made matters worse by being bitter and hurtful towards her and the girl. Two years ago, before the tractor had pinned Marcus beneath it, causing damage to his back and legs, their lives had been fairly comfortable. Now the responsibility of keeping a roof over their heads had fallen to her and Eva, and the burden was a heavy one. Yet she tried to keep a happy heart.

'Get on with yer work now,' she chided herself, 'before the man himself comes crawling after you on his knees.' She knew he was capable of such a thing. She glanced nervously towards the orchard; from here she couldn't see the house, but her thoughts carried her there, to the sitting room where she had left the two of them earlier. 'I hope he's not being too difficult with the girl.' She knew from experience how hurtful he could be.

Determined now to return as quickly as possible,

she raised the axe again and while she worked, she sang.

Like Eva, she loved to sing. There was a time when Marcus used to sit and listen while she and Eva entertained him with folksongs her old granddaddy had taught her. She would always remember those times with delight. Now, though, it was forbidden to sing in the house, so whenever she worked outside, her voice would lift in song to help her through the long, hard days.

She swung the axe in time to the melody, unaware that Eva, half hidden by the trunk of an old apple tree, had paused to listen to her.

The song she sang was 'I'll take you home again, Kathleen'. The words and melody evoked many bitter-sweet memories in Eva. As the poignant words filled her troubled soul, she was transported back over the years to when her mother was young and carefree and her father a strong, wonderful man. On a winter's night he would sit before a warm, cheery fire while his wife and daughter sang to him. Afterwards there would be clapping and laughter, and lots of hugs and kisses.

Now, while her mother sang, Eva cried soft, helpless tears that ran down her face and dampened the collar of her blouse.

After a while she wiped her eyes, composed herself and joined in the song, as she hurried towards her mother.

Colette laughed out loud. 'You never could resist joining in, you bugger! Not even when you were small enough to sit on yer mammy's knee.' Colette gazed fondly at her daughter; she saw such loveliness and promise in Eva. The girl was already a beauty, but not in a bold, striking way. She was a quiet young woman, very self-assured and strong-willed.

Like her mother, Eva was small and strong, but while Colette had light brown eyes, her daughter's were the colour of a deep, calm sea, sometimes green, sometimes darkest blue, always beautiful. Her waist-long hair was the colour of ripened corn, her skin smooth and gently tanned by the many hours she spent outside in God's fresh air. Eva was a simple girl, with simple tastes. She loved the countryside with a fierce, abiding passion. An only child, caught between her parents and with no desire for material things, this place and the countryside around were her only real sources of contentment.

As she studied her, Colette noticed the trickle of blood running from Eva's hairline. Her features hardened. 'Did your father do that?'

'It's nothing.'

Reaching out, Colette pushed back the long fair hair. The gash was deeper than she had thought. 'To the stream,' she urged, and pushed Eva forward.

At the stream, the two of them knelt on the hard ground while Colette used the cuff of her blouse to wash away the blood. 'Sometimes yer father can be a right bastard!'

After a moment or two, Eva drew away. 'It's just a scratch,' she said.

'What's his excuse this time?' Colette asked as they walked back to the barn.

Helping her mother gather the kindling, Eva was careful not to alarm her. 'He wants you home, that's all.'

'Oh, aye? Let me guess. He's thrown his breakfast across the room and threatened to skin yer alive if yer don't do as he says.'

'He says he's ill. He needs you.'

'I see.' With a knowing smile, Colette threw the last of the kindling into the basket. 'Then I'd best get back, eh?' She would have heaved the basket across her shoulders, but Eva took it from her, swinging it easily to her own shoulders.

She said, 'Maybe he really is ill this time.'

Colette shook her head. 'Somehow, I don't think so. Yer father's been hurt and he's often in great pain, but he's never ill.' She looked up wistfully. 'Except in his mind.'

The two of them set off back to the house.

'I thought to leave him sleeping until I'd finished chopping the wood. Did he wake in a foul mood?'

Eva gave a half-smile. 'You could say that.'

'Refused his breakfast?'

Eva nodded.

'Threatened all and sundry if yer didn't fetch me?'

'That's about right.'

'What was it this time?'

'Your best china.' Eva gave her mother a side-ways glance, her lips twitching in a smile.

'The vase, eh?'

'The same.'

Colette nodded. 'The wily old bugger knows how to get his own way.' Then she grinned. 'I wonder what the old devil would say if he knew the vase was worth no more than the price of a pint.'

Eva laughed out loud. 'It's not him who's the wily old bugger, it's you!'

'I have to be one step ahead of him,' Colette answered with a wink. 'An' if the ol' misery catches on to the vase trick, I've one or two more up me sleeve, so don't you worry.'

'Oh, I'm not worried.' And she wasn't.

'Never let a man know what yer up to,' Colette said knowingly. 'Keep 'em guessing, that's what I say.' She gave Eva a nudge. 'Did I ever tell yer about the first time me and yer daddy made love?'

'No, you never did.' Shyness flooded her soul.

'It was in a field, right over a hornets' nest. Talk about panic!' She began chuckling. 'I've never heard such language in all me life. An' believe me, if you've never seen a naked man running full pelt through the hedgerows with a swarm of hornets after him, well, you've never lived!'

'Were you badly stung?' Eva couldn't help but smile.

'Stung?' Colette's brown eyes rolled. 'Everywhere yer could possibly think of. Yer daddy came off worse though. One angry hornet attacked his nether regions and he couldn't walk straight for a week.' Taken by a fit of giggling, she fell against a tree. 'It damped his ardour, I can tell yer that.'

'You've a wicked sense of humour,' Eva chided. As they hurried on, the two of them were helpless with laughter and the sound of their mirth echoed through the orchard.

He heard it. And his face went dark with rage.

A T THE FRONT door, Colette put her finger to her lips. 'Ssh.' She reached up and took the basket from Eva's shoulders. 'Leave yer father to me,' she said quietly. 'An' when yer chores are done, get yerself ready an' go into town. It's Saturday, an' didn't yer promise Patsy you'd go with her to that new nightclub in Bedford? It'll do yer good to get away from here for a while – put the roses back in yer cheeks.'

Eva had been looking forward to a night out with Patsy but she was worried about her mother.

'I don't like leaving you when he's in this kind of mood.'

Colette sighed. 'Yer not to worry about me an' yer father. I know how to handle the old devil. He'll not get the better of me.' She gave Eva a little push. 'Go on, lass. The sooner you've finished your work, the sooner you can be out of it.'

Eva wasn't so sure. 'We'll see.'

Colette knew better than to press her. Eva was too much like herself to be pushed into doing something she didn't want to do. All the same, it pained her to see how her daughter was beginning to take on more and more responsibility for her and Marcus. When all was said and done, Eva was only eighteen years old, with her whole life before her.

Colette found Marcus seated in his armchair, reading the paper and chewing on a ham sandwich. 'It's cold,' he snapped, peering at her from over the paper. 'The fire wants banking up.'

'Why did yer need to send Eva after me?' Taking a moment to warm her hands before the fire, she chided gently, 'Shame on yer, Marcus. One o' these days you'll really be in trouble an' nobody will believe yer.'

Crumpling the paper between his great fists, he answered in a harsh voice, 'I was feeling badly but you didn't care a sod, did you, eh? Took your bleedin' time getting back here, didn't you? For all you cared I might have been lying face down on the floor, helpless – dying even.'

'Aye, but yer weren't, were yer?' More's the pity, she thought bitterly, and was immediately filled with remorse. 'Oh, now, I didn't mean to sound cruel,' she told him. 'I'm tired, that's all. I was up first light and me back feels like it's broke in two.' Coming to him with a smile, she said, 'I hoped you'd sleep till I got back.'

'Hoped I'd kick the bucket, you mean.' Throwing the half-eaten sandwich to the floor, he snapped, 'No bloody breakfast, and a cold house, that's what greeted me when I got out of bed.'

'The house wasn't cold, Marcus,' she protested. 'I made up a good fire before I left. And Eva tells me she offered you breakfast, but you refused.' In an effort to appease him, she said kindly, 'I'll get you a nice cup of tea and a hot breakfast, how does that sound?'

To her dismay, his face set in a sullen expression. 'Don't want it,' he snarled. 'I woke up feeling fit, feeling like a real man for the first time in ages. I wanted *you*, but you weren't there. You're never bloody well there when I need you.'

Misunderstanding, she answered softly, 'Well, I'm here now, so tell me what I can do for you, an' I'll do it.'

'Get back upstairs.' His face smug, he settled more comfortably into the chair. 'Make yourself ready and I'll be there as soon as I've finished reading my paper.' Slowly and deliberately he began straightening the battered paper.

*Now* she understood.

With a determination to match his own, she quietly refused. 'No, Marcus.'

'What's that you say?' He couldn't believe his ears.

Colette stood her ground. 'I've been up since first light. I've washed a pile of clothes and hung them out, gathered the eggs, set the shop out ready for Patsy, and chopped enough wood to see us through the week. I've worked myself into the ground. I'm cold and tired, and I need a bath. So when I've got you a hot breakfast, I mean to soak me aching bones. Afterwards, I'll give Eva a hand with the day's chores so she can take herself off for an evening out with Patsy.' Struggling to control her anger, she reminded him, 'God knows, the girl deserves it.'

While she talked, his face grew white, his thick, misshapen fingers gripping the arms of the chair. There was murder in his eyes as he said in a low voice, 'I don't think you heard me, so I'll say it again. *Get upstairs and make yourself ready!*'

Afraid but defiant, she resisted. 'It's no use you getting yerself into one of yer fits. I *won't* go upstairs for you, and I won't make myself ready, as you call it. What I will do is bank up the fire then make your breakfast.' She smiled at him. 'I expect yer feeling a bit miserable, what with me out all hours doing this or that, and the pair of us never being able to sit and talk the way we used to.' She chatted on, looking away as she said, 'With a hot meal inside yer belly, you might be in a better mood.'

She turned to the fireplace and stooped to pile some logs in a semi-circle over the coals. The flames leaped high, licking at the fire-back. 'There now, isn't that cosy?' She turned to the chair where he'd been sitting.

He wasn't there.

For a moment she was confused, then she looked up and here he was, standing to one side of the fireplace, his arm resting on the mantelpiece and his face grinning down on her. 'I can move quick as a snake when I've a mind.'

'I can see that,' she acknowledged suspiciously. 'What else can you do that you've never told me about?'

'That's for me to know and you to find out.'

She didn't reply. Oddly disturbed, she continued to look up at him. There was something about his manner that frightened her; the way he lurked close, the way he spoke, soft yet not gentle. And his eyes – small, dark eyes that she knew like the image of her own face. She had seen those eyes smile on her, and she had seen them crumple in pain, but she had never seen them as they were now, rock-hard and staring, alive with hatred.

'Don't be angry,' she murmured. She often put his needs before her own and gave way to his demands, for the sake of peace, but this time she was so bone-weary she couldn't face having him roll on top of her.

Reaching down, he took hold of her arm, pinching it so hard she gave a small cry. 'You'll never see the day when I'm too crippled to take a woman,' he growled. 'So it's either up in the bedroom or on the floor here and now.' He licked his lips in anticipation. 'What's it to be then, my lovely?'

'Take yer hands off me!' Sometimes, it was more than she could cope with. Marcus was not the same man she had married all those years ago. That man was dead and gone, just as surely as if the tractor had crushed the life out of him. God forgive her, there were times when she wished it had. He should be thanking the good Lord for saving his life but instead he spent every waking minute cursing the hand fate had dealt him. But, for all that, she would never desert him. In spite of his contempt for her, she would stay and make his life as bearable as possible. He was her husband for better or worse, and she had given her vows before God.

As she struggled to free herself, she said what was in her heart, her voice hard with disgust. 'There

was a time when I went weak with pleasure at the
touch of yer hand, but not now, not any more. Yer
not the man I married. You're a lazy, idle bugger
and, God help me, I'm stuck with yer. That's a
burden I have to live with, like it or not.' There
was fire in her eyes as she faced up to him. 'Listen
to me, for I mean every word. Yer bullying will get
you nothing. I swear to Him above, I'll die before
you see me give in to yer demands ever again.'

Stunned by her outburst, he just gaped at her.

She'd gone too far to stop now, and she emptied
her heart of all the bad things that had gathered
these past years. 'You take pleasure in using me
and the girl to wait on yer hand and foot, when
all the time yer capable of doing things for yerself.
Other men have been hurt and maimed, and they
don't lie back and cosset themselves. What kind of
coward is it that would blame their family for what's
happened? You can walk as well as me when you've
a mind, and you still have the strength of ten men
when it suits yer.' She held nothing back. 'Yer a bad,
lazy feller, Marcus Bereton. Instead of whining an'
moaning, why don't yer get out and do some of the
hard work round this place? You'd be a happier man
for it, and me and the girl would have a better life,
and not before time neither!'

'*You dare talk to me like that?*' Marcus roared. She
struggled desperately to free herself, but he pinned
her down, perilously close to the fire, until the sweat

ran down her face and she could hardly breathe. She began to fear for her life.

'Let go of me, Marcus,' she ordered, trying hard not to show her fear. 'Yer won't solve anything by hurting me.'

'That's for me to say.' He spread his legs to balance himself and used his free hand to undo his trousers. 'I can see I'll have to take what I want – unless you want me to get it elsewhere.' His eyes glittered madly. 'The girl hasn't had a man yet. Think on *that* before you refuse me again.'

His words filled her with white-hot loathing and fury, and as he laughingly bore down on her, her strength rose to match her rage. Without thinking of the consequences, she pitted herself against him.

———⊰◦⊱———

IN THE COLD and damp of the shed, Eva shivered. The old wooden building was long past its prime; there were long, widening cracks in the walls and a hole in the roof the size of a man's fist. Eva had meant to patch it up, but somehow there was never the time.

She paused in her work, folding her arms for warmth. The damp had crept right into her bones. Beneath her feet the flagstones felt like hard slabs of ice, and above her head the sky was clearly visible through the sagging roof. 'The old place really needs pulling down,' she mused. 'But where would we get the money for a new one?' The land gave them a living, that was all. There was no money for luxuries.

Stacking the last of the kindling, she turned the basket upside down and hung it on the peg.

She padlocked the door behind her when she left. As she slipped the big iron key into her pocket, she chuckled. 'Anyone would think I was locking up the crown jewels.' The shed contained crates of eggs and a selection of winter vegetables, kindling, sacks of coal and the few tools they possessed. It didn't amount to much, but it was worth more than jewels to them.

Last winter somebody had broken into the shed and stolen a leg of pork and a fat Christmas turkey that Eva had earned picking Brussels sprouts with frozen fingers on a neighbour's land. Colette was furious. She dug out an old padlock and from that day on the shed was secured every night, though she had to agree with Eva that if anyone really wanted to get in, all they had to do was sneeze hard and the whole place would tumble like a pack of cards.

As Eva made her way back to the house, she thought she heard a scream. Unsure, she paused to listen. When she heard it again, she realised with horror that it was her mother's voice. 'Dear God! What's he doing to her?' As she broke into a run, she heard Colette call her name and her heart froze with fear. 'Please God, let it be all right,' she prayed as she flew down the path and burst, breathless, into the house.

———⊰•◦•⊱———

S HE COULD SMELL smoke the moment she threw open the door. She rushed to the sitting room and stared, horrified, at the sight that met her eyes.

Kneeling on the floor, with Colette in his arms, her father rocked back and forth, his face buried in his wife's hair. Colette lay limp and quiet, her dress burned, her face smudged and dirtied. Flames licked up the walls, caught hold of the curtains and fired the ceiling. The smoke was suffocating.

'Get out, Father!' Surging forward, Eva took hold of him by the shoulders. 'The fire's out of control, we have to get out!' She tried to loosen his hold on her mother, but his grip was like iron.

'Why wouldn't she listen?' he gasped. The tears ran down his face, making thin pink tracks through the soot on his skin. 'I didn't mean to hit her . . . didn't know she would fall backwards . . . the fire took her.' He could hardly speak for the smoke filling his lungs.

With her own lungs close to bursting, Eva stooped down, slid her arms beneath Colette's small body and, with a strength born of desperation, lifted her mother out of his grasp. She staggered out of the room, into the smoke-filled kitchen and on towards the back door. Behind her, Marcus slumped to the floor. Eva was only conscious of the awful stillness of the weight she carried. She dared not think and, afraid of what she might see, did not look down.

The back door was shut. Kicking out with all her might, she breathed a sigh of relief when it sprang open. Head down, she lunged forward, heat and smoke following. With a surge of fear, she realised the hem of her skirt was on fire.

'It's all right, we've got you!' Voices invaded her head as she fell to the ground, her arms still round her mother's small body. 'Let me have her. You're safe now.' Neighbours had seen the flames and made their way here, anxious to help. In the distance Eva could hear the unmistakable sound of sirens.

'My father . . .' Eva looked about for him. He was nowhere to be seen. Grabbing hold of the nearest person, her eyes wide with fear, she cried, 'My father's still inside!'

'Don't you worry,' the man said. 'A couple of the lads are bringing him out now.'

They laid him on the ground, next to Colette. A woman knelt beside him. Catching sight of Eva's stricken face, she shook her head. 'I'm sorry,' she murmured. 'The smoke was too much for him.'

Marcus was gone.

Colette lived for only a few moments. 'You've been my reason for living,' she whispered, her brown eyes quietly smiling up at Eva's haunted face. 'Try not to remember the bad times, sweetheart.' Her gaze went to the man who had once given her such joy. Reaching out, she touched his hand. Whispering softly to Eva, she said, 'Deep down, your daddy was a good man.' In her eyes shone a great sadness for the wasted years.

They clung to each other in their last moments together, their tears mingling as their lives had mingled. Then, with a gentle sigh, Colette closed her eyes.

Eva held on to that small figure, her grief terrible to see. 'Whatever will she do?' asked one old woman who lived in the valley. 'With all her family gone, where can she turn?'

People shook their heads. They couldn't see a future for Eva.

And, for a long time to come, neither could Eva.

# Chapter Two

T HE SECOND WEEK of July 1954 was glorious.
The birds were in full song and flowers spilled
an abundance of colour over every wall and in every
garden. Everywhere the heady smell of blossom
filled the air.

The vicar made mention of it, and tired spirits
were lifted by it, but Eva didn't notice. All her senses
were focused on the two wooden boxes standing side
by side before the altar.

The church was full; people who knew the
Beretons had come and so had people who didn't,
always mindful of the fact that tragedy could strike
anyone at any time. Their hearts went out to Eva,
a lovely, hard-working girl who had lost everything.
While the vicar prayed for the souls of the departed
and asked that their only child might find peace, all
eyes were on Eva, so young and alone.

Her gaze never left the coffins of her parents. In
her mind's eye she saw it all as it had been, before
the accident, before the badness set in. Her heart
was full of memories; the images flitted through her

shocked mind, touching her with such bitter-sweet pain she could hardly breathe. Occasionally, shining through the sorrow came the touch of a smile, gently lifting the corners of her mouth and lighting her eyes with the brightness of tears.

The years had been kind before love had turned to indifference and then to a kind of hatred. The bad years had been like a long hard winter, yet the family had stayed together, bound by ties of blood and a shared life. Now it was the most beautiful summer and they were parted, and all that had gone before was just a whisper in the wind.

Suddenly the congregation broke into song. Her thoughts shattered, Eva looked up. She could not bring herself to sing; what was there to sing about? Instead, her quiet green eyes roved over the congregation and she wondered why they were here. Most of them were strangers to her. A round-faced woman caught Eva's glance and looked away. A tall, grey-haired man at the end of the pew reverently bowed his head. Eva thought she had seen him once before, when her mother sold the kindling sticks at market. She seemed to recall he bought two bundles and afterwards stayed to pass the time of day.

There were pitifully few relations. The Beretons had been a small family; Marcus had no brothers or sisters and his own parents were long gone. Colette had one sister, who was married with two sons, and an aged aunt. They were all here. Eva had welcomed them only this morning, but it was like welcoming strangers. All but one. Bill. It warmed her heart to see him again.

———⬧◆⬧———

T HE SERVICE WAS over. The mourners filed out behind the coffins, into the pretty churchyard, where the two were laid to rest.

When everyone had gone, Eva stayed behind to speak to her parents. In her heart she did not believe they had gone far away. In fact, she felt closer to her father at that moment than she had at any time over the past few years. She felt that, somehow, these two people who had been her whole life would be with her wherever she went, for as long as she herself was alive.

Her mother had once told her that hate and love were two sides of the same coin. Now she knew what that meant, because the love for her father was still there. 'I love you both so much,' she murmured. 'I will always love you.' The tears came, and she let them fall, her heart sore with pain.

From the doorway of the church, Bill thought how small she seemed standing there, all alone, so vulnerable, so tragic. He wanted to go to her, but his instincts warned him that this was her time. A time to recollect, and mourn. It was not for him to intrude. But he felt for her. Eva had always been special to him, she always would be. And because of

27

what he had learned from his father earlier he knew she would suffer more before the day was through.

God alone knew how hard he had tried to protect her from what was to happen, but his hands were tied and there was nothing he could do. Except maybe warn her. But that was pitifully little.

He continued to look at her, thinking how lovely she still was, and how very young she seemed, though he recalled how fiercely independent she had been as a child. Remembering, he smiled. Would she remember how it was, he wondered, or had she forgotten? He hoped not.

After a time he turned away, murmuring, 'I'm sorry, Eva.'

Eva caught sight of him walking away. The last time she had seen him, they had both been just children, but the years had not changed him all that much; the way he walked was the same, with a kind of long, easy stride, and his dark brown hair still seemed to have a mind of its own.

She looked away. 'It was a long time ago,' she whispered. 'So much has happened since then.' Seeing him had moved her deeply.

She glanced back to her parents. With a brave smile and a small prayer for their safekeeping, she wrenched herself away.

Bᴀᴄᴋ ᴀᴛ ᴛʜᴇ farmhouse, Patsy put the finishing touches to the buffet. At thirty years of age, she was a big, handsome woman, with baby-blue eyes and untidy auburn hair. Anxious that everything should be just right by the time the mourners returned, she cleared away the dirty crockery.

She went back into the sitting room. Looking round, she praised herself in a strong Irish voice. 'Sure, I've done meself proud, so I have.'

And she had. On the table were plates of dainty sandwiches, small sausage rolls, sliced ham and squares of cheese, enough new bread and butter to feed an army, and a selection of scones made by Eva the night before. She checked the place settings. 'Plates, knives, cups and saucers, milk and sugar . . .' She squealed with horror. 'Be Jaysus! Sure, I've forgotten to put out the napkins.' She looked frantically about, until her eye caught the pile of blue paper napkins standing on the dresser where Eva had left them. Rushing across, she grabbed them. 'Patsy Noonan, sure you'd forget yer head if it weren't screwed on to yer stupid shoulders.'

After arranging the napkins between each plate, she stood back to survey the scene again. Thanks to the hard work of the neighbours, restoring and replacing treasures after the fire, the room was warm and cosy, with a number of small pictures across one wall – prints of sunflowers and fields, and a pretty flower-framed cameo of Colette and Marcus on their wedding day. Her grin of pleasure faded as she caught sight of the fire-blackened chimney breast. 'It's a sad thing, so it is,' she sighed. 'Now then, it's time to get meself washed and tidy before they come through the door.'

In the hall she glanced at herself in the mirror; staring back was a strong, pleasant face, with small splashes of red plum jam round the mouth and chin. 'Yer a sloppy article, so yer are!' she told herself. But it didn't matter. What mattered was Eva. Patsy loved her dearly and had appointed herself Eva's guardian. It broke her heart to see how her whole world had come to such an end, and she worried about how quiet Eva had been.

When Patsy was worried, she got hungry, and she was hungry now: 'I think I'd better have my share now, before it's all gone.' Turning on her heel, she returned to the sitting room and helped herself to a jam tart. It was gone before she was even halfway up the stairs. Licking her fingers, she continued smartly towards the bathroom.

Outside the main bedroom she stopped. The door was open. She could see the big old bed which Eva's parents had shared. Patsy sighed. 'I hope you've both found a better place,' she murmured, making the sign of the cross on her forehead. She knew that life in this house had not been easy these past two years. 'Oh, Eva!' She brushed away a tear. 'You helped me through a bad time once and I hope

I can help you do the same now.' Eva was the kind of friend that only came along once in a lifetime. 'Yer shouldn't be put through such pain, my love, but it's strange how life punishes the gentlest of creatures.'

Eva had told Patsy she could use her room; a bright, sunny place with chintz curtains and pretty rugs on the floor. After washing in the bathroom, she combed her hair in front of Eva's mirror and then put on the straight black dress which Eva had hung on the wardrobe door.

Regarding herself in the long, oval mirror, she groaned. 'Yer still a fat little thing, even in black. One of these days you'll have to slim down or there won't be a frock to fit yer this side of heaven.' She *would* slim down, but not yet. There was no incentive. Certainly no boyfriend. For some reason she could not understand, young men didn't fancy her.

Downstairs she checked everything again. She brought the kettle to the boil and then threw open the sitting-room window to let in some air – the afternoon sun flooding into the room was making it uncomfortably warm. That done, she went to the door and looked down the lane. 'No sign of them yet,' she muttered. She was half tempted to help herself to another jam tart but thought better of it.

Settling down to wait, she sat on the front step, her chubby legs crossed and her back against the door jamb. The warmth of the sun on her face made her feel sleepy.

Half an hour later, the first car drew up and Eva stepped out. Her gaze was drawn immediately to the front doorstep and the familiar figure curled up there. She couldn't help but smile. Patsy was fast asleep.

'Looks like it's all been too much for her,' the driver chuckled. He was a kindly man, used to ferrying people to and from the churchyard. He had done the job these past twenty years, until now he could almost do it with his eyes closed. On these serious occasions there was little cause for amusement, but seeing that fat little urchin on the doorstep, his old heart was warmed. 'Seems a pity to wake her,' he said to Eva. 'A neighbour, is she?'

'A friend,' Eva gently corrected him. 'A very dear friend.'

He nodded. In his work he got to know most things, and what he knew about Eva was that she had lost her entire family in one fell swoop. Life was a bastard sometimes. 'Do you want me to wait, love?' Often the relatives were in a hurry to get away. Other times they lingered, like vultures over a meal.

Eva shook her head. 'I don't think so,' she told him, watching the other two cars draw up. 'From what Aunt Margaret said, they have everything arranged.'

It surprised her when he took hold of her hand. 'I haven't had a chance to say how sorry I am,' he said. 'The job I do is not a thankful one, and to be honest I'm glad to leave it behind at the end of the day. It isn't often I let myself be affected. I can't afford to, but I'd just like you to know I think you've been dealt a lousy hand, you being so young and all.' As he looked into those strong green eyes, he felt humbled. 'God bless you,' he murmured. 'I wish you all the best.'

Eva didn't know quite what to say.

He understood. 'Right you are then.' Glad to be off home where he could put his feet up for the rest of the day, he shuffled back into the driving seat, started the engine and shifted into gear. In no time at all he had made a tight and difficult turn and was heading in the opposite direction.

Eva watched him for a moment before returning her attention to Patsy. When she saw her Uncle Peter violently shaking the poor girl, she was horrified. 'What do you think you're doing?' Hurrying across the garden, she grabbed him by the arm. 'Leave her alone.' Her voice trembled with anger. 'Please, go inside. I'll see to Patsy.'

'Lazy little bugger!' Straightening his shoulders, he glared at Patsy who had woken in a fright. 'What's she doing lolling all over the step like that? Doesn't she realise there's been a funeral? Has she no respect?'

Wide awake now, Patsy retaliated. 'Yer gave me a bleedin' fright, so yer did!' Scrambling to get up, she almost knocked him over. 'An' if yer ask me, it's *you* who needs to have a bit of respect. You're the one shouting and bawling, so yer are!'

Peter's face turned bright red. 'Do you realise who you're talking to, young lady?'

'No, and I don't wish to, you bad-tempered old sod.'

Muttering under his breath, he squared his small, stiff shoulders and turned to Eva. 'Get rid of her,' he demanded sourly. 'We've important matters to discuss, and they are not for strangers' ears.'

'I'll do no such thing,' Eva replied. 'Besides, Patsy is no stranger. She's my best friend, and Mother loved her as much as I do.'

'Do as you're told, young lady,' Peter snapped. 'I do not want her in this house.'

Eva's impulse was to get rid of *him*. But, mindful of the fact that this awful little man was married to her mother's sister, she remained calm and dignified. 'I'm sorry, Uncle Peter, but I've already explained, Patsy is a friend. She's been here all morning, preparing the food. And, with all due respect, I think you should remember this is *not* your house. Patsy will always be welcome here.'

Sucking air through his nose, he said crisply, 'In spite of her faults, your mother always had good manners. It's a pity you're not more like her.'

'We all have our faults, Uncle Peter. Yourself included, I'm sure.' The sly criticism of her mother hurt Eva deeply. Another time she might have taken issue with him, but not today. This was a day she wanted to remember with dignity. He was her uncle, after all, and he had come all the way from Canada to pay his respects. That at least called for a small measure of restraint.

'Very well,' he conceded with ill grace, 'if you insist she must stay, then I suppose she must.'

Eva's Aunt Margaret had seen and heard it all. Looking ashamed and worried, she gave Eva a nervous smile. Eva smiled back, and the poor woman relaxed.

When the two visitors had entered the house, Patsy spoke her mind with bruising honesty. 'Sly little sod. No wonder yer mammy didn't like him.'

Eva agreed. 'He worries me. I can't believe he's travelled all the way from Canada just to pay his respects.'

'Perhaps yer Aunt Margaret persuaded him to make the trip.'

They peered discreetly into the house, where Margaret was rushing about waiting on her husband, as though she was a servant and he the master. 'I don't think he'd come over here just because she asked him to, do you?' Eva said.

'Happen you're right.'

'Poor woman. She seems frightened of him.' Much like her own mother had grown frightened of her husband in the last two years.

When Peter turned and smiled at her through the window, Patsy whispered, 'Watch him, Eva. He's a bad divil.'

'I know what you mean, but don't worry,' Eva assured her. 'I'm a match for the likes of him.'

'What did he mean when he said you had important matters to discuss?' Patsy had always felt free to speak her mind with Eva.

'Your guess is as good as mine.' It had been years since Uncle Peter had visited England, and for a long time there had been no contact between their two families. Eva couldn't imagine what he had in mind, but one thing was certain, whatever he was up to, it would not be to her advantage. Though she was sure there was nothing he could do to hurt her, Eva couldn't help but feel threatened. He was too confident; too arrogant by half.

'Come on, Patsy,' she urged. 'We'd better go in.'

Patsy groaned. 'Jaysus, look at what he's done.' Raising her arm, she twisted it so she could see the elbow. 'The bugger's skinned my elbow on the wall.'

'It's not too bad, Patsy.' Eva deliberately made little of it. Taking out her handkerchief, she dabbed at the blood. 'There's some Germolene in the kitchen. That should take the sting out of it.' She helped Patsy brush the dust from her dress.

The entire episode had spanned only a few

minutes, but in that time Peter's two sons and the aged aunt had made their way into the house.

'Time to put my best face on,' Eva murmured as she and Patsy went in, 'though to tell the truth, I'd rather just be on my own to think things through.'

Patsy made no comment. She knew exactly what Eva meant, for hadn't she been through something very like it herself?

Peter was the first to greet her. 'You're slipping in your duties, my girl,' he announced with irritating authority. 'You should have been at the door to see everyone in.'

'I would have been if you hadn't caused such a fuss outside,' she reminded him. Turning to Patsy, she told her where to find the Germolene then, mindful of her duties, she approached the aged aunt.

Great-Aunt Judith was the sister of Eva's grand-mother. 'How are you, my dear?' she said, greeting Eva with a half-smile. 'Margaret and I have been so worried about you. I couldn't believe it when I heard,' she added brokenly. 'God only knows how hard it must be for you.' In her late eighties now, Judith was small and wizened, with soft brown eyes and a halo of wispy silver hair. There was an air of serenity about her.

'You mustn't worry,' Eva replied fondly. 'I'll be all right.' Her gaze strayed to where Patsy was check-ing the food. 'Patsy has been a tower of strength to mc, and it does help, you being here.'

'I did love your mother,' the old dear murmured. 'She was a sweet little thing, always singing, as I recall.'

Eva was too filled with emotion to speak.

Lost in her memories, the old woman went on, 'She was such a lovely little thing, much like yourself, my dear.' She stroked Eva's long fair hair. 'I remember when she and Margaret were girls. Margaret was the quiet one, while Colette was always up to mischief. Full of fun, she was.' Taking out a snow-white handkerchief, she shook open the newly ironed folds. 'Too young,' she whispered, noisily blowing her nose into the handkerchief. 'Your mammy was too young to be so cruelly struck down.' Big, sorrowful eyes looked at Eva. 'And I'm so old. It isn't right that I should outlive her.'

Eva put a comforting arm round her. 'Don't upset yourself,' she said gently. 'You'll only make me feel worse.'

'Oh, I wouldn't want to make things worse for you, my dear,' Judith answered, a little smile breaking through her tears. 'But . . . whatever will you do now, child?'

Taking hold of the old woman's hands, Eva replied in a quiet, reassuring voice, 'You mustn't forget I'm my mother's daughter.'

The old woman smiled. 'Not only in looks but in spirit too.'

'So you'll stop worrying?'

The old woman nodded.

When Eva leaned forward to kiss her, Judith clung to her. This was Colette's girl and, God willing, she would come to no harm.

—————⇒●⇐—————

B ILL TURNED FROM looking out of the window just at the moment when Eva and the old lady were embracing. When he saw them, the whisper of a smile touched his dark eyes. Then he lowered his gaze, thrust his hands into his pockets and strolled out of the house, into the sunshine.

Unaware of his attention, Eva drew away from her great-aunt, a bright smile lighting her features. 'Now, how would you like a big slice of cake? I made it last night – one of my mother's recipes.'

'Go on then,' the old woman replied. 'Not too big a slice though. My girdle's tight enough as it is.'

At the table, Margaret spoke to Eva. 'I'm not sure if we've done the right thing coming here,' she said. 'I did so want to see Colette again, but I never thought . . . never dreamed . . .' She stopped, her voice quivering with emotion. A moment, that was all, and she had her feelings under control. 'I had no idea your Uncle Peter had kept in touch with someone at this end . . . a solicitor . . . name of Dollond, I think. It was he who passed on the awful news, and of course we had to come.' After pausing to gauge Eva's reaction, she continued in harsher tones, 'Your Uncle Peter has a secretive way with him. It can be very unsettling at times.'

Eva recalled Peter's remarks about 'matters of importance'. 'How do you mean exactly?' Somehow, she trusted Aunt Margaret.

'I'm not sure, only he can be devious.' It was obvious Margaret didn't know what was on Peter's mind either. 'I wouldn't blame you for not wanting us here. We're almost like strangers to you now.'

'You mustn't think like that,' Eva reassured her. 'I really am glad you came.' With the exception of Peter, she thought. He was better out of sight, out of mind.

'I'm sorry he behaved like that.' Margaret's gaze momentarily flicked to Peter. 'My husband can be a very difficult man when he sets his mind to it.'

'We're all a bit fraught.' Eva thought it only polite to make excuses for him.

Margaret looked at Eva for a moment, before saying in a soft, kindly voice, 'Peter is a selfish, arrogant man, and I'm more aware of that than most.'

Sensing her sadness, Eva changed the subject. 'I'd better make myself useful,' she said brightly. 'I promised Aunt Judith a piece of chocolate cake.'

'Then you mustn't keep her waiting.'

As Eva turned to go, Margaret called her back. 'Eva?'

'Yes?'

'Thank you.'

Eva nodded. There was obviously more to this family than met the eye; dangerous undercurrents. Margaret seemed a good woman. It was a pity she was tied to a man like Peter.

Eva cut a generous slice of chocolate cake for Judith. Todd, Margaret's younger son and the image of his father, was helping himself to a sausage roll. Eva greeted him politely and then made her way back to the old woman. She could feel Todd's eyes burning in the back of her neck. She didn't like him, any more than she liked his father.

She found Judith sound asleep in the armchair, head to one side, snoring gently.

'Will yer look at that?' Patsy remarked. Before Eva could protest, she took the plate of chocolate cake from her. 'I'll hide it,' she muttered. 'When they've all gone, we'll have it with a cup of tea.'

Silently, Eva wished they would *all* go soon, even Patsy, God bless her. The day seemed never-ending, and the thought of her parents weighed heavily in her heart. But it seemed no one was in a hurry to leave. For the next half-hour, the old woman slept on; Margaret asked Eva if she could see the family photograph album and, once engrossed in that, she was a world away. Deep in conversation, Peter and Todd stood in a corner of the room, far enough away from the others not to be heard.

Patsy busied herself toing and froing, and when

Eva came to help, she was banned from the kitchen. 'Will yer not be told? Tomorrow you can cook us a meal and wash up afterwards. Yer can go through the house like a dose o' salts and wash every curtain in the place if yer like.' Her voice took on a softer tone. 'Yer Aunt Margaret seems a kindly woman, so she does. Why don't yer talk to her? Sure she grew up with yer mammy, didn't she? Mebbe the pair of youse could help each other.'

Eva was leaning, arms folded, against the work-top, her gaze drawn outside to the rose garden, where her mother used to sit and be quiet after a long, hard day.

For a moment Patsy watched her, silent and saddened. She put a comforting arm round her shoulder. 'There's me blabbering away, and yer not even listening, are yer?'

Startled, Eva swung round. 'Sorry, Patsy. What did you say?'

'What I said was . . . Yer look worn out.' Gently she propelled Eva towards the door. 'Why don't yer go out and sit in the garden? It'll only take me a few minutes to clear this lot away. After-wards, I'll get us both a cool drink and we'll sit together for a while. What do yer say to that, eh?'

'I'd like that.' Suddenly she didn't want Patsy to go. Once the others had left and the house was empty, she would be alone. In all her life she had never been really alone. Her mother had always been there. And her father.

Patsy peeped through the door into the front room. 'Yer uncle and the young one are still whispering in the corner,' she told Eva. 'The old woman's still asleep and Margaret's crying over the photos. No sign of the handsome feller, though I don't suppose he's too far away.'

Eva felt ashamed. 'I don't know what he'll think of me, I haven't spoken two words with him yet.' Shyness engulfed her.

'He'll understand, so he will. He seems different from the others. Keeps to himself. I've seen him speaking to his mother and the old one, but he seems to be keeping his distance from the other two. Is there bad blood between him and his father, d'yer think?'

'There didn't used to be. Mind you, I wouldn't have noticed even if there was, not then. Whenever Aunt Margaret came to visit us, me and Bill would be outside. Winter or summer, it didn't matter, we'd fish in the brook or swing from the old crooked tree in the orchard.' The memories were vivid now, as was the affection she'd always had for him. 'We had a secret den in the barn, hidden away between the apple crates and the manure bags.'

'Stink, did yer?' Patsy wrinkled her nose. It was good to hear Eva reminiscing.

Eva laughed. 'We did stink but we didn't care. You know how it is when you're kids. Mum used to ask where we'd been to get in such a state, but we never told.' It was all coming back, bringing a rush of joy to her heart. 'Oh, Patsy, we did have such good times then.'

'Fond of him, were yer?' Patsy's romantic heart melted. 'Childhood sweethearts and all that?'

Eva shook her head. 'We were only kids.' Her smile was revealing. 'Though I do remember that we used to talk about getting married when we grew up.'

'Did you miss him after he went to Canada?'

'Like mad.' Just for a fleeting moment she felt the pain she had felt then. 'For weeks I cried myself to sleep.'

'Did yer never hear from him again?'

'For a while, yes. When Aunt Margaret wrote to Mam, there'd be a little note inside from Bill. But, like I said, we were only kids, and kids soon forget.'

'*You* haven't.'

'No.' She never would. 'But then I never forget anything.' For a long time, she dreamed that Bill would come back and they could pick up where they'd left off. But that was just a childish dream. 'Anyway, after a time, Aunt Margaret stopped writing and that was that.'

'Why would yer Aunt Margaret stop writing?'

Eva hesitated. Something her mother had confided in her came back to her. 'I think Peter must have ordered her not to keep in touch.'

'Why would he do that?'

Eva shrugged her shoulders. 'Who knows?' She did know, but it wasn't wise to raise the past.

'You're keeping something back, aren't you?' Patsy was like a dog with a bone. 'If it's bad, it's better to share, then it can't hurt you, me darlin'.'

'Between you and me, and nobody else?' Eva knew Patsy would keep on until she'd found out the truth. 'I don't want it known outside these four walls.'

'Ah now, have yer ever known me to gossip?'

'No, I haven't.'

'So get it off yer chest.'

'It's just that Mam told me how Peter tried to flirt with her. No,' she corrected herself, 'it was more than that. He came here one day when Dad was out in the spinney. Mam was upstairs and heard him come in. When he called out, she told him to wait a minute and she'd be right down. But he didn't wait. Instead, he went upstairs and made a pass at her. He got his arms round her waist and tried to push her on to the bed. Mam put him in his place, and he never forgave her. You see, he was used to getting what he wanted.'

'He's even more of a bastard than I thought!'

45

Eva was quiet for a moment, before confiding, 'That was why he wouldn't let Aunt Margaret keep in touch, in case Mam told her. But she wouldn't have. That wasn't her way.'

'All the same, Margaret was yer mammy's sister. Why didn't she ignore him and write anyway? How would he ever find out?'

'I should imagine he watched her like a hawk. I don't expect things were easy. Just now, she told me he was devious and selfish.'

'I'm surprised he took the old one to Canada with them,' Patsy said caustically. 'He seems the sort who'd make arrangements to have her put down like an old dog. I mean, she'd be a burden, wouldn't she? He might have to feed and house her. My God, sure that's a terrible burden for a foine man to be lumbered with!'

Smiling, Eva shook her head. 'You don't mince your words, do you?' She regarded Patsy fondly. 'And you're right. I can't be certain, but I suppose at the time Aunt Judith was in her early seventies.' It was difficult to know. Aunt Judith's age had always been a bit of a mystery. 'Anyway, according to Mam, Margaret dug her heels in – "First time I've ever known Margaret stand up to him," that's what Mam said. Apparently there was quite a fuss. Aunt Margaret wanting one thing and Uncle Peter wanting another, with the poor old dear stuck between the two.'

'Families, eh?' Patsy tutted. 'Makes you wonder if it's all worth it.'

'Peter threatened to leave Aunt Margaret behind if she didn't toe the line.'

'So how did she persuade him to take Judith in the end?' Patsy leaned across the table, her homely face cradled in large, capable hands. 'Don't tell me, he realised that if Margaret stayed behind, he'd have to wait on himself and there'd be nobody for him to nag at. *That's* why he agreed to take the old woman after all, isn't it?'

'Wrong.'

'All right then, *Bill* threatened to stay behind, and your Uncle Peter hadn't got the guts to go it alone.'

'Wrong again.'

'Then why?'

'Money.'

'What money?'

'Aunt Judith's money. She had a bank account, and she owned her own house, two up, two down, on Hardwick Street. She planned to keep the house and rent it out, in case she didn't like it in Canada. Uncle Peter talked her out of that plan and put one of his own to her.'

'He's the devil's own, so he is!'

'Anyway, she sold the house and handed Uncle Peter a sizeable sum – an investment in his new business, that's what he told her.'

'Well now, she must be worth a bob or two because if he's anything to go by, the business must be doing all right.'

'I'm afraid not, Patsy.' Eva's face was grim. 'The business collapsed and she lost the lot. Aunt Margaret wrote and told Mam how bad it was, and how they might have to come home. But somehow, Uncle Peter got financial backing for another business and he's never looked back.'

'Did he ever repay the old woman?'

'I should think that would be the last thing on his mind.' Eva glanced towards the living room. Satisfied there was no one nearby, she went on, 'This is a clever, cunning man. When he drew up the agreement with Aunt Judith, I dare say he made sure that if anything should go wrong, he wouldn't be held responsible.'

'The man's a bastard, so he is!'

Eva wholeheartedly agreed. Talking about him left a bad taste in her mouth. 'I'm neglecting my duties,' she said. 'I'd better go in and be sociable.'

'Sure they haven't even missed yer.' Once again, Patsy steered Eva towards the back door. 'If they want yer, they know where to find yer. So be off now. I'll follow yer in a few minutes, so I will.'

E VA MADE STRAIGHT for the rose garden. For a while she strolled round it, picking off dead flowerheads and dropping them into a plant pot, the way her beloved mother used to do.

After a while she paused and smiled, her tear-filled eyes raised to the sky. 'Look at me, Mam,' she murmured. 'Following in your footsteps, bringing you as close to me as I can.'

All day she had kept back the heartache, making herself remember the good times and keeping her mind on the family who had gathered here. Now, though, hugging the plant pot close to her breast, she bowed her head and let the heartache take its course.

Sobs racked her body and tears ran down her face. There was so much pain inside. Her mother, and her father, were gone for ever, and she was left with only the earthly things they had left behind. Suddenly the world was incredibly lonely and frightening. How would she cope? What would she do without the love and companionship of that dear, darling woman?

She chided herself for being selfish. What about her mother? So young and vital, with much of her own life before her. And what about her father? Maybe in the fullness of time he would have become a better, kinder man. Now she would never know. But it was her mother she yearned for.

'Wherever you are,' she murmured, 'I'll always

love you, every day, every minute for the rest of my life. But what now? What will I do without you, Mam?'

'*You'll be strong, like you always were, like she would want you to be.*'

Startled, Eva swung round, almost falling into Bill's arms. 'I'm sorry.' Embarrassed and ashamed, she didn't know what to say.

For a moment he didn't reply. Instead he gazed down into those troubled green eyes and his heart went out to her. He had loved Eva when she was small and he loved her now. When the time was right, he would tell her that, but for now she needed comfort, that was all. 'I heard you crying,' he said, 'and I couldn't walk away.' He held on to her, his hands warm and strong about her shoulders. 'I'll go if you want me to,' he offered. 'I'll understand if you'd rather be alone.'

With the smallest of movements she shook her head. 'Please stay.' His nearness was comforting. In that moment when she saw him there, it was as if they were children again. The perfume of roses filled the air and the birds sang, and as they stood there, each heart was filled with joy. 'It's good to see you, Bill,' Eva said, and his slow, easy smile carried her back over the years.

'It's good to see you too,' he replied, 'but I wish it was under different circumstances.'

She glanced down, the grief overwhelming her.

'Eva?'

She looked up, her eyes moist but on her face
a look of determination. 'I'd better go back inside.'
Her instincts warned her that her uncle was watching her every move. The last thing she wanted was
to be less than her mother would have expected.
But it was so good to be here in the garden where
her mother had been happy, and with Bill beside
her she felt a kind of peace she hadn't felt for a
long time.

'Don't go back inside just yet.' Gesturing to a
rough-bark seat Bill said, 'We could sit and talk
over old times. Or just stroll round the garden if
you'd rather.' She was so vulnerable, he wanted to
put off the moment when he must burden her with
more bad news.

'I don't suppose a few more minutes will matter,'
Eva decided. 'Let's sit and talk.' Already she was
feeling better. It was almost as though her mother
was watching and had sent an old friend to ease
her grief.

As they walked to the bench, Eva sneaked a
glance at him. He had always been a good-looking
boy and now he was a handsome man. He still had
the same dark, laughing eyes he had had as a boy,
though they were sombre right now.

'I'd know you in a crowd,' she said as they
sat down.

'Oh? I expect what you really mean is I still

look like that snotty-nosed, raggy-arsed kid you used to chase.'

'That's right,' she said with a laugh. 'You do.'

Patsy was on her way with the cold drinks, but seeing them laughing together, she turned on her heel and made her way back to the kitchen. 'They're in love and don't even know it.' She smiled to herself, then promptly drank both glasses of lemonade.

Bill took hold of Eva's hand. 'I'm so sorry, Eva. Is there anything you'd like me to do? Anything at all?'

'I'm all right,' Eva told him. 'I'm grateful for your offer but there's nothing you can do to help me – nothing *anyone* can do.' Taking a deep breath she told him in a firm voice, 'But you were right when you said I must be strong. I have to get on with my life, just as she would want me to.'

'I know you will,' he said. 'I remember what a determined little thing you were. Whenever we got in trouble, you always insisted on having your share of the punishment.'

She laughed at that. 'You hated it, didn't you? How I'd always own up just when you'd taken all the blame.'

'You were always such an independent little madam.'

'And you always wanted to be my knight in shining armour.'

'I often recall our little adventures,' he said with a smile. 'They were the best part of my growing up.'

'Mine too.' It was such a pity that life had to change.

'Did you know I married?' There was no use hiding the fact.

Taken aback, Eva concealed her disappointment. 'No, but I'm not surprised. Did you bring her with you?'

'She wasn't able to come. Other commitments and all that.'

'I see.' Eva understood. Funerals were difficult, especially when you didn't know the family.

'Eva?' He looked into her face and wanted to hold her tight. But she wasn't his, and they were not children any more.

'What is it, Bill?'

He took a deep breath, ready to explain, but then he stalled a moment longer. 'As I recall, you were always a loner. You said it was hard to make friends. Is it still like that, Eva?'

Eva thought for a moment. It was true what Bill said. As a child she saw very few children of her own age, and on the odd occasion when she did, they seemed so confident and self-assured that she felt inadequate. When she started school, it wasn't any easier, though she desperately wanted to be part of a group, or to find a friend of her own.

'Yes, it's still the same,' she answered. 'I wasn't blessed with the knack of making friends. But I'm luckier than most.'

'Why is that?' He couldn't take his eyes off her. Oh, but she was so delightful. Much prettier than he remembered, and with such a gentle, lovely nature.

'I've had three wonderful friends in my life,' she said. 'My mother. You. And Patsy.' She sighed, a flicker of sadness crossing her features. 'First of all, *you* went. Now my darling mam's gone.' A small smile brightened her face. 'But I still have Patsy who I love dearly. She's like my own sister.'

A frown creased his forehead. 'Patsy? Oh, she's the one who fell asleep on the doorstep, right?'

Eva nodded. 'I know what you're thinking. That I should find a more responsible friend, more my own age.'

'Not at all. A friend is a friend, and should be cherished. Tell me about her.'

'Her name is Patsy Noonan.' Eva chuckled. 'Irish as the Blarney Stone, she is.'

Bill laughed. 'She doesn't mince her words, I know that. I heard her giving my father a piece of her mind, and my God he deserved it.'

Eva was surprised. 'You heard?'

He nodded. 'I didn't intervene because I didn't think you'd thank me for it, and anyway the two of you were giving him a hard enough time as it was.' Delight lit his face. 'It did my heart good, I can tell you.'

'You were right not to intervene. I prefer to fight my own battles.'

'Oh, and don't I know it!' He reminded her of the time they had made a den in the middle of a neighbouring farmer's cornfield. When the farmer ran them off, Eva pelted him with rotten apples. 'He told your dad about it in the pub the next night, and everyone had a laugh. The farmer said he thought you were too dangerous to be let loose.'

For a precious moment their laughter brought them closer together. Then he spoke softly. 'Eva, there is something you must know. Something I must tell you before you go back inside.' The time was right.

Eva looked into his eyes. 'I'm listening.' She wondered if he was about to open his heart to her, tell her how he felt the same way she did. With him so near, it was as if no time had passed and the same strong bond that had drawn them together all those years ago was still there. Still wonderful.

He might have told her just that. He might have told her far more. But, for the moment at least, there were other, more pressing issues. 'Two days ago, I learned something you need to be aware of,' he began. But before he could go on, they were interrupted.

'Eva! Eva, where are you?' Todd's voice cut

through the air. 'Oh, there you are.' Approaching from the direction of the house, he ran towards them, a small, hard-faced young man, wearing a false smile over his air of self-importance; and as he came nearer, it crossed Eva's mind that his father must have looked exactly like that when he was the same age.

'What is it, Todd?' He made her feel as if she had been caught out like a naughty girl hiding away. 'I was just coming back to the house,' she said guiltily.

She was about to get up but Bill reached out to restrain her. 'Not yet,' he softly pleaded. 'There are things you need to know.'

Realising Bill's intention, Todd stepped between them.

'What is it you want?' Bill demanded, glaring at him.

Addressing himself to Eva, Todd explained, 'Father's been looking everywhere for you. He needs to see you now.'

'Well, he'll just have to wait, won't he?' Bill knew why his father wanted to talk to Eva, and it fired his anger.

Still addressing Eva, Todd told her, 'He said to tell you it can't wait, that we have to be away soon.'

In a quiet, firm manner, Bill said, 'Tell him Eva will be along in a few minutes. We have things to discuss first.'

Sensing the tension between the two brothers, Eva intervened. 'It's all right, Bill. Really. We can talk after I've heard what your father wants.' A quick, intimate smile lit her eyes. 'That is, if you still want to.' She couldn't be certain. After all, a lot of water had passed under the bridge since last they met.

He nodded. 'I'd like that,' he said, and the words came from his heart, although he couldn't help wondering if Eva would want to talk once she learned what his father had to say to her. 'I'll wait for you,' he promised.

'Thank you. I'm sure I won't be too long.'

As Todd hurried her away, Bill's face was grim. 'Don't let him destroy you,' he murmured.

———— ◆ ————

PETER WAS WAITING in the sitting room, alone. Eva wondered if he'd purposely cleared the room, waking Great-Aunt Judith in the process. His hands were thrust deep into his pockets and his back was to the fire. His face was red from the heat. 'Come in, my dear,' he said as Eva stepped into the room, followed by Todd. Peter gestured to the armchair. 'No need to stand to attention. Make yourself comfortable.'

Eva declined. 'If you don't mind, I'll stand. Just say what you have to say.' There was something about him . . . She felt he was nursing some kind of secret, and it had to do with her, she was certain. It irked her, too, the way he stood with his back to the fire, inviting her to sit in her own chair, in her own house. The man was too arrogant for words.

'Very well,' he conceded, 'though I think it might be better if you sat down.' A smile crept over his shrewish features. 'I'm afraid I have some rather unpleasant news for you.'

'I'm listening.' She sounded calm and composed, but inside her stomach was churning.

'As you wish.' He began pacing up and down. 'It's to do with your future, my dear,' he began. 'What had you in mind, now that your parents are . . . well, now that you're all alone here?'

'Why, carry on of course,' Eva answered without hesitation. 'My parents built up a good business here. I have no intention of throwing it all away.'

'A few acres and a small farm shop – what is it you sell? Eggs, kindling and whatever else you can coax out of this godforsaken land?' Peter's chest puffed out as he began strutting once more. 'Hardly a good business, my dear.'

'Good enough for my parents, and good enough for me. This godforsaken land, as you call it, has provided well for a family of three all these years.'

'Then you must consider yourself fortunate, my dear.' Suddenly he was looking at her in a different way. This was *his* child; born out of rape and lust. If it had suited his purpose to hurt her with the dreadful truth, he would have taunted her with it, but there was nothing to be gained. With a darkened expression and a cutting edge to his voice he said, 'It's time for you to leave all this behind and start a new life.'

Infuriated, Eva replied in a cold, quiet voice, 'I think that's for *me* to decide. This little business might not measure up to your high standards, but it's what I want.' She stepped forward. 'I'm grateful that you saw fit to attend my parents' funeral, but now I think it's time for you to leave.'

'That, my dear, is for me to decide, to echo your own words. There are matters here that need attending to.' He raised his hands to encompass the room.

'What do you mean?'

'None of this is yours. Not the land, or the house, or even the sad little business.' His sly smile enveloped her. 'It's *mine*, my dear. It always has been.' The price he paid for taking Colette by force was to continue providing the roof over their heads. Now though, with Colette gone, he owed this girl nothing.

Eva's face went white with shock. 'You're lying! How can it be yours? My parents bought this house soon after they were married. I've lived here all my life.'

He shook his head. 'Nothing is ever what it seems.'

'I don't believe you.'

'Then you must see your solicitor. He knows the truth.' Impatient now, he strode past her to the door. 'I won't turn you out here and now,' he said over his shoulder, 'but I'll be back tomorrow evening, eight o'clock sharp, by which time I'll expect you to be packed and ready to hand over the keys.'

When he had gone, Eva went to the window and looked out over the land that her mother had loved. 'It can't be true,' she whispered. 'Mam would have told me.' Beneath the big old oak, she could see Bill in angry conversation with his father. Now she knew what he had been trying to tell her. 'He's lying!' she whispered over and over. 'He's lying!' And yet somehow she knew he was not.

'He's *not* lying,' Todd's voice said in her ear. 'I've seen the papers. It all belongs to him.' She swung round, to find his gloating face inches from her own. He dared to put his hand on her shoulder. 'I have some influence with my father,' he murmured. 'Be nice to me, and I'll see what I can do.'

Before Eva could reply, he was violently jerked away. Bill had him by the scruff of the neck. 'I ought to thrash you good and proper, but this is not the time or the place. This is *still* Eva's home, and you'd do well to remember why we're here!' And with that, Bill marched his brother to the door. Todd twisted to glare at Eva. 'It won't be your home for long, not if I know my father!'

'We'll see about that,' Bill hissed. 'He has me to reckon with yet!' With a shove he pushed Todd out of the room. Turning to Eva, he apologised. 'I'm sorry about that. But I meant what I said, I'll do everything in my power to stop him.'

'I can't believe it,' Eva said. 'How could your father get possession of this house? When? And why wasn't I told?'

'I'm sorry, Eva, I can't answer any of your questions. I only found out about this business the day before we arrived, and that was only by accident when I heard the two of them discussing it.' Bill crossed the room and took her hand in his. 'I've tried to reason with him, even offered to buy it from him for you. But he won't listen. For some reason, he flatly refuses any offer I make.' He squeezed her hand. 'But I won't let him get the better of you, Eva. Somehow or other, I'll make certain that you keep what's rightfully yours.'

'Dear Bill, still my knight in shining armour,' Eva said with a brave smile. Then her shoulders slumped. 'I don't understand any of this.'

'Neither do I.' Bill thought back to the journey from Canada, the way Todd and his father had huddled together, furtively plotting. 'What really puzzles me is the way he's gone right against his business instincts. Money is his god. I've made him an offer over and above what he could hope to get for this property on the open market and yet still he refuses.'

'That's because he's a bastard!' As soon as she'd said it, Eva felt ashamed. 'I'm sorry, I shouldn't have said that. When all's said and done, he's still your father.'

'He's *not* my father.' Unsettled, Bill moved away, standing for a while with his back to the blackened chimney. 'I was adopted. I never learned to love him, but I adore Margaret. She's been the mother I never had.' His voice shook. 'He's been a swine to her. I've tried time and again to persuade her to leave him, but she never would – never will.'

Eva's heart went out to him. 'Some women are like that. However badly they're treated, they stay with their man through thick and thin. My mother was like that. She said that when you gave your marriage vows before God, you were duty bound to live by them, especially if there were children involved.'

'Make your bed and lie on it, eh?' he said wryly. 'You don't know what it's been like, seeing her buckle under to his every demand. All these years he's chipped away at her confidence until now she's just a shadow of her old self. The peculiar thing is, when I was man enough to challenge him, Margaret took his side and I found myself out on the streets.' His lip curled. 'Seems I read the situation wrong.'

'She loves you though.' Anyone could see that. 'More than she loves her own son, I think.'

'Why am I telling you all this?'

'Because old friends should be able to tell each other everything.' She deeply valued these moments with him.

Bill made no reply. Instead, he cupped Eva's face in his hands, smiling into her eyes with the look of a man in love. But then, just as she was about to speak, he shifted his gaze and went on. 'Todd has never been any comfort to her,' he confided. 'He's moulded in his father's image. The older he gets, the more he admires him, and the more like him he becomes.'

'I can see that.'

Bill sighed. 'There's something odd here though, Eva. My father's a wealthy man, with more land and property than he knows what to do with. He doesn't need this house, or the land.' He hesitated. 'It's almost as though . . .' He wasn't quite sure how to put into words what he was feeling.

Eva finished his sentence for him. 'Almost as though he has a grudge against me, is that what you're trying to say?' The same thought had occurred to her.

'But it doesn't make any sense.'

'All the same, you're right. It's as though he's trying to punish me.'

'But you were just a child the last time he saw you. What reason would he have for wanting to punish *you*?'

'I think I may know why. There was a time when he took a fancy to my mam, and when she turned him down he was furious.' That was as much as her mother had admitted; praying the awful truth would never emerge.

'But he can't blame you for that.' He wasn't surprised by what Eva had told him. In Vancouver where they lived, his father's weakness for other women was no secret – except maybe to his wife.

'No, he can't blame me,' Eva said, 'but maybe he thinks that by repossessing her home and throwing me out, he's getting his revenge on her.'

Bill nodded. 'It's the sort of thing he might stoop to.'

'I can't help thinking there's something else, though,' she said quietly. 'Why would he hold a grudge all this time? And why did he wait until now to make his move? If he really does own this house as he claims, why didn't he throw us out long ago, while Mam was still alive? That would have hurt her deeply. It has to do with me, I'm sure of it.'

'I think you're wrong. I think it's more to do with his obsession with power. I know it's difficult, Eva, but please, for your own peace of mind, try not to dwell on it for now. You've been through so much already.' He raised her face to his. 'This house, the land, it's very important to you, isn't it?'

Too choked for words, she nodded, her eyes appealing to him.

'Don't worry,' he murmured. 'One way or another we'll get to the bottom of it. For now, let's just concentrate on keeping him at arm's length.' His expression hardened. 'He won't have it all his own way, Eva, I can promise you that.'

Eva squared her small shoulders. 'And I promise, whatever happens, he will never have the satisfaction of bringing me down.'

Bill looked at the way she stood, head high, determination shining from her, and he knew he would never love her more than he did at this moment. 'I've no doubt you're a match for him,' he said, a smile creeping over his handsome features, 'and I've no doubt you mean to leave your mark on him.' The smile gave way to a frown. 'But you must never underestimate him, Eva. I know him too well. He's a very clever, dangerous man.'

'I'm not afraid of him.' Though, there *was* the tiniest part of her that quailed at the thought that he might know something about her that she didn't. 'First thing in the morning I mean to go into Bedford and see the solicitor. Everything my parents ever did was through Dollond and Travers in Ainsworth Street. If anyone can get to the bottom of this, they can.'

'That's very wise,' he agreed, 'but don't be too disheartened if you don't get any joy from them.' He winked conspiratorially. 'I have a few ideas of my own.'

'No, Bill.' For her aunt's sake, Eva hated the idea of deepening the rift in the family. 'I'm not ungrateful, but this is something I have to do on my own.'

'Trust me, Eva.'

'I do trust you.'

'Good!' Taking her by surprise, he kissed her on the mouth. 'Tomorrow night, eight o'clock,' he promised, 'we'll be waiting for him.' And with those few words, he departed, leaving Eva softly touching her lips. His kiss had been a disturbingly pleasant sensation.

———⊷◦⊶———

IN THE MORNING, Eva and Patsy prepared to drive into Bedford. Eva swore when the car wouldn't start. 'I wish our money could have stretched to a more reliable one,' she groaned. 'But I suppose beggars can't be choosers.' Impatient, she gave the car a kick.

When, with a shuddering sigh, it burst into life, she looked at Patsy and laughed. 'I wonder if a good kick up the backside would do the same for you?'

Patsy was never at her best first thing. 'Fancy dragging me outta bed this time of a morning. Are yer trying to kill me or what?'

'What's wrong with you?' Eva asked, amused. 'It was gone six when I woke you. You've been up earlier than that before.'

'Oh aye! After a drop too much o' the good stuff and the bed won't keep still.'

'Stop moaning and look for a parking place.'

'Look yerself, yer bossy young bugger!' Patsy was thirty, going on ninety. 'I'm that tired, I can't see a hand in front o' me.' As she sank down into the car seat, her bleary eyes peered at the dashboard clock. 'Will yer look at that!'

'What?' Eva kept her eyes on the road.

'It's still only quarter past eight, so it is. What an uncivilised hour for a lady like meself.'

In spite of her worries, Eva had to laugh. 'Some lady. Take a look at yourself in the mirror. Go on!' She glanced at Patsy's sleepy face and unkempt hair. 'You look like something the cat dragged in.'

Patsy stole a look at herself in the vanity mirror, and sure enough she gave herself a fright. 'Ah, sure, I can't be perfect *all* the time!'

'You did insist on coming with me, remember. I would have told you all about it when I got back. After all, I'm fighting for your home as well as mine. If he takes the land, he takes your cottage too. We mustn't forget that.'

'I know.' Patsy glanced in the mirror for a second time. 'And yer right, I do look like something the cat dragged in. But don't you worry, give me a minute an' yer won't believe yer eyes.' Spitting into the palms of her hands, she ran her hands over her hair to flatten it until it looked like an ill-fitting cap. 'There! That's better. Now for a bit of lipstick. Where's yer bag, me darlin'?' Without waiting for an answer, she plucked Eva's handbag from the back seat and began rummaging. 'Jaysus! You've got everything in here but the back door.'

While Patsy groomed herself, Eva negotiated the narrow entrance into the car park. There was one space. 'That's lucky.' Reversing into it, she shifted the car out of gear and switched off the engine. 'You don't have to come in if you don't want to.' Turning to Patsy, she had a shock. 'Good God! Whatever have you done to yourself?'

Patsy's red hair had a mind of its own and it took more than spittle to keep it down. Like a mass of coiled springs that had been suppressed for too long, it framed her head like an electrified halo. Her lips and teeth were covered with lipstick and her long lashes clotted with mascara.

'Oh, Patsy!' Eva didn't know whether to laugh or cry.

'What? Yer don't think it suits me? The truth now, how do I look?'

'Different.' Biting her lips, Eva managed to stem her laughter. 'Yes, that's it. You look different.'

For a long, anxious moment, Patsy examined herself in the mirror. Then, with a solemn face, she turned and stared at Eva. 'I look like a circus clown,' she said, the grin erupting into laughter.

A short time later, sobered by the purpose of their journey, the two of them made their way to the High Street and up towards Ainsworth Street.

'If I remember rightly, their offices are just past the church.'

'Are you sure they'll see us?'

'No, but I'm hoping they can fit us in before they start their appointments for the day. That's why I wanted to get here early. I knew I wouldn't have a hope of getting an appointment at such short notice.'

As it turned out, Eva's instinct was right.

'Ten minutes, Miss Bereton, that's all I can spare. Sit yourself down, before I change my mind.' Thomas Dollond was an elderly man, with a sharp mind and a kind, round face. When the two of them were seated, he carefully eased his old bones into his chair; Eva wasn't certain whether the loud, creaking sound was him or the chair.

'We wouldn't have come without an appointment,' Eva said, 'only it's very urgent.' Patsy tugged at her sleeve. 'Oh, I'm sorry, this is Patsy Noonan.'

'Really?' His surprise betrayed itself for only a second. 'Ah yes, Miss Noonan has been doing your mother's accounts for some time. She also works in the farm shop and rents the field cottage.'

'You know a great deal.' It was Eva's turn to be surprised. As far as she knew, it was some time since her mother had visited these offices.

Patsy didn't know whether to be flattered or annoyed. 'Who told you all that?' she asked him.

'A solicitor is paid to know these things,' he said importantly. Adjusting his spectacles, he added, 'Incidentally, your account ledgers are a pleasure to the eye. Meticulously kept, as I recall, and very commendable, especially as I believe you are not a qualified accountant.' What a wild-looking thing she was, he thought. Not at all what he'd imagined from her neat work. 'Mrs Bereton told me how highly she valued you.'

Turning his attention to Eva, he said, 'You say the matter is urgent?'

'Desperately.'

Leaning back in his chair, he nodded like one of those monkeys on a stick. 'I know about your parents,' he said sympathetically, 'and I'm very sorry. In fact, I dictated a letter only yesterday but in view of the delicate situation I thought it best to delay sending it.'

Eva sat bolt upright. 'What letter?'

He cleared his throat. There were moments when he hated his job. This was one of those moments. 'It's to do with the property, but I think you already know that, don't you?' He was visibly uncomfortable. 'Isn't that why you're here?'

'My uncle says the property is his.' Eva hardly dared go on, afraid of the answer to the question she had to ask. 'It isn't true, is it?'

He sighed.

'I'm sorry,' Mr Dollond's voice was filled with

genuine regret, 'your uncle has owned the property for many years. Long before he went to Canada, in fact.'

'But my parents bought it before he went.' At least that was what she had always believed.

He shook his head slowly. 'Your uncle purchased the property when your parents went through a period of financial difficulty. Your parents then became paying tenants. The agreement was drawn up in this very office. I myself oversaw the transaction and was given responsibility for its smooth running over the years.' Getting out of his chair, he went to the filing cabinet and took out a buff-coloured file. 'It's all here,' he said, seating himself to thumb through the file. 'Deeds, rental agreement made by your parents, records of payments and such.'

'May I see?'

'Of course.' Handing her the file he explained, 'Your uncle rang me the day he arrived. He was most adamant that, should you ask to see proof of his ownership, as he believed you might, I must have all documents readily available.'

Patsy had heard enough. 'Mercenary bastard!' she muttered.

Mr Dollond leaned forward. 'I sincerely hope you don't mean me, young lady?' Thirty she might be, but compared to him she was a mere babe in arms.

'Er, no, sir.' Patsy went red with embarrassment. 'I meant Eva's uncle from Canada.' Her embarrassment didn't last long. '*He's* the mercenary bastard!'

The old gent smiled. 'Then, as long as you don't quote me outside these four walls, I wholeheartedly agree. The fellow is a scoundrel!' Such a personal comment went against his many years of professional discipline. But he was due to retire soon and these days he found himself speaking his mind more and more.

Eva perused the file. With every page her heart sank deeper. At last, despairing, she handed back the file. 'All this time,' she murmured, 'and I never knew it was all his.'

'I'm sorry, but he has the right to evict you.'

'Is there nothing I can do?' Eva felt close to tears.

'I'm afraid so.' He dared not give her any false hopes. 'I've spoken with your uncle at great length. He's adamant he won't keep you as tenant.' He ventured an idea. 'Perhaps *you* might be able to persuade him.'

'I would rather die.'

'Then I'm afraid there is nothing to be done. The harsh truth is, your uncle is here to reclaim his property and I'm duty bound to assist.'

Eva wondered why he was 'duty bound'. If he really didn't want to act on behalf of her uncle, he should say so. To her mind, he was no better than her uncle. Money was a powerful leveller, she thought cynically.

'I tried everything,' he said. 'I did think he might let you buy the property from him but he flatly refuses to sell any part of it, to you or to anyone else.'

'Not even to Bill.' Her mind kept harking back to him; her heart too.

'I'm sorry, I didn't hear that.'

'His son, Bill – adopted son,' she corrected herself. 'He made a very generous offer for the property and was refused.' Eva would always be grateful to him for trying. 'Bill is a good man. He had an idea that he could buy it and then sell it to me at a price I could afford. But my uncle would have none of it.'

'I see. Well, I'm afraid it only confirms what I've said. For whatever reason, he means to reclaim this property for himself.'

'Can I fight him through the courts? Tenants' rights or something like that?' She was grasping at straws.

He shook his head. 'A waste of time. It was your parents who were the tenants, not you.'

'What if I refuse to budge?'

Patsy answered her. 'The bugger will send in the bailiffs and have you thrown out, and your belongings behind you.'

'She's right, I'm afraid.' Nodding his head in that peculiar way of his, Mr Dollond added grimly,

'In the end he will win, and you'll be left with bitter memories.' He seemed embarrassed. 'You probably think I'm as heartless as your uncle, but it isn't that simple. Unfortunately, your parents and I were bound by the same agreement and now, however unpleasant it might be, it's left to me to tie up all the loose ends.'

In fact there were very few 'loose ends'. He had kept the records straight over the years, and Colette Bereton had looked after the house and land exceedingly well. Her loving care of the place had greatly added to its value. To his mind, Peter Westerfield's spiteful treatment of Colette's daughter bordered on wickedness. But who knew what lay behind the man's decision, and anyway, who was he to question it, especially when he was being paid, and had been paid, very handsomely indeed?

Eva was silent. It seemed like only a heart-beat ago she had a father and a mother, a home and security; and Patsy, too, had been settled and content for the first time in years. Now it was all being snatched away, and there was nothing she could do to stop it. 'I'm sorry you couldn't help,' she said eventually. 'I'm sorry we've wasted your time, and ours.' There was bitterness in her voice, and a certain amount of condemnation.

'I'm sorry too.' Getting out of his chair, Mr Dollond came round to sit on the desk in front of her. 'I *have* tried to reason with your uncle.'

'I'm sure you have.' Eva relented. 'I don't hold you responsible for any of this, though I wish I hadn't been kept in the dark all this time.'

'Look, I may be an experienced solicitor, but I'm also an old man coming towards the end of his career. I'm fortunate to have children and grand-children, and it would break my heart to see them treated in the shocking way your uncle is treat-ing you.' He coughed and scratched his chin, and seemed to be struggling with his thoughts. 'I've been more fortunate than most. I own a few acres of land, and a small cottage set aside for the new gardener. But he isn't due to start for a month. You're welcome to stay there for a few weeks. It will give you breathing space, time to think and make plans.'

'Thank you. It's a very generous offer and I'm truly grateful.' Eva was deeply touched by his gesture. 'But I can't accept.' It was no solution. She had to stand on her own two feet or she might never move forward.

'But what will you do?' Suddenly he felt guilty. Had he really done enough to help her? More to the point, in view of the huge fee he was being paid, had he really wanted to?

'I'm not quite sure what I'll do,' Eva answered softly. 'But one thing I do know.' She stood up then, her shoulders straight, her expression harder than Patsy had ever seen it. 'My uncle can take the roof

75

from over my head and leave me destitute, but he will never break my spirit.'

The old man admired her courage. 'I can believe that,' he said, 'but it's a sorry day when families fall out among themselves. Still, once he's returned to Canada, I don't suppose you'll ever need to have any contact with him again.'

Eva looked solemn. 'There are things here I still don't understand, but I will. One day, I'll find out the reason behind his spite. Meanwhile, just as it's up to you to tidy up all the loose ends, it's up to me to prevent *him* from ever again setting foot in my mother's house.' Her quiet smile was unnerving.

'What do you mean by that? I've already told you what will happen if you insist on staying there. He'll have no choice but to send in the bailiffs and they can be very aggressive – and they have the law on their side!'

Digging into her purse, she asked, 'How much do I owe you?'

'Well, nothing . . . I mean . . .' Her calm, collected manner flustered him.

Eva closed her purse. 'Thank you for your time,' she said and left the office with Patsy before he could say another word.

'WHERE *will* we go?' Subdued by the outcome, Patsy was only now beginning to realise the seriousness of their situation.

Once outside the office, Eva slowed her steps. 'I don't know,' she admitted. 'We need to talk about it – what to do, which direction to go. We need to pool what resources we have and draw up some kind of budget.'

'Ah, sure, *I* can do that.' Patsy was beginning to feel useful. 'But it's the *other* things. I don't own much more than the clothes on me back, but there's some lovely things belonging to your mam in that cottage, and in the house too. And what about all her precious ornaments? That delightful little clock that sits on the mantelpiece and chimes the quarter hour, all her blue china, and the wooden dolphin yer daddy carved for her when you were born?'

Eva smiled at that. Her mother had told her how he had sat, night after night, working on that dolphin. Oh, but he must have loved her in those early days.

'Yer mammy wouldn't want yer to leave that behind.'

Drawn into the past, and deeply troubled by the present, Eva lapsed into silence.

Patsy gabbled on. 'We'll have to ask your uncle for time to send in the removal van. We can't leave it all behind. The bugger would only sell it for what he could get, and you'd never see a penny of it!'

'I'll see to it, Patsy. Don't worry.' Eva didn't want to talk about it right now. What she needed was time to think, to get her mind in order. So much had happened and it was all bearing down on her, like a great, heavy weight.

'Such lovely things,' Patsy persisted. 'Yer uncle will *have* to give us time to get them out, so he will.'

'I don't want any favours from him.' Eva's heart ached. 'Besides, they're just things. Holding on to them won't bring her back, will it?' Mr Dollond had been her last hope; now it was all up to her. Even Patsy was counting on her to forge a future for them both. The more Eva thought about it, the more she wondered if she was up to the responsibility.

Patsy linked her arm through Eva's. 'No, me darlin',' she conceded, 'having her things won't bring yer mammy back. Nothing will. But we have each other, and that's something to be grateful for, isn't it?'

Eva clasped her hand over the podgy fingers. 'Oh, Patsy,' her eyes shone with affection, 'you're all I have now. And you're right, about the furniture and things. I have no intention of leaving them for him to get his hands on. They belonged to my parents, their lives were wrapped up in them.'

Shrugging, she gave a deep sigh. 'I can't leave them, and I can't take them. We have to travel light. We don't even know where we're going, or how we'll earn a living, or even whether we'll have a roof over our heads.'

'You make it sound frightening.'

'We'll be all right,' Eva said confidently. 'We're not afraid of hard work, and we've done all manner of things – accounting, stock-keeping, running a shop, maintaining a smallholding. Besides, we're young and strong enough to tackle anything.'

Patsy laughed out loud. '*You* might be young,' she cried, 'but I'm way past my prime and far too fat to *tackle* things.'

'Give over, Patsy. You're only thirty.'

'Well, I'm still too fat.'

'I shouldn't worry too much about that,' Eva grinned. 'If we have to starve for a few days, the weight will fall off you.'

'I don't intend to starve, I can tell you that now,' Patsy said stoutly. She loved her food.

'You know, Patsy, I really believed the solicitor would say my uncle was lying and that everything was all right.'

'But it isn't, is it?'

'To tell you the truth, Patsy, I am frightened.'

Patsy was shocked. 'Sure, I never thought I'd see the day when you were frightened of *anything*.'

'Deep down, we're all frightened of something.'

And for once, Patsy didn't argue. She, more than anyone, knew the wisdom of those words.

———»•«———

B Y LATE AFTERNOON, Patsy had divided her worldly possessions between a small suitcase and a cardboard box. 'Well, that's it,' she declared, carrying them to the car. 'Where do you want them?'

'Stack them in the car boot with my stuff.' Eva stared at the suitcase and box. 'Is that all?' she asked. 'Are you sure you haven't forgotten anything?'

Patsy shook her head. 'It's all there.' She swung the suitcase up and into the back of the boot, then wedged the box on top. 'Anyway, I thought you said we had to travel light.'

'Oh, look at that!' Eva pointed to the top of the copper beech and there, trembling on the lower branches, two baby pigeons were preparing for flight. 'Aren't they lovely?'

'Ugly, yer mean. I've never seen such ugly things as baby pigeons.'

Captivated, Eva couldn't take her eyes off them. 'Oh, Patsy, look again,' she urged. 'Look at their bright, shining eyes and fluffy new feathers, and think of the courage it takes to fly off into the unknown.' She would miss it here, in this lovely, quiet place.

Patsy looked again at the birds. 'Well, mebbe.

But you would be excited, wouldn't yer? I know how long you've waited for them birds to fledge. Now they're ready to leave, yer must be feeling like a mother hen, watching her babies take to the skies.'

'They're ready to spread their wings, just like us.'

Patsy felt a great sadness. She wasn't at all ready to spread her wings. In her lifetime, she had travelled to many places, and whenever she moved on, it had always been with a sense of adventure and excitement. But not this time. This time she had put down roots and pulling them up was painful. And if it was painful for her, then she couldn't begin to imagine how Eva must be feeling.

'Eva?' Patsy so much wanted to help but she didn't know how.

'Yes?' As Eva turned, the light caught the gleam of tears in her eyes, and all her sorrow and pain were written there.

Patsy's words of comfort stuck in her throat. Instead she said lamely, 'I think we both need a cup of tea. What do you say, me darlin'?'

'It's best if we go quickly,' Eva replied. 'That way we won't be prolonging the agony.' There was another reason too. 'I don't want to still be here when he turns up.' The thought of her uncle gloating as he saw them off the premises was too much to contemplate.

'But it's only six o'clock. He won't be here for

another two hours. Anyway, didn't Bill say he might find a way for us to stay here?'

'That's what he said.'

'Then shouldn't we wait? At least until eight o'clock?'

'No.' Eva had already decided. 'I'm sure Bill would move heaven and earth if it meant we could stay, but we can't, and it's no good fooling ourselves. There is nothing he can do to make my uncle change his mind. He won't be budged by anyone, not by the solicitor, not by Bill, and especially not by me.'

'Will we ever come back, do you think?' Patsy's voice shook.

Eva looked at her, her own heart aching terribly, and in a moment they were seeking comfort in each other's arms. 'Don't worry,' Eva said through her tears. 'We'll be all right. We'll look out for each other, just like we've always done.' Simple words, softly spoken, but they soothed Patsy, and that was enough. 'Go and tidy the cottage,' Eva suggested. 'I'll finish off in the house and then we'll be gone from here.'

Patsy was confused. 'What about your mam's things? I thought you'd arranged for the man from the charity to come and collect them?'

'I changed my mind.'

'Why?'

'Please, Patsy, not now.' She didn't feel like explaining every move she made. Besides, she knew

Patsy would never agree with what she had decided. Best not to tell her until afterwards, she thought.

While Patsy busied herself tidying the cottage, Eva did the same in the house. 'Must leave it all as Mam would have wanted,' she said to herself as she went about her work. First she washed and stacked the few dishes she and Patsy had used over lunch; then she dusted and hoovered, and last but not least, she collected together all her mother's smaller possessions and packed them into her father's tatty leather hold-all.

Gazing at a photograph of her mother, she murmured, 'I'm only taking these few things, Mam.' For a while her loss overwhelmed her. 'I don't need anything to remind me of you, Mam,' she said. 'I'll carry you in my heart for ever.'

The photograph showed her mother sitting on the swing beneath the apple tree. It was a sunny day, and Eva had been trying out her new camera. Neither she nor her mother thought the photograph would be much good, because the sun was in the wrong position and Colette was making her laugh. Just as Eva snapped the picture, her mother swung towards her, hair flying in the breeze and skirt lifted high. 'I'm sorry, sweetheart,' she said afterwards, 'but I felt like a little girl again, and oh, it was such fun. I didn't mean to waste your film.'

And yet, as it turned out, it was the best picture Eva ever took. Colette was delighted. Eva bought a frame and sat it on the mantelpiece where it had been ever since. Even Marcus had liked the picture. 'You didn't have to show your arse though,' he complained, but there was a twinkle in his eye every time he looked at the photograph.

Now, taking it down from the mantelpiece, Eva gazed at the picture for a long, precious time, reliving the day, moment by moment.

When it was too painful to look any longer, she carefully undid the back of the frame and lifted the photo out. It seemed like an act of sacrilege.

———⟫•⟪———

B ILL MADE ONE last, desperate plea to his father. 'For years you've been after that piece of land I secured in Whistler,' he said. 'I'll make a deal with you. Sell the Bereton place to me, and we'll talk about the Whistler land.' They were in the office of a suite of rooms Peter had taken in Bedford's grandest hotel.

Peter's eyes glittered with greed. 'What? You mean you'd consider selling that to *me*?' He couldn't believe why Bill would do such a thing. 'Good God, man! It cost you an arm and a leg to secure that land. It must be worth a small fortune now – right at the foot of the Rockies and ripe for development. If it got out that you were prepared to sell, you'd have people biting your hand off.'

'Well, do you want to talk, or don't you?'

'How good a deal will it be for me?'

Bill thought he had him hooked. 'It'll be good enough, but I can tell you now, I don't intend to give it away.' He knew how badly Peter wanted that land. He wanted it too, but it was Eva's needs he had in mind now. Besides, with the right investment, the Bereton place could be a little gold mine, and if it was what Eva wanted, he was more than prepared to inject the capital needed.

'I can't believe you're really offering that land to me,' Peter said. 'You've known all along how badly I wanted it. I had planned to develop it myself, or sell it on for a handsome profit. Thanks to you, all that went right out the bloody window.' His weasel-like features lifted in a sly grin. 'You didn't get it all your own way, though, did you, eh? At least I had the satisfaction of forcing up the price. I was the one bidding by proxy. You never knew that, did you?'

'I had an idea it was you,' Bill said easily. 'Don't forget, I know the way you operate. So. Name your offer for the Whistler plot, and I'll see if it's good enough.'

'Why do you want the Bereton place?'

'That's my business.'

Peter grinned. 'You always were soft on her, weren't you? For weeks after we took you to Canada you couldn't settle. She was on your mind then, and she's still on your mind. Even when you married and settled down, I bet you still hankered after her.'

He knew how to hit hard. 'I wonder what your wife would say if she knew you were making a play for your own cousin.'

Incensed, Bill fought to retain his dignity. 'That's enough!' Everything Peter had said was the truth, he couldn't deny that. But he had never once been unfaithful to Joan, and he had no intention of being so now. Eva was special to him, and always would be, but he suspected she didn't feel the same towards him. Moreover, their lives had long ago gone their separate ways. 'I spent many happy hours on the Bereton place when I was a boy,' he admitted. 'Eva will always be part of that time. I just don't want to see her thrown out of her own home. That's my reason for coming to you now, and only that.'

Peter was still sneering. 'After all, you and the Bereton girl aren't blood cousins. You're one of the unknowns, dumped by your own mother, whoever she was. And fool that I was, I took you in. Ten years of marriage and I still had no heir. How wrong I was. I picked you. I needn't haven't bothered. Within two years I at last had a son who was my own flesh and blood.' He paused; Eva was his own flesh and blood too, but she would never know it. 'So if you wanted to set up home with the Bereton girl, what's to stop you? Not the law, that's for certain, and not me, because I couldn't care one way or the other what you do with your life. In fact, all I want you to do is to get out of my sight, for good! Now!'

Bill frowned. 'I thought we had some business going here.'

'I wouldn't do business with you if you got down on your knees and begged me – though it might be a pleasing sight.'

The bastard means it, thought Bill with a sinking heart. 'I thought you wanted the Whistler land.'

'Oh, I want it right enough, make no mistake about that. I'll have it too.' His voice stiffened. 'But I'll have it on my terms.'

'Over my dead body!'

'Don't tempt me,' Peter snarled. 'Anything can be arranged.' Striding to the door, he called out, 'Todd, your brother is ready to leave.'

Todd promptly appeared. 'What's wrong?' His bulbous stare went from his father to Bill.

'See him out,' Peter ordered.

Todd looked at Bill. 'It seems you've outstayed your welcome.' He put a hand on Bill's arm.

White-faced, Bill shrugged him off. 'Move away.'

Todd glared at him, his face filled with hatred. 'You're not one of us. You never will be.' With that he swung his fist. Bill caught it and roughly thrust Todd aside. He lost his footing and fell at his father's feet in an undignified heap.

'You bastard!' Todd shouted.

'Maybe so,' Bill answered quietly. 'But there are bastards and bastards. And you two are the worst kind. I'm glad you think I don't belong.' He stared at them with contempt. 'I'm only sorry I'm branded with the same name.'

On his way out, he was shocked to see Margaret in the adjoining room, head down and softly crying. 'I'm sorry you had to hear that.' He put his arm round her and drew her close. 'I love you dearly. You know that, don't you?'

She nodded, looking at him with pained eyes. 'I know,' she said, 'and I know how badly they've always treated you.'

'Why don't you come with me? I'll take care of you.'

When she shook her head, his heart sank. 'Oh, Mother. You'll never leave him, will you?'

'Not yet,' she whispered. 'One day though . . .'

'I'll keep in touch,' he promised her.

# Chapter Three

'WE'VE ONLY HALF an hour before they arrive, so we have.'

Patsy was panicking. Now that she had accepted they had no choice but to leave, she was anxious to be gone. 'I don't want you to see that awful man again,' she told Eva. 'Come on, me darlin', we've done all we can, and now it's time to go.'

'I won't be long, Patsy. Just another few minutes.' Her whole life was in this house, she thought wistfully. Leaving it all behind was the most agonising thing she had ever had to do.

'Did yer say the solicitor phoned?'

'About ten minutes ago. He wanted me to take the house keys to him after we've locked up.'

'And will you?'

Eva looked round the room. 'I keep thinking I've forgotten something.' She didn't want to talk about handing over the house keys.

Patsy took the hint. 'Did yer phone the furniture man?'

'I did.'

'And yer say he offered yer a fair price for yer mammy's lovely things?'

'I've already told you.'

'So we're to collect the money from the shop then?'

'That's what he said.'

'We're to take the key to the shop and wait there, have I got that right?'

'Don't worry about it, Patsy. It's all organised.' She wished Patsy would leave it alone. The more questions she asked, the more Eva felt obliged to lie. Although not all of it was lies. She had phoned the man, and he had made a fair offer, subject to seeing the articles. They were to take the key to him and he would come straight up to view and collect the goods. When he returned to the shop, if he was happy with the deal, he would pay out the agreed sum. The only thing was, Eva had already decided to turn down the man's offer. But she daren't say anything, or Patsy would only start worrying all over again.

Patsy ran her hand over the pine rocker where Colette used to sit in the evenings. 'Sure, it's a sin and a shame, so it is,' she muttered.

Eva's heart was close to breaking and Patsy was only making matters worse. All Eva wanted was a moment or two alone. All of her life was here, within these four walls. Leaving it was tearing her apart.

'Patsy, will you do something for me?' She had

to be diplomatic. The last thing she wanted was to make Patsy feel unwanted. She owed her so much. All through this dreadful time, Patsy had been a rock to her, even though she was losing her own home and livelihood. Friendship like that was rare.

Happy to help, Patsy grinned. 'Just say the word an' it'll be done in the wink of an eye.'

Eva beckoned her over. 'Look there, Patsy.' Pointing to the hen enclosure and the few proud creatures strutting about in ignorance, she said, 'I've been wondering what to do about the poultry. If I sell them to the farmer, he's bound to wring their necks, and if we leave them here I've no doubt Peter Westerfield will do the same, but with a great deal more enjoyment.' Her features hardened. 'I'll never forgive him for turning us out of here. Mam always used to say we shouldn't harbour grudges, but he's a wicked man. I won't forget what he's done. I know my father was very difficult, and sometimes he was spiteful. But that was because he'd been struck down in his prime and he couldn't cope with it. Uncle Peter has no such excuse. He's just bad through and through.'

'I can't understand why yer mammy never told yer he owned this property.'

'I've no idea why she would keep something as important as that from me.' Eva had agonised over it, but she could think of no reason to explain the secrecy. 'We used to talk about everything, or at least I thought we did. But I mustn't think about it too much. There's nothing I can do to change things, and I don't want it to mar my memories of her.' Although nothing could ever do that, she thought. 'If Mam chose not to tell me, then I can only think she had good reason.'

'Yer right.' Patsy felt better for knowing that Eva was as puzzled by the question as she was. 'Now then, me darlin', what do yer want me to do about these wretched hens?'

'Let them loose, Patsy.'

'What? Yer mean just open the gates and let them run off?'

Eva nodded. 'Yes. Why not?'

'Well, at least that'll give them a chance to survive. And while I'm at it, I'll see if they've laid any eggs since this morning.'

'Good idea.' The two of them had already loaded the trailer with fruit, vegetables, eggs and kindling, and hooked it to the back of the car.

Through the window, Eva watched her hurry across to the enclosure. With her wild, red hair and that funny way she had of bobbing along, arms swinging, her trousers looking as if she'd jumped too far into them, she was always a sight. 'You're a mess,' Eva chuckled, 'but whatever would I do without you?'

She laughed as Patsy tried rounding up the birds; they led her a merry dance and one even had the gall to flutter on to her shoulders and squirt down her back. 'Gerroff, yer scrawny parrot!' she screeched, doing a lively jig to frighten it away. 'Or I'll wring yer bloody neck meself, so I will!'

Eva laughed so much the tears ran down her face. Then she turned round and the empty house was like a dark blanket thrown over the sunshine.

Quickly now, before Patsy could return, Eva hurried about the task she had set herself. 'I'm sorry, Mam,' she muttered, 'but it's better this way.'

First she went into the hallway to collect all the bits and pieces she had decided to keep – small things she didn't have the heart to leave behind, like the notebook her mother used to jot ideas down in, and the little rag peg bag she had made with her own hands. Small, inconsequential things that wouldn't take up too much room and were an integral part of Eva's memories.

After making certain that everything the two of them were taking was safely stacked in the car boot, she satisfied herself that Patsy was still at war with the poultry – though she needn't have bothered looking because the squawks and shouted abuse told its own story.

Back in the house, she took pen and paper and wrote a note. It was a difficult note to write, and one which she had given much thought to.

Dear Bill,

I hope you find this note. I daren't leave it at the house.

Like you, I've never forgotten where we played as children, nor the happy times we had then. But that was a lifetime ago; we both know there comes a day when you have to put it all behind you, and try to survive in the real world. I have to go away from here now, and I don't know if I shall ever be back.

I just want to say thank you, Bill, for the happy times we had when we were children, and for what you are trying to do for me now. But please understand when I say I would rather you didn't cross swords with your father because of me. I would not want that on my conscience, especially when your relations with him are already strained.

Please don't worry about me, and don't come after me. If I don't learn how to make my own way in the world, I will never amount to anything.

Goodbye, Bill. Give my love to Aunt Margaret. I know you will both understand why I had to do what I did. Have a safe journey back to your wife.

Be happy, Bill. I will never forget you.

Love,

Eva

P.S. If you have any thought for me at all, please respect my wishes.

Folding the note into an envelope, she made her way out, through the kitchen and along the path to the barn, where she and Bill used to play. 'Nothing's changed,' she murmured, entering the barn and lingering by the door, 'and yet *everything's* changed.' Nostalgia swept over her. 'The magic of childhood doesn't last long. You blink, and it's all gone.'

In her mind's eye she could see herself and Bill in this old barn. She could imagine them climbing the apple crates and building the den they were so proud of. She looked at the low timber beam where the two of them sat and gazed out of the window, unseen by the world. 'I was wrong,' she said, smiling, 'the magic hasn't gone. It's still here.' She laid the palm of her hand across her heart. 'It's all still part of me. Part of my life.' It was a comforting feeling.

She stuck the note on an old nail in the timber beam and stared out of the window at the very same scene she and Bill used to look at. She raised her gaze to the sky. 'Please let him find the note.' If he didn't, he would always believe she had gone away ungrateful. That was no way to say goodbye to a friend. As it was, a few hastily scribbled words were small return for what he had tried to do for her, but it was all she could offer. If things had been different and he hadn't had a wife, maybe they could have seen each other, talked over the old times and renewed a very special friendship. But, the way things were, it was better to let sleeping dogs lie.

For a time she let her thoughts wander. 'It's no good dwelling in the past,' she told the bare walls. 'I have to forge a life for myself and Patsy.' Though how she would do that she had no idea as yet. 'Bill already has a life,' she whispered with the smallest tinge of regret. 'Once he's home he won't give me a second thought' – though somehow she couldn't really bring herself to believe that.

'Pull yourself together, Eva,' she told herself grimly. 'You know what you have to do.'

As she left, she closed the barn door behind her; she didn't want her Uncle Peter or that obnoxious son of his to wander in. 'Though I'm sure they'll get around to it eventually,' she said scornfully. 'But not before Bill finds the note, I hope.' On the way back to the house, she went into the shed and took out a number of articles which she crammed into an old sack.

Patsy caught sight of her going back into the house. 'Next time yer want any monsters set free, yer can do it yerself!' she called. 'The buggers don't want to go. Sure, I reckon they'd rather have their necks wrung than take their chances out there.' All around her the birds fluttered and panicked, and the more she went after them, the more frantic they became. 'See what I mean? There's not a penn'orth o' brains between 'em!'

Reluctant to cross the yard with her sack, Eva called back, 'Keep still, Patsy. You're making them panic.'

'It's *me* that's panicking!' Patsy replied. All the same she did as Eva suggested and stood still, and in no time at all the birds strutted away in orderly fashion, out of the pen and into the field. 'Yer deserve to be eaten alive!' Patsy shrieked at them.

Eva hoped they would be safe. 'Keep your wits about you,' she whispered to them as they disappeared from sight. 'It's a dangerous world out there.' As she and Patsy would find out soon enough, she thought anxiously.

'Wait for me in the car,' Eva told Patsy. 'I'll only be a minute.'

'I'll just clean meself up first,' said Patsy, heading for her cottage. 'Messy buggers, those parrots.'

Once inside the house, Eva carefully secured the door before undoing the sack. Laying the articles on the sitting-room carpet, she checked to see if she had forgotten anything. No. It was all there – a half-filled petrol can, old newspapers and oily rags. Her hands were trembling as she undid the top of the can.

There was a moment when she almost abandoned the idea, but thoughts of her Uncle Peter taking possession of this lovely house where she had been so happy were more than she could bear; and the idea of him pawing over her mother's things hardened her resolve. 'I have to do it, Mam,' she murmured, 'and may God forgive me.'

She waited, her gaze locked on the window. 'Come on, Patsy!' she muttered. 'Hurry up, or I won't have the courage to do it.' She daren't set light to the place until Patsy was safely in the car. Eva suspected Patsy would not be able to cope with what she was about to do.

Washed and tidy, with her hair scraped into a pigtail, Patsy emerged from the cottage and hurried to the car. 'Ready!' she called, seeing Eva looking from the window.

Eva smiled and waved, relieved when Patsy looked away.

One last check through the house and Eva was horrified to see she had almost forgotten her mother's photograph, which was still on the mantelpiece. Quickly now, she popped it into her skirt pocket. Taking a deep breath, she screwed the newspaper into soft balls and set them before her mother's chair; that done, she piled some kindling on top and soaked the mound in petrol. She then dipped an oily rag into the petrol and trailed it from the mound to the door, treading warily as she retreated.

She let the rag fall to the floor, then stepped back to a safe distance, struck a match and dropped it directly on to the rag. At first, it seemed she might have to do the whole thing again, but just as she took a step forward, the rag ignited. Alarmed, she jerked backwards, unaware that the photograph of her mother had tumbled from her pocket.

For a moment her stricken gaze followed the narrow trail of fire as it slowly meandered across the room. It should take a while before it reaches the chair, she thought. Then she hurried out of the house. She had already made sure that every window was closed and now she locked the front door and ran to the car, praying that the fire would not show itself before she and Patsy got away.

'Where've yer been?' Patsy demanded.

'Just making sure the house is secured. I don't want to leave it too easy for that bastard to get in.'

'Have yer got the keys?'

Eva started the car and shifted into gear. 'They're in the dustbin,' she answered. 'If he wants them, he can grovel about in there.'

Patsy laughed. 'Yer a girl after me own heart, so yer are.'

At the bottom of the lane, Eva sneaked a look back. There was no sign of the fire having got a proper hold yet, thank God. All the same, her heart felt like a lead weight inside her as she drove on.

'What's wrong, me darlin'?' Patsy knew her every mood.

Coming to the crossroads, Eva headed towards the churchyard. 'Just thinking,' she said.

Patsy understood, remaining quiet for the short journey to the church. Once there, she let Eva go to the graveside alone. 'Ah, sure, you've a lot to think about an' all,' she murmured, wiping away a tear. 'We've neither of us got anybody else. That's why we've got to look out for each other.'

Alone in the pretty churchyard, Eva felt as though she was the last person alive in the whole world. Empty of words, she let the tears fall freely, easing the awful grief inside. Then she dried her eyes, stooped to caress the flowers that were still fresh on the grave, and promised softly, 'As soon as I've made enough money, I'll get you the loveliest headstone I can find.' Then she turned and walked back to the car.

⊰⊱

A s THEY HEADED into town, not a word was spoken. Patsy was thinking about her own parents somewhere in Ireland, yet just as lost to her as if they, too, were in some remote and pretty churchyard. Eva was still too full of emotion to speak. And yet they were perfectly comfortable with each other's silence.

Eventually they turned into a narrow back street. It wasn't an easy task, driving the bulky trailer down it, but Eva wanted to sell to someone out of the way, where she was sure she wouldn't be recognised. The wholesaler she had chosen, a little red-faced man, was in a foul mood. 'Mind you don't knock me bleedin' premises down,' he shouted as she drew up outside.

'Watch yer tongue, yer little weasel!' Patsy snapped indignantly. 'I'll have you know, Eva's as good a driver as any man.'

'Bloody women, who needs 'em! What do you want? State your business then bugger off.'

'I've got produce for sale.' Eva got out of the car and uncovered the goods on the trailer. 'Eight crates of fresh eggs, a dozen baskets of firm apples and pears, straight off the trees, and enough kindling to satisfy your customers for a month.' She picked out a full, round cabbage. 'And you won't find better greens than this if you search from one end of the country to the other.'

Eva was justifiably proud of the harvest she and her mam had gathered. The land they had farmed was good and fertile, but it was muscle and heart that coaxed the food from the ground. 'Flowers too,' she said. 'Freshly picked. And roses like you've never seen.'

'You'd make a good salesman,' the man quipped, 'but I've learned not to trust anybody, however pretty they might be.' His eyes roamed over Eva's face, noting the fine chiselled features and soft, full mouth. But she was a woman, and he'd had enough of them to last a lifetime. 'It don't matter how wonderful *you* think this 'ere stuff is,' he told her crossly, 'I like to see for myself.'

With his fat hands straining his pockets and his flat cap askew, he strolled round the trailer, occasionally plucking out an apple or a pear and sinking his teeth into it, sticky juice dribbling down his chin. 'Hmm. Not bad. Not bad at all.'

Ever mindful of what she had done back at the house, Eva was impatient to get away. 'Well, are you buying or not?' she demanded. 'If you're not, we'll be on our way. There are plenty of other merchants looking for good produce.'

'I'm buying, but I took delivery of fifty boxes of roses and chrysanths only this morning. So I don't need the flowers.'

'It's everything or nothing.'

'How much for the lot then?'

'Make me an offer.' Eva had a figure in mind but she wasn't going to reveal it in case it was less than he was prepared to pay.

'Twenty.'

Without a word, Eva climbed back into the car.

'Hey!' He scurried round the trailer and flung open her door. 'Don't be in such a bleedin' hurry!' It took him a full minute to recover his breath. 'All right, twenty-five.'

Eva closed the door. 'Sorry, I haven't got time to haggle.'

Just as she finished speaking, the sound of a fire siren screamed out. Her heart leapt. They've found the fire, she thought. We've got to get away.

'Thirty,' she told the merchant. 'And that's my last word.'

'What about the trailer? My bugger's knackered.'

'Sixty the lot.'

'Fifty-five, and that's *my* last word.'

'Cash?'

'If that's what you want.'

'It is.' She had closed her bank account. If she was to start afresh, it had to be from scratch.

'Go on then, it's a deal, but you're a hard bugger to do business with.' Secretly he admired her stubbornness. He had an idea she might be in some kind of trouble, especially since she seemed to be in a desperate hurry to get away. Either she was short of a bob or two, or this little lot had fallen off the back of a lorry.

Eva hopped out of the car. 'You get the cash,' she suggested, 'while we unhitch the trailer.'

'I'll give you a good price for the car, if you're interested in selling that as well.'

One stern look from Eva was enough to send him on his way. 'Bleedin' women!' he muttered as he went. 'Steal the arse from your trousers if you let 'em!'

Ten minutes later, Eva was on the road again. 'If

I'd had more time, we could probably have squeezed more out of him,' she told Patsy, 'but I want to get away from here as quickly as I can.'

Suspicious, Patsy stole a sideways glance at her. Eva was looking unusually pale, she thought. 'Eva, you worry me,' she said.

'What do you mean?'

'I don't know. It's just that you seem in an almighty hurry all of a sudden.'

'I've told you, Patsy. I don't want to be around when my uncle turns up at the house.'

'I know that, but we're not at the house now. And will yer slow down! You're doing seventy, so yer are.'

Eva eased her foot off the accelerator. 'I'm sorry,' she apologised. She must be careful not to make Patsy suspicious. What she had done back there at the house was a crime. It was better if Patsy knew nothing about it. That way she could not be implicated. 'We'd better decide exactly where to make for.'

'I thought we'd agreed to go south.'

'Yes, but where south? Which is the best area for us to find work? More to the point, what kind of work are we looking for?'

'Anything that pays a wage or puts a roof over our heads.'

'It won't do, Patsy. We have to be more specific.'

'What then?' Patsy was good at figures but hopeless at making plans.

Eva concentrated her mind. 'First, we need to choose a place and head for it. Then we should book into a hotel or guest house for the night. In the morning, when we're fresh and rested, we'll have a good look round. If we like the place enough to put down roots, we'll go to the labour exchange and see what's on offer. How does that sound?'

'Sounds all right to me.' Patsy's thoughts were driven by her stomach. 'Maybe we should find a cafe and get something to eat while we look at the map.'

'Okay. If you're that hungry, we will. But I'd rather look at the map now and keep going. We've a long journey ahead of us.'

Patsy didn't understand. 'Have we? I thought we didn't know where we were going yet.'

'I'm wondering if we should go north rather than south.' Somewhere her uncle would never think of looking.

Patsy's eyes opened with astonishment. 'North?'

'It's just a thought.'

When Patsy thought of 'north', she thought of Ireland. And when she thought of Ireland, she thought of the council home she'd run away from. 'I'm not sure,' she said. 'How far north?'

'Wherever we go,' Eva assured her, 'we both have to agree. Would you rather we slept on it?'

Patsy nodded. 'I'm too hungry to think straight anyway.'

'All right, we'll find somewhere to eat. Then we'll make for Leighton Buzzard since we're heading that way and find a guest house.'

'Can we afford to stay in a guest house?' Patsy was a born worrier. 'Nothing's cheap, is it?' She had just five pounds. 'I was never one for the saving. Earn it, spend it, that's the way I am.'

'Then you'll have to change your ways,' Eva suggested kindly. 'At least until we're settled.'

Eva had thirty pounds from her bank account, and fifty left from her parents' money; there had been more but the cost of burying them had taken the lion's share. With the merchant's money, she had one hundred and thirty-five pounds altogether.

'We've enough to get us a meal, a night at a respectable guest house, and a good start wherever we decide on,' she said.

'That's grand,' Patsy declared.

And, feeling lighter of heart, the two of them drove on to Leighton Buzzard.

<hr />

THE FIRST THING Peter Westerfield saw as he turned off the main road was a column of grey smoke above the skyline. Not for a moment thinking it would have any bearing on his own plans, he drove on, down the narrow lane, through the thicket, and on towards the Bereton place. 'She'd better be packed and ready for off,' he grunted. 'It's mine now, lock, stock and barrel.' He laughed, a dark, sinister sound. 'Do you hear me, Colette?' he murmured. 'Your precious daughter's been shown her marching orders. I warned you there'd come a day of reckoning. *This* is the day.' There was a time when he had loved her. Now he felt nothing but hate. 'You made me pay for my bit of pleasure,' he snarled. 'Maybe I should have let the truth be known and beggar the consequences.' Yet he knew that all hell would have been let loose if she had talked. 'Pity it cost me for keeping your mouth shut!'

Bill had arrived earlier. When he drew up, the firemen were frantically trying to extinguish the fire. 'Stand back, sir,' he was ordered. 'The roof could go at any minute.'

No sooner had the fireman spoken than the roof collapsed into itself with a deafening roar. Great timbers jutted into the sky like huge stiff fingers, the flames licking up and around. Another ear-splitting roar and the entire structure caved in like a pack of cards, spewing up a mighty shower of sparks and debris. The once pretty house had become no more than a pile of burnt rubble.

Bill had been devastated to find Eva gone and the house in flames. Convinced that his father might have done it, and maybe even harmed her, he searched the grounds high and low, calling Eva's name. But she was nowhere to be found. Helpless, all he could do was stand and watch while her home burned to the ground. It was a sad and terrible sight. In spite of all their efforts, there was nothing the firemen could do; the house was already beyond saving when they were alerted.

Bill became aware of Peter rushing towards him, his face drained of colour. 'My God!' He stared at the ruins, then at Bill, his face darkening with fury. 'That bitch!' He raised his hands, fingers bent, as if ready to strangle someone. '*She* did this! It's her way of making sure I never lay my hands on it.'

Until then it had not entered Bill's head that Eva could have set light to her own home, but now he realised his father might be right, and he was deeply concerned. If Peter believed she was responsible, he wouldn't rest until she was brought to account.

Bill didn't betray his feelings. 'It's strange you should think it was Eva who did this,' he said. 'I thought it might be you who'd fired the place.'

Peter was startled. 'What the hell do you mean?' he demanded. 'I've been nowhere near, and anyway, why would I go to all the trouble and expense of getting back my own property, only to set light to it?'

Having planted a seed of fear, Bill decided to nurture it. 'You've got every reason to fire the place,' he insisted. 'You told me yourself you've no intention of selling the property, and you flatly refused to rent it to Eva. You won't be here to keep an eye on it yourself since you're returning to Canada soon, so it stands to reason the place would have fallen into disrepair.' He gave Peter a knowing look. 'That being the case, its insurance value is its only asset. I expect you've got it insured to the hilt. I know the way you think – set fire to it, then collect the money.'

He glanced towards the firemen who were now crawling all over the ruins, making certain there were no dangerous pockets of heat that might start the fire up again.

'You're out of your mind!' Peter was visibly shaking with anger. Everything Bill said made sense; to an outsider it was all too plausible, and it put the fear of God in him. 'You know as well as I do, she did this.'

'Well, *I* might believe you, but I doubt anyone else will. You know what insurance companies are like, always suspicious. And the fire service will no doubt want to ask you some questions.'

Peter glanced apprehensively towards the chief fireman who, satisfied that the fire had run its course, was now taking off his helmet and looking their way.

Bill was enjoying himself. 'Could be days, *weeks* even, before the whole thing's sorted out and they let you go home, which won't help your business interests. I mean, how can you control your business when you're this far away? And you've made quite a few enemies over the years, haven't you? You know what they say, when the cat's away, the mice will play. It wouldn't surprise me if they got up to all manner of tricks behind your back.' Then a final dig. 'I shouldn't think they'd want to question me though. So if Todd wants to stay here with you, don't worry, I'll look after your interests back home. You can count on me.'

'Like hell I will!' The chief fireman was making his way towards them. 'Keep your mouth shut,' Peter muttered. 'Least said soonest mended.'

---

T HE FIREMAN ASKED whether they had reported the fire.

'We've only just arrived,' Peter told him. 'This is my property and I was due to meet my niece here.' In a sombre voice he added, 'She's just lost both her parents, you know, and now we're the only family she's got.' He feigned sympathy. 'We arrived a few days ago from Canada, for the funeral, you understand. And now this. Terrible business. Poor girl.' He shook his head and sighed.

'Is she here now?' The fireman glanced about, a look of anxiety in his face. He was an old hand at putting out fires, but he had never learned how to cope with human tragedy.

It was Bill who answered. 'She's gone away for

a few days, with an old friend. My cousin has been through a bad time, as you can imagine.'

'Of course.' He returned his attention to Peter. 'But you're the owner, are you, sir?'

'I've already said.'

'Have you any idea what might have happened here?'

'No idea at all. Like I say, I only arrived a few minutes ago.'

'And you've no idea who made the emergency call?'

'None whatsoever.'

Another voice spoke out, a stranger's voice. 'It were me that placed the call, officer.' The farmer had been a neighbour of the Beretons for many years. 'I only wish I'd got you here earlier, but I'm not as young as I were. I were out rabbiting when I saw the smoke. I knew right away it must be the Bereton place.'

'How did you know that?'

'I'm not senile yet, you know!' the old man retorted. 'The reason I knew it must be the Bereton place is because, as a rule, I can see the rooftop from where I was standing, and all I could see were black smoke swirling to the heavens. Besides, this is the only smallholding in this vicinity, apart from mine, o' course.'

'I see, sir.'

'I had to run all the way home to use the phone.'

Taking his hat off, he wiped the sweat from his brow. 'An' as you can see, I'm not all that nimble on me old legs.' As round as he was tall, he had short, bowed legs and walked with a peculiar dipping motion.

'Did you see anyone else in the vicinity?' The fireman was sure the blaze had been started deliberately.

'Nope.' The old man turned his gaze on Peter. 'Just now, when I were approaching from the spinney, I heard you and the young man talking.' He paused, his eyes never leaving Peter's face. 'I never knew young Eva had an uncle, and I'm sorry this has happened, on top of everything else. Nice girl. Lovely family, they were.' His expression hardened. 'I'd hate to hear anyone bad-mouthing 'em.'

Peter looked away, uncomfortable under the farmer's scrutiny.

The old man rammed his hat back on his head. 'I've said me piece, so, if you've finished, I'll get back to me rabbiting.' He turned and walked away with that peculiar bobbing motion.

'Strange old bird,' said the fireman with a smile. He told the two men he would have to put in a report to the local police station and then rejoined his crew.

Peter climbed into his car, slammed shut the door and wound down the window. 'I'll make her pay for this!' he snarled at Bill. 'The pair of you. You're probably in this together. You tell her from me, she's going to rue the day she crossed swords with Peter Westerfield.'

'Hurt her, and you'll answer to me,' Bill said grimly. It was all he could do to keep his hands to himself, but he knew violence would solve nothing.

Peter sniggered. 'You ought to be very careful about getting too protective of the lovely Eva. You have a wife waiting for you back home, don't forget.'

'Don't ever underestimate me,' Bill warned quietly. 'I'm more than a match for you. If it wasn't for my mother, I'd have finished you long ago. The Whistler plot was a prime example. You wanted it, and I took it. Remember that.'

'And you remember this. Better men than you have tried to finish me off and failed miserably, to their cost.' Peter slammed the car into gear and sped away with a screech of tyres.

<hr>

IN THE SHORT while before he must leave, Bill strayed to the barn. Pushing open the door, he peered inside, a bitter-sweet smile shaping his handsome features. He wandered about, touching this and that, his eyes taking in all the familiar things. 'Dear Eva,' he murmured. 'Thinking of you, and the times we shared, kept me sane when I was at my lowest.' Going to the corner beam where he and Eva used to sit, he looked out of the window at the view that Eva had gazed at only a short time before.

Thoughts of his wife filled his mind, and another kind of love came into his heart; Joan was a sweet person, but she was not Eva. It was odd how life sometimes steered you along, taking you into situations that were not of your making. As a man of principle, he would not break his wife's heart to fulfil his own desires. 'For better or worse', those were the vows he had made. His path had been chosen a long time ago, and however much he wanted to, he was too far down that path to change direction now.

As he turned, he saw the note pinned to the beam. Taking it down, he opened it.

As he read Eva's letter, all manner of emotions swept through him. When at last he finished, he carefully folded it and laid it tenderly on a broken crate. 'I can't take you with me, Eva,' he murmured. He looked out at the blue sky and the way the clouds were beginning to curl overhead. 'But I'll be thinking of you, wherever you are.' Closing his eyes, he sighed deeply. 'Keep safe, my love.' It would take all of his willpower not to search her out.

His heart heavy, he went out into the warm sunshine.

As he approached the pile of black rubble that had once been Eva's home, the acrid smell of burning stung his nostrils and coated his tongue. He stood and surveyed the damage. Nothing had been saved. Everything had been either burned to ash or charred beyond redemption. He bowed his head, wondering what Eva must have felt when she set light to this lovely house. He couldn't even begin to imagine what it must have cost her to do it.

As he turned to leave, something caught his eye, a small piece of paper right at his feet. Intrigued, he bent to pick it up, astonished to see that it was a photograph of Eva's mother, older than when he knew her, but little changed. The edges of the photo were scorched and crumbling, but the face was intact. It was a pretty face, much like Eva's, with a bright happy smile and eyes that shone with the joy of life. 'You shouldn't be here to see this,' he murmured. 'I can't believe Eva would have wanted to leave you behind.'

He wondered about that. Had she simply forgotten it? No. Eva was devoted to her mother. What then? He searched his mind. Of course. In her haste to leave she must have dropped the photo. That could explain why it was not in a frame and lying close to the door.

Carefully, he peeled away the charred edges, then he took out his wallet and placed the photo inside, hoping that one day he might be given the opportunity to return it to Eva.

# PART TWO

# OCTOBER 1955
# NEW FRIENDS

# Chapter Four

PATSY WAS TOO excited to work. 'Ah, sure, yer a sly wee bugger, Eva Bereton. I *know* yer planning something for me birthday. Yer might as well tell me.'

Eva continued stacking the freshly laundered linen into the cupboard.

'It's no use yer ignoring me, because I won't go away until I know what's going on.' Persistent to the end, she put down her tray of dirty crockery and placed herself between Eva and the linen basket. 'Well? Are yer gonna tell me or what?'

Reaching round her, Eva drew out two perfectly folded white sheets. 'Nothing to tell,' she lied.

'Aw, go on! I saw you and Frank whispering in the corner the other day. When yer saw me coming yer looked guilty as thieves. Before I could say a word, yer shot off in different directions, so yer did.'

'Rubbish. We did no such thing.' Eva wondered how she was ever going to keep the truth from

Patsy until the day of her birthday. She was as stubborn as a mule. The whole staff were planning a surprise, but it would all be spoiled if Patsy got wind of it.

Patsy's fertile mind was working overtime. She leaned closer, whispering intimately, 'If yer weren't planning something for me, yer must have been planning something else.' Glancing about furtively, she leaned even closer. 'There's something going on between you and Frank, isn't that the truth? Go on, me darlin', yer can tell me. Sure, I'll not say a word.'

Blushing to the roots of her hair, Eva pushed her aside. 'Give over!' she said. 'You know very well there's nothing going on between me and Frank.' Though if he had his way, there would be, she thought. He was a nice enough man, and good-looking into the bargain. She liked him, but with Bill still on her mind, she wasn't ready to get involved with Frank, or anyone else.

'Yer blushing, so yer are.'

'No, I'm not.' Collecting her linen basket, Eva came out of the cupboard and closed the door, turning the key in the lock.

Blackpool hotels had suffered a spate of break-ins lately. The proprietor here took it very seriously, fitting sturdy locks to every cupboard and putting Eva, recently promoted to housekeeper, in charge of their safe-keeping. She had a dozen keys hanging from her belt, which she put on in the morning and kept on until she returned to her room in the evening. She often commented that it was like carrying a sack of coal round her waist. She had a permanent bruise on her leg where the keys dangled and bumped as she walked.

'Frank *does* fancy you though.' Patsy prided herself on knowing everything.

'It doesn't mean I fancy him, does it?' Eva didn't mind discussing the subject. At least it had taken Patsy's mind off her birthday, which was in two days' time.

'He'd be a good catch, so he would, what with his mother owning this grand hotel an' all.'

They went down the back stairs and on towards the kitchen. 'Will you stop trying to marry me off.' Pairing her with a good man seemed to be Patsy's sole aim in life. 'I don't doubt Frank would be a good catch for anyone who might be on the lookout for a man. But don't look at *me*.' She batted her hands as if trying to fend off something threatening. 'You know I'm not interested in men at the minute.'

'That's because yer won't let yerself forget Bill Westerfield.'

'Maybe.' She couldn't deny it. Not to Patsy anyway.

'Holy Mother of Jaysus!' Drawing in a long, loud breath, Patsy let it out in a withering sigh. 'Will yer never learn? The man's in Canada, so he is. And he's happily married. Sure, it's been fifteen months since we were forced out of house and home. If yer haven't heard from him in all that time, what makes yer think yer ever will?'

Arriving at the kitchen door, Eva stopped and turned. 'Don't forget he doesn't know where I am.'

'All the same, if he wanted to find out where you were, I'm sure he wouldn't let anything stand in his way. Sure, the man's got money, hasn't he? And money talks, so it does.'

'You don't understand, Patsy.'

'Is that so?'

Eva knew if she didn't put Patsy straight, she'd never get any peace. 'I don't want him to find me. Like you say, he's happily married and far away in Canada.' Momentarily closing her eyes, she saw his face as clearly as if he was in front of her. Recalling every word in the letter she had left him, she told Patsy, 'Nobody knows better than me that Bill would never try to find me.'

'Because he doesn't want to, yer mean.'

'No.' Eva had never told Patsy the truth. She thought this might be the time to do so. 'Because I asked him not to.'

'What are yer saying, Eva?'

Eva told her how she had left Bill a note in the barn where they used to play as children. 'For a time, I wondered whether he might not have found it. Now, after all this time, I know he did.'

'And now yer sorry, is that it?'

Eva shook her head. 'No. I'm glad he found the note, and I'm glad he respected my wishes not to come in search of me.' She sounded so definite, yet in truth she harboured just the tiniest regret.

'All the same, yer love him, don't yer?' Quieter now, Patsy felt ashamed for pressing the point.

Her heart aching, Eva looked into her friend's eyes, and for a brief moment she was tempted to bare her soul, but some deep instinct held her back.

'Well?'

'Nothing.'

'Yer meant to say something. What was it, me darlin'?'

Eva put on her brightest smile. 'How do you fancy going out tonight?' Left to herself, she would much rather curl up in bed with a hot water bottle and a cup of steaming hot chocolate.

'Out? In this weather?' Aware that Eva had deliberately changed the subject, Patsy played along. 'It's enough to freeze the balls off a brass monkey out there. If yer think I'm walking along the seafront, you've another thought coming, so yer have!'

'No, Patsy. I don't mean walking along the

seafront. Besides, the front will be packed with tourists, here for the illuminations. I meant dancing at the tower. What do you say to that?' Eva was suddenly warming to the idea of going out. After all, it was Saturday night, and it was weeks since she and Patsy had done anything exciting. Working all hours to earn money so they could buy a roof over their heads didn't allow time for enjoyment.

Like a child, Patsy clapped her hands with pleasure. 'What a brilliant idea!'

'You're game then?'

'I'll say!'

'Good. I'll meet you in the lobby at quarter to nine, and don't be late.'

'I have to get bathed and changed, and I'll need time to make myself up, so I will. I mean, who knows what talent might be there?' Grinning like a Cheshire cat, Patsy rolled her eyes. '*You* might even find yerself a feller.'

Eva said nothing but gave her a disdainful look. It was enough.

'All right then, nine o'clock on the dot, and yer can have me hide if I'm a minute late.'

'What time, Patsy?' There were occasions when Eva felt she could cheerfully strangle this delightful Irish bundle, but there were other times, like now, when it was all she could do not to laugh out loud.

'Aw, all right then. Quarter to nine it is.'

---

I N THE KITCHEN, Cook was dishing out more help-ings of food. 'Thank God another day's nearly over,' she groaned. 'It seems everybody wanted to eat in tonight. The dining room was packed to the hilt. I've been on my feet since four o'clock and I haven't stopped since.' She glanced at the wall clock. 'And here it is five minutes past eight.'

'It's the illuminations, so it is.' Coming into the kitchen, Patsy took the tray to the sink and began unloading it. 'I looked out the window upstairs and the streets are crawling with traffic. I should think every hotel in Blackpool is full right through October.'

Eva agreed. 'Give it another week and it will be so quiet we'll be wishing they were back.'

Patsy's tray clattered to the floor. She bent to pick it up and knocked over a teapot, which went the same way, and shattered. 'Whoops.' She looked sheepishly from Cook to Eva. 'I'll have it cleared away in no time at all, so I will.' She dived into the cupboard for the dustpan and brush.

'It'll cost you to replace that,' Cook reminded her. 'Mrs Dewhirst's rules – breakages have to be paid for by them that does the breaking.'

'That'll leave a big hole in Patsy's wages,' Eva said.

Cook liked these two girls. Patsy was a lovable Irish rogue, who wore you out just watching her. She took each day as it came and bore few responsibilities. Eva, though, was the kind of girl who took the world on her shoulders. A deep-down sort, with a heart of pure gold.

She relented. 'Oh, well, accidents will happen, I suppose. As far as we know, the teapot just fell to the floor, all by itself, isn't that so?'

Patsy and Eva nodded solemnly.

'I'd rather have the tourists here,' Patsy said as she dropped the shards into the bin and replaced the dustpan and brush. 'Remember last winter when we worked so hard we were knackered by the time the tourists started coming in again? All that wallpaper stripping and scrubbing, it fair wore me out. I'd rather rush about cleaning rooms and changing beds, so I would.'

Cook shook her head and pointed to the sink, piled high with crockery. 'Just look at that little lot.'

Eva looked around the room. 'Where's Libby?'

Flicking a wayward greying hair from her face, Cook explained, 'Libby's had to help out with the serving. Billy's still away with the flu and poor Rose couldn't cope, so I had to let Libby loose.' Sniffing, she added, 'It's a good job we've got enough crockery, or I'd be pulling my hair out.'

'I'll help,' Eva offered.

Cook would have none of it. 'Me and the girls didn't start till half past seven this morning, and we had it easy right up to six o'clock tonight, whereas you two started at half past five and you've been run off your feet all day, so be off with you. You look worn out, the pair of you. Go on to your beds.'

'We're going dancing,' Patsy announced.

Cook laughed out loud. 'Dancing, is it?' Plopping a generous helping of cabbage on the plate, she tutted and sighed. 'By! What it is to be young.'

'We can't leave you in a mess like this,' Eva protested. 'It won't take me and Patsy long to clear it away.'

'I said be off with you. Enjoy yourselves and don't come rolling home in the early hours, or Mrs Dewhirst will have something to say. And if you oversleep in the morning, she'll have your guts for garters.'

'My feet ache too much to dance,' said Eva. Besides, dancing usually meant being held in a man's arms, and she wasn't in the mood for that. 'Patsy can dance and I'll watch, but come midnight I'll be ready for my bed.'

'Oh, I'll be snoring long before that,' Cook said as the two of them left the kitchen.

Up in her room, Eva took a moment to relax. Seated on the edge of her bed, she kicked off her shoes and flexed her toes. It was a good feeling. Before she knew it, she had fallen back on the bed and was lying there, eyes closed and arms cradled behind her head.

Relaxed and comfortable, she let her mind wander. She went over everything they had been through since leaving home. She worried in case the fire had been discovered in time and Peter had been able to stand in her mother's house, gloating. She wished she hadn't lost the photograph of her mother. That, more than anything else, had given her many sleepless nights. It wasn't long before she'd discovered the photo was missing, and for one moment she was tempted to drive back to the house and look for it. But that was impossible, of course. She thought about Bill, and her heart turned somersaults. If only things could have been different for them.

She let her mind sink into sleep. Her eyes became heavy, and her arms limp.

The sound of a door banging shut woke her with a jerk. Rubbing her eyes, she mentally shook herself. 'Patsy will kill me!' Eva was suddenly wide awake. The clock on the wall told her she had twenty minutes. It was time enough.

Grabbing a towel and robe she ran out of her room and along the corridor to the bathroom. This cramped part of the hotel was given over to resident staff, with only one bathroom between the four of them. Cook travelled in daily, as did her two assistants and the receptionist. Frank had his own house some half a mile away, and his mother lived in the fancy quarters at the front of the hotel.

The bathroom door was locked. 'Who's in there?' She prayed it wasn't Patsy.

Back came the familiar voice. 'Who the devil d'yer think it is? Sure, I thought you'd already been in and out, so I did.'

'How long will you be?'

'I've only just got in here and I want to try out this new bubble bath. It's supposed to make you smell like something out of heaven. I'm telling you, Eva, the fellers won't be able to keep their hands off.'

'Aw, come on, Patsy. How do you expect me to get ready if you're hogging the bathroom?'

'Use the main one on the next floor down.'

'You know that's not allowed.'

'So?'

'If I get caught, it's instant dismissal.'

'Frank would never let his mother dismiss you.'

'Patsy!'

'Go away, why don't yer?'

'Right!' Eva could be just as stubborn. 'If you're not ready in ten minutes, I'm going back to bed.'

There was a quiet moment, before Patsy started singing. Angry though she was, Eva had to smile. 'You bugger!' she muttered, making her way down the winding stairs to the lower floor.

Unfortunately, the maid was changing the towels there. 'Oh, it's you, miss.' A small young thing with big frightened eyes, she had been working at Sealand Hotel for only two days. 'I'm ever so sorry, miss, I thought you said to change them once in the morning and again at night, while most of the guests are in the dining room.'

'Yes, Meg, that's right. Don't worry. You carry on.' Like a schoolgirl caught smoking behind the bike shed, Eva slunk off. 'I'll never be ready in time,' she muttered, running up the stairs. 'It'll be so late by the time we get there, everyone else will have gone.' And, the way she felt right now, that would suit her very well.

---

Twenty minutes later, in spite of everything, Eva made her way downstairs; she had on her best black patent shoes with a bow at the side, a grey swinging skirt, pale blue blouse, and a short jacket in a darker blue.

'Well now, don't you look lovely?' Annie Dewhirst was a tall, slim woman, with short dark hair and a look of authority. The sharp tone of her voice belied her ready smile. 'Where are you off to?'

'Patsy and I are supposed to be going dancing at the tower, but if she's as late as she usually is, it probably won't be worth going.'

'Of course it will be worth going,' Mrs Dewhirst

said. 'You work very hard, Eva, and you need to socialise more. You haven't even got a young man. An intelligent, pretty young lady like yourself, it doesn't seem right.'

'I'm not in the market for a young man,' Eva answered warily. 'I'll leave all that to Patsy.' There were times when she wondered about this woman's probing comments. She got the feeling that beneath that smart, friendly surface lurked a nature that was less than pleasant.

'I see.' The smile disappeared. 'Well, make sure you're in at a respectable time, and mind how much you drink. I don't take kindly to members of my staff coming home the worse for drink.'

'You don't have to worry about that, Mrs Dewhirst.' Eva was deeply offended. 'I have never been the worse for drink, and as for Patsy, she's not as irresponsible as people like to think.'

Annie Dewhirst felt rebuked by Eva's quiet dignity, and suddenly old and drab before her youth and beauty. She could see only too well why her son Frank was so besotted with her, and it was almost more than she could bear. She felt obliged to make amends. Frank would never forgive her if she upset this girl.

'I didn't mean to imply anything,' she apologised. 'You're the last person I would want to criticise. I mean, I'm very grateful for the way you stood in when my housekeeper left in such a hurry. I might even go as far as to say you're the best housekeeper I've ever had.'

'Thank you.' Eva was flattered but not duped.

'You keep yourself to yourself, and I've had no cause at all to complain about you. Patsy, though – well, she can be a bit unpredictable, wild even. At her age I should have thought she might have more sense, but there you are, some people never grow up, do they?'

'Patsy won't be a problem.'

'Just keep an eagle eye on her. I don't want this hotel getting a bad reputation. It's taken me years to establish its good name.'

To Eva's relief, Patsy chose that moment to come hurrying into the hall. 'Hello, Mrs Dewhirst,' she said, all smiles. 'I expect Eva's told you we're going dancing.'

'Yes. I was just saying you should both enjoy yourselves.' She might have repeated her warning about not coming in late, or getting drunk, but thought better of it. What she had told Eva about her being the best housekeeper she had ever employed was the truth. Considering that Eva was not yet twenty, she was surprisingly conscientious. Until such a time as she could get rid of these two and replace Eva with someone equally reliable and competent, she would have to curb her tongue.

Tugging at Eva's sleeve, Patsy said, 'Come on, Eva. Let's go.'

Eva was only too happy to oblige.

Annie Dewhirst watched them leave, one so slim and elegant, the other plump and loud. 'The sooner I get rid of you two, the better,' she muttered. 'As for you, Eva Bereton, keep your hands off my son. I'm saving him for a better catch than *you*!'

'YOU WERE LATE,' said Eva as they stepped into the street. It was cold outside and she buttoned up her jacket.

'I'm really sorry.' Patsy didn't look sorry. 'A bath is still such a luxury after living in the cottage for all that time, I like to make it last.'

'Oh, you did that all right.'

'I think yer look lovely, Eva. Do I look nice? Will the fellers fancy me?'

'I can't speak for the men, but yes, you do look nice.'

Patsy was dressed in a tight black skirt and red blouse under her black coat, and black suede shoes. Impulsively, she did a twirl and almost fell over. Eva grabbed her arm to steady her, and looked at her suspiciously. 'Have you been drinking?' Leaning forward she sniffed at Patsy's face. Sure enough, the faint smell of alcohol wafted up. 'Oh, Patsy!'

Mortified, Patsy lowered her eyes. 'Aw, sure, it were only a wee drop at the bar to give me courage.'

'Just think yourself lucky Mrs Dewhirst didn't

smell the drink on you. You know her views about staff drinking in the bar; only last week she sacked a porter for doing just that.'

'I haven't forgotten.' Patsy made her best Annie Dewhirst face; the voice, too, was good. 'No member of staff to drink in the hotel bar at any time.'

'You're nothing but trouble.'

'I know.'

Eva laughed. 'I must be as mad as you because I love you all the same.'

'Sure, I know that too. I should be ashamed o' meself, so I should.'

'It's no good you playing for my sympathy.' She looked at Patsy's face and couldn't help laughing. 'Come on you,' she said, throwing her arm round Patsy's shoulders. 'Let's enjoy ourselves like the woman said.'

'Now you're talking,' Patsy grinned, and they made their way on foot to the seafront like two excited children.

Thousands of colourful illuminations hung from the street lamps. They were strung across the road, making a zig-zag promenade all of their own, from one end of the Blackpool Mile to the other. There were all kinds of weird and wonderful shapes, figures and caricatures, in colours and patterns of every description, each casting its own special glow. People thronged the promenade and there was an air of excitement all around.

When they got to the tower, Eva was relieved to see there was still a lively crowd in the place. 'That should please you,' she told Patsy, shoving her through the door. 'There's bound to be some fellers on the lookout for a spare woman.'

'They'll be looking at you, not me, so they will.'

'Don't be daft!'

'I'm telling yer. There won't be anyone in this place to touch yer.' She regarded Eva with pride. 'The fellers will be all over yer an' no mistake.'

'No they won't, because, unlike you, I won't be giving them the come-on. Now go on. Hand your coat in and get your ticket, then we can go inside.'

'If a good-looking man asks yer to dance, yer won't say no, will yer?' Patsy never gave up.

'Chance would be a fine thing,' the girl behind the cloakroom counter butted in through her chewing gum. 'I've been on this desk since seven o'clock and I ain't seen *one* good-looking feller all evening.'

Patsy just glared at her and handed in her coat. Then Eva passed her jacket across and they went into the dance hall.

'That silly arse wouldn't know a good-lookin' feller if she saw one,' Patsy announced. 'Experience, that's what counts.'

'You'd know all about that then, would you?' Eva asked, heading for the nearest chair.

'Of course.' Patsy was full of herself. 'Men are no strangers to me.' In the blink of an eye her mood changed. A shadow crossed her face as she recalled one man in particular. 'Mind you,' she added soberly, 'once they've got yer in their clutches, it's hard to escape.'

Realising that Patsy was losing herself in the past, Eva told her, 'Just remember, you're here to enjoy yourself.' Flopping down in the chair, she dug into her purse and took out a one-pound note. 'I'll have a packet of plain crisps and a Babycham, please. You get what you like. My treat.'

'I think I'll have a pint.' Patsy drank like a man.

While Patsy pushed her way to the bar, Eva relaxed. 'My feet feel like hot puddings,' she sighed, taking off her shoes and stretching her toes under the table. 'Ohh, that's better.' Leaning back in the chair, she closed her eyes. 'What I wouldn't give to be in bed right now,' she groaned.

As she spoke the music stopped and her words were clearly audible to the young man at the next table. He leaned over with a smile. 'I'm available,' he said. 'Your bed or mine?'

With an embarrassed smile, Eva shifted her chair away from him. But she could feel his eyes burning into the back of her neck.

That young man wasn't the only one to notice Eva. 'I like your friend,' the barman told Patsy.

He was in his late twenties, short and thick with a coarse face and staring eyes. Sliding the drinks towards her, he said, 'I'm off duty in half an hour. What do you think? Would she mind me chatting her up?'

'She'd probably love it,' Patsy told him. 'She's a devil for the men. But I wouldn't if I were you – unless yer fancy a spell in the hospital, like all the others.'

He turned pale. 'What others?'

'The men she chases. It drives her husband mad, so it does.'

He went paler still. 'She's got a husband then?'

'Built like a bull and with a temper to match.'

'Jesus! I can do without that kind of trouble. What flavour crisps did you want?'

On the way back to the table, Patsy saw how other men were eyeing Eva. 'It's always the same,' she muttered, but there was no malice there. In fact, she was pleased; wherever they went, Eva drew the interest, and Patsy capitalised on it. But it wasn't just that. She had always been proud to be with Eva. As different as day and night, they complemented one another. It didn't matter that there were twelve years between them. They laughed together, cried together, and talked about the kind of things they could never confide to anyone else.

'Took you long enough, didn't it?' Eva was glad

to see her. She felt conspicuous sitting on her own. 'It's a good job you're not a waitress, a girl could die of thirst before you appeared.'

Patsy plopped the Babycham in front of her. 'Here. Get that down yer and think yourself lucky it's all there.' Gazing woefully at her own pint, she grumbled, 'I lost half of mine when a big-footed ape knocked into me.' Choosing a three-legged stool to sit on, she almost lost her balance. 'Jaysus! Can't the buggers afford a stool with four legs?' She pushed it aside and dropped on to a sturdier seat. 'First I lose half me pint, then the bloody stool collapses under me.'

'Didn't you make the bloke buy you another pint?'

'I did.' Patsy winked. 'He's bringing it over now.'

Eva laughed out loud. 'You did it on purpose, didn't you? It wasn't him that knocked into you, it was you that knocked into him.'

Shrugging her shoulders, Patsy chuckled, 'Desperate needs call for desperate measures.'

The man in question was big and muscular. 'I'm sorry again,' he apologised, placing the drink before Patsy. 'I'm not usually that clumsy.' He looked over at the dance floor. 'I'm not that good a dancer but would you like to give it a go?'

'Why not?' Before he could change his mind, Patsy was on her feet and leading him on to the floor. 'Don't go helping yerself to me drink,' she warned Eva. 'I'll know if you have!'

Eva chuckled softly to herself. 'Didn't take you long to get yourself a man, did it, eh?'

For a while, she watched them dancing; the man wasn't as bad as he'd led them to believe. He moved with surprising grace, unlike Patsy who kept treading on his feet, making him wince with pain. Eva tried not to laugh out loud.

'I'm glad she's not dancing with me.' From his place at a nearby table, Frank Dewhirst had been watching Eva for some minutes, before deciding to approach her.

Surprised by his sudden appearance, Eva looked up. 'Frank!' To his mother's fury, they had been on first-name terms for some time now. 'I didn't realise you were back. Your mother said you'd be away for a week at least.'

'Ah, she underestimated my negotiating skill.' At thirty years of age, tall and slim, with brown hair and browner eyes, he had a boyish charm. 'I got the business of buying over much quicker than anticipated. Work on the new foyer will start the second week in January, our quietest time.'

'Your mother says she wants a grand winding stairway.'

'And the rest.'

'I rather like it the way it is.' Eva thought the entrance had a homely, welcoming look.

'So do I, but it's what she wants.' Gesturing to Patsy's seat, he asked, 'Mind if I steal a minute of your time?'

'Of course I don't mind.' She really liked him, though she thought he ought to stand up to his domineering mother a bit more. 'Don't drink Patsy's pint though,' she joked, 'or it will be more than your life's worth.'

Together they watched Patsy and her partner. 'Make an odd couple, don't they?' Frank remarked with a grin. 'How did she latch on to him?'

'She bumped into him on purpose. He spilt her pint and she made him buy another.'

'Was it Patsy's idea to drag him on to the dance floor?'

'No, that was his idea, but I think he's regretting it.' Patsy seemed totally oblivious of her partner's distress. 'I've been wondering whether to rescue the poor devil, but he's such a big, ugly ox, I'm not sure. And anyway, my feet are still aching from a long walk after a long day.'

'Let him take his punishment like a man,' Frank remarked. 'I'd rather you stayed here with me.' In the soft light he thought how beautiful she was, and how childlike. From the first moment he had seen Eva, he was lost. 'There are things I want to ask you.'

Eva was intrigued. 'What things?'

He didn't know how to start. What he really

wanted was to ask her to be his wife, but it was too early. He knew instinctively she didn't feel that way towards him, though he was sure of her affection. It was only a small shift to love, and he could wait; though not too long.

Noticing his hesitation, Eva gently pressed him. 'Is something troubling you, Frank? If helping with Patsy's party is taking up too much of your time, I don't mind doing it all, honestly.'

'No, it's not the party,' he assured her. 'Besides, I offered to help, and I'm having fun.'

'If it isn't the party, what is it?'

'It's you.'

Eva felt apprehensive. 'What about me? Has your mother complained? I know we have words now and then, but I thought she was happy with my work.'

He touched her hand, a thrill running through him. 'No,' his voice was caressing, 'she hasn't complained.' When, embarrassed, Eva drew her hand away, he assumed a casual, businesslike air. 'One thing about Mother, she knows quality when she sees it.' And so do I, he thought. 'You could run that hotel with your eyes closed and she knows it.'

'I don't run the hotel,' she said, though it sounded like a wonderful idea. 'I look after the linen and oversee three young girls.'

'Don't undervalue yourself, Eva. You do much more than that. Since you've been housekeeper, the whole place seems to run like clockwork. You know what they say, if the wheels turn from the bottom, everything is easy. The staff think the world of you, and they're much more content these days.'

'Frank, where is all this leading?'

'Just tell me, Eva, do you intend staying with us a long time, or have you got plans to move on?'

That set her thinking. These past weeks she had grown restless; she didn't see herself as a hotel housekeeper for the rest of her days and she wondered what she might find out there in the big wide world. Patsy, too, was beginning to get restless. But she didn't want to get involved in a discussion about herself and Patsy, so she simply said, 'I haven't given it too much thought.'

'I consider you a friend, Eva.' He felt she was fobbing him off. 'Anything you tell me will remain strictly between the two of us.'

It was true. Frank was a good friend, and he deserved an honest answer. 'I'll admit there have been times lately when I've been tempted to set off and look for something else,' she told him. 'I may have a good job, but it isn't what I wanted. Besides, Patsy isn't cut out to wait on people and clear away their leftovers. We started out with higher hopes, and I feel I owe it to her as well as to myself to set my sights a bit higher.'

His face lit up. 'I was hoping you'd say that,

because I have a proposition to put to you.' His heart said marriage, but his head said wait.

'What kind of a proposition?'

Moving closer he lowered his voice. 'Some time back, I got talking to some men who stayed at the hotel. They were agents, men who scoured the country looking for cheap land. They buy it for next to nothing, hold on to it for a time, and then sell at a handsome profit. "Money for old rope", that's how they described it.'

'Maybe. But you need money to make money. Even I know that.' That was the only thing holding her back. Since she and Patsy had been in work, they had scraped together a tidy sum, but it wouldn't take them far. A number of ideas had gone through her mind, and always it came back to the same argument. There was never enough money.

'What if I were to put in all the capital needed?'

'I'd have to say no.' Bill had offered to help her, and she had refused. She would stand on her own two feet.

'Why not?'

'Because I don't want to be beholden to anybody. It doesn't mean I'm not grateful for the offer, but the answer has to be no, thank you all the same, Frank.'

'A loan then? Pay me back when we start making a profit.'

She shook her head. 'No.'

'Won't you at least think about it? I know we could make a real go of it, Eva, you and me.' The idea was like a worm in his insides; first business partners, then marriage. 'Please don't dismiss it out of hand.'

'All right, I promise I'll give it some thought.' But she knew her answer would be the same.

'That's all I'm asking.' For now, he thought.

———⊰◦⊱———

IN SPITE OF her earlier reservations, Eva enjoyed the evening. She and Frank chatted, mostly about Patsy's birthday party, which was to be held in the local pub. And they danced a few times. As always, they were relaxed in each other's company. Patsy was a hit with her new friend, and though Eva urged her to come and join them, she and her 'big feller' kept clear of them. 'Sure, I'm not playing gooseberry. I can see you and Frank have something cooking.' She winked in that irritating way she had, when she was totally wrong and would not be told otherwise. 'Don't think I haven't seen the two of youse, heads bent and whispering all the while.'

Embarrassed that Frank might overhear, Eva made an excuse to go to the ladies. She knew Patsy would follow.

'There is nothing between me and Frank,' she told Patsy firmly, 'and I'll thank you to remember that.'

'All right, yer not sweethearts. So what were youse whispering about?'

'Can't tell.' Eva mentally crossed her fingers that Patsy wouldn't start on about her birthday again. 'What do you know about that man?' she said to distract her.

'What man?'

'Your new boyfriend.'

Patsy rolled her eyes dreamily. 'Well, he's good-looking—'

'That's a matter of opinion.'

'He's a big, strong hunk—'

'I won't argue with that.'

'An' he's taken a real shine to me, so 'e has.'

Hesitating, Eva wasn't sure how to say what was on her mind, but say it she must. 'I don't like him, Patsy. There's something about him that gives me the shivers.'

'Aw, yer jealous, so yer are.' Dabbing on her lipstick, she got some on her teeth. 'Now, look what you've done!' she cried, throwing her lipstick down. 'Give us a tissue and stop bullying me. It's a long time since I've had a man, and here yer are, making me feel bad.' The trouble was, Eva had struck a raw nerve. There *was* something about the man that was unsettling, but Patsy chose to believe it was the 'chemistry' between them that made her nervous.

Handing her a tissue, Eva said, 'Be careful,

Patsy, that's all I'm asking. Don't let him get you drunk.'

'I can look after meself. You just keep yer mind on Frank. Sure, the two of youse are getting on like a house on fire. It's the first time in ages I've seen you easy with a feller, so it is.' As she went to the door, she remarked, 'I'm going for a walk with me new sweetheart, but I'll not be long, I promise.'

'Don't go too far. I'll be making my way back soon.'

Returning to the table, Eva conveyed her fears to Frank. 'I know she's old enough to take care of herself, and I know I shouldn't poke my nose in, but I can't help feeling she's jumped in at the deep end with this man. I'm sure he just wants to have his way with her.'

'You're a cynic.'

'You think I should mind my own business, don't you?'

'In a word, yes.'

Eva laughed. 'Well, at least you're honest.'

Somehow his rebuke seemed to calm her fears and she contentedly sipped her drink.

Frank talked about the contractors he had signed up to refit the hotel foyer. 'I've seen some of their work,' he said. 'It's quality, and it doesn't cost the earth. In fact, some of the other contractors I talked to were almost double the price on certain fittings. For instance, I've made a saving of fifty pounds on the new balustrade. And the counter front will be in finest walnut – a warm wood, I always think.'

'If you don't mind me asking, does the hotel have a big enough turnover to warrant such expense?'

'You're very astute,' he said. 'That's why I want you with me on that business project. I just know we could make a lot of money.' Seeing her frown, he put up his hands as if in surrender. 'Sorry! I won't mention it again.'

'I'm not saying the hotel doesn't have a good turnover. I know it does. But I wouldn't have thought it was making huge profits.'

'And you would be right.' He had no reason to hide the truth from Eva. 'You're in as good a position as anyone to know the number of guests that come and go. You know the prices, and you can probably make an educated guess about outgoings. I've argued with Mother about spending money on a perfectly respectable foyer, but will she listen? Not her. She has a mind like a woodcutter's axe: once it's been cast, there's no going back.'

Eva smiled at his description but tactfully said nothing. She tapped her foot to the music and watched the dancers, twisting and turning to the rhythm, their bodies close. 'I sometimes wonder where I've been all this time,' she said wistfully. 'I don't ever remember dancing like that.'

'I've never seen you dance,' Frank said. 'You work all hours and when you're not working you sit on the beach looking out to sea. I've seen you there, and I've always thought it would be a sin to disturb you. You seem so deep in thought.' He knew very little about Eva, she hardly ever spoke of her past.

'I have a lot to think about,' she confessed. Where to go from here, what to do, how to live. How to rid herself of the impossible love she felt for Bill. And, above all, what would she do with the rest of her life? Her one great comfort was that her mother was always with her. Wherever she went, whatever she was doing, her thoughts were never far from that beloved woman. She would think of her father too, but there was never the same depth of feeling there. Frank is right, she thought. I work and sleep, and in between I'm all alone. There were times when even Patsy couldn't help.

Frank was quietly observing her, aware that there were depths to Eva he might never fully know. The knowledge was not welcome, but he hid his displeasure. 'You're something of a mystery to me,' he said. 'You never talk about yourself, Eva. You're always holding back, as though you're afraid to be hurt.'

Smiling wryly, she told him, 'We're all afraid to be hurt.'

Growing bolder, he asked, 'Were you hurt, Eva? Did you love someone once?'

She looked away. 'I've never had a deep relationship,' she answered truthfully.

'But you loved someone?'

Eva lapsed into silence, surprised that he should ask such a personal question. And when she answered, it was with simple truth. 'I never loved anyone in that way. I never really thought about it.' Not until Bill came back, she thought.

'Was it a lonely life, on that farm of yours?'

'We kept chickens and grew farm produce, but it was a small place, only a few acres.'

'Sounds like hard work.'

'It was. But it was so beautiful, Frank, unspoilt by the rush and panic of life. I'm not saying it wasn't busy, but there was a tranquillity there, it was a sort of quiet haven where only the changing seasons marked the passage of time.'

'Sounds wonderful.' Not for him though. For him the bright lights and rush of city life. That was where the money was, and that was where he meant to be; Eva, too, only she didn't know it yet.

'One day I'll have it all again,' she went on. 'Just like it was – a small cottage with gardens all around, and an orchard, and fields with a running brook beside them.' It was her goal in life. Her mother's place was gone for ever, but somewhere, in a quiet and lovely place, she would find what her heart desired. Until then, she would have to be patient and do what she had to do to keep body and soul together and make sure she and Patsy had a roof over their heads. But her time would come, she was determined on it.

'I've never had that kind of contentment,' Frank confided. 'My father died when I was very small, and Mother has always been the core of my life.' His expression darkened. 'The trouble is, she still thinks she can rule me. She won't let go. Everything she does, every plan she makes, it's all centred round me.'

'That's only natural, surely.' Eva couldn't understand his animosity. 'You're her only son. It's plain to me that she loves you very much.'

'It's not love,' he said sharply. 'What she feels for me is not natural. She wants to *own* me, control me, like she does everyone else she comes into contact with. Every time I try to strike out on my own, she uses all her wiles to keep me under her wing.'

Eva couldn't disagree; certainly, she was aware that Annie Dewhirst resented her friendship with Frank and did what she could to discourage it in all sorts of subtle ways. 'How old were you when your father died?' she asked.

'He died on my third birthday, a vicious flu virus. He couldn't fight it off, pneumonia set in and he was gone in a matter of days. I have no memories of him at all.' He clenched and unclenched his fists, his eyes cast downwards. 'You've no idea what it's like, growing up without a father and having a mother who tries to dominate your every thought.'

'I know what it's like to be at odds with one of your parents,' she admitted. 'My father was a wonderful man until a tractor overturned on him and he was crippled. After that he changed. He hardly ever smiled, and neither I nor my mother could do anything to please him. In the end we gave up trying. Sometimes life can do that to you.' She sighed deeply. 'One minute you can be a loving, happy family, and the next you're divided and life is never the same again.'

For a while they sat quietly, listening to the music. Frank never took his eyes off Eva. She haunted him. He wanted her so much he was prepared to kill for her. 'Patsy tells me you've done all kinds of work since leaving home.'

Tearing her gaze from the band, Eva smiled. 'You could say that. We stayed in more places than I can remember – Leighton Buzzard, Buckingham, Aylesbury, and others I can't even recall because we were in and out so fast.'

'Did you never want to stay?'

Eva's mind went back to the few weeks they had spent in Leighton Buzzard. 'There was a place. It was a big rambling house, owned by a car dealer; his wife was a dental surgeon working from a room at the back of the house. They were a large noisy family, four boisterous children, two ponies, a Siamese cat, and a German shepherd with a new litter of puppies.'

'Sounds like mayhem.'

'It was, but it was such fun. I looked after the children, while Patsy did the gardening. We were paid well, and on top of that we had a rent-free cottage overlooking the canal. In the evening we could see the barges travelling up and down, the men with their big burly arms and the women in their colourful turbans. We were really happy there, but they decided to sell up and move away. Six weeks we were there, and it was one of the happiest times I can remember.' Except for the memories of home, she thought.

'What else did you do?' He wanted to know everything about her.

'We've turned our hands to all kinds of work. Some of it was hard, and some of it badly paid. But occasionally we got paid well and enjoyed the work. We've washed up in cafes, cleaned offices and, would you believe, we even worked in a zoo for a time, taking money at the ticket kiosk.' She chuckled. 'Once, we got paid a couple of bob each for sweeping the pavement outside Woolworths.'

'My God!' He couldn't help but admire her. 'I don't mind telling you, I'm impressed. And, more to the point, you've managed to impress my mother, and I can tell you from experience, that is *not* easy!'

Eva laughed. Frank was so easy to talk to. He had the knack of making you feel special, as though what you did really mattered. He seemed to take a genuine interest; some men just took pleasure in belittling a woman's achievements. But Eva did not believe she had achieved very much. She was no closer to realising any of her dreams and aspirations. Yet it wasn't for the want of trying.

'Has it been very difficult, Eva?'

'Difficult enough,' she answered thoughtfully, 'but there have been a few laughs along the way, and we always managed to get back on our feet, even when things went wrong. One of the best jobs we had was serving in a baker's shop. We had two rooms above the shop as part of our wages, and as many pastries and pies as we could eat.' She chuckled at the memory. 'Trouble was, Patsy began eating away all the profits. The owner had a word with her, she took offence and the upshot was a blazing row. The next morning, we were thrown out.'

'It seems to me Patsy must be a burden at times.'

'She's *never* a burden,' Eva said immediately. 'Patsy is like a sister to me.'

'I understand.' He didn't though, and he was just the tiniest bit jealous.

'She worked for my mother, did you know that?'

'I believe she mentioned it when she was being interviewed for the job at the hotel.'

'She did the accounts, and helped at the farm

shop. She was a godsend. When my parents died, I was devastated. It was Patsy who got me through it. She was always there. Always supportive.'

She didn't tell him about the other times; how, when her father was at his worst, Patsy would carry them all along as though everything was normal. It was that kind of spirit that kept them going. Life was often impossibly difficult, but Patsy could always make them laugh. 'Oh, no,' Eva said emphatically, 'Patsy could never be a burden. Not to me.'

'She told me you are very like your mother.'

Eva smiled softly. 'I like to think so.'

'She also told me about the fire.'

Shocked, Eva asked, 'What else did she tell you?'

He cast his mind back. 'Only that your parents died because of the fire.'

Tears involuntarily sprang to Eva's eyes, and she was silent.

'Eva, I'm so sorry.' Still she was silent. 'What happened to the house? Did it burn down?'

Suffused with shame, she shook her head.

'Why didn't you stay there if you loved it so much?'

With every word he uttered he opened up old wounds. 'I don't want to talk about it,' Eva said, standing up. Surreptitiously she wiped away her tears. 'Patsy's been gone too long. I'd better go and find her.'

He didn't want her to go, especially not when he was just getting her to open up about herself. 'Patsy won't thank you for going after her,' he argued. 'She'll come back when she's ready. Stay here with me. Please. There is so much more I want to ask you.'

'I'm ready to go home.' Eva couldn't deny she had enjoyed herself, but now she felt tired. It had been such a long, hard day. Besides, Frank was too probing, and she had spent too long trying to put all that behind her. 'If I don't let her know I'm leaving, she'll come back and wonder where I've gone.'

'I'll come with you, and then I'll walk you home.' Fearing he might be rushing her, he swiftly added, 'If you'd like me to, that is. We still have a few things to decide about Patsy's party.' He didn't care a jot about Patsy's party; in fact it was a bloody nuisance. As if he didn't have better things to occupy his time! But it brought him into contact with Eva, and that was good enough for him.

——&gt;&bull;&lt;——

OUTSIDE, PATSY WAS fighting her new man off. 'I said no!' Flattening both her hands against his mighty chest, she managed to shove him back a step; being full of drink, he wasn't all that steady on his feet, but then neither was she.

'You're a bloody tease, that's what you are. It were you that led me out here. You wanted it as much as I did, and now you think you can cry off! Well, you can't! Not when you've got me all worked up.' Pushing his rough hands up the hem of her skirt he propelled her back to the wall. 'And don't yell out, 'cause I can silence you with one blow.' Licking his lips, he grinned inanely. 'Stop fighting. Let yourself enjoy it. I've never had any complaints yet.'

'Touch me and I'll have the authorities on you, so I will!' Patsy sounded confident, but inside she was trembling. She had badly miscalculated this oaf. He was big and strong, and against him she was like a fly in a gale.

Ignoring her protests, he tore her skirt from hem to waist. When, terrified, she screamed out, he pressed a rough hand over her mouth. 'I warned you!' He smashed his clenched fist into her face and she slumped unconscious in his arms. He laid her on the ground. Then with big clumsy fingers he began removing her undergarments.

<hr />

E VA WAS FRANTIC. 'I *know* I heard her call out.'

'You must have been imagining it.' Frank hadn't heard a thing, and was hoping he wouldn't. He wanted to walk Eva home alone.

'Ssh!' Through the silence of the night, Eva imagined she heard a kind of scuffling. 'Listen, Frank. I know she's here somewhere and I'm not leaving until I've made sure she's all right.' She ran towards a disused building a few yards away. 'I think the sounds came from somewhere round here.' Frank ran after her.

As soon as they turned the corner of the building, they saw him.

'Piss off, you!' Stinking drunk, the burly man was having trouble getting astride Patsy. 'Can't you see we're busy?'

Eva ran forward. 'Quick, Frank! He's hurt her!' Lying beneath him, Patsy's bloodied face stared up, her eyes grey and pained, as though she was trying to make sense of what was going on.

'You cowardly bastard!' Frank yelled. He grabbed the fellow by the collar and forced him to his feet; the big man could hardly stand.

'She asked for what she got,' he slurred.

Struggling to sit up, Patsy leaned heavily on Eva. 'Please, Eva,' she muttered, 'tell Frank . . . let him go.' Eva opened her mouth to protest, but Patsy shook her head. 'He's right . . . I did . . . lead him on. Please . . .'

'Let him go,' Eva reluctantly told Frank, and to the man she said, 'If it was up to me, you'd be marched off to the police station, but for some reason Patsy says no. I'll tell you this though,' she warned. 'If you ever show your face round here again, or come anywhere near Patsy, you won't get off so lightly.'

They watched him go, unsteady and aimless, lurching from one side of the road to the other. 'He deserves a damned good whipping!' Frank said, though he was glad he hadn't had to do it. He was relieved, too, that the police weren't going to be involved. He didn't want to get caught up in anything tawdry.

'Let's get her home,' Eva said. She was worried about Patsy. 'Or maybe we should take her straight to the infirmary. She looks terrible.' In the glow from the street lamp, she noticed that Frank's nose was trickling blood. 'Are you all right?'

With the back of his hand he wiped away the blood. 'It's nothing,' he told her. 'I caught a glancing blow, that's all.' It got better, he thought. Blood on his face made him a real hero. 'Don't worry about me, it's Patsy who needs tending.'

Patsy heard, and put on a brave face. 'I'll be right as rain, so I will,' though her jaw ached as though it had been run over by a steam roller, and her legs felt like jelly. 'A good wash, that's all I need. There's nothing broken.'

'All right, Patsy, if you're sure. We'll get a taxi.' Eva turned to Frank. 'See if you can find one, will you, Frank?'

'I'm not leaving you two in this alley. If I remember rightly, there's a taxi rank just round the corner.'

With Patsy between them, supported on either

side, the three of them slowly made their way back to the road.

'You're lucky we found you when we did.' Frustrated because his chance with Eva was gone for tonight, Frank was annoyed with Patsy. 'He could have killed you, don't you realise that?'

'He didn't though, did he, eh?' Through one swollen eye she peered at Eva. 'I'm sorry, gal. If ye had any sense, you'd send me packing, so ye would.'

Eva shook her head forlornly. 'I've never had any sense where you're concerned.'

'I'm pissed as a nook.'

'I can see that.'

'Sure, I wouldn't blame ye if ye bawled me out.'

Eva's only concern was for Patsy's well-being. It was no time for recriminations. Tomorrow maybe, but not now.

---

BACK AT THE hotel, Annie Dewhirst was frantic. 'It's gone midnight!' She had been pacing her bedroom floor since eleven thirty. 'Wherever is he?'

She went back and forth, head bent and eyes blazing. Occasionally she would glance out of the window, muttering to herself. '*She's* not back either. If he's with her, he'll not hear the last of it. Scheming little baggage. If she thinks she can get her grubby little hands on this hotel and my money, she's got another think coming.'

She grabbed the phone receiver and rang reception. 'Margaret?'

'Yes, Mrs Dewhirst?'

'Have you seen my son?'

'No, Mrs Dewhirst. Not since he went out some hours ago.'

'Has Eva Bereton come back yet?'

'I haven't seen her, and I've been at the desk the whole time. She and Patsy have gone dancing, I believe.'

'You're sure they're not back?'

'Well, yes. If they'd come through the front door I would have seen them.'

Annie slammed the receiver down and began her pacing again, then stood by the window, wringing her hands. Her eyes bulged out of her head when she saw Frank and Eva carrying the dishevelled Patsy between them. What was worse, Patsy was in full song, her voice ringing out in the clear night air: 'Catch me if yer can, my name is Dan, and I'm yer man . . .'

But Annie wasn't smiling. 'Bastards!' She ran to the door and down the stairs.

'You're not coming in here,' she screeched, flinging open the front door. 'Take her in the back way. When she's safely out of sight, I want to see you, my boy!'

'Patsy needs a doctor,' Frank argued.

Forgetting the professional front she had per-fected over the years, she hissed at him, 'I don't give a bugger *what* she needs!' She kept her voice low. 'You are not bringing that drunkard in through this front door. The back way, I said, and be quick about it. If anyone sees her in that state, our reputation will be destroyed.'

Shaking with temper, she glared at Eva. 'Trouble, that's what you are. Real trouble, the pair of you!' Then she quickly closed the door in their faces and leaned on it to gather her composure.

'Are you all right, Mrs Dewhirst?' Margaret asked timidly. She had heard every word exchanged at the front door and prayed her employer wouldn't turn her anger on her.

'Of course I'm all right!' Glancing up at the large clock over the reception desk, she saw that it was almost 2 a.m. With great deliberation, she turned the key in the lock. 'Keep your eye out for any latecomers,' she told the nervous receptionist, 'and mind who you let through that door. Do you hear?'

'Yes, Mrs Dewhirst. Whatever you say.'

⇒➤◦⇐

SWINGING THE HAPLESS Patsy on to her bed, Frank groaned. 'I had no idea you weighed so much.' Leaning over the bed to recover his breath, he looked straight into her bruised but mischievous face. 'You've knackered me.'

'Well now, it don't take much to knacker you, does it, eh?' She managed a naughty chuckle. 'Ye can stay and see me in me nightie if ye like, but I warn ye, I'm not a pretty sight, even at the best of times.'

'In that case, I think it's a pleasure I'll refuse, if you don't mind. I've seen enough of you for one night.'

As Eva walked him to the door, Patsy called out, 'Don't forget yer mammy wants to see ye – *my boy*!'

Her remark struck home. He stiffened, but made no comment.

'I'm sorry about Patsy,' Eva apologised. 'She means no harm.'

'It's all right,' he lied. 'No offence taken.'

Before Eva closed the door, she kissed him gently on the mouth. 'Well, *I* want to say thank you. Honestly, Frank, if you hadn't been there, I dread to think what might have happened.'

From down the corridor, Annie saw the kiss, and she could hardly restrain herself from calling out. But she chose to remain hidden. Presently, she hurried to her room to wait for Frank.

He didn't come, and she seethed with anger.

Her resolve to get rid of Eva and Patsy hardened into a plan of action which would achieve her aim without Frank ever knowing of her part in it.

———⟫•⟪———

FRANK DIDN'T SLEEP well that night. Filled with thoughts of Eva and tasting her kiss until the morning light, he began to make his own plans to woo Eva and get her down the aisle as soon as possible. After all, she had kissed him, hadn't she? And what was a kiss if it wasn't an expression of love?

To Eva though, the kiss had been no more than a friendly thank you. 'That was a cruel and unnecessary jibe,' she chided Patsy. 'How could you say a thing like that after what he did for you?'

'Don't know what yer talking about.' With the drink beginning to wear off, Patsy was getting sulky and difficult.

Propelling her to the bathroom, Eva was severe. 'You know what I'm talking about all right,' she said angrily, 'but we'll say no more about it tonight. Let's get you washed and cleaned up, and into your bed. Tomorrow we'll decide what to do.'

Instantly, Patsy was alert. 'What do ye mean, decide what to do?'

'Nothing.' Eva didn't want to talk about anything right now; she felt dead on her feet. But she had no doubt that neither she nor Patsy would be welcome here any more. It was such a shame, especially when she was beginning to understand the hotel trade from top to bottom.

————»-•-«————

IN THE MORNING, Annie was all sweetness and light. 'Of course I was angry,' she told Frank, who had come to see her in her office. 'The three of you intending to come in the front entrance like that, whatever would the guests think?'

'You're right, Mum. It was a stupid thing to do. It won't happen again, I can promise you. By the way, where is Eva?' He hadn't been able to find her on the way here.

'I've given her the day off,' Annie said benevolently. 'It's one of our quieter days and I can manage without her for a while. I've been in to see Patsy, and she looks terrible. Her face is swollen like a football.' She shuddered with distaste. Then her expression changed and she bestowed a wide, proud smile on him. 'Eva told me what you did. I'm so proud of you.' Secretly she thought he was a fool. What if he'd been hurt? Killed even? God Almighty, it didn't bear thinking about!

'I didn't do much,' he said lightly. 'There's nothing pressing you want me for, is there, Mum?' he asked. 'I'd like to make sure they're all right.' It was Eva he wanted to see. As for Patsy, he couldn't care if he never clapped eyes on her again.

'I'm afraid they'll have to wait. There's a bit of a crisis and you're the only one who can sort it out.'

'Not today. I've enough to do as it is.' Asking Eva to marry him was top of the list.

'Palmer's have just been on the phone. They're refusing to deliver the tablecloths and decorations for tomorrow's wedding party. If I don't get them by this afternoon, I'm in real trouble.'

That focused his attention. 'Palmer's? There's been some stupid mistake. I placed that order myself weeks ago. Get them back on the phone,' he urged. 'I'll have a word with them, find out what the devil they're playing at.'

'It's no good,' she lied. 'I've been on the phone half an hour with them already this morning. With Carson away for a week, the whole place seems to be falling apart at the seams. I've been passed from office to office, and nobody seems to know what they're doing.'

'Maybe it's time we dropped Palmer's and went elsewhere. Have you phoned any of the other suppliers?'

'Every one and they can't help. Besides, Palmer's are the best. You know that, Frank. When he gets back, Carson will shake that place up like you've never seen. Heads will roll, I can promise you that.' She leaned over the desk towards him. 'There's no other way, Frank, you'll have to go round. You placed the order, and it's you who has to sort it out. Get them to deliver, or we're in real trouble. It won't take you long.'

'But they're forty miles away.'

'An hour there and back, that's all. Please, Frank.'

He sighed. 'But I've got to see Eva before I go.'

'You can't.'

'Why not?

'Because she's driven Patsy to the doctor's and they may have a long wait before he'll see her on a Sunday. Don't waste time, Frank. Sort this thing out with Palmer's, and Eva will be here when you get back. I'll tell her there's been a crisis and you're seeing to it.' A happy thought entered her head. 'I'm sure Eva realises there are times when only you can put things right.'

It worked. He nodded. 'You're right, Mum. A crisis, you tell her that.'

Well satisfied, Annie watched him hurry off. Then she made two calls. The first was to Palmer's. 'Mr Carson's secretary,' she requested officiously.

The two women had a very curious conversation, the upshot of which was that the secretary would expect her 'payment' soon, and that yes, everything would be ready when Frank arrived.

'It's always good to have friends in low places,' Annie chuckled as she put down the phone. 'Especially ones who owe you a favour or two.'

Her next call was to send for Eva and Patsy; they had not gone to the doctor but were in Patsy's room, where Eva was tending her bruises.

When, a few moments later, they were standing before her, Annie regarded them with contempt. She might well have taken to Eva, had it not been for the fact that Frank had taken to her first. She was so lovely and bright, her fair hair falling loose about her shoulders, her green eyes looking at her expectantly, and a trifle warily. Patsy was bruised and sore, her top lip grotesquely swollen and her nose puffed and red. They were a strange pair, Annie thought.

'I want you out of here in half an hour,' she said brusquely. 'Pack your bags. Be off, and don't ever come here again.'

'Jaysus!' Patsy was shocked to her roots. 'Surely to God ye ain't throwing us out?'

Eva's shock was short-lived; this was no more than she had expected. 'I understand,' she said. 'We'll be on our way. The last thing we want is trouble.'

'Good. That's all I have to say. Now, get out of here.'

Patsy half turned, but Eva held her back. 'Hang on, Patsy. I think Mrs Dewhirst has forgotten something.'

Annie stiffened. 'And what might that be?' she asked tightly.

'Our back pay and holiday money, Mrs Dewhirst.'

Annie's face went pale with anger. 'There'll be no back pay or holiday money for you two, not after what happened here last night.'

'Then we'll have to wait for Frank and see what he has to say,' Eva bluffed. 'He was with us last night, after all.' She wondered where he was. Probably despatched on an errand to get him out of the way.

Annie couldn't help but feel a stab of admiration for Eva. Realising she had met her match, she conceded. 'Very well. I shall expect you back here, with your bags packed, in half an hour. I'll have your money ready.'

When Eva and Patsy returned to the office, coats on, bags in hand, Annie paid over what was owed. The only words spoken were by Eva, as she was leaving. 'Frank is a good man,' she said to Annie, her tone gentle. 'I like him a lot. But I wasn't trying to steal him from you.'

With those profound words she made her departure. Behind her, Annie was left to wonder about this young woman who had come into her life and gone out of it in so short a time. 'Maybe you weren't trying to steal him,' she murmured to herself, 'but you were a danger that had to be removed. I have never seen my son look at any woman the way he looked at you.'

Annie sat at her desk and studied Eva's signature on the wage receipt. Then she took pen to paper and laboriously copied it over and over, until she had almost perfected the lettering. 'I could have done this for a living,' she chuckled.

A short time later, she read the letter she had written back to herself.

Dear Frank,

    I have to leave. I meant to tell you last night, but there was no opportunity.

    I know this will come as a shock to you, but I lied to you, Frank. There is someone else. I treated him badly, but it's time for me to face up to my responsibilities. I still love him, you see.

    You've been a good friend. I won't see you again, so take care of yourself.

        Eva

When Frank came home, full of his accomplishments and eager to see Eva, his mother handed him the note. 'I'm sorry,' she said. 'Eva told me before she left.'

While he read with a stony face, she hoped and prayed it would turn him against Eva.

When a moment later he screwed the letter into a tight ball and threw it on the fire, she breathed a sigh of relief. Eva was out of their lives and he had learned his lesson.

# PART THREE

---

# JUNE 1960
# OLD FRIENDS

# Chapter Five

B ILL NEVER LIKED travelling by air. He preferred
to have some control over his fate. If anything
unexpected happened up in the air, he would have
no say at all in the way his life ended.

But when business took you from Vancouver to
Victoria, you either took the ferry, or you flew. The
ferry was undoubtedly the more relaxed way, and
some claimed the most scenic, which was certainly
true as the land was not obscured by clouds, but it
was slow, and for Bill, time was precious.

The sky was cloudless today; it was a glorious
morning in June. The sea stretched beneath them
like a deep blue, shimmering carpet. Here and there
islands speckled the water, with tiny white-sailed
yachts bobbing between them. This part of British
Columbia was breathtaking.

'It's so wonderful!' Sheila stretched her neck to
look out of the window.

Bill smiled in agreement. 'However many times
I see this view, I always feel humble, insignificant.'

'Yes,' she replied, keeping her eyes on the waters

below, 'I know what you mean.' She shifted her gaze to sneak a look at some of their fellow passengers. One of them had his nose stuck in a business paper; a young couple had eyes only for each other; another man was slumped down in his seat, eyes closed and head nodding. 'Though I don't think *they* understand what you mean,' she chuckled.

Bill's eyes followed her gaze. 'Too early in the morning for him, poor devil.' He looked at his watch. 'Half past eight. I wouldn't have minded a lie-in myself this morning.' They had got to bed last night at midnight for the third night in a row, and still they had two days' hard graft in front of them before they could begin their long journey home to Vancouver.

He glanced at Sheila. 'I expect you're tired too, aren't you? You've worked alongside me all through, and never once complained.'

Three years his secretary and two years his friend, Sheila was a godsend to him. She had been forty-seven when he took her on in preference to umpteen young things with feather brains and long legs.

His wife had been surprised when she met Sheila. 'You must be mad, choosing her over someone younger,' she told Bill, but secretly she was delighted. Sheila, though pleasantly attractive, with a slim figure and good legs, would not pose a threat to her.

Bill had never regretted his choice. Sheila worked hard and was unswervingly loyal. Her reputation brought plenty of attractive offers from other property agents, but she always dropped them into the nearest wastepaper bin. Bill knew what a gem she was, and treated her well. Whenever he went away on business, it was with the knowledge that he would return to an orderly office, with every crisis taken care of. When he went on a business trip involving a string of meetings over a period of time, he would take her along and put an experienced temp in to hold things back in Vancouver. This didn't happen often and so far the arrangement had caused no great upheaval.

'Sheila?'

'Hmm?'

'You seem far away. I just wondered if you regretted being away from the office.'

Her kindly face crinkled in a smile. 'How could I regret seeing all this?' she asked, gesturing to the islands below. 'Of course I'm not regretting it. You know I like to accompany you from time to time. Someone has to keep an eye on you.' She grimaced. 'All the same, I hope that young woman isn't messing up my files!'

Bill laughed. 'She wouldn't dare! Not after the lecture you gave her before we left.'

She stared at him. 'Shame on you, Bill Westerfield. You were eavesdropping.'

'I should think everyone within a five-mile radius heard you laying down the law.' When she looked mortified, he added, 'Only kidding.'

'It was only a short lecture,' she said. 'You have to make sure these temps know their place.' She looked out of the window again. 'We're nearly there, I think.'

As she gazed out of the window, Bill took quiet stock of his secretary. He had grown very fond of her. Slim to a fault, with greying hair and robust outlook on life, nothing seemed to faze her, not even his father. One day she would leave, he knew it was inevitable. Her only living relative was a younger sister who lived in Scotland, and Sheila always said that when she was old and weary, she would go home to be with her sister. Bill hoped that day was still very far away.

His thoughts turned to England, and Eva, and almost without thinking, he took out his wallet and opened it. There, smiling back at him and looking exactly as he remembered Eva herself, was the scorched picture of Colette.

He had been sorely tempted to ignore the plea in Eva's letter and search her out, but he hadn't, in spite of his love for her. His conscience stopped him. He was a married man. The marriage might not be a happy one for him, but he believed his wife loved and needed him, especially since the loss of their only child. Besides, Eva didn't love him in that way. She was probably married herself by now.

'Penny for them?' Sheila's voice broke into his thoughts.

'Just thinking.' Quickly folding his wallet, he returned it to his pocket, drawing her attention to the world outside. 'We're landing,' he observed.

Sheila's heart went out to him. She knew of the photo; it wasn't the first time she'd seen him looking at it, though she had no idea who it was.

Bill was a good man, one of the best. But he was not content. He had not been content for a very long time. The situation at home was fraught, what with the loss of their child last winter, and now his wife's drinking. There had been all kinds of cruel rumours, as there often were about a tragedy. Whispers were growing that Bill's wife was responsible for their son's death because she had left the infant wandering the gardens alone while she entertained a man friend.

Thankfully, Bill seemed unaware of the rumours, but they were spreading, and sooner or later he was bound to hear them. Sheila dared not dwell on it too much. True or not, they could well destroy a marriage that was already struggling to survive. But then, if the marriage were to end, it might not be such a bad thing, she thought, for Bill in particular.

&#10148;&#10674;&#10703;

T HEIR LIMOUSINE WAS waiting; long and black, with tinted windows, it had a sinister appearance. 'I hate these things,' Sheila said as she scrambled into the car. 'Everyone stares as you drive along.'

Bill climbed in after her. 'It's human nature. When the windows are blacked out, people naturally want to know who's inside.'

'I feel like a fraud.' Settling down in the luxurious seat, Sheila looked round. The floor-covering was thick and plush; there was a small television, a cocktail bar encased in walnut, and above that a neat row of expensive crystal glasses. 'I'm not used to this. Whatever would people say?'

'Pretend you're a celebrity,' Bill laughed. 'Wind down the window and wave as you go by.'

Wisely ignoring him, she changed the subject. 'How far to the railway station?'

'About twenty minutes, if my memory serves me right.'

The railway waiting room was packed; there were tourists in shorts, children running around, and also, much to Bill's interest, a number of serious-faced men in suits.

'I expect they're here for the same reason as we are,' he remarked to Sheila. 'Whistler is an up and coming area. The development potential is growing, and land prices have taken off again.'

'I wonder if your father will be there.' Sheila voiced what was already on his mind.

'If he is, I'll be ready for him.'

Sheila knew what lay behind Bill's grim tone. Without going into any detail, Bill had told her that his father had made the Bereton girl homeless, and that she had disappeared before he could help her. But Sheila knew Bill well enough to realise there was more to it than that. She even suspected he might be in love with Eva, but she never pried. If there ever came a time when he might want to talk, he knew she was there, and he knew she would never sit in judgement. Until then, Bill's secrets were his own.

'I'm glad I hung on to that parcel of land.' Bill focused his mind on the business in hand. 'It's a hard decision to make, whether to hold on for a bit longer, or develop it now.' He lapsed into thought.

'Follow your instincts,' Sheila told him. 'They haven't let you down yet.'

She was right. It seemed that everything he touched turned to gold. He was sitting on a small fortune with the land at Whistler, and he had made a huge profit from selling off a string of commercial properties in Vancouver. Four years ago he got them for a song because they were rundown and nobody seemed prepared to take them on. Everyone said he was mad, but within two years the whole area had taken off. It was where every businessman wanted his offices located.

The train pulled into the station and everyone began to move towards it.

'Now, *this* is more my cup of tea.' Sheila settled down near a window, with Bill beside her. 'I love trains, and I've always wanted to ride through the Rockies.' She was more excited than the children with their noses pressed to the windows.

Trying not to smile, Bill said, 'You're here to work, my girl, not to enjoy yourself.'

But she did enjoy herself, and so did he.

They ate a hearty breakfast. Sheila had cornflakes with milk and sugar, followed by a fresh croissant and strawberry jam, washed down with a cup of tea. Bill opted for a fried breakfast – egg, tomato, sausage, crispy bacon, the aroma of which permeated every carriage – and plenty of strong black coffee. 'To clear my mind,' he told Sheila, who chided him for drinking so much coffee.

'Bad for your health,' she responded.

The journey was a memorable experience. They passed lakes and forests that were older than Methuselah, and more magnificent than words could describe. The tumbling waterfalls and extraordinary rock formations were an awesome sight, and growing right up to the track were the prettiest flowers of every shape, colour and size.

Some way along the track, the train began to ʌ down. 'What's happening?' Sheila asked.

ʌassing guard heard her. 'Look out of your

window to the right.' Smiling knowingly, he moved on.

When Sheila cried out with excitement, Bill leaned over her shoulder. 'Brandy Wine Falls,' he told her; he had seen them on his last trip. 'The water falls from high up in the mountains.' He paused. 'There can't be many sights like that on God's earth.'

Eyes glued to the window and hands clasped together, Sheila whispered, 'It's amazing!'

Falling away from beneath the rails, the rush of clear, sparkling water roared down towards the rocks, where it swirled and meandered before flowing into the forest like a silver snake going to ground. 'I've never seen anything so wonderful!' Sheila murmured. And Bill had to agree.

All too soon, the journey was over. Through the train window, Bill read the station sign, Whistler. 'Now it's down to work.' He was ready. Work took his mind off Eva for a time, but always she returned to haunt him. In his deepest heart, he knew one day he would have to find her. When the time was right.

⟫◆⟪

THE HOTEL WAS small but comfortable. Bill had instructed Sheila to ask for rooms with a mountain view, and that was exactly what they got. Sheila's was on the ground floor, while Bill had opted for a loftier view.

After satisfying himself that she was comfortable, he made his way upstairs to his own room. It was pleasant enough, big and square, with a pine bed and dresser, and a brightly painted bathroom.

Placing his overnight bag on the bed, he took off his jacket and went to the window. This was not the first time he had stayed here, but the grandeur of these mountains always made him feel humble. 'No one should build here,' he murmured. But it was too late for regrets. Already there were numerous buildings – small shops and general supply stores, all catering for the people who came here from all walks of life. There were those who wanted to escape the routine of everyday life and there were the enterprising people who had settled here as soon as it had begun to open up to the outside world; others came for the ski-ing, and many came merely to admire the natural beauties that Whistler had to offer.

At 2 p.m., Sheila and Bill met in the foyer. Bill ordered coffee to be brought through to the lounge. Once there, he and Sheila got straight to work.

'Three meetings,' Sheila reminded him. 'The surveyor at two fifteen, with the architect joining you both on site half an hour later. I booked a quiet room here in the hotel for your discussions afterwards. I've checked at the desk and there's no problem.' She grimaced. 'It's just a small room overlooking the gardens, which they put aside for business meetings, though I'm told they have a full conference room planned for next year.'

'Have they given me the two hours I asked for?'

'What with the auction and all, the room is apparently booked solid from midday, but yes, you've got your two hours.'

The waitress brought the coffee and Sheila shifted her papers to the sofa. 'I've put the schedule and all relevant documents in here.' She handed Bill a slim plastic folder.

He glanced through it. 'Thorough as usual,' he commented, giving her a grateful smile.

'It's what you pay me for.'

'It's make your mind up time,' he said. 'By the end of the day, big decisions will have to be made. If I make the wrong ones, I may well live to regret it.'

'That won't happen.'

He laughed. 'You never doubt, do you?'

'Not where you're concerned.' She had often wished things might have been different. Sometimes life cast a dark shadow and it was hard to get out from under it. Bill was more a part of her life than he would ever know and that was how it should be.

'I'll have to keep my wits about me, that's for sure,' Bill remarked thoughtfully.

'You've tangled with them all before. They know they'll get no change from you.'

'I need you there,' he told her. 'Take notes. Miss nothing. I don't want surprises.'

'Trust me.'

'Don't I always?'

His remark made Sheila feel ashamed. As for not wanting surprises, he would be shocked to his roots if he knew the truth. And, oh, how she longed to tell him. The temptation was never far away, but conscience and fear were stronger, so she remained silent.

———⊰•⊱———

THE DAY WAS perfect, warm and bright, with a cool breeze falling from the mountains. The surveyor commended Bill on his choice of site. 'This whole place must have been wide open when you bought this,' he observed. 'You had the choice, and you settled on what I reckon is the best piece of real estate in the whole area.'

'I did my homework.'

'I can see that.' Now and again a man like Bill Westerfield came up from nothing to take on the old veterans. It took a younger, more agile mind to see into the future. All the same, the surveyor felt a tinge of regret. 'It seems a pity to build stores and such here,' he remarked, for a moment letting his heart rule his head. 'Such a tranquil place. Still, I suppose we have to move with the times. Or stand still and be trodden underfoot.'

'No, you're right,' Bill answered thoughtfully. 'It does seem a pity, and to tell you the truth, I'm not entirely convinced that "stores and such" are the right way forward. That's why I wanted you and the architect here at the same time. I have several ideas I want to chew over.'

For a moment they stood at the foot of the mountains, gazing at the site and projecting their minds forward to what might eventually stand here. Now, it was a vast empty area, pitted with ancient dips and rises. Boulders, delivered from the mountains at some time in the distant past, dotted the landscape. The ground swept upwards towards the mountains; on one side was a brook, on the other a dramatic, curving swath of pine trees. Directly in front was a panoramic view of the small community below, and beyond that a wide shimmering lake. The site itself lay like a precious jewel in a timeless garden.

'There are men who would pay an absolute fortune for this,' the surveyor remarked enviously.

'They're too late.' Bill thought of his adoptive father. 'They missed their chance long ago.'

With Sheila always two steps behind, the two men strode about, measuring, discussing, bandying ideas, and though he was alert to the task in hand, Bill's heart was with Eva.

There was something here, in this quiet, beautiful place, that reminded him of her. He could build her a home here, which she would cherish; they could have a wonderful life, blessed with children, God willing, and live here for the rest of their days. A lifetime in paradise, he thought.

He laughed inwardly. What was he thinking of? Things like that were the stuff of fairy tales.

Some time later, the architect joined them, and the discussions took on a new dimension. 'It's going to be a viable, commercial proposition,' he advised Bill. 'But we might have to cut deep into that area there.' He gestured towards the swath of trees.

'That's not an option.' Bill was adamant. 'We're not here to destroy. *If* I decide to build rather than sell, it must naturally complement what's already here. To spoil it would be sacrilege.' From out of the corner of his eye, he caught Sheila's quiet smile of approval.

When the outdoor work was concluded, they retired to the hotel. The room booked for the meeting was soulless, with harsh green walls and a large central table surrounded by straight-backed chairs. It was not very welcoming, but conducive to business.

Bill placed himself at the head of the table, with the surveyor and architect on either side of him. Sheila remained close by, pen and pad at the ready.

'Down to business,' Bill declared. 'Before we leave this room, I need to know that we're all of the same mind.' The surveyor and architect began emptying their briefcases on to the table. 'Put away your notes and plans,' Bill told them. 'We're starting from scratch.'

━━━◆━━━

WHENEVER BILL WAS away, Joan Westerfield was never lonely. 'Don't you feel ashamed?' she teased, stroking the man's erect penis.

Groaning, he pushed up to her. 'Why should I feel ashamed?'

She giggled. 'Not many men would make love to their son's wife – in his bed, too.'

'He's *not* my son!'

She laughed softly, opened her legs and drew him down on top of her.

Unable to resist, he smiled wickedly. 'You're a devil!'

'Devils together,' she whispered and pushing her tongue into his mouth, gave herself up to him.

The following evening Bill returned. 'I've missed you,' Joan murmured, meeting him at the door with open arms. 'You've no idea how lonely it can be when you're not here.'

That night they made love. For her it was a triumph. For Bill, though he was a man, with a man's needs, it just made him want Eva all the more.

Tonight, as always after he and Joan had made

love, he went downstairs and made himself a cup of strong coffee. 'If I thought Joan could be happy without me, I'd go right now,' he whispered. But believing that he was the one at fault because of his love for another woman, he swept aside his secret longings.

In her cosy apartment, Sheila, too, was finding it difficult to sleep. Seated in an armchair in her sitting room, she gazed at the photograph. Tears ran down her face. 'I should never have let it happen,' she muttered. 'Why did I let it happen?'

The photograph was of two babies; one a boy, the other a girl. 'I made one mistake,' she whispered, clasping the photograph to her breast, 'and I'll be punished for the rest of my life.'

# Chapter Six

'TAKE YOUR FRIEND home, before I kick her out on the end of my toe!'

Eva gave the man a withering glare. 'It was the waitress who started the argument. Patsy was only defending herself.'

'Out, I said!' With a dozen customers looking on, he was in no mood for listening. 'It's not the first time she's caused trouble in here, and now I'm barring her.' He paused, looking into Eva's defiant face and thinking how lovely she was. 'You're welcome any time,' he said more kindly, 'but not her. Not that one!' For good measure he gave Patsy a little shove towards the door, and received a mouthful of abuse in return.

'If you bar Patsy, you bar me,' Eva told him.

He shrugged. 'As you like.' He ushered them out and on to the pavement.

The waitress who had goaded Patsy made a rude gesture. Patsy saw it. 'The little bastard, I'll rip her eyes out!' she shrieked, and Eva had to physically restrain her from barging back inside.

'One of these days, Patsy Noonan . . .' Giving up, Eva sighed. 'What's the point? You'll never change.'

'Sure, it weren't my fault!' With her lip dragging the ground, Patsy trailed behind. 'Didn't ye see how she kept on at me?'

Eva paused for Patsy to catch up. 'Can you blame her?'

'What d'ye mean by that?'

'You know perfectly well what I mean, Patsy, telling the poor girl how you'd spent the night with her young man. And not content with that, you had to go into every sordid detail.'

'Serves her right. She's no good for him any-way.'

'Oh? How do you know that?'

Sulking now, Patsy retorted, 'I don't want to talk about it.' She began going at a faster pace, forcing Eva to keep up with her. 'If she can't take the truth, it's not my fault, is it?'

'Wait a minute!' Catching Patsy by her coat sleeve, Eva drew her to a halt. 'Is this the same man you said you were serious about? The one you thought might walk you down the aisle?'

'I said I don't want to talk about it.'

'He's dropped you, hasn't he? Like all the other men you take a shine to, he's had his fun and games, and now he doesn't want to know.'

'All right! Go on, say it!'

'What?'

'"I told you so." Say it, I don't mind. It's what I deserve.'

Now, everything was clear. Eva felt desperately sorry but at the same time she did wish Patsy would be more careful with the men she chose. 'Oh, Patsy, when will you ever learn?'

As they walked along, Patsy was broodingly silent, and Eva kept her own counsel, thinking how true it was that men seemed always to be at the root of a woman's problems. As for herself, she had never lost sight of Bill. He was always in her mind. In her heart.

Eva drew Patsy into a tiny cafe opposite the castle. 'Let's go in here,' she suggested. 'We never did get around to ordering food.'

'Don't want to.'

'You're not hungry then?'

'I didn't say that.'

'They do a delicious ham and salad roll in here, remember?' Eva was starving. This was their lunch break and there would be no more time for food until they finished at six tonight. 'Come on, Patsy. We have to be back at work in half an hour.'

'If I do come inside, I'm not talking.'

Eva despaired. When Patsy was in this mood, it was like trying to shift a mountain. 'That's okay. Whatever you want.'

In the event, the lunch was very enjoyable; hot

ham rolls with salad on the side, and a steaming mug of strong coffee topped off with cream. 'I don't love him.' Patsy had a mouthful of ham and a piece of cucumber in her mouth. 'He was just a passing fancy. Somebody to take me out and treat me like I was special.'

Eva made no comment.

'He *did* dump me,' she confessed, 'like I was nothing at all.'

Still Eva made no comment.

Unperturbed, Patsy went on, chewing and chatting at the same time. 'We were getting on like a house on fire, I told ye that, didn't I? Then, out of the blue for no reason, he told me he was going back to *that* little sourpuss!' She made a sour face. 'That's what I can't understand.' Her eyes grew round. 'What the devil does he see in *her* when there's me for the taking?'

Eva took a bite out of her ham roll. She knew that whatever she said, Patsy would disagree. If she let Patsy talk without interruption, she could get it all off her chest and hopefully they would have a peaceful afternoon.

'What's wrong with you?' Patsy demanded. 'Are ye deaf or what?'

'Afraid to open my mouth, that's all.'

'Why?'

'In case I get my head bitten off.'

'Don't be so bloody daft!'

'Patsy?'

'Don't go asking me about him, 'cause I'm not talking!'

'No. I was just thinking, about us.'

'What about us?'

'I've been wondering if it's time to move on.' In fact, Eva had thought of nothing else this past year. Now they had a healthy sum of money saved, she felt an irresistible urge to try and build a business of their own.

'I thought you liked it here in Wales. Especially Cardiff. One of the prettiest places you've seen, that's what you said.'

'And I meant it. The people are very friendly too.' Sometimes it was a real wrench moving away. 'But our contract has nearly finished. In three weeks' time, the site will be completed and we'll be out of a job.'

'Jaysus!' Wrapped up in her personal trials, Patsy had never given it a thought. 'What about the house? Will we be turned out?'

'It was part of the contract, Patsy. Several years' work and a house for the duration. In three weeks, it all comes to an end.'

'What will we do?'

'There are two things we can do, Patsy,' Eva answered. 'We can stay here and scout about for work and a place to live. Or we can go and search out something altogether different. Go somewhere

where no one can ever turn us out. Find something that really belongs to us – bought and paid for.'

'What? Like our own house, you mean?'

'And maybe our own business.' Excitement filled Eva's soul. 'Oh, Patsy, it's what we've scrimped and saved for these past years. We've got a tidy sum put by, not a fortune but it might get us a little business of our own. We'd have to keep our sights low at first, borrow from the bank too I expect, but if we could make a start, oh, Patsy, wouldn't that be something?' A dream come true, that's what it would be.

'Do you really think we could do it? A house and everything?'

'We'd have to go on sharing a house for a time, but if we do well, it wouldn't be long before you could have your own place, Patsy. Think of that.'

Suspicious and insecure, Patsy rounded on her. 'Why should I want my own place? Haven't we been content enough under the same roof? Are you trying to get rid of me, is that it?'

'You know that's not the case, Patsy.' Sometimes Eva longed for a little house of her own. All these years, she and Patsy had lived under each other's feet and though she loved Patsy, she found herself dreaming more and more of her own place. She wanted space to think. Space to be alone with her thoughts and memories. 'I'm thinking of you as well. What if you meet someone special? You might be glad to have your own place.'

Patsy's face lit up. 'You might be right at that. I could fetch him home and we could make all the noise we wanted, instead of being afraid to wake you.' Leaning over the table, she wiped the crumbs from her mouth and clenched her fists in the air. 'It sounds good. So tell me what the plans are.'

While Eva outlined her ideas for their future, Patsy ordered another ham roll, and to hell with the time!

———◦———

T HE NEXT THREE weeks flew past.
'I wish I could keep you both on.' A tall willowy man in his early sixties, Larry was the owner of the Castle Construction Company. 'But I promised myself that this would be the last project.'

The three of them stood in his portable office, staring out of the window at the sprawling new housing development. Wide roads and landscaped gardens lent an air of grandeur to the rows of mock Tudor houses, every one sold by Larry and Eva, with the help of Patsy's exuberant telephone manner. 'Now that it's finished, and I'm still in good health, thank God, I mean to retire.'

He looked from one to the other. 'You can stay

on in the house for a few weeks if you like, but after that I'll need to sell it. I have to rake in as much as I can for my retirement.'

Eva thanked him but declined. 'You've been very good to us,' she said, 'but we've got plans of our own.'

Satisfied, he shook hands with them, then handed each a small brown envelope. 'It's just a small token of my appreciation. With Patsy's flair on the phone, and your genius in selling to anyone who showed an interest, Eva, I feel I owe you. And don't say it's what you were paid for, because there are others who are paid the same and don't give a monkey's.'

They left the office and Eva made her way across the site to the foreman.

'You're away then, the two of you?' Mick Forester was a kindly soul, short in stature with a wiry frame and a laugh that would frighten donkeys, but he had a heart of gold, and it was full of aspirations for a life with Patsy Noonan.

'The place won't be the same when you're gone,' he sighed. 'Me and the lads will be here for at least six months, landscaping and tidying up. But I wish you all the best.' His blue eyes strayed to where Patsy was waiting for Eva. 'Take care of the lass,' he said. 'It's a job I'd willingly do, if only she'd let me.'

Eva said what was in her heart. 'Patsy's a

fool. She wouldn't know a good man if she fell over him.'

'Where will you go?'

'Blackburn, I think.' In fact, she was certain.

'Why Blackburn?'

'Because Lancashire is not too far away, and I've heard there's a lot of new enterprises opening up.'

He chuckled. 'Looking to make a fortune, are you?'

Eva smiled. 'I can but try.'

'Look after yourselves,' he called, and Patsy, tormenting as ever, blew him a kiss.

'You're heartless,' Eva chided, 'breaking his heart the way you did.'

'Not him,' Patsy replied. 'It was over between us almost as soon as it got started.'

'That's a shame.'

'No, it's not. He's too quiet, too easily satisfied with his lot – work every day, home every night and out once a week. I need something more exciting out of life.'

'It's not because he's a widower with a small daughter, is it?'

'Maybe, I don't know. But I can't say I relish the thought of being tied to a kitchen sink or looking after a snotty-nosed brat.'

'That's a bit harsh. Mick's child is a sweet little thing.'

'You're right, she's a little darlin'', but I'm not ready to play Mammy.' Patsy's own hard childhood had coloured her vision of family life. 'Anyway, I'm too irresponsible and set in me ways to settle down, so I am.'

'He adores you, Patsy, anyone can see that.'

'I know it. But I don't want kids and I don't need a husband.'

In fact, Patsy had taken a real shine to Mick, until he began to talk of marriage. It had unnerved her and now she was afraid to go anywhere near him. 'To tell you the truth,' she murmured, 'I hope he forgets all about me.'

Eva knew there were times when you spoke your mind, and other times when you let Patsy be. This was a time to let her be. 'So, we're off to Blackburn then, are we?'

'Whatever you say.' Patsy was not one for making decisions. 'But why Blackburn?'

'Some time ago Frank told me about men who make a killing on buying and selling land. It sounds perfect, and the north is a very lucrative area. I just have a good feeling about it.'

Patsy's mind had already turned to other matters. 'What did old Larry give us?' She took out her brown envelope and tore it open. She gasped when she saw the small bundle of notes nestling there. 'Jaysus! Will ye look at that?' Quickly she counted them. 'Sixty quid!'

When Eva counted hers, she was astonished to find one hundred pounds in crisp new notes. 'He's obviously very grateful.'

'Sure, the old sod must have made an absolute fortune!'

'And good luck to him,' Eva declared. 'Now, God willing, it's our turn.'

Patsy dreamed of new high-heeled shoes and black stockings, of nightclubs and men who wouldn't get too close. As for Eva, she could see herself and Patsy with their own thriving business. That was her dream.

She had another dream too, and it clouded her visions for the future. The face was handsome, with laughing eyes and a lock of hair that fell mischievously over his forehead.

The man was Bill. A man with a wife and probably children by now, a family in which she played no part.

Their last sight of Wales was the shimmering river and the hills beyond. 'I'll never forget this lovely place, and its people,' Eva said. 'One day we'll come back.'

'When we're stinking rich,' Patsy added.

Eva smiled. 'Money isn't everything. Always remember that.'

# *Chapter Seven*

O N  THE  FIRST day of November 1965, Eva
and Patsy arrived in Blackburn.

'Where are we going?' Patsy asked, clambering
into the taxi Eva had hailed.

Eva took out a folded note from her coat
pocket. 'Number fourteen, Albert Street, please,'
she told the driver, reading from the note. Then
she turned to her impetuous friend. 'Let me do the
talking, Patsy. And if she tries to up the rent she's
already agreed on, don't start swearing, or we'll
find ourselves sleeping in the park tonight.'

'Anybody would think I were a blabbermouth,
so they would,' Patsy complained. 'Don't ye think
I know when to behave?' She grinned and gave
the driver a wink in his mirror.

Albert Street was narrow and cobbled, with
terraced houses on either side, and a lamppost
in front of every other door. 'Couldn't ye find
something a bit posher?' Patsy was disappointed.
'We've got money now. We're important.'

'We're no more important than when we set

out from me mam's place,' Eva reprimanded her. 'We've just been luckier than most. Besides, we haven't got money to waste, Patsy. Not if we want to find a place of our own and set up a little business.'

As they drove past the houses, Eva thought how well kept they were; the front doorsteps were scrubbed and the net curtains glowed like white teeth from every window. 'You can always tell when a house is loved,' she remarked, drawing Patsy's attention. 'See how they sparkle?'

'Pretty,' replied Patsy, her eyes on the driver, who by now was sure he was on a promise.

Eva wondered what their new landlady was like. Old? Young? Married or single? Was she crotchety or good-natured, and how did she come to advertise in a Welsh regional newspaper? 'No men need apply,' it said, and 'No dogs, ornamental or otherwise.' Nothing about rent in advance though, and, as a rule, landlords always demanded a month's rent in advance.

Number fourteen stood by itself at the end of the road; it was tiny with two windows upstairs and two downstairs. It had a brown wooden door and a wrought-iron balustrade which hid the cellar steps. On one side of the house was a pretty bridge over a brook, and on the other an empty space where a house had been demolished. From the look of the rubbish piled in the middle, it seemed someone had a mind to build a bonfire. A stuffed bird stood in one of the downstairs windows of number fourteen.

'Jaysus! A dead parrot.' Patsy was horrified. 'Ye didn't say we were lodging with Long John Silver.'

A thin, waif-like boy, with protruding ears and a mop of lank brown hair, answered the door.

'Could I please speak to your mother?' Eva asked.

'What's it about?' He had a strong Cockney accent, which took Eva aback.

'Is your mother in?'

'Are you from the social?' He looked quickly up and down the street, his startlingly blue eyes filled with fear.

'No, we're not,' Eva assured him. 'Could you tell your mammy her new lodgers are here?'

He visibly relaxed. 'Are you Eva Bereton and Patsy Noonan?'

Eva nodded.

'Me mam ain't 'ere.'

'Is it all right if we come in anyway?' Producing the letter she'd received from the lady of the house, she explained, 'We've already agreed terms.'

'No! Yer can't come in.' Agitated, he began to close the door.

Patsy promptly stuck her foot out to block it. 'You cheeky little sod!' she exclaimed. 'Turning away paying folk — I hope yer mammy clips yer ear when she comes back.'

Both Eva and Patsy were stunned when he began to weep. 'She ain't coming back,' he sobbed. 'Me mam's dead an' buried, an' me dad's buggered off. Tell the authorities if yer like but they'll not put me away 'cause they'll never find me.' He pushed past them and fled down the street.

'Good God above!' Eva's heart ached for him. 'Stay here,' she told Patsy, 'I'm going after him.' And before Patsy could object, she too was gone, running down the street as though her life depended on it.

With Eva gone and the door wide open, Patsy began calling, 'Hello. Is anyone home?'

No answer.

She leaned into the corridor. 'Hello?'

She almost jumped out of her skin when a tabby cat darted out from behind the door. 'Jaysus, Mary and Joseph! Are ye trying to finish me off or what?' Shooing the cat away, she decided to wait for Eva before going inside. 'This place gives me the creeps, so it does,' she muttered, inching the door shut until it was only open a crack.

Patsy noticed that the downstairs net curtains in the house opposite were twitching; it was obvious someone was watching. 'Nosy old sods!' she grumbled. 'Mind yer own bloody business.' She glared at the window, and whoever was peeping seemed to go away. Satisfied, Patsy drew the two small suitcases closer and sat astride them, legs apart and arms folded. 'Don't be too long, Eva,' she whispered. 'Me arse isn't built for straddling suitcases.'

※━◆━※

Eva felt as though her lungs would burst. Having followed the boy across two streets, then over a bridge and down a bank, she found herself beside a stream. There was no sign of the boy, but she sensed he was near. 'I only want to talk,' she called out. 'I don't mean to hurt you. I'd like to help, if I can.'

'Go away!'

Eva turned towards the direction of his voice and spotted him. Crouched low and peering fearfully round the trunk of a tree, he darted back when she caught sight of him. 'It's all right,' she said, edging nearer. 'I really do want to help you.'

'Stay back!' There was a sob in his voice and, like her, he was out of breath.

Eva stopped in her tracks. 'It's not fair,' she said, hoping he wouldn't up and flee again. If he did, she didn't think she could race after him any more.

Her comment had confused him. He stayed silent and hidden.

'It's not fair,' Eva said again. 'You know my name and I don't know yours.'

Silence.

'Will you tell me?'

A slight movement, but no answer.

'I'll guess.' After all that running, her legs ached. She moved cautiously towards a large round boulder. 'I'm not going away,' she told him. 'I'm going to sit down here, and we can talk.' From the boulder she had good sight of the boy. He was facing her, his face stained with tears.

'I bet you're called Bill, aren't you?' Shocked that this particular name had come to her without thinking, she went on, 'When I was your age I knew a boy called Bill. He and I were best mates, and I was very sad when he went away.' Sadder now than she was then, she thought.

'Me name ain't Bill.' With the back of his hand he wiped his tears away.

Encouraged that he hadn't yet taken flight, Eva asked, 'Is it Jack then?'

'I'm not telling yer.'

'I bet it's Michael.'

'Don't be daft!'

'I give up. What is it then?'

Silence.

'Me mam says she called me after a film star. He can sing and dance and everything.'

'Frank Sinatra?'

'Naw.'

'Dean Martin?'

'Never 'eard of 'im.'

'Mickey Rooney?'

'I'm glad she didn't call me that. The kids at school would have called me Mickey Mouse.'

'Fred Astaire?'

'That's me dad's name, Fred.' His voice caught in a sob. 'He left us. That's what made me mam poorly. I could hear her, every night, crying herself to sleep.' Unable to hold back his tears, he bent his head and wept again.

Eva slowly got up and moved closer. He made no attempt to run.

'I want me mam,' he groaned, looking up at her with big sorrowful eyes. 'Please. I want me mam!'

Without a word, Eva sank down beside him and gathered him in her arms. For what seemed an age she let him cry, holding him tight, sharing his pain.

After a time, she looked down and said, 'My mother died too. I missed her so much – I still do. Just like you miss your mother.' Placing a kiss on the top of his head, she went on in a whisper, 'It's hard to lose someone you love, and sometimes it makes you feel so sad you think you can never smile again. But you do, you know, even though the pain is still there, deep down.'

'I'll never see her again, will I?'

She had faced the same question herself after her own mother died. 'I don't know,' she answered truthfully, 'but in your heart you'll always see her. She'll be there every time you think of her, even years from now. You have to remember her when she was smiling, when she was happy. Can you do that?'

'I'll try.'

Eva hugged him. 'That's right,' she said. 'And besides, she wouldn't want you to be sad all the time, would she?'

'No.'

'Do you want to go home now?'

'You won't let 'em put me away, will yer?'

'We'll work something out.'

'Promise?'

Eva nodded.

'What about your friend?'

'What about her?'

'She doesn't like me.'

'What makes you say that?'

'She swore at me.' He gazed at her with his blue eyes. '*She* might tell the authorities.'

Eva laughed. 'She swears at me too sometimes, but it doesn't mean she wants to put me away.'

A few minutes later they were on their way back to Albert Street. 'You won't run away again, will you?' Eva asked anxiously. 'Not now we're friends.'

'Depends.' He jumped over a pavement crack. 'On what?'

'Whether Patsy Noonan tells the authorities.'
Tucking one leg up, he hopped on to the next
flagstone.

'Patsy won't tell.' Taking his hand, Eva propelled him across the road.

'I'm old enough to get across the road.' Indig-
nant, he drew his hand away.

'How old are you?' He looked about twelve,
but he was so undernourished, he could be
older.

'Old enough,' he said. 'I used to fetch stuff from
the market when me mam got too bad to go out.'
Close to tears again, he fell silent.

'What was your mother's name?'

'Mary.' He smiled as though saying her name
gave him pleasure. 'Her name was Mary, and she
was beautiful.'

'That's a lovely name.'

He wasn't jumping the pavement cracks any
more. And he wasn't talking. He was quietly brooding.

Eva tried to jolt him out of it. 'You still haven't
told me your name.'

'I need to trust yer first.'

'I thought you did.'

'Not yet.' He gave her a wary glance. 'Me mam
said I weren't to trust nobody. She said some folk
could knife yer in the back and smile at yer while
they were doing it.'

'Unfortunately that's true.' Peter Westerfield sprang to mind. 'I knew a man like that once.'

The boy was wide-eyed. 'You mean he knifed you in the back?'

Eva smiled. 'No. What your mother meant was that some people will do you harm even when they pretend to be your friend.'

'I'd like a friend.'

'Everybody needs a real friend, someone who will stay by them through thick and thin. I'll be your friend, if you'll let me.'

'I might.'

'If I meet with your approval, is that it?'

'Mebbe.'

Eva laughed. 'You're a hard man to do business with.'

With a proud smile he said, 'Me mam said I've got the makings of a landlord.'

It was all Eva could do to contain her laughter.

She suspected his mother's comment was a teasing compliment. As she knew from experience, a landlord could be both sharp and kind-hearted. And, from her brief knowledge of this little bundle of manhood, she thought his mother's description was perfect.

When they got back to Albert Street, the door was closed and there was no sign of Patsy. 'She's run off,' the boy said, 'just like me dad.'

'No, she wouldn't do that.'

'Where is she then?'

The door flew open. 'Come inside, why don't ye?' Patsy invited them, eyeing the boy with suspicion. 'The kettle's on, and I've made a fire.'

The boy sprang forward and rushed past her, down the passage and into the back parlour. The fire was roaring and spitting, warming the room like it used to when his mam was here. 'I were saving that coal!' Angry, he rounded on Patsy. 'I only make a fire at nighttime.'

'Ye ungrateful little bugger,' Patsy snapped. 'The house were freezing cold. I thought I were doing you a favour, so I did.'

'Well, yer weren't, and I don't want yer here, neither of yer.' He glanced at Eva and there were tears in his eyes. 'I told yer she didn't like me!'

Behind his back, Eva gestured for Patsy to leave them be. When Patsy flounced into the scullery, Eva spoke firmly to him. 'She didn't mean any harm. I know she should have asked you before coming into your mother's house, but she was only trying to help. Patsy sometimes makes mistakes, like any of us. She's a good, kind soul really.'

'She shouldn't have done it.'

'I know, and we're both very sorry.' Going to him, she asked softly, 'Do you want us to leave? You've only to say the word and we'll be gone before you know it. We can always find other lodgings.'

Behind her back she kept her fingers crossed, praying he wouldn't turn them away; not for their sake, but for his. 'Well? Would you like us to go?'

He didn't look up. '*You* can stay, but not her.' His gaze went towards the scullery.

'Do you remember what I said? About being your friend?'

'Yes.'

'Well, Patsy has been *my* friend for a long time. When my mother died, she helped me to smile again. She stayed with me when everyone else went away. I won't desert her now.'

'She doesn't like me.'

'Do you like her?'

'No.'

'Then what shall we do?'

He thought awhile. 'Will she do what yer tell her?'

Eva gave a small laugh. 'Not always, but I can try.'

'Will yer tell her not to shop me to the authorities?'

'She won't do that, I promise. And I'll do everything in my power to keep you here, in your own home. Will that do?'

'Do you want her to stay?'

'I'm afraid we come as a pair.'

'All right. She can stay. But only because you want her to.'

'Thank you.' She paused. 'You still haven't told me your name.'

'It's Tommy.' He seemed embarrassed. 'Tommy Johnson.'

Eva held out her hand. 'Hello, Tommy Johnson.'

Wrapping his small fist round hers, he said shyly, 'Tomorrow I'll show yer where they took me mam.'

Eva felt highly honoured.

From the scullery doorway, Patsy watched the tender scene, her eyes moist. 'You'll never know,' she whispered sadly.

⋙—⋙◆⋘—⋘

WHILE PATSY WENT off to the shops to buy food and a small bag of coal, Eva and Tommy set about cleaning the house.

Like all the houses down the street, the Johnson place was very cramped: three tiny bedrooms, a small, square bathroom and a steep staircase with steps so narrow that you had to walk down it sideways. It had a parlour with a large range, and a scullery that was big enough to take a table and chairs. There was a front room for best, and curtains at every window. But it was filthy dirty.

'Me mam couldn't get about like she used to,' Tommy said, 'and I didn't have no time for cleaning.' Giving the big brush a push, he sent a swirl of dust into the air. 'When me dad ran off, I were the man of the house and I had to fetch money in.'

'How did you manage that?' Little by little, Tommy was opening up.

'Selling old paper to the paper merchant fetched a bit, and there was always the market on a Saturday. The stallholders used to pay me for sweeping, picking up fallen fruit and veg, things like that. Me and me mam used to eat the fruit of an evening, then on Sunday she'd put the veg into a big stewpot.' He licked his lips. 'It were good, and sometimes it lasted all week.'

'What about school?' When he didn't answer, Eva persisted. 'How long have you been on your own, Tommy?'

Still wary, he shrugged. 'Don't know.'

'It's all right,' she assured him, 'but we'll have to talk about it all sooner or later, you know that, don't you?'

'S'pose so.' Disturbed, he put away the brush and disappeared into the back yard where he sat hunched up on the step. He didn't come in again until long after Patsy was back with the shopping, and only then because he couldn't resist the smell of cooking. He ate in silence and then disappeared upstairs.

'I should think it's the first time in a long while

that he's gone to bed with a full stomach,' Eva
remarked. 'Did you see him wolf that food down?'
It had done her heart good to see it.

Patsy was unusually quiet.

'Cat got your tongue?' Eva asked.

'I don't think we should stay here.' Patsy stared
into the fire. 'I think we should go now, while the
going's good.'

Eva didn't understand. 'What is it, Patsy? What's
wrong?'

She raised her eyes, and they were troubled.
'I don't like this set-up, that's all. How come he's
still loose? Why hasn't the social got their hands
on him?'

'How come you've taken such a dislike to him?'
It wasn't like Patsy.

'He's not our responsibility.'

'So we should leave without trying to help him,
leave him to fend for himself, is that what you're
saying?'

Patsy's mood deepened as she stared into the
flaring flames. 'The boy's trouble, and he's not our
problem.'

Eva couldn't believe this was Patsy talking. She
was about to say so when there came a knock on
the front door. 'Who the devil's that?' Her first
thoughts flew to the boy. 'Could be his father.
Maybe he heard his wife died and he's come for
the boy.'

'Or it could be the authorities,' Patsy said, 'come to take the responsibility off our shoulders.' Impatient, she got up and went to the front door, reappearing a minute later with three women in tow: a tall, skinny being in a long coat that reached the ground; a small, round body wearing a hat and gloves; and a third, homely and smiling. Her name was Maggie Bell, and she was the spokeswoman. 'We've come because we're concerned about the boy,' she said.

'It's the neighbours,' Patsy explained. 'I'll go and pack.' Without another word, she departed upstairs, leaving Eva to deal with them.

Eva invited them to sit down. She learned that the Johnsons had moved into the area just a few months ago. 'In no time at all, the boy's father cleared off,' Maggie Bell said. 'Soon after that the wife fell ill. We all did what we could, but she was a proud, independent sort. The lad seemed to be coping well, and so we let things drift.'

'Have you told the authorities?'

'None of us would want to do that.' Maggie looked Eva in the eye. 'Are you related?'

'No, I'm a lodger.'

'That doesn't matter. All we want to know is, do you mean to look after the boy?'

When Eva answered yes, she had every intention of taking care of Tommy, and that he would come to no harm, Maggie nodded, smiled, and said,

'That's all we wanted to know, and if you need our help, you've only to ask.'

After they'd gone, Eva went upstairs. 'You don't have to pack,' she told Patsy. 'We're staying. And if you two can't get along, then you'll have to learn how to stay out of each other's way.'

Patsy clearly wasn't happy, but she made no protest.

Later, when they were all in bed, the boy's crying was clearly audible.

Eva went to comfort him while Patsy, for reasons known only to herself, lay in her room, pretending not to hear. Like the boy, she could not hold back the tears.

# Chapter Eight

T HE SUNDAY CHURCHGOERS didn't even notice them. It was too cold for lingering; heads down they hurried away, the biting November wind cutting through their Sunday best. Numbed to the bone, all they had in mind was to get home as quickly as possible, make a cup of tea and sit beside the fire with their knees bared.

Kneeling beside his mother's resting place, the boy fumbled to arrange the flowers – long-stemmed white roses and a scattering of pinks. 'I can't do it,' he said, looking up pitifully at Eva. 'They won't stand up in the vase.'

Rolling back her coat sleeves, Eva knelt beside him. 'That's because they're too long,' she said, taking them out of the vase. 'We'll have to shorten the stems.' One by one she carefully broke them and Tommy arranged the flowers in the vase.

This was the third time Eva had accompanied him to the churchyard, and each time his heart broke anew. Today, though, he didn't cry, and Eva was glad of that. He sat on the hard, cold ground, staring at the name on the headstone; Eva had asked Patsy if they could pay to put the stone over Mary Johnson, and begrudgingly Patsy had agreed. 'It'll come out of *your* money when we start making profits,' she'd retorted.

'It's lovely, ain't it?' Tommy smiled, blinking in the wintry sunshine. 'It feels good to see me mam's name there. Before when I came here, it were all bare and horrible, and I wanted to tell her it weren't my fault. Now she's got pretty flowers and everything.' He gulped back a sob. 'One day, when I'm rich, I'll pay you and Patsy back. Every penny, you see if I don't.'

'Oh? You mean to be rich then, do you?' Eva had an instinct that he probably would turn out all right, in spite of everything.

'I'm gonna have a big, flashy car and drive you anywhere you want to go.'

'What about Patsy?' No matter how hard she tried, Eva couldn't get these two together. There was a barrier between them, put there by Patsy.

'I'm not bothered about her.' His face always darkened when Patsy's name was mentioned. 'I'll only let *you* come in my car.'

'Thank you, but I've got a better idea.'

'What's that?' He scrambled to his feet.

'I'll buy my own car, not a big flashy one but a smart blue one with leather seats and lots of shiny chrome.'

He laughed. 'That's a poncy car!'

Throwing her arm round him, she walked with him from the grave. 'How about if I clip your ear?' she joked.

'Me dad used to say that.' His mood instantly changed. His feet began to drag and he seemed to lose interest.

'Tommy?'

He looked up.

'Why don't you tell me about your dad?' Eva had brought him close to the subject a number of times, but always he backed off.

'He's no good.'

'Is that what you really think?' It seemed a harsh thing for a lad to say about his own father, but on the face of it he had good reason.

'He ran off and left us. If it hadn't been for him, me mam would never have took poorly.'

'Is that what your mam told you?' Sometimes Eva felt Tommy loved his father more than anything in the world. Other times, like now, there was bitterness in his voice when he spoke about him.

'Me mam was always soft. She said he wasn't a bad man – he's a bit of a gypsy, that's what she said. He couldn't stay in one place for long at a time, she told me, and he didn't make her poorly, that's what she said, but he did. I know he did.'

'Would you forgive him if he came back?'

'He won't come back. He's gone back to his

precious London and I won't be clapping eyes on him again.' He clammed up after that, and nothing Eva could say would persuade him to divulge any more.

On the way back to Albert Street, Tommy grew excited. 'Do you want to see my den?'

Frozen to the bone, Eva wanted nothing more than to get home.

'It'll only take a minute,' he promised, taking off at a run. 'Come on!'

Eva went after him. 'Slow down!' she called. Under her breath she muttered, 'It's a long time since I was your age.' Her thirtieth birthday wasn't too far off.

Running, walking and occasionally stopping for breath, the two of them went towards Preston New Road, where the big houses were. At the bottom of Corporation Park, Tommy stopped. 'This is where the posh people live,' he said knowledgeably. 'Dr Franklin lives in that house.' He pointed to a large, red-brick house set back in pretty gardens. 'One night when me mam was really bad, I had to run up here and fetch him.' His chest swelled with pride. 'I got to ride in his big car – like the one I want when I'm rich.'

Gasping for breath, Eva could only nod.

'Come on then,' he cried, and took off again, doubling back to Park Street. 'All the solicitors and important folk live here.' Standing in the middle of the pavement, his arms spread wide to encompass the grand old houses, he had the confident air of an estate agent making a sale. 'Some of these have been made into old people's homes,' he said. 'Me mam said it's really nice for 'em, living near the park.'

Exhausted, Eva sat on a low brick wall. 'I'm not going any further,' she said. When she had started out her nose was numb with cold and her skin proud with goosebumps. Now she was hot and bothered, her underslip sticking to the sweat on her back. 'Just where is this den of yours?'

'In there!' Laughing, he dashed into the front garden of a derelict house. 'It's all right, it's been empty for years.' He opened the front door and went inside. 'Tramps sleep here. I've seen one of 'em lighting a fire an' all.'

Intrigued, but a little wary, Eva followed.

In the hallway, she stood and stared. 'What a terrible shame,' she muttered. 'I bet this house was beautiful in its prime.' In a strange way, it was still beautiful.

Before her were many doors, two to the left and more to the right, and directly in front another, all hanging sadly on their rusted hinges. The ceiling was high, its plaster cracked. Through one corner you could actually see right into the room above. A damaged chandelier creaked dangerously on its chain.

Eva shifted her gaze. A wide stairway wound up to the gallery. There was a window on the half-landing, its stained glass unbroken, remarkably.

Daylight filtered through the green and blue panes, illuminating the hallway eerily.

Eva and Tommy wandered round the house. The oak-panelled walls in the living rooms were missing huge chunks. No doubt that's what the tramp that Tommy saw was burning, Eva mused.

The kitchen was vast. Surprisingly, all its cooking facilities remained intact. There was a long, narrow walk-in pantry at one end, and cupboards reaching to the ceiling over one wall. The windows were smashed and the walls stained with damp. There were holes in the floor, and a pungent smell from the burst pipes beneath the sink. But for all that, Eva thought, it was a bright, pleasant room.

Upstairs the story was the same: neglect and violation, the elements taking over, and in one bedroom creeping ivy had found its way in through the decaying walls.

Taking Eva by the hand, Tommy led her past the main bedrooms towards the smallest room right at the back of the house. 'This is my den,' he said proudly, pushing back the broken door. 'When they took me mam away, I stayed here for two whole nights.'

Eva wanted to ask him what had happened when his mother was taken away – who organised her burial, and who paid for it? Why was he allowed to roam about without being taken into care? But now was not the time. Later, when he got to trust her more, she would find out. Maybe the neighbours knew more than they were saying. Perhaps she should talk to Maggie Bell again.

Eva was astonished by Tommy's den. The view from its window was breathtaking. 'Oh, Tommy! It's beautiful.' It was like coming into heaven from the darkest corner of hell. 'I never dreamed this dilapidated house could be hiding such a view.'

The house stood in extensive grounds. There was a pond filled with green algae; a magnificent stone statue stood in the centre, its nose broken and one arm lying half submerged by its feet. Beside the pond was a decaying set of garden furniture – a round table with fancy legs and four barrel-backed chairs with rotting cane seats.

The grounds led down to a valley, beyond which was a forest and a lake. For one magic moment, Eva's thoughts went back to her mother's house and the fields where she had played and worked. A great sadness filled her lonely heart.

'Ain't it lovely?' Tommy was bursting with pride. 'An' it's all mine. There ain't nobody who knows about it except me and those tramps, an' I ain't seen them for ages.' He wrinkled his nose. 'Phew! They didn't 'alf stink, like summat gawn bad.'

'Who owns this house, Tommy?'

'Nobody.'

Ruffling his hair, she laughed. '*Somebody* must own it.'

'I ain't seen nobody.' He glanced out of the window. 'Except her. She's always telling me to clear off.'

Careful not to touch the broken glass, Eva peered out of the window. A small, round woman was hanging out washing next door. 'I think I'll go and talk to her.'

With Tommy in tow, she hurried down the stairs. The back door was nearest. 'What's she called?'

'I don't know her name.' Tommy hung back. 'Dunno why yer want to talk to the old witch anyway,' he snorted. 'She'll only tell yer to piss off.'

Eva told him he wasn't to use such language, and that he was to stay quiet while she talked to the woman. 'I don't want her thinking we're here to cause trouble.'

Parting the overgrown hedge, Eva called out, 'Excuse me!'

Startled, the woman swung round. 'Who's that?' she shrieked. 'Piss off or I'll fetch the police!'

'Told yer!' Tommy sniggered. 'That's what she always says.'

Taking her courage in her hands, Eva pushed her way through the hedge, emerging dishevelled and scratched. 'I just want a word,' she started, but before she could say any more, the woman flew at her with the line prop.

'Get away from here!' she screeched. 'Bloody tramps!' Catching sight of Tommy loitering behind, she went red in the face. 'You! I've told you before, you little sod! Clear off!'

'No, you've got it wrong.' Eva waved her hand in protest. 'We're not tramps. I want to talk to you, about the house.'

The woman was not convinced. 'If you come a step nearer, I swear I'll run you through.' She brandished the line prop as if it was a bayonet.

'Please, I mean you no harm, I promise you,' said Eva.

The line prop bayonet wavered.

'I wouldn't be bothering you at all, but I really am interested in the house next door. Who owns it, do you know?'

The woman decided that maybe she had overreacted. She put the line prop down. 'You should have come to the front door,' she said. 'You're trespassing, coming through that hedge.' She pointed to Tommy. 'And what's that little bugger doing here?'

'Do you know who owns the house?' Eva persisted.

The woman regarded Eva, wondering whether she could trust her. With the lady of the house gone away and all manner of work to catch up on, she could do with a bit of company. She made her decision. 'You'd best come inside,' she said, shivering. 'It's enough to freeze your insides standing here. The wind whistles up this valley day and night, winter and summer,' she grumbled as she led them to the back door. There she turned and pointed at Tommy. 'You, boy. Either wipe your feet and come in, or be obstinate and stay out. It seems like me an' your mam's got things to talk over.'

Neither Eva nor Tommy corrected her assumption that Eva was Tommy's mother. Somehow it didn't really matter.

When Tommy's feet were wiped clean and Eva's too, the woman continued on into the kitchen.

'Cor!' Tommy's nose twitched in the air. 'Meat pie! Me mam used to bake meat pies. Yer could smell 'em right through the 'ouse.'

The woman surprised them both by smiling. 'Do you want a slice?' She was proud of her culinary skills and to have them appreciated was a real treat. Certainly, the lady of the house never gave her much praise.

'Yeah!'

'Haven't you forgotten something?' Eva said.

'Please.'

'Right.' The woman pulled out a chair. 'Sit yourself at the table, me lad, and I'll get the pie out the oven. It should be done to a turn by now.'

The woman was, what, forty-five, fifty? Eva couldn't be sure. She had greying hair and a slight limp. When she wasn't scowling, she had a face that could pass for pretty. Her eyes were deepest brown, with a bright, merry twinkle.

'I'm Olive, the housekeeper here,' she introduced herself as she pulled a huge pie out of the oven and placed it on a wooden server. She cut a generous slice for Tommy. The pie crust was crisp and light, crumbling as the knife sliced through. Dark brown gravy spilled out, spearing the air with a warm, delicious aroma.

'It's bubbling hot,' Olive warned Tommy. 'Blow on it before you bite or it'll stick to your mouth and have the skin clean off.' She turned to Eva. 'Would you like a slice?'

Eva's mouth was watering. But she mustn't be tempted, she told herself. Patsy would have a meal ready for them when they got back. Tommy might relish two meals, but she couldn't. Not wanting to offend Olive, however, she answered, 'Yes, please, but just a tiny piece to taste.'

While Olive cut another slice, Eva glanced round the room. It reminded her of her mother's kitchen – warm and cosy, with a large sideboard dressed with blue china, and all manner of copper hanging over the fireplace.

'It's old-fashioned, I know.' Olive caught her looking. 'If I had my way, I'd have the whole lot torn out and a new kitchen put in. There are no mod cons here, you know. The house hasn't been changed since the mistress's grandmother was alive.'

When all three were seated round the table, she talked as though she hadn't seen a human being in years. 'The mistress is a kind soul,' she revealed, 'but she's never really been happy since the master and their only daughter were killed in a car crash. Dreadful thing. Her daughter was twenty-two . . . lovely girl.'

'Has she any other children?' Eva asked.

'No, there were no other children, just Rosie. Adopted as a baby, she was, but you'd never have known she wasn't their blood kin.' She frowned. 'Funny how like the mistress she was, same dark eyes and hair, same wide smile.' As though talking to herself, she muttered, 'Like she was made to order.'

'So she lost all her family? That's a terrible thing,' said Eva sadly, memories rushing back to haunt her.

'You talk as if you know a thing or two about losing someone you love.' If Olive hoped for an answer, she was disappointed. Eva quietly ate her pie.

'Cor! This pie's even better than me mam's.' Tommy had scoffed his slice and was looking for a second. With gravy running down his chin he asked hopefully, 'Is there any more going spare, missus?' Snaking out his tongue he sucked the gravy into his mouth.

'No, Tommy,' Eva intervened. 'You've had more than enough.' He and Patsy were already at loggerheads. It would do no good if he was to turn his nose up at her cooking when they got back. 'Besides, you've been very well looked after by this kind lady. A thank you wouldn't hurt.'

'Thanks, missus.' Tommy gave Olive a smile to warm her heart.

'A drop of sarsaparilla to wash it down, that's what the boy needs.' Olive fetched it from the pantry cupboard. 'Now then, m'dear,' she said to Eva, 'what was it you wanted to know about the house next door?'

Eva had many questions, but Olive could not answer them all. The house had been empty these past five years, and all manner of vagabonds and no-goods had slept there. 'We even had them folks with sandals on their feet and bells round their necks. Played fiddles all night, they did. In the end the police ran 'em off.'

'Hippies,' Tommy contributed.

'If you say so,' said Olive. She didn't know who owned the house. It had been put up for sale years ago, but there had been no takers, as far as she knew. 'If anybody has bought it,' she remarked, 'they're certainly taking their time doing anything about the place.'

'Who was handling the sale?' Eva asked. 'Do you know?'

Olive frowned with thought. 'It was a local estate agents. Dunmore . . . No, not Dunmore, Dunnon. That's it, Dunnon and something. I can't remember the second name.' And with that, Eva had to be content.

Soon afterwards, Eva and Tommy rose to leave.

'If I remember any more about the house, I'll let you know,' Olive promised as she showed her visitors out. 'Come and see me again, won't you?' Lonely and often neglected by the woman she worked for, Olive had taken to Eva, and Eva to her.

———⟫•≪———

PATSY WAS BESIDE herself. 'Where the devil have ye been?' she demanded as they came into the back room. 'I've been imagining all sorts of terrible things, so I have!'

Eva apologised profusely. 'I've lots to tell you,' she said excitedly. 'I think I might have found us our little business.'

'Not before time either,' Patsy snapped. 'We've been here weeks and it's doing us no good living on our savings.' Her gaze went involuntarily to Tommy who was wolfing down his egg and chips. 'Especially when we've been lumbered with another mouth to feed.'

The spiteful comment silenced Eva. She knew there was something chewing away at Patsy, but for the life of her she couldn't imagine what it was. Each time she commented on it, Patsy denied it and flounced out of the room. The more Patsy protested, the more Eva felt certain there was something behind this hostility towards Tommy. He could be cheeky, yes, and there were times when she had to reprimand him, but Patsy had never even given him a chance.

From that first minute she'd clapped eyes on him, she'd been hostile, and Tommy was all too aware of it, which only made matters worse.

It was eight thirty when Tommy made his way upstairs. 'Goodnight, God bless.' As always, too shy to kiss her, he touched Eva's shoulder as he passed.

'Goodnight, Tommy.' Eva rested her hot drink on the fender. 'Don't forget to wash and clean your teeth, will you?'

At the bottom of the stairs, he paused. 'Can I come with you to find the agent?'

'We'll scc.'

'Goodnight then.' He made no move to leave. Instead, he shuffled his feet, bringing his uncomfortable gaze to Patsy, who was in the armchair, pretending to read. 'Goodnight, Patsy.' It was the first time he'd tried to breach the barrier she'd put up between them.

For one heart-stopping minute, Eva really believed Patsy might warm to him. She looked up and stared at Tommy, her features momentarily softening as she studied his eager face and small, wiry form. Opening her mouth to say something, her face suddenly stiffened and she turned away. 'Get off to bed,' she muttered. Her voice was unyielding, her face the same.

Shoulders hunched, he glanced sadly at Eva before he, too, turned away. With slow, weary footsteps, he made his way upstairs.

Eva followed.

In his room, Tommy sat, dejected, on the edge of his bed. 'Why does she hate me?' he asked. 'I ain't done 'er no 'arm, have I?'

Eva sat beside him and put her arm round his thin shoulders. 'No, you haven't done her any harm, Tommy.' Normally he didn't seem to care whether Patsy liked him or not. Tonight, though, he was different. More vulnerable somehow.

'Sometimes, like just now when she told me to get off to bed, she reminds me of me mam.' His voice trembled. 'I really want her to like me, Eva. I want us all to be good mates.'

'So do I,' said Eva with feeling.

'I wish me dad hadn't run off.'

'Have you no idea where he might be?'

A dark mood settled on him. 'I don't care if I never see him again!' Staring down at the bedclothes, he twiddled them between finger and thumb. 'I hate him.'

'Look at me, Tommy.'

The boy looked into her eyes. 'I mean it,' he said sombrely. 'I hate him for what he did to me and me mam.'

'Hatred is a terrible thing, Tommy,' Eva said gently.

'He shouldn't have left us. He *made* me hate him! But I ain't done *nuffin'* to make Patsy hate me.'

'I'm sure she doesn't really hate you, Tommy. I'll talk to her again, try to find out what's wrong.'

'You really like that house on Park Street, don't you?'

Eva nodded. 'I think it's beautiful.'

He laughed. 'It's falling down!'

'I know.'

'I'm tired.'

'We've had a busy day. I expect you'll sleep like a log.' She ruffled his hair. 'But not before you've had a wash, I hope.'

Grimacing, he shook his head. 'Goodnight, Eva.'

'Goodnight, Tommy.'

Going out of the room, she glanced back. Tommy was bending over the dresser, taking out a towel. In the mirror she caught sight of his unhappy face and her heart twisted. Poor Tommy. Patsy was being so unfair to him.

Downstairs, she wondered how to confront Patsy about her feud with Tommy. Her previous attempts had proved fruitless, and Patsy was in such a foul mood tonight. Still, the evening was young. She'd leave it till later and hope that Patsy's mood would mellow.

Taking up pen and paper, she began working out some figures. If she was going to persuade Patsy to accept her ideas about the house on Park Street, she needed a strong, convincing argument to put before her.

There was so much she didn't yet know. For instance, what was the agent asking? How much would it cost to renovate the place? They wouldn't have nearly enough money of their own, so how much would it cost to borrow the rest, and who could they turn to? The bank manager had been all sweetness and light when they had made that large deposit, but how would he feel about lending them money to get a business project off the ground? More to the point, would he think her idea was even viable? Patsy, too, would want to know the answers to all these questions.

As Eva tried to do some calculations, she occasionally glanced at Patsy reading her paper, hoping she might show some interest. She wanted Patsy to make the first move, given the mood she was in.

Patsy discreetly watched her from behind her newspaper. 'What's the little bugger up to now?' she wondered. When she could bear it no longer, she got out of her chair. 'Do you fancy another drink?' Waiting for an answer, she stood over Eva, arms folded, peeping at what she had been scribbling but unable to make any sense of it.

'Let me get the cocoa, Patsy. After all, you cooked the dinner.' Eva made to get up, but was pushed back down.

'You stay right there, ye bugger!' Patsy pointed a finger at the sheet of paper. 'I want to know what all this is about. And while you're at it, ye can tell me what you and the boy have been up to half the day. And what were ye talking about just now, up the stairs, eh? It's like a bloody conspiracy round here, so it is!'

'Forget the cocoa, Patsy. Why don't we just sit and talk?'

'Ye know very well I think better with a drink in me hand,' Patsy retorted. 'As there isn't a decent drop of anything else in the place, I'll have to settle for cocoa. So, do ye want one or not?'

Eva nodded, afraid to open her mouth.

When the two of them were seated beside the fire, Eva told her everything. She explained how Tommy had taken her to see his den, and that she had been astonished to find it was a big old house in need of repair.

Patsy regarded her suspiciously. 'Yer after buying this place, aren't ye?'

'Maybe.'

'Where's it at?'

'Park Street.'

'An' where's that?'

'Alongside a beautiful park.' Eva grew excited. 'Oh, Patsy! It's a lovely area, tree-lined streets and big, posh houses. The house has a big garden and the most fantastic view. You'd love it, I know you would.'

'Yer a mad woman, so ye are,' Patsy chuckled.

'One minute yer off taking flowers to Tommy's mam, and the next yer full of cock-eyed ideas about spending our hard-earned money on a big house in a tree-lined street.'

'Only if you're agreeable.'

The smile slipped from Patsy's face. 'Ye said something about it being in need of repair. What exactly d'ye mean? The walls want painting? A new bathroom? Just how bad is this place?'

Taking a deep breath, Patsy admitted, 'It's virtually derelict.'

Patsy was horrified. 'Ye *are* bloody mad!'

Undeterred, Eva went on, 'Oh, Patsy, it's really lovely. In its day it must have been the best house up there. There's a pond and a statue, and you should see the land behind. There's the most beautiful valley, which runs into a forest. There's a lake, and the view is just magnificent.'

'Forget it, me darlin'. We're not ready for a big house with a pond and a magnificent view. We'll have to settle for a house something like this one, and a little business too. Have ye forgotten that's why we came here? To get a business going and earn ourselves a tidy living?'

'I think the house can be where we both live *and* work. There's a real business to be had there, Patsy, I'm sure of it.'

'What kind of business are we talking about?'

'I don't even know if we can do it. There's so

much to be gone over. Formal things like finance, and permission for change of use.'

'Eva! Will ye answer me? What kind of business are we talking about?'

'A hotel.' There, it was said, and as she had suspected, it stunned Patsy.

'Jaysus, Mary and Joseph!' Patsy stared at her. 'With the money we've got, we might just be able to open a cafe in the bus station. But a hotel? Jaysus! I thought *I* was the dreamer.'

Grabbing her by the hand, Eva told her, 'We can do it, Patsy, I know we can!'

'I don't see how. Where would we get the money? And even if we could get the house in order, just think of all the other things we'd have to find.'

Eva refused to give in. Grabbing her sheet of paper, she shoved it under Patsy's nose. 'It's all here, what we need – furniture, crockery and cutlery, linen—'

'Beds and towels,' Patsy interjected, 'pots and pans, a reception desk, a till, hotel stationery, receipt books. And staff. Sure, we'd never run a hotel on our own, not a respectable one.'

Eva felt Patsy's excitement growing and she knew she had her. 'It won't be easy, I know, and at the end of the day we might be disappointed, but we have to try, Patsy, or we might always regret it. I've been thinking about it ever since I came back, and I have some ideas.'

'Go on.' Patsy settled into her chair. 'I'm all ears, so I am.'

Collecting her thoughts, Eva got out of her chair and began pacing the room. 'We haven't got anywhere near the kind of money needed but we do have a few thousand pounds, and it's a start.'

Patsy laughed. 'A drop in the ocean compared to the money we'd have to find. And where would we get that, I ask ye?'

'From the bank.'

'Sure, that's like getting blood from a stone. An' even if, by some miracle, we *did* get finance, how would we pay it back? The interest alone would cripple us before we got off the ground.' Patsy knew about money. It was her strength.

'Like I said, it won't be easy. Nothing worthwhile ever is. But look at it this way, Patsy. We have to buy somewhere to live, don't we?'

'A terraced house, that's what we said. Something that would leave us enough money to start a little cafe or a shop.'

'Yes, but if we got the house on Park Street cheaply enough, we might even have enough left over to renovate the place, and there's your collateral. Wouldn't the bank go for that?'

'I'm not sure. They're not very favourable to women opening a business. But you're right, Eva, if we got the house cheaply enough, we might have something to bargain with.' Holding out her hand for the sheet of paper, she said, 'Let me see the figures.'

Reluctantly, Eva handed it over. 'It's just scribble,' she said, 'a few ideas. I'm not good on finance and accounts, you know that. That's your department.'

'If we're serious, we'll have to persuade the bank manager, and to do that, we'll need to show him a financial forecast. If he's not convinced, that's the end of that.'

Eva hugged her. 'Oh, Patsy, I'm sure we can do it!' Suddenly there was something to aim for. Something that would make everything worthwhile.

So it was decided that, first thing in the morning, they would visit the estate agent for the house. Eva had found only one with the name Dunnon in the telephone book for Blackburn – Dunnon and Haines. There seemed little point in Patsy going to look at the house before they knew for certain it was still on the market. Eva was a little apprehensive about what her reaction would be when she saw the state it was in, but she would deal with that when, or if, the time came.

Patsy had one condition about their plans for the morning. 'I don't want the boy tagging along.'

'Why not? He's no bother. Give him a chance, Patsy,' she pleaded. 'He so much wants you to be friends with him.'

'Sure, there's no chance of that.' Collecting the two mugs, Patsy hurried into the scullery.

Eva went after her. 'Don't you think it's time we talked about this?'

'I don't know what ye mean.'

'I think you do. Ever since we came here you've been dead set against that boy. Why? What's behind it all, Patsy?'

'I'm off to me bed.' Patsy made to push by, but Eva held firm.

'Talk to me, Patsy. We've always shared things. There's something very wrong here, and I need to know what it is. I can't help if you won't talk.'

'Sure, there's nothing to talk about.'

'It's not fair on Tommy, and it's not like you to be so hostile.'

Patsy kept her gaze lowered. 'Mebbe it's time you went to the authorities about the boy. He should be at school, out from under our feet, so he should.'

'You know as well as I do they'll put him away. Do you really want that on your conscience?'

'What do you mean to do about him then?'

'I'm going over to talk to Maggie Bell. She seems to care about what happens to Tommy. Maybe she'll have a few ideas. But I'm not going to the authorities.' Eva's voice grew hard. 'And neither are you, Patsy Noonan!'

Patsy turned on her. 'If you think I'd snoop on him, you don't know me,' she snapped.

'Then I'm sorry for jumping to conclusions, but what am I supposed to think?'

For a long moment, Patsy looked at her, thinking what a kind heart and loyal nature Eva had, and she felt ashamed. She would have given anything to confide in Eva, as Eva had always confided in her, but she couldn't bring herself to do it. There were things here that she could never share with anyone; awful, sad things that had haunted her for too long. 'Oh, Eva, I don't want us to fall out. We've been through too much together to let that scrap of a boy come between us. Let him come with us tomorrow if it means that much to you. But don't let him think he'll be living with us. And don't expect me to be friends with him, because I never could be.'

Eva was about to speak, but Patsy shook her head. 'Please, Eva,' she begged, 'leave it at that.'

She made her way across the back room, and on up the stairs, her heart sore, and her eyes filled with tears.

Eva sat in the armchair. What *was* the matter with Patsy? In all the time Eva had known her, Patsy had never taken against anyone like this unless they richly deserved it. But there was nothing she could do if Patsy refused to confide in her.

Eva glanced at the clock. It was almost 10 p.m. 'I wonder if it's too late to go knocking on Maggie Bell's door,' she muttered. There was so much she needed to ask that kind soul. She ought really to go to bed, but there was so much playing on her mind she probably wouldn't sleep anyway. So she quietly put on her coat and crept out of the house. 'Ten minutes, that's all it should take,' she promised herself. 'Twenty at the most.'

'THIS IS A fine time of night to come calling.' Maggie Bell stood at the door, her figure silhouetted in the hallway light. Her hair was wrapped in curlers and she had obviously taken out her dentures to soak overnight. 'Whatever it is, can't it wait till morning?'

'It's about Tommy.'

'Oh aye, I might have known.' Rolling her eyes, she tutted. 'You'd better come in then.'

The house was surprisingly modern. The furniture was teak and colourful rugs covered the floors. The old range had been taken out and there was a new fire surround, with a chrome clock on top of it and wall lights either side.

'D'yer want a brew?' Without waiting for Eva to answer Maggie went off to put the kettle on. 'Come in here and tell me what the little bugger's been up to,' she called from the kitchen.

'He's a good lad, Mrs Bell—'

'Maggie to my friends.'

'Right, Maggie. He's not been up to anything. It's just that I can't imagine how he's managed on his own, or how he didn't get taken into care. I was hoping you could fill me in a bit more.'

'There's folk round here that don't trust the authorities, and we've all looked out for him.' When the kettle began to whistle, she took the lid off the teapot, poured in a small amount of boiling water and swilled it round. 'He doesn't look it, but the lad's gone fourteen. He'll soon be able to work, then he'll be nobody's responsibility.'

'He doesn't look older than twelve.'

'He's small-boned, like his mam. And he's had a hard time of it, poor little bugger.' Pouring out the tea into two flowered mugs, Maggie asked Eva, 'Do you want him off your hands, is that it? Because if you do, you'll not be allowed to stay in that house. You'll need to find fresh lodgings, you do realise that, don't you?'

'No, I'm not trying to get him off my hands. I've grown very fond of him. I just need to know more, and I've got a feeling you can tell me a lot more than you're letting on.'

Maggie laughed aloud. 'You're a cheeky young bugger! But you've a right to know, seeing as you've been fair enough with the boy.' She carried the tray into the sitting room. 'He looks well,' she declared. 'I've been keeping a crafty eye on him.'

'Tell me about his parents.'

Eva was told to sit down.

'Right.' When Maggie was sitting opposite, she

took a great swig of her tea before launching into a very detailed account of the Johnson family. 'Mary was a northerner born and bred. Her husband, Fred Johnson, was a southerner. He was also a restless, moody man, given to disappearing for days on end and turning up when it suited him.' She gave a snort of disapproval. 'The pair of them were ill-suited, you could see that a mile away. He never did settle here, as far as I could tell.' She sniffed, took another gulp of her tea and added, 'He was a Cockney, and that was where his heart remained. The north was where Mary was born, so she was pulling one way and he was pulling another. But I suppose he wasn't a bad man, just unhappy.'

'But he left his wife and child, so he couldn't have been much good, could he?'

There was a moment when it seemed Maggie might clam up, but then she relented and opened her heart, and what she had to say was a shock to Eva. 'He didn't leave of his own accord. Mary threw him out, bag and baggage. Two o'clock in the morning, it was, and the two of them out in the street, arguing. She said he couldn't come back inside unless he promised to settle down and make a proper home for her and the boy. He said he could make no promises, but he'd try his best. Mary ran inside and fetched a suitcase and an armful of clothes. She threw the lot at him. "Bugger off out of it, and good shuts!" that's what she said.'

'Good God! Where was Tommy while all this was going on?'

'In bed I should think, fast asleep.' She recalled the night it happened. 'He must sleep unconscious,' she remarked, 'because the row woke the street, I can tell you.'

'So Fred Johnson never knew his wife died, and the boy was left all alone?'

'How could he? He's never set foot in the street since that night, and I know Mary never heard from him again.' She sighed, a deep weary sigh. 'Poor Mary, she had a temper as bad as his. The two of them parted bitterly, and the lad ended up taking the brunt of it all. I might well have tried to contact his dad, but I had no idea where to look, and besides, the boy seemed dead set against seeing him again. He blamed Fred for everything, when of course it was six of one and half a dozen of the other.'

'How did you manage to keep the boy out of council care?'

'With difficulty and determination.' Leaning forward she asked, 'Did the boy tell you I had him living here for a time?'

'No.'

'Did he tell you his mam inherited the house from her father, so by rights it now belongs to him?'

Eva was astonished. 'No, I had no idea.'

'There's a lot more you don't know either.'

'What? Things that Mary told you, you mean?'

Eva had taken a liking to Maggie. 'I expect you were a good friend to Tommy's mam, weren't you?'

Maggie laughed. It was an empty sound. 'Enemies, more like. After they arrived here, I never exchanged one word with her. I went out of my way to avoid her, and she did the same when she saw me.'

'But why?'

'It's a long story.' A slow, easy smile spread over Maggie's old face. 'But, if you've got time, I wouldn't mind getting it off my chest after all these years.'

'I've got all the time in the world,' Eva answered, and settled back in her chair.

# Chapter Nine

PATSY WAS FLABBERGASTED. 'What?'

'It's true, Maggie Bell is Tommy's aunt.'

'Why didn't she tell us this before? And why isn't she looking after him instead of parking him on us? Anyway, how do *you* know all this?'

'After you and Tommy went to bed last night, I went over there. I had a few questions to ask, and she told me everything.'

Falling into the armchair, Patsy stared at her. 'Then you'd better tell me, hadn't ye?'

Eva related what Maggie had confided in her. 'Mary was Maggie's sister. She was brought up here in Blackburn, in this very street. She was born in this house. She left home when she was sixteen and travelled about for a time, working in nightclubs and bars. She met Tommy's father when she took a job in the East End of London. When Mary became pregnant, they got married. When Mary's father, a widower by then, fell ill, he became desperate to see her again, Maggie says. Being the youngest she was always his favourite and it broke his heart when she left and cut off all contact with her parents. When her mother died, Mary didn't know, because she couldn't be found. Her father didn't want the same thing to happen with him. He wanted to see her again before he died, but it wasn't to be. He didn't know where to begin to look for her. In his will he left Mary everything – this little house which he and his wife had bought soon after they were married, all the furniture, and a sizeable amount of money that he had saved.'

'What did he leave Maggie?'

'Just enough money to bury him beside his wife.'

'Why in God's name would he do that?'

Eva shrugged. 'Who knows? Maggie says it took her years to forgive him. His grave went untended and she couldn't even bear to hear his name. She had given up the idea of marriage to look after her mother when she became ill, and then she stayed on to take care of her father. She nursed them both through their ailing years, and in all that time there was never a word from Mary.'

'How did she find her sister?'

'The solicitor did that, through the Salvation Army, Maggie said.'

'So, when Mary came back to live here, Maggie bought a house over the way?'

'No. She had no money to buy a house. She found a job at the local hospital and rented the place across the street. Apparently the landlord had let the house go to rack and ruin and most of her wages went into making it a home. Two weeks before Mary returned, Maggie was pensioned off with a small sum of money, which she spent on her home. She's got nothing else. In fact, as she told me, she lives day to day, and asks nothing from anybody.'

'Does Tommy know all this?'

'No. Maggie never told him she was his aunt, and she asks that we don't tell him either. When her father cut her out of his will in favour of Mary, he hurt her deeply. When Mary came back, Maggie tried to make friends, but her sister sent her packing. "If you're after some of what our dad left, you can think again," she said. She wouldn't even let her over the doorstep. Then, when she threw Fred Johnson out—'

'Threw him out?' Patsy sat up. 'I thought the boy said he ran off?'

Eva shook her head. 'No. Apparently she threw him out when he wouldn't promise to settle down. After he'd gone, Mary took to the bottle. In no time at all the money was all gone, and she went downhill. The rest you know.'

'Why did Maggie bother to keep an eye out for the boy when she'd been treated so shamefully?'

'Because she's a good woman, Patsy, that's why.'

'So if we got a place of our own, she could take care of him and you need have no conscience about it.'

'It's not that easy, Patsy. She's done her duty, and now she doesn't want to know. She took the boy in and kept him out of council care. When he asked if it was right what they'd said, that she was his aunt, Maggie told him she had lied to them so they wouldn't put him away. Afterwards, she watched out for him when he came back to this house, but now she's washed her hands of him. He'll be fifteen soon, she said, and out at work.'

'After what that family did to her, I can't say I blame her.'

'Tommy's done her no harm.'

'Maybe not.' Patsy's expression hardened. 'But if we get our own place, I still don't want him living with us.'

Eva said nothing. There seemed little point. But she refused to give up hope that Patsy would change her mind.

⟶•◄

MR HUGHES OF Dunnon and Haines ushered Patsy and Eva into his office and bade them sit down. 'I'm just having coffee,' he said, his bird-like face jutting from his shoulders as though he was about to peck. 'Would either of you like a cup?'

Patsy looked at Eva and Eva answered for them both. 'No, thank you all the same.' Tommy wasn't with them. In the event, there had been no more argument about whether or not he accompanied them to the estate agents because he had asked if he could go to the museum to see the stuffed animals instead. Eva agreed, and told him to meet them outside the estate agents at twelve o'clock. Excited as a puppy, he'd gone away whistling.

'Could you please tell us what the position is with regard to the unoccupied house on Park Street?' Eva asked Mr Hughes. 'I understand you were handling its sale.'

'Well now, let me see.' Mr Hughes scratched his nose until it resembled a ripe cherry. 'As I recall there *was* someone very interested in that property, but for some reason or another, the sale never did go through. The gentleman in question said he would come back, but he never did.'

'Who owns the house?' Eva wondered how Dunnon and Haines managed to stay in business with agents as vague as Mr Hughes seemed to be.

'I'll have to look that up,' said Mr Hughes with an apologetic smile. 'It's been some time since anybody enquired about the place.'

Rising from his chair, he skirted round Patsy and began delving in a tall metal filing cabinet by the door. 'Robinson . . . Roberts . . . I'm sure it was something like that.' His fingers alighted on a blue folder. 'Ah! That's it! Roman, Francis Roman, Acacia Lodge, Park Street. Here we are.' Placing the folder before him on his desk, he thumbed through it. 'No, it seems the house was never sold. The owner has since died and the house is scheduled to go to auction in six weeks' time.'

'Auction!' Eva's heart sank. 'That means we'll be up against lots of other buyers.'

'Auction is often the ideal way to buy a property like this.'

'Why do you say that?'

'Not everyone has the ready cash or the means to borrow. Those that have can pick up real bargains if they're lucky.'

'Jaysus!' Patsy was out of her depth. 'We've neither of us ever been to an auction, except for the fruit market on a Saturday, but that's a different kettle of fish from buying a house, so it is.'

'Well, the executors will consider any offers made before the auction.'

'What is the reserve price?'

'There isn't one. Having tried, and failed, to sell the house in the usual way, the executors will take what they can get for the property. However, the original asking price was six thousand pounds, and only an offer in that region would secure the property. Otherwise, the executors will take their chances at auction.'

Eva's heart sank. 'We only have limited funds.' She glanced at Patsy. She seemed too stunned to speak, which was probably just as well. 'Certainly not enough to buy the place outright,' Eva went on. 'We have ideas about developing the house, and that would take even more money.'

'Could you borrow?' asked Mr Hughes. 'The banks might well be interested.' Privately, he doubted that any bank would give these two obviously inexperienced women the time of day, but it wasn't his job to discourage potential buyers. 'A number of these properties have been converted to small, select apartments. It's a good area, close to the park and within easy reach of the town centre.'

'Well, we can certainly try,' said Eva, trying to sound a lot more positive than she felt. She stood up. 'Thank you for your time, Mr Hughes. We'll be in touch.'

'The bugger!' Patsy exploded as soon as they were in the street. 'The place is falling down, you said. How can he ask so much for it?'

'It's got potential,' Eva replied. She scanned the street, looking for Tommy, but he was nowhere in sight. Still, it wasn't quite twelve yet. 'Maybe we should take our chances at the auction. What do you think, Patsy? We might get lucky.'

'Have yer taken leave of yer senses? What chance would we have against professional property developers? None at all, that's what.'

Eva couldn't argue with that. She wasn't going to tell Patsy, but the thought of bidding thousands of pounds in a room full of sharp businessmen terrified her anyway. 'We'd better go and see the bank manager, then.'

'First,' said Patsy firmly, 'I want to see this dream house of yours for meself.' Her face suddenly stiffened as she saw Tommy loping down the street towards them.

'Did you buy the house?' he asked breathlessly as soon as he came to a halt in front of them.

'It's not as easy as all that,' Eva laughed. 'But it's still on the market, and that's a good start.'

On the day Eva took Patsy to see the house, Tommy stuck to them like glue. Patsy declared how he was 'A bloody nuisance, and why did he have to come along in the first place?'

When Eva argued that it was Tommy who found the house, and had every right to be there, Patsy grudgingly conceded. 'All right then,' she grumbled, 'but I don't want him showing me this and that. Nor do I need the pair of youse trying to persuade me into your way of thinking. I'll make me own mind up, so I will!'

On first seeing the house, she gave a groan. 'Jaysus, Mary and Joseph! It's a dreadful ruin, so it is!'

For one awful minute, Eva thought Patsy would turn and run. 'Just look inside,' she pleaded; taking Patsy's arm she drew her closer to the door. 'You've always been better than me at seeing how a place can be improved,' she lied. 'Please, Patsy!

Just a peep? Now we've come this far, you can't not go inside.'

'Just a peep then.' Delighted by Eva's flattering remark, how could she refuse? 'Don't bully me,' she warned, 'or I'm off! And keep that little bugger from under me feet.' Giving Tommy a scowl of a look, she allowed herself to be taken forward.

At the door she shook her head. 'Like I said,' she tutted, 'it's nothing but a ruin. Be Jaysus! It'll take a bloody fortune to put this lot right, so it will.'

As she ventured further into the house, looking into one room and then the other, and after a while going up the stairs, Eva followed and wisely said little. She was afraid to, in case she said the wrong thing and Patsy took off.

Picking out all the faults; the sagging ceilings and the rotting floors, and the way every nook and cranny had been worn by the elements, Patsy sounded as though she hated every inch of the place.

And yet, deep down, Eva suspected Patsy was warming to the house.

Once or twice Tommy looked as if he might take Patsy up on a point or two, but when Eva silenced him with a determined shake of her head, he scurried off into his den and didn't show his face until Patsy had led Eva outside again. 'It's worse than I thought,' she said. Then a smile appeared and Eva knew she liked it. 'You've a good eye, Eva me darling,' she confessed. 'And sure, it isn't me that knows a thing or two about how to bring a place back to life . . . it's you, so it is, and well you know it.'

So, they were in agreement. The place had real possibility.

'But we've got our work cut out, so we have,' Patsy remarked as they made their way home.

Eva made no comment. She knew, possibly more than Patsy did, how much of an uphill battle it would be.

FOR THE NEXT couple of weeks, Eva and Patsy threw themselves into drawing up a financial forecast. They checked out the price of furniture, linen, carpets, kitchen and dining necessities, studied hire-purchase terms, and calculated running costs. They also visited the house a number of times with various builders to obtain estimates of renovation costs. At last Patsy had enough facts and figures to draw up a comprehensive financial projection. They dropped it off at the bank and then waited, and hoped. A week later they received a letter from the bank manager suggesting they meet at the house. He wanted to see the place for himself.

They duly met him and watched as he wandered about, making copious notes and muttering to himself. When the three of them stepped out into a bitterly cold day, Eva asked his opinion, but he declined to comment until he'd discussed the situation with senior colleagues at the bank. He asked them to come into the bank at three o'clock the following day. When they agreed, he merely nodded, looked from one to the other, and hurried away.

'We'll get nothing at all from that one,' Patsy said with a snort.

Eva felt the same, but she wouldn't give up. 'What makes you say that?'

'Sure, the bugger couldn't get away quick enough.'

'I hope you're wrong,' Eva said, but deep down she wasn't hopeful.

The following day, her fears were confirmed. 'I'm sorry,' said the manager, 'the bank isn't prepared to take such a risk. I'm afraid we will have to say no.'

'But why dismiss it out of hand like that?' Eva demanded. 'You haven't even talked through our business proposition.'

'This is your first business venture. Your financial projections are pure guesswork. And you have no collateral. If the business failed, the bank would be liable for all your debts.'

'If it was two men sitting here, it would be an altogether different matter,' Patsy scoffed.

He shifted uncomfortably in his seat. 'I assure you, the bank's decision is based on financial issues alone. We believe it's too big a venture for two people with no business experience, and too great a risk without collateral, as I've already said. Now, if you don't mind, I have another appointment.' With that he stood up and strode to the door, which he opened for them. 'If you were to hit on a less ambitious idea, we might possibly talk again.'

'I don't think so,' Eva answered calmly. The next time she and Patsy walked into this bank, it would be to close their account. 'If you'd had the decency to read through our forecast properly, you would have learned that I *have* run a business before, my parents' business, and Patsy kept the books. She probably understands figures better than you do.'

Outside, Patsy rounded on Eva. 'I told you it was a crazy idea but you wouldn't listen.'

'Oh, Patsy, he's not the only one in the world to lend money. We can try elsewhere. We've got time, the agent said so.'

Patsy would have none of it. 'No, Eva. The bank manager's right. It's too big a venture. We'd only end up broke – years of hard work, with nothing to show for it.' She paused, looking at Eva's stricken face. 'I know how much you'd set your heart on it, me darlin', but it wasn't right from the start.'

'It *is* right, Patsy. That house is perfect for a small hotel. We both know it. Don't let him turn you against the idea.'

'I don't want us to lose everything on that place. There'll be other opportunities. Maybe that arrogant bastard was right. Maybe we should lower our sights.'

'I can't force you to go along with it,' Eva said. 'It's as much your money as it is mine, and whatever we do, I want it to be for the two of us. But please, Patsy, won't you give it one more try? Maybe the agent can help us find a backer. Let's go and see him before we throw in the towel.'

'No.' There was something else preying on Patsy's mind. 'The boy obviously thinks he's coming with us when we move. I know you think I might change my mind, but I won't. The further away from me he is, the better I'll like it.'

Eva was shocked. 'Do you really hate him that much?'

'I don't hate him.' Patsy turned away.

'Is that the real reason why you're refusing to try again for the Park Street house, because you're afraid we might have to take Tommy with us?'

'All I'm saying is forget the house on Park Street. It would never have worked out anyway.'

'He's living with us now, so what's the difference?'

'That's another thing. I know we're only weeks away from Christmas, and it's a bad time for house hunting, but as soon as the New Year is over, I want us to start looking for a place of our own. Something we can afford without breaking the bank.'

Patsy's mind was made up, and nothing Eva could say would change it.

Later that night, Eva heard Patsy's fretful footsteps pacing up and down, back and forth. Climbing out of bed, she went along the landing and tapped on her door. 'Are you all right, Patsy?'

The door opened. 'Go to bed!'

'You're not to worry about the house,' Eva told her. 'I didn't realise you were so against it. But it's all right. We'll forget it, like you said.' From the look of Patsy's red eyes, Eva was sure she'd been crying. 'We'll find something else, so you're not to worry, you hear?'

Reaching out but keeping the door only inches open, Patsy took hold of Eva's hand. 'You're a good friend,' she murmured. 'I don't deserve you.'

'Try and get some sleep, Patsy. Goodnight.'

Patsy closed the door and Eva returned to her room.

Neither of them slept much. Eva felt responsible for pressing Patsy into something she didn't feel comfortable with. Acacia Lodge was a real find, she knew that. But if Patsy wasn't happy with the idea, then she had no right to pursue it. She smiled wryly. If she had money of her own, wild horses wouldn't hold her back.

Seated on her bed, Patsy held the photograph in the palm of her hand. For a long time she stared at the images there: a woman, a man and a boy. The man had one arm round his wife, and the other round the boy's shoulders. The boy was Tommy. Patsy assumed the woman was Mary.

It was the man who held her attention. Tall and

rugged, he seemed to be in his early to late forties, with the kind of smiling brown eyes that instantly befriended you. Wearing a chequered shirt and cord trousers, he looked fit and able. The sunshine dappled his face and, in the split second the photograph was taken, the boy was looking up at him with adoring eyes.

As she looked, the tears ran down Patsy's face.

Carefully, she put the photograph back in the envelope and replaced it in the bedside drawer where she first found it.

# Chapter Ten

A CACIA LODGE WAS due to be auctioned on 4 December. 'I'd like to attend the auction, wouldn't you?' Tommy was fast asleep in bed. Eva and Patsy were sitting by the cheery fire, while Patsy mended her long coat.

Patsy looked up in surprise. 'What for?'

'I just want to see what kind of a person buys it. I'd hate to think of it going to someone who might tear it apart or, worse still, pull it down and build a monstrosity in its place.'

'What would it matter? It won't be us that buys it.' Swearing under her breath, Patsy made another attempt at tidying the sleeve of her coat.

'It *would* matter, Patsy. It's a beautiful house and deserves better.' Eva lowered her voice. 'I only wish we could have given it a new lease of life.'

'It's only a house when all's said and done. Ycr too sentimental, so ye are.'

'So you won't come with me?'

'I've got better things to do, so I have,' Patsy tutted.

'Like what?'

'Like going to the shops for a new winter coat.' With a snort of disgust she threw the garment aside. 'I've had this one for ever. Just look at it!' Raising the sleeve of the coat, she pointed to the frayed cuff. 'It's falling apart, so it is. It's time I treated myself to a new one.'

Startling them, Tommy appeared at the door, his small frame shivering and trembling, more from fear than cold. 'It weren't my fault.' Making a beeline for Patsy, he leaned over and stroked her shoulder, his voice breaking into a sob as he begged, 'Don't hit me, will yer, Mam? Please. I won't do it again.'

Patsy leaped to her feet. 'I'm not yer mam!' she cried. When Tommy seemed not to have heard and just stood there, softly crying, she turned to Eva. 'Jaysus! What's wrong with him?'

Eva had rushed to his side. 'Ssh!' Looking at Patsy, she put her finger to her lips. 'He's sleep-walking.' Tenderly, she turned him round and walked him to the door. 'Quick, Patsy, he's freezing cold. Fetch a blanket out of the linen cupboard, will you?'

Patsy did as she was asked. 'I'm not cut out for this sort of thing,' she protested, though her gaze was constantly drawn to Tommy. 'He put the fear of God in me, so he did!'

And the fear of God stayed with her until she

had gone to her own bed and closed her eyes to sleep.

---

THE AUCTION ROOM was packed to capacity. Eva stayed at the back, though she would rather have been at the front bidding with the rest of them.

Several parcels of land were to go under the hammer: half an acre in the middle of town; a disused generation plant; a block of vandalised garages; and other miscellaneous items which no one seemed to want.

When item number seven came up, there was a buzz of excitement. 'Acacia Lodge,' the auctioneer announced. 'A grand old place, in need of repair but not beyond saving. With eight acres of prime land behind, and a magnificent view, this is a very desirable property.'

'It wants a bloody fortune spent on it.' The portly man close to Eva was talking with his colleague. 'You mark my words, it'll go for a song.'

He was wrong. The bidding was lively and Acacia Lodge was sold for seven thousand pounds, to a man Eva couldn't see properly. He was half hidden by a column at the side of the room.

People began filing out. Eva went forward, curious to see the man who had stolen her dream. But he had already gone. Feeling cheated, she followed the others out and headed towards Albert Street.

Behind her, the business of the day was concluded. 'You've got a good buy there,' the auctioneer told the man. 'A property like that comes up only once in a while.'

The man smiled. 'I've gone above my budget,' he confessed, 'but I've been looking for a long time for a property in this area. This one fits the bill, and I didn't want to let it go.'

'Ah, well, some get what they want,' the auctioneer said wryly, 'and others go away empty-handed.' His gaze went to a balding man who had bid strongly for the house. 'John Lowes is a builder hereabouts. Not a very nice man,' he confided, 'I enjoyed seeing him struggle. You're the first one who's snatched a property from under his nose in a very long time.'

'John Lowes, eh? What did he intend doing with it, do you know?'

'There's only one thing he does with the properties he buys, knocks them down and builds tight little developments that sell for a fortune.' He regarded the man in front of him. Tall and slim, with brown hair and inquisitive eyes, he had the air of someone who knew what he wanted. 'What business might you be in, sir? If you don't mind me asking, that is.'

'I'm a hotelier. My mother died some years back and left me a thriving business. Since then I've built up a network of hotels right across the country.' He pulled out his chequebook.

'Hotels right across the country, eh? What name do you go under?'

Looking up with a smile, the man handed over his cheque. 'Frank Dewhirst,' he answered. 'I'm not known hereabouts.'

The auctioneer passed him a receipt, and all documents relating to Acacia Lodge.

As Frank walked away, the auctioneer muttered, 'Not known hereabouts, eh?' He chuckled. 'I've a feeling you'll be known well enough before too long.'

<hr />

W HEN EVA WALKED in the door, Patsy saw how preoccupied she was. 'Ye shouldn't have gone,' she chastised her. 'Sure, that place wasn't meant for us, me darlin'.'

'Maybe.' Taking off her coat, Eva gave a deep sigh. 'Maybe not. But it doesn't matter now anyway because it's been sold.'

Patsy paraded up and down in her new astrakhan coat. 'Does the coat suit me? I paid more than I wanted but I tried it on and had to have it.'

'It looks lovely,' Eva answered honestly. In fact Patsy looked very attractive. She was made up and her shoulder-length hair shone like roasted chestnuts.

Taking off the coat, Patsy threw two more pieces of coal on the fire. 'Jaysus, yer look frozen to the bone, so ye do.'

Rubbing her hands in front of the fire, Eva looked round. 'Where's Tommy?'

'Gone to the market, that's what he said.'

'How long ago?'

'Can't be sure – an hour, maybe longer.'

'It's half past six. He shouldn't be out in the dark, especially on a cold night like this.'

'I'm not his keeper.'

'Oh, Patsy! He's only a kid.'

'He's fourteen. When I were fourteen, I had to find me own way in the world, so I did. Nothing came easy, and there was no one to worry where I was neither. Stop fretting, will ye? The boy will be back when he's good and ready, so he will. Now then,' she flopped into the armchair, 'will ye tell me what happened at the auction, or what?'

Still concerned about Tommy, but trying not to show it, Eva related the events of the afternoon. 'I don't know who the man was, but he meant to have that place, I can tell you.'

'You're bitterly disappointed, aren't ye?'

'I'll get over it.' She glanced nervously towards the door. 'He should be in by now.'

'Like I said, he'll be in when he's good and ready.'

'You didn't have an argument, did you?'

'We never argue because we never talk.'

'I wish you would.'

'What? Argue?'

270

'You know very well what I mean.'

Wary, Patsy changed the subject. 'We'll soon be looking for a place of our own,' she reminded Eva. 'A business, too. Christmas will be on us before we know it and, to tell you the truth, I'll be glad when it's over. What with thinking of turning a derelict house into a hotel, and then all this unnecessary worry about a boy who isn't even our responsibility, sure, I reckon we've wasted enough time here. We came here to set ourselves up in home and business, and we've done neither.'

'We could have done both if only you'd listened to me.' Eva hated herself for saying it, but it was the truth. 'Sorry, Patsy. That was unfair.'

'Sure, I can't blame ye. I know what it's like to set yer heart on something only to have it snatched away. In the past, whenever we've had a difference of opinion, you've been right every time.' Patsy gave praise where praise was due. 'But not this time,' she said determinedly. 'This time, you were wrong an' I was right. And I'm making no apologies.'

The door opened and Tommy staggered in with a large Christmas tree. 'I had to fight another lad for this,' he said. 'The man on the stall gave it to me for helping load his lorry. After he'd gone, Billy Bully from Montague Street tried to take it off me, but I gave him a thrashing and he ran off.' Peering out from beneath the branches of the tree, he grinned with pride, his black eye beginning to shine blue, and his face stained with blood. 'It's a grand tree, ain't it?'

'It certainly is,' said Eva, taking part of the weight from him.

Patsy made her excuses and left the room.

'Let's have a look at that face of yours,' Eva said, propping the tree in the corner. 'You should have let the bully have it.'

'I did!' Tommy's chest swelled with pride. 'I gave him a bloody nose and ripped his shirt half-way up his back.' He giggled. 'His mam's got a terrible temper. She'll half kill him when he gets home.'

Seeing that he wasn't badly hurt, Eva had to smile. 'When I said you should have let him have it, I didn't mean . . .' She laughed out loud. 'Oh, never mind. Wash your face and I'll get you something to eat.' With Tommy, there was never a dull moment.

While he sat by the fire, scoffing his cheese sandwich, Eva went upstairs. Knocking on Patsy's door, she asked, 'Are you coming down?'

Patsy opened the door. 'You can come in if you want.'

Entering the room, Eva caught sight of a brown envelope lying on the bed. Patsy quickly tucked it into the drawer, her face red with embarrassment. 'What's that little bugger been up to?'

'He's been fighting over a Christmas tree.'

'Huh!' Going to the dresser Patsy took out a brush and began running it through her hair. 'I'm not coming down.'

'Why not?' Lately, Eva couldn't fathom her. 'I've brewed a pot of tea and made us a cheese sandwich. It's that new crusty bread from the corner baker's.'

'Ten minutes then. But I'm having nothing to do with the boy, or the Christmas tree.'

The evening was painful. Tommy tried time and again to involve Patsy in the conversation, but she would have none of it until, at nine o'clock, she marched off up to her room. Exhausted, Eva wished she hadn't persuaded Patsy to come downstairs. 'You'd best get off to your bed now,' she told Tommy.

He kissed her goodnight on the cheek. 'She wants to take you away from me,' he said soulfully.

'Why do you say that?'

'I just know. I try to be nice to her, but she'll never like me.'

'Go to your bed, Tommy,' Eva urged. 'Tomorrow we'll go and find some decorations for the tree.'

That put the smile back on his face.

After he'd gone to his room, Eva stayed downstairs for a while. But there was no smile on her face.

She looked at the tree slumped in the corner. 'You look like I feel,' she laughed, wondering how Tommy had managed to get it home. 'All the same, we'll dress you up and make you sparkle. Then, with a bit of luck, we might *all* feel more Christmassy.'

━━━━━➤✦❖✦⬲━━━━━

BRIGHT AND EAGER the following morning, Tommy seemed to have put Patsy out of his mind. 'Where are we going now?' he asked as he and Eva went away from the town centre where they'd stocked up on shiny baubles and tinsel.

'Going to look for some holly.' She swung into Preston New Road.

'But *where*?'

'You'll see.' Eva quickened her steps.

'This is the way to Corporation Park.'

'That's right.'

'Park Street too.'

'Right again.' She had come to know the area very well.

'Are we going to see Olive?'

'If she's there.'

'Do you think she'll offer us some of her delicious pie?'

Eva laughed. 'I hope not. It's Patsy's turn to cook the evening meal, and you know how stroppy she gets if we don't eat every last crumb.'

He thought about that. 'Is she really your best friend?'

'Yes.' Playfully chucking him under the chin, she added, 'And so are you.'

'I wouldn't want her for *my* best friend.' Suddenly his mood had darkened.

Eva slowed. Looking him in the eye she asked, 'Are you sure about that, Tommy?'

Keeping his gaze on the pavement, Tommy didn't answer.

Eva waited.

'I'd *like* her to be my friend,' he admitted eventually, 'but she won't let me.'

'I know.'

'I ain't done nuffin' to upset her neither.'

'I know that too.'

'Me mam were moody an' all.' He kicked a stone out of the way and thrust his hands into his pockets, shivering. 'Brr! It's bleedin' freezin', ain't it?'

'What do you mean, about your mam being moody?' This was the first time he'd spoken in that way about his mother, and Eva hoped he might open up to her.

Tommy shrugged his shoulders. 'Dunno. I didn't mean nuffin'.'

Eva thought it best to make no comment, believing that people were more likely to confide if you didn't push them too hard.

Not Tommy though. Tommy changed the subject. 'Patsy wouldn't even know if we'd had some pie.'

Eva laughed out loud. 'I wouldn't count on it.'

'Olive might not offer us any. She might not even be there.'

'That's true.'

In fact, Olive was there and she had just taken a delicious rhubarb crumble out of the oven. Eva couldn't resist it. When she was finished, she was so full she could hardly breathe. 'That's the best rhubarb crumble I've ever tasted,' she told the smiling Olive, who had to be restrained from spooning out another helping.

As for Tommy, he had his mouth crammed full. Grinning appreciatively, he showed a mangled mixture of rhubarb and crumble. 'Close your mouth, Tommy!' Eva told him, and he did.

'I don't know what's going on next door,' Olive chatted, 'but there have been all kinds of people coming and going. One big fellow in a duffel coat and boots went all over the grounds, taking pictures. He seemed to be here for an age. This morning, two others turned up in a big red lorry. They were in the house for ages. Afterwards, they stood at the bottom of the garden making notes and talking. Then they drove off, and I haven't seen them since.'

Eva told her about the auction, and Olive said

she was glad that the house might be renovated. 'It's such a terrible waste.'

'Eva wanted that house,' Tommy butted in.

'Oh, dear!' Olive thought she might have said the wrong thing, but Eva put her mind at rest.

'I couldn't afford it,' she said.

'It would have been lovely having you next door, but I believe in fate. It seems to me you weren't meant to have it.'

'That's what Patsy said.' Tommy had finished his crumble and was feeling talkative.

'Who's Patsy?'

'She's Eva's best friend, but she doesn't like me.'

When Olive looked surprised, Tommy went on, 'If Eva was my mother like you thought before, then Patsy couldn't make her leave me behind when they go.' Olive looked even more bewildered.

Eva intervened. 'That's enough, Tommy. Why don't you go and find some holly?'

Tommy nodded and went outside.

Olive watched him through the window as he foraged. 'Oh, look,' she said suddenly. 'That man's there, the one I told you about who went all over the grounds, taking pictures and measuring.'

Eva joined her at the window and saw the man, talking to Tommy. 'I'd better go,' she decided, knowing how Tommy let his tongue run away with him, 'but I'll come and see you again.' Olive was delighted.

Outside, just as Eva suspected, Tommy was relating his life story. 'Me dad's a Cockney too,' he was saying, 'but he couldn't settle in the north so he ran away and left me with me mam. If he came back now, I'd pretend I didn't know him.'

'I'm sorry,' Eva said to the stranger, putting a hand on Tommy's shoulder, 'we have to go.' Gripping Tommy's coat collar, she urged him away from the man and on past Acacia Lodge. 'You're too free with strangers,' she warned. 'We don't know that man from Adam.'

'He's a good bloke. He's from London, that's what he said. I were just telling him about my dad, and how he run off like the coward he was.'

As Eva turned to say something to him, she caught sight of a second man emerging from the doorway of the house. 'My God!' For a minute, Eva thought her mind was playing tricks. But then he looked straight at her, and though he was older, there was no mistaking him. 'Frank Dewhirst!' The name came from her lips like a ghost from the past.

'What did yer say?' Tommy looked from her white face to the man in the doorway. 'Who's that geezer?'

For what seemed an age but was in fact only a few seconds, Frank and Eva stared at each other, unable to believe their eyes. Suddenly he was rushing towards her. 'Eva? Eva Bereton?'

'He knows yer name!' Tommy cried.

Overcome with emotion at seeing her again, Frank hugged her to him and then held her at arm's length. 'I can't believe it,' he kept saying. 'Eva Bereton! Lovelier than ever. I can't believe it.'

Eva hardly knew what to say, she was so amazed.

Tommy thought it was like one of those films he'd seen when he'd sneaked in at the pictures. 'I'm Tommy,' he said boldly, but Frank was too preoccupied to respond.

When he asked to take Eva out that evening, she accepted. 'We can talk over old times,' he said. 'I've got so much to tell you.'

⸻ ⸙ ⸻

Patsy was so shocked, she almost dropped the dishes. 'Frank Dewhirst, of all people! How is he? What's he doing in this part of the world? And why would he be nosing about the house on Park Street?' The questions came thick and fast. 'Ye don't think *he's* the one who's bought it, do ye? Jaysus! Wouldn't that be a turn-up for the books?'

'I don't know any more than you do.' Wiping the dishes, Eva stacked them away. 'He asked me out to talk over old times, and I've said yes.'

Pausing in her chores, Patsy swung round. 'Oh? And when's this?'

'Tonight.' Eva was wondering if she'd done the right thing. 'He's collecting me at eight o'clock.'

279

Patsy smiled. 'And why not?' she declared. 'He was a good friend, so he was.'

'Now I've agreed to it, I'm not sure I should have.'

'Oh? Why?'

'Water under the bridge and all that.'

Patsy frowned. 'Does he know his mother sent us packing?'

'If he does, he didn't say.'

'Then he doesn't know.' She regarded Eva's quiet face. 'He was in love with you though. You do remember that?'

Eva nodded.

'Is that why you wish you hadn't agreed to go out with him?'

Now that Patsy had spelled it out, Eva felt foolish. 'I expect so, but what does it matter now? And anyway, you're right. Frank was always a good friend, and I'm still very fond of him.'

Before Frank arrived, Eva helped Tommy put up the tree in the front room. 'It's too early to dress the tree,' Eva told him, 'but you can make some paper chains and trim the holly.'

Tommy was preoccupied. 'You won't marry that man, will you, Eva?'

'Who's talking of marriage? He's an old friend, that's all.'

'If you did get married, you wouldn't leave me on my own, would you?'

Eva laughed. 'I'll be back in a couple of hours. And when I do get back, I'll expect to see this room nice and tidy.'

When Frank arrived, the reunion with Patsy was less emotional. 'You don't look any different,' he said, though he thought she was a bit slimmer than before.

Tommy remarked on his 'big posh car', Patsy said how good it was to see someone from the old days, and in minutes Eva was whisked away. 'You look beautiful,' he said, opening the car door for her.

Eva had brushed her blonde hair into a glowing frame about her face, and her green eyes shone with excitement. She wore a light-grey, long coat, and beneath that a straight-cut black dress. The high-heeled shoes accentuated her slim ankles, and altogether she made a very attractive figure.

'I've found this lovely old inn,' he told her as they drove out of town. His hand wandered from the steering wheel to take hold of hers. 'Oh, Eva, you can't know how excited I am at finding you.'

After all this time, and two disastrous relationships, he still had marriage on his mind. But there was time enough for that, he thought. He guessed Eva had no man in tow now, or she would not have accepted his offer to take her out. So, what had she been doing all this time? What had brought her to Blackburn, and what were her future plans? He and

Eva needed to catch up with the past. So, for now, that would have to suffice.

The inn was indeed lovely. It was on the outskirts of Preston, old and beamed, with small windows and intimate rooms. The restaurant backed on to a river. Frank asked for a table by the window.

Eva was enjoying herself immensely. 'It's a long time since I came to a place like this,' she told him. In fact, she had never been to a place like this.

She thought Frank had not changed much; his appearance was slightly more rounded, and he had a few more lines round the eyes, but he still had that scrubbed, fresh-faced look and, with his smooth hands and expensive suit, he looked the picture of affluence.

Her first question took the smile from his face. 'Are you still running the hotel with your mother?'

'Mother died six years ago.'

'Oh, I'm sorry.' Eva felt awful.

'The hotel was left to me,' he said. 'It's been totally refurbished, and now caters to an elite clientele. In fact, I've made a speciality of catering for top businessmen – company directors, high-level conferences, that sort of thing.' The smile returned. 'You might be surprised to know I own eight top hotels right across the country.'

Eva was not surprised, and told him so. 'I always believed you would do well.'

'Acacia Lodge will be my ninth hotel.'

'You bought it?' So Patsy was right.

Frank nodded.

'It's so strange,' she said. 'I had plans of my own to turn Acacia Lodge into a hotel.'

'Did you?'

'I was at the auction. I had no idea it was you who bought it.'

'If I'd known you wanted it, I might have backed off.'

'It wouldn't have made any difference,' she confided. 'I couldn't raise the money for it. I just went out of interest.'

'We have so much to talk about, don't we? What's happened to you in the years since you left? Is there a man in your life still, Eva? Have you any children? What are your plans for the future?'

Eva laughed. 'So many questions!'

'Oh, there are many more,' he confessed. Not least of which was asking her to marry him. But first things first. He raised his glass to hers. 'To you and me. May we be blessed with everything our hearts desire.' Now that he had found her again, all he wanted was Eva.

Eva clinked her glass with his, and they drank a toast.

'TOMMY!' PATSY'S VOICE sailed through the house. 'Answer that bloody door.'

Running to the window, Tommy looked out. 'There's no one there!' he yelled back; whoever it was must have gone away.

In the other room, Patsy was drying her hair by the fire. Irritated now, she rubbed the towel hard into her scalp. 'It's them damned carol singers, so it is! I swear they start earlier every year.'

When the knock came again, this time louder, she wrapped the towel round her head and marched to the front door. Flinging it open, she glared at the lad standing there; a round-faced fellow about the age of Tommy, but twice the size. 'What the devil d'ye want?' she demanded. 'Carol singing, is it?'

'No, missus.' Looking the essence of innocence, he smiled at her. 'I've come to see Tommy. He promised me a game o' marbles.'

Patsy continued to stare at him. In the half-light from the street light, he seemed fairly well dressed, and he had a friendly sort of face. 'Tommy's friend, eh?' There was something about him that bothered her, but she couldn't put her finger on it. 'Ye shouldn't be out at this time of night on yer own,' she chided.

'It's all right,' he answered with a sweet smile. 'Me mam knows where I am.'

'I see.'

'So will you please tell him Mike's here?'

Patsy nodded. 'Wait there.' Half closing the door, she went to the front room where Tommy was surrounded by strips of paper and mountains of holly trimmings. 'There's a lad here to see you.'

'Who is it?'

'You'd best go and find out, hadn't ye?' Her hair was dripping wet and she had no shoes on her feet; Eva was out enjoying herself, while *she* hadn't been out in so long she'd begun to feel her age. She'd almost forgotten what it was like to lie in a man's arms and feel the thrust of his body on hers. And now, as if that wasn't bad enough, she couldn't even have a peaceful evening indoors without some bloody kid banging on the door at all hours.

'Just get rid of him,' she snapped, 'or bugger off out, I don't care what ye do.' With that she stormed off, back to the fire.

Slipping his shoes on, Tommy ran to the door. 'Hello?' It was pitch-black outside, and there was no one in sight. 'Who's there?'

'Tommy, it's me.' From across the road, a young figure stepped out from behind a parked van. 'I was told this was yours.' He seemed to be lifting something from the back of the van. 'You'd better come and help. I can't carry it on my own.' The voice sounded vaguely familiar but Tommy couldn't be certain.

'What is it?' Cautiously, he stepped down from the doorstep, and crossed the road. 'Who sent you?'

As he neared the van, the figure stepped away. 'Here, lad. Come here.' The voice was that of an older man. 'It's a present, see.'

Tommy's young heart soared. 'Dad! Is that you, Dad?' All his hatred was forgotten.

'It's me, son. We have to talk. But not here. Get inside. Quick!'

Something about the tone of voice and the furtive urging made Tommy hesitate. 'Let me see who you are,' he demanded. 'How do I know you're my dad?'

The man laughed. Tommy turned to run, but it was too late. Grabbing him by the scruff of the neck, the man hauled him into the van. No sooner was he inside, than the van drove off. Through his terror, Tommy saw the boy slam the doors shut. It was the lad who had fought him over the Christmas tree.

'Thought you'd give my boy a thrashing, did you?' The man's unshaven face was pressed close to Tommy's, his warm, booze-ridden breath like a fog in Tommy's wide, stricken eyes. 'Well now, I reckon I should give you a taste of the same, don't you?'

'Let me out!' Fighting with all his might, Tommy tried in vain to escape. 'It were *my* tree, not his! I paid for it, with work.'

The van careered round corners, throwing them from side to side and sending all manner of articles down on them – the van was packed with items of furniture, lamps and what looked like tied-up bundles of bedding. 'Steady on, you silly cow!' the man yelled. 'Are you trying to kill us all, or what?'

'I don't like this business, Josh, taking a kid from his family.' The driver was his wife. She was clearly nervous. 'If we get caught, we'll be in real trouble, have you thought of that?'

'Drive the bloody van and mind your own business!' Incensed, Josh twisted his grip on Tommy. 'Nobody beats my Billy up and gets away with it,' he growled. 'I need to set the record straight, that's all.' Addressing his son who, like the coward he was, remained at the back by the doors, he said, 'The truth now, Billy. Who paid for that tree?'

'I did! It were a surprise for you and Mam.'

'And did this little bugger sneak up on you? Is that why you got the worst of it?'

'It were just like I told you. He didn't even give me a chance.'

'Well now, that's what I thought. My boy is twice your size, so I knew you couldn't beat him fair and square.'

'I didn't sneak up on him!' Tommy was terrified. 'He's a liar! I *did* beat him fair and square.'

'Stop the bloody van!' Josh shouted at the woman.

She did as she was told, bringing the van to a halt at the side of a spinney. 'Don't do it, Josh.'

'I told you to mind your own bloody business.'

She appealed to Billy. 'Tell your dad the truth.'

'I already did,' he answered rudely. 'The coward sneaked up on me from behind.'

Josh dragged Tommy into the spinney. 'Right then, we'll soon see who's the liar.' Turning to the woman, he ordered, 'Fetch the rifle.'

Both she and Tommy stared at him wide-eyed with horror. 'I'm not fetching no rifle,' she said, backing away. 'I won't be part of no murder.'

'Don't be so bloody stupid, woman.' Josh laughed out loud. 'I'm not gonna shoot anybody. I just want to make certain the coward doesn't run away from a fight with our lad.'

When she hesitated, Billy ran and brought the rifle to him. 'She's a softie,' he sneered, 'like all women.' Deep down he was shaking. Tommy was the better fighter, and Billy knew it, but he dare not admit it or his dad would have the flesh off his back.

Suddenly Tommy felt himself being thrown forward. 'It's up to you now, Billy boy!' Josh yelled, and while Tommy looked round in a daze, Billy leaped on his back.

It was a fierce fight. After only a few minutes both boys were exhausted, but Tommy stayed on his feet, ready to fight on.

'Buck up, Billy!' Josh urged angrily. 'Don't let the brat get the better of you.' Coming up behind him, he gave his son a great shove. 'Stop bloody dithering! Use your fists like I showed you. Your feet as well if you have to.'

Hurting and afraid, Tommy hit out, the well-aimed blow sending Billy sprawling. Humiliated, and knowing his dad was watching, the older boy scrambled up and ran at him. Tommy side-stepped; Billy tripped, and as he fell he knocked his head on the ground, momentarily dazing himself.

'Get up!' his father ordered.

When the boy lay there, his bloodstained face upturned, he yelled again, *'Get up!'*

Billy raised his head. 'I'm not fighting no more.' He knew when he was beaten.

Enraged, Josh darted forward, yanked him off the ground and sent him head first towards the woman. Then he stripped off his coat. The woman's frantic voice called out, 'For God's sake, he's only a bairn, and he's hurt bad. Leave him be! The boy got a fair enough thrashing – they both did.'

Tommy's legs felt wobbly, his head was throbbing and a trickle of blood was running from his hairline into his eyes, half blinding him.

Behind the woman, Billy grinned. 'Go on, Dad,' he goaded. 'Teach him a lesson!'

Stepping forward, Josh stood before Tommy's small, unsteady form. 'Oh yes, I'll teach him a lesson all right. The best lesson he's ever likely to get.'

And, as he came forward, Tommy braced himself.

PATSY LOOKED AT the clock. 'Ten thirty.' She wiggled her toes in front of the fire, trying to ignore the fact that Tommy had been gone for almost two hours. 'Eva's making a night of it.' A little smile crept over her face. 'Lucky devil, so she is.'

Beginning to grow restless, she went to the front door and looked out. 'I'll give him what for when he gets back, the little sod! All the same, where can he be until this time? Jaysus! I'm getting as bad as Eva, so I am. That boy should know better than to stay out till all hours. He'll hear from me when he gets in, so he will.'

Returning to the back room, she paced the floor. 'Come on, Eva,' she muttered. 'What the devil's keeping yer?' She didn't know what to do. She had thought of going to Maggie Bell, but so far had persuaded herself there was no need.

<hr />

THE VAN HAD travelled only a few miles when Josh ordered his wife to stop outside a country pub. 'I've a terrible thirst on me,' he complained. 'The landlord here is a good bloke. He's well known for serving a pint out of hours.'

A moment later, man and boy both climbed out of the van. When the woman went to follow, he turned on her. 'You stay here. Keep an eye on the boy.'

'I'm hungry.'

'Do as you're told! I'll send you something out.' He gave her an unwelcome, sloppy kiss. 'Somebody's got to watch him.'

In a few minutes Billy was back with a ham sandwich and a pint of beer. 'Dad says to get that down you,' he told her. 'We'll not be long.' With a sly glance into the back of the van, he grinned. 'Got taught his lesson, didn't he, eh?' When she didn't answer, he swaggered away.

Unable to eat the sandwich, she put it aside. But she sipped at the beer, her throat dry with shame. She glanced round. The boy lay on a bundle of bedding, one arm flung out, the other buckled beneath him. In the light from the pub window, his face had a sallow, unreal appearance. Gulping hard, she took another sip of the beer. If it came to it, she could handle her son. But Josh was a bastard without mercy. He was the one she feared.

Half an hour passed. An hour. Inside the van the silence was eerie.

Getting out of the van, she peered through the pub window. Some of the men were saying goodnight. 'Give us a call at six in the morning.' Workers, staying overnight, the woman deduced.

Josh was at the bar, talking to the landlord. They were knocking back whisky now and from the look of them had already drunk more than was sensible. Billy was slumped in a chair, sound asleep. Suddenly, Josh slid to the floor. The landlord laughed out loud.

Looking up, he saw her watching. In a minute he was outside.

'Come in,' he said. 'Your lads are staying the night, so you'll have to do the same.' He put his arm round her. 'I've a nice warm bed waiting. Your man's dead to the world. We can have a bit of fun, the two of us. He'll never know.' Pushing his arm up her skirt, he felt for her thigh. 'Ooh!' Grabbing her hand he guided it to his trousers. 'Feel that! You've made him stand up like a bloody ramrod.'

'Bugger off!' She slapped him hard across the face.

'Please yourself,' he grumbled. 'Get back in your bloody van and freeze, for all I care.'

Back in the van, she waited for the light in the bar to go out. A moment or two later, she went to the back of the vehicle. She opened the door and reached inside. The boy was icy cold. Taking two ends of the bedding, she wrapped it round him, afterwards gently stroking his face.

She glanced across at the pub. All was in darkness. It was now or never, she decided.

Quietly, she closed the van doors and climbed back into the driving seat. Keeping the lights switched off, she turned on the engine and waited, her eyes raised anxiously to the pub window, fearing a light might come on and someone would see her.

Upstairs, the landlord drew back the curtains

and looked out. 'Running the engine to keep warm, eh?' he laughed. 'She'll be knocking for me to let her in before the night's through.' Still laughing, he dropped on to the bed and fell into a deep, drunken stupor.

After a while the woman drove slowly away. At the end of the lane she accelerated, speeding along the road and praying that she would not be stopped by the law.

Beyond all pain, Tommy didn't move or make a sound.

———◆———

EVA WAS BESIDE herself with worry. 'Tell me again, Patsy. Who did the boy say he was? What did he look like?'

For the umpteenth time, Patsy went through what had taken place.

'And you say he didn't tell you he was going out?'

'Not a word. Like I said, I told him his pal was at the door, then I came back in here. I just assumed he'd decided to go off with the lad.' Like Eva, she was beginning to feel very uneasy about the situation. 'Eva, what are we to do?'

'You stay here, Patsy. If he comes back and the house is empty, he'll only panic.'

'Why? Where are ye going?'

'I'm going to look for him.'

'What? At this time of night? You don't know who's prowling about. Let me come with you.'

'No, Patsy.' Throwing on her coat, Eva hurried to the door. 'Keep a lookout for him, and whatever you do, don't leave the house.' Only when Patsy had promised did Eva set off.

Frozen to the bone, she searched the streets, looking in every nook and cranny, calling his name, but he was nowhere to be found, and her heart was in her boots. The further away from Albert Street she got, the more she wondered whether Tommy really wanted to be found. Recalling how concerned he was about being left on his own, she murmured, 'I would *never* leave you on your own, Tommy, you should know that.'

Thoughts of going to the police crossed her mind, but she thrust them away. Numbly, she continued to search.

Back at the house, Patsy sat in her chair, her eyes like lead weights. 'Stay awake, Patsy, my girl,' she told herself. 'When he knocks on that door, he'll get the length of my tongue an' no mistake!'

It was nerve-racking, waiting for Tommy, looking out for Eva. Worried and angry at the same time, Patsy paced the floor. 'Ah, sure, I knew the little sod would be trouble the minute I clapped eyes on him.' The strange thing was that now, when she believed he might be in trouble, Patsy felt a surge of love for him.

Some time later, when there was a knock on the door, she fled along the passage, excitedly calling out as she ran, 'Eva! Have yer got the boy? Jaysus! I thought I'd never see the pair of youse again.'

Close to tears, she flung open the door. She was astonished to see there was no one there. 'What the devil!' Staring into the night, she thought she saw a figure running, but with the night so dark, she couldn't be certain.

'Kids!' Tossing her head, she snorted angrily. At the top of her voice, she yelled into the street, 'Little monsters! There'll be a bucket o' water waiting if yer try it again, so there will!'

As she closed the door, her gaze fell to the step. For a moment she couldn't make out what was lying there; must be something left by the kids who'd knocked on the door, she thought.

Stooping to examine what she suspected was a bundle of dirty rags, or something filthier from the gutter, she froze with horror. 'Oh, Jaysus Mary and Joseph!' It was a boy, bloodstained and looking like death itself. Shaking her head in disbelief, she knelt beside him.

A light went on in the house opposite and Maggie hurried across the street. 'What's all the yelling and shouting? Folks are trying to get some sleep.' When Patsy looked up, her face stricken, Maggie fell silent, her gaze going from Patsy to the bundle she had lifted ever so gently into her arms. 'God Almighty, it's our Tommy!'

When they got him inside and saw the extent of his injuries, both women were moved to tears. 'There's nothing we can do for him. The lad needs hospital treatment and quick!' Maggie rushed to the phone. 'Mind him gently now while I call an ambulance.'

'No!' Patsy stopped her. 'We can't wait for an ambulance. We'll take him by taxi. It'll be quicker. We'll get one easily down the road.'

Maggie nodded. 'You're right. It's the weekend, and the ambulances might be out on all manner of calls. Besides, the infirmary is only three miles away.'

While Maggie went to fetch a taxi, Patsy sat holding Tommy. Wiping the blood from his face she whispered, 'Who did this to ye? Who was it, Tommy?' But he was silent, and she could not stop her tears. She loved the boy. All this time she had rejected him because of something not his fault, and now she would give anything for him to be all right. The truth rose up in her like an angry, beautiful thing. She could let the feelings loose now, and not be afraid. Only Tommy mattered now. *Not the other one.* Only Tommy.

Bending her face to his, she asked him in the softest whisper, 'Will ye ever forgive me?'

W HEN EVA RETURNED, weary and concerned,
she found the note left by Patsy:

> Eva, me darlin',
>     I'm taking Tommy to the infirmary. The
> boy's suffered a terrible beating. Maggie's
> going with me.
>     Come quick.
>         Patsy

Shocked to the core, Eva ran out into the street. She
didn't stop to call a taxi or ask for help. Instead she
ran all the way to the infirmary, a prayer on her lips
the whole journey.

⇒◦◦◦◦←

F OR THE NEXT few days, Tommy hovered between life and death. Distraught, neither Eva
nor Patsy left his side and, from the moment Frank
was informed, he was a great source of comfort to
both women, especially Eva. 'I won't leave you,' he
promised.

As good as his word, he stayed with them, a rock
of strength; suffering their distress, tending to their
needs, while they tended to Tommy's, and sharing
their delight when the doctor announced, 'Tommy's
out of danger.'

After that, but only when they knew he really was

recovering well, Patsy and Eva took turns to go home of a night.

When it was Eva's turn, Frank would stay a while and make sure she was comfortable, before reluctantly leaving. What he really wanted was to stay and hold her through the night, but Eva never encouraged that, and he wisely did not outstay his welcome, always believing there would be a time when it was right.

And, just as he had hoped, the time came soon enough.

The lack of sleep was showing on them both. Eva was at her lowest ebb, and he sensed she would not refuse if he suggested that he stay. 'Don't send me back to an empty hotel room,' he pleaded. 'It's a soulless place, Eva. I'd rather stay here and keep an eye on you. You look so tired and washed out.'

Eva looked at him, studying the pale features and the unshaven face, and she felt ashamed. 'You've been such a good friend,' she said with a quiet smile, 'and I do know how bleak a hotel room can seem when you've no one to talk to.' In fact, she felt lonely without Patsy and Tommy. Suddenly the house was cold and unfriendly, and her heart was not in it.

'Are you saying I can stay?'

When Eva nodded approval, he couldn't believe his luck.

Worming his way into her affections, he made

a cheery fire, ushering her to sit in the big arm-chair beside it, while he busied himself making a pot of tea.

Afterwards, they talked well into the small hours, until Eva fell asleep in the chair. Seeing his chance, he carried her up to her bed.

As he was laying her down, she woke and looked up at him. 'I love you,' he said and, tenderly caressing her, he lay down beside her. When she made no effort to move away or protest, he kissed her softly. 'Do you have any feelings for me, darling Eva?' he whispered and, weary and lonely as she was, Eva could not think of an answer true to her heart. But, he was here, warm and comforting, and she had always liked him.

Encouraged by her silence, he kissed her again; this time touching her breasts and daring to go further.

Eva had forgotten how wonderful it was to have a man love you. And here was a good man, who had seen her through a bad time, without asking for anything in return. She could send him away. But she had come to accept and enjoy his company. Besides, right now, she didn't want to be alone.

He grew bolder. Peeling off her clothes, he touched every part of her body. Cupping her small firm breasts, he lapped his tongue round the nipples, sending shivers of delight all over her.

When he felt she was ready, he entered her.

Eva clung to him, wanting his love . . . *not* wanting his love. But he was the only one; for the moment.

And the moment was wonderful.

# *Chapter Eleven*

THE NURSE PEEPED out through the office window. 'Just look at those two.' Drawing her colleague's attention to Patsy and Tommy, she smiled with pleasure. 'It's a joy to see them.'

The plump nurse followed her gaze. 'You're right.' Patsy was helping Tommy with his model aircraft. Every now and then they would erupt in fits of laughter. 'To look at them, anybody would think they were mother and son.'

'I'll be honest with you, I didn't think the lad would pull through when they brought him in.' She recalled the night. 'Like death he was – four broken ribs, a fractured arm, and multiple internal injuries. Whoever did that to him must have been out of his mind.' She sighed. 'The police will never catch him now. He's long gone.'

'I'd like to get my hands on the swine!'

'So would the other woman, Eva Bereton. Beside herself, she was. I tell you, Lilian, I wouldn't want to be in his shoes if she ever catches up with him.' Turning away, she dipped a thermometer into a beaker of blue liquid.

'Still, all that really matters now is that the boy has recovered. He might be small for his age, but he's a tough little monkey.' The nurse's face beamed with pleasure. 'Nearly three months it's been, and now, at long last, he's going home.'

A few moments later, Eva appeared. Maggie Bell was with her. 'I'll go and sign him out,' she told Eva. As his aunt, she was the only one who could legally arrange his discharge from the infirmary.

'There you go.' Eva dropped a bag containing Tommy's new clothes on the bed. 'Me and Maggie have been shopping. There's even a pile of comics for you to read on the way home.' Bending to kiss him, she studied his face; pinker now, with bright, alert eyes. Thankfully, the memory of what had happened to him seemed to be fading. Eva thought it amazing how resilient children could be. 'Are you ready to come home now?'

Patsy gave Eva a wink. 'Whatever makes ye think he wants to leave here? Sure, the lad won't want to come back to a poky little house when he can be waited on hand and foot in this lovely place.'

'I *do* want to come home!' Tommy cried. 'I've had enough of being in here.' Then, when he saw the two of them smiling, he laughed out loud. Grabbing the bag, he unpacked it. There was everything he needed. 'Can I get dressed now?' he asked eagerly. 'Can we go?'

At that moment, Maggie returned. 'Everything's done,' she told them and, smiling at Tommy, said, 'Soon as ever you're ready, we can take you home.'

Tommy was ready in record time. 'Why did Maggie go to the office instead of you?' he asked Eva as she wheeled him to the lift. 'It's you and Patsy who look after me, not her.'

Eva had wondered how she would explain Maggie's involvement and had an answer ready. 'I asked Maggie if she would fetch your medicines, that's all.'

Later that evening, Eva popped over to Maggie's house. 'Why don't you tell Tommy you're his aunt?' she urged. 'It'll be a comfort to you both.'

'No.' Maggie was adamant. 'I'll always look out for Tommy, but it's best to leave things as they are. He wouldn't understand. I could have helped when his mother needed me, and I didn't, God forgive me.'

'Because she wouldn't let you, that's why.'

'I know that, and so do you, but it might look different to Tommy. She told him things about me – nasty, untrue things. Even when I helped to keep him from being taken into care, he was always wary of me. I could sense it, but I expect he thought I was the lesser of two evils. Besides, I'd be no good to him. Not now.'

'You do yourself an injustice, Maggie.'

'It's a sad thing when a family falls apart like ours did, but it happened and there's no going back now.' A slow smile crept over her kindly features. 'You and Patsy have taken the boy to your hearts, and you'll never know how grateful I am.'

'He's easy to love,' Eva answered softly. 'You need never worry about him. Patsy and I will always take care of him.'

'Isn't it wonderful how Patsy has taken to Tommy?' Maggie remarked. 'There was a time when I thought she actively disliked the boy.'

'Yes, it is wonderful.' Eva, too, had delighted in the growing affection between Patsy and the boy. 'They spend so much time together these days, Patsy and I haven't even got round to thinking about looking for a little business.'

Patsy never mentioned finding a place of their own any more, and Eva was glad of it. But they would soon have to think about earning a living, or they'd have no savings left.

When she got back to the house, she broached the subject with Patsy.

She had been having similar thoughts. 'You're right, we've got to do something. Then there's this house, and Tommy.' She took a deep breath. 'If

Mary's father left it to her, and now she's gone, who does it belong to?'

'Maggie thinks it might belong to Tommy, by rights. But unless Mary left a will saying so, and I don't think she did, it belongs to Tommy's father.'

'But the bugger's done a bunk!'

'Makes no difference. He is still her legal husband, so I think the house is his.'

'It's a crying shame, so it is.'

'What are you getting at?'

'Just thinking.'

'Come on, out with it.'

'I thought, if the house belongs to Tommy, and we've been putting aside all our rent for whoever might claim it, why not make the money over to him? And, while we're at it, why not buy the house from him and put the money into a trust or something so he'll have a tidy sum to look forward to when he comes of age?' These days, Patsy always put Tommy's interests first.

'It's a good idea, but if I'm right in thinking the house is legally Fred Johnson's, there's no question of us buying it. The rent money we've been putting aside for whoever might come and claim it is earning good interest, so we can always put that away for Tommy. So we're back where we started, with no house of our own and no business. If we bought a place, it would mean moving away from here, with Tommy, and I know Maggie wouldn't want that.'

'If she won't be honest with the boy, why should we give a sod about what she wants?'

'She's been good to him, Patsy. Don't forget he might have been put away if it hadn't been for her. And when he was hurt, she was never far away.'

Patsy relented, feeling a little ashamed. 'So, what do we do?'

'Tommy has to go to school after Easter,' Eva reminded her. 'We're very lucky the authorities were so sympathetic to his case. Why don't we leave it be until then? It's only a matter of a few weeks.'

'Fine by me.' She then voiced another worry that had been chewing away at her. 'Is it getting serious between you and Frank?'

Taken aback, Eva replied cagily, 'Why do you ask?'

'Because you've been seeing a lot of each other.'

'I'm not denying that. He's been a godsend while Tommy's been in hospital. He was there almost every other day.'

'All the same, I'm beginning to wonder if it was more to see you than Tommy.'

'That's unfair, Patsy. Frank is a good man, and he really likes the boy.'

'I'm not saying he isn't a good man. I'm just saying Frank loves you. He always has.'

'I know.'

'Do you love him?'

'I'm not sure.' She blushed deep pink. There were things Patsy didn't know.

'Can I say something you might not like?'

'I expect you will anyway.'

'It's about Frank.'

'What about him?'

'He's insanely jealous about you. That could be a dangerous thing.'

'He's no need to be jealous about me.' Unless he can read my mind, she thought wryly. Because if he could read her mind, he would see another man there – Bill Westerfield, the man she loved with all her being.

'All I'm saying is, be very careful, me darlin'. He set his cap at you once before, and I've a feeling he won't let you escape him twice.'

'I thought you just agreed he was a good man.'

'And so he is. Rich, too. Sure, Frank is a good catch for any woman.'

'But not for me, is that what you're saying?'

Patsy quietly regarded her; in her thirtieth year, Eva was a stunning beauty. Her long hair was still corn-coloured, her eyes the loveliest sea-green, her skin soft and clear, and her smile shone through the dullest of days, and yet there was always the faintest regret in those eyes. Patsy had always known the reason for that regret. Wisely, she had kept quiet over the years. Now, though, she felt compelled to speak. 'Do you ever think about Bill?'

For a moment it seemed as though Eva might not answer, she was so still and silent. Presently, she looked up. 'Yes, I still think about him,' she confessed. 'I always will.'

'Even though you know you can't have him?'

'Even then.' Her lovely eyes glistened with tears. 'I know Frank isn't Bill, and I know I can never love him the way he deserves, but I'm lonely, Patsy. So lonely.' Not Patsy, or even Tommy, could fill the void in her heart.

'Tell me something, Eva. Does Frank make you happy?'

'Sort of.'

Patsy's smile told Eva she understood. 'Sometimes that's all we can expect.'

'Maybe.'

Patsy stood up and went to where Eva sat. She put a friendly arm round her. 'You deserve a bit of happiness, me darlin',' she said, 'and if Frank can lift your heart, then who am I to spoil it? But don't make mistakes you might regret later on.'

Eva smiled up at her. 'You're like an old mother hen.'

'Not so much of the "old", if ye don't mind!'

They chatted a little longer, about nothing in particular, each keeping her own secrets.

'Ye look tired, so ye do.' Patsy yawned. 'An' yer not the only one.' She struggled out of her chair. 'I'm off to me bed. Goodnight, Eva. Sleep well.'

'A minute, Patsy.'

'What is it, me darlin'?'

'You don't know how glad I am that you and Tommy are such good friends now.'

'I'm glad too, so I am,' Patsy confessed. 'It took a terrible thing for me to realise how much I love him.'

'I never understood why you set yourself against him.'

Patsy shook her head. 'Goodnight, Eva.' Some things were best left unsaid.

<hr>

T HE NEXT FEW weeks saw many changes. Tommy went from strength to strength and actually began looking forward to the day he would, belatedly, start school again.

Eva saw more and more of Frank, and Patsy worried about that, especially when Frank twice questioned her about Eva's past men friends. Of course Eva had gone out with other men, and some of them were serious, but as far as Patsy knew, Eva had never felt the same way about any of them.

How could she, Patsy thought, when she had only ever loved one man in the whole of her life? Bill Westerfield was etched in Eva's heart for all time, and no one, however attentive and loving, would ever take his place. Patsy knew that, even if she knew nothing else. But her lips were sealed where Frank was concerned. She had a feeling he would not be able to handle the truth.

Acacia Lodge began to take shape. Frank's plans for it had changed. He had not told Eva, but he meant it to be their home, after they were married.

One Saturday afternoon in March, Maggie kept an eye on Tommy while Patsy and Eva went to the market. Passing the winkle stand, Patsy made an astonishing revelation. 'I'm going to London,' she told Eva, 'and I'm not coming back until I've found Tommy's dad.'

'But *why*?' Eva knew something had been brewing.

'Because Tommy needs his dad, and because . . .' She paused, pretending to inspect the winkles.

Eva waited.

'It doesn't matter.' Patsy clammed up. 'All that matters is that Tommy needs his dad, and I mean to fetch the bugger back where he belongs.'

'You wouldn't even know where to look.'

'I can try.'

'Does Tommy know what you're thinking of doing?'

'No, and you mustn't tell him, d'ye hear? He thinks I'm going to Cardiff.'

'What?'

'I've made up a story about an old friend needing to see me.'

'Did he believe you?'

'Of course. And why shouldn't he?'

'I think it's a crazy idea.'

'Whatever ye say, I'm off first thing in the morning.'

Sure enough, Patsy was ready to leave at 8 a.m. sharp the following morning. 'The train leaves in half an hour,' she told Tommy. 'You look after yourself and I'll be back before you know it.'

'I don't want you to go.' Tommy had come to adore her, and now to lose her, even for a short time, was painful.

Eva gave him a hug. 'You've still got me,' she reminded him. 'And Patsy's right. She'll be back before we know it.'

The parting was brief and soon the taxi was drawing up at the door.

'Mind ye take care of each other now,' Patsy said as she climbed into the taxi.

'Don't forget to telephone when you get there.'

'I will.'

'And don't stay away too long.'

Patsy didn't hear. The taxi was already out of sight.

Eva dedicated the day to Tommy. In the morning, he helped her with the housework, then the two of them worked on the jigsaw puzzle Maggie had bought him. 'I'm glad you didn't go with Patsy,' he told her gratefully. 'I wouldn't like you both to be away at the same time.'

'And we won't be,' she replied. Not if she could help it, she thought, and Patsy was so attached to the boy now that she would never contemplate leaving him. Even her trip today was on Tommy's behalf. 'What shall we do this afternoon?' she asked him.

'I'd like to go to the fish market.'

She grimaced. 'Not my favourite place, the fish market.'

'We won't go if you don't want to.'

'I'll be brave for your sake.' Oh, how she hated that fish market, all those dead things lying there, staring up with flat, unseeing eyes.

An hour later, wrapped up against a keen wind and threatening rain, she and Tommy walked down Albert Street and on to Penny Street; the boulevard was just a few steps away. 'Tell me if you begin to get tired.' Though he was very much stronger now, he still had a tendency to get weary very quickly.

The bus ride was fun. There were two ladies in front who argued the whole way, and a boy with a yo-yo, which had Tommy mesmerised. The conductor sang at the top of his voice, making the worst sound Eva had ever heard, though it did cause laughter among the passengers when an old man in a flat cap complained, 'My cat makes a better noise than that when she's after her supper.'

As always, the market was packed. The stench of fish reached them before they even rounded the corner. 'While I'm here, I might as well get a nice piece of fish for our tea,' Eva decided.

'And chips?' Tommy's mouth watered. 'Make some of your nice fat chips.' It didn't take much to please him.

They had a wonderful afternoon. Instead of buying fish, Eva decided Tommy had earned a treat, so she took him to a nearby fish and chip shop where they cooked and served at table to order. 'Cod and chips twice,' she ordered. 'And mushy peas swimming in their own gravy.'

Tommy wolfed his food down, and Eva was delighted to see how his appetite had recovered. They talked about school, and how much he was looking forward to it, and afterwards they strolled along the canal to see the barges.

The day was beginning to close in when Eva decided it was time they made a move towards home. 'I ain't tired.' Tommy wanted to roam round the shops.

But Eva could see the red rims round his eyes. 'Well, *I'm* tired,' she lied, 'so take me home.' And he did.

'I ain't going to bed until Patsy rings.' Tommy was adamant. He bathed and got ready for bed but, tired though he was, there was no budging him. 'She promised to ring, and she will.'

'All right,' Eva conceded, 'but only until half past eight. If she hasn't rung by then, it's bed for you, young man, and no argument.'

The clock struck the half hour. Then it chimed eight times, and still no phone call. Tommy sat by the fire, his nose stuck in a comic, ears tuned to the phone.

Eva watched an animal rescue programme on television. After a while she switched it off and made them both a drink. 'If she rings after you've gone to bed, I'll tell you everything she says in the morning.' Her eyes went to the clock. It was almost eight thirty.

Reluctantly, when the clock struck the half hour again, Tommy dragged himself upstairs. He was on the landing when the phone rang. 'It's her!' he yelled, and much to Eva's dismay he ran down the steps two at a time. Breathless and excited, he got to the phone before she did. 'Patsy!' he shouted down the receiver. 'Patsy, it's me, Tommy!'

He talked to her for ages while Eva waited patiently, until she thought he looked tired and drawn. 'That's enough for now, Tommy.' She took the receiver from him. 'Off to bed now. I'll be up later to say goodnight.'

This time, Tommy didn't argue. 'Goodnight,

Eva,' he said, kissing her fleetingly. 'I've 'ad a lovely day.'

Patsy had no news. 'I've been up and down all over London,' she groaned. 'I've asked everyone who I thought might know something, and I've searched every bar in the East End, but so far nothing. It's like Fred Johnson has disappeared from the face of the earth, so it is.'

Eva asked if she ought not to make her way home. 'You've done your best,' she said, 'and Tommy is missing you. We both are.'

'Ha! And so ye should.' There was the sound of a coin being dropped into the box, and then, 'Look, me darlin', that was me last coin. I'll stay another day or so, and keep looking for him. I've found cheap lodgings and they're clean enough, so don't you worry about—' The line went silent. Patsy's money had run out.

Replacing the phone, Eva climbed the stairs and peeped into Tommy's room. He was fast asleep. Drawing the covers over him, Eva bent to kiss his forehead. Satisfied that he would sleep through the night, she went back downstairs.

No sooner had she washed her and Tommy's cups than there was a knock on the door. Fearing Tommy might be woken, she went quickly down the passage.

Eva was not surprised to see Frank on the doorstep. 'Come in,' she invited him, opening the door wider. 'But be quiet. Tommy's only just got off to sleep.'

As she closed the door, he took her in his arms. 'Two days away and I've missed you like the devil.' He kissed her on the mouth. 'It's good to be back.'

Eva led the way back to the sitting room. 'Did the Manchester opening go well?'

'Fantastic. The hotel is up and running, and already the bookings are flooding in.'

'That's wonderful.'

'It would have been more wonderful if you'd been there.'

'It's just as well I wasn't.' He had asked her, and under other circumstances she might have accepted, but she'd had a little job to do, which was best done on her own. 'Patsy's gone away.'

'Gone away? Where?' He hung his coat on the back of the sitting-room door.

Before answering, she went to the door and softly closed it. 'She's gone to find Tommy's dad.'

'Does she know where he is?'

Eva laughed. 'You know Patsy. She's scouring the East End of London for him.'

Clearing Tommy's comics off the chair, she glanced towards the door. 'Even if she found him, I'm not sure it would be a good thing. Tommy's been through so much, I dread to think what might happen if his dad walked in. Tommy believes he ran off. He doesn't know his mam threw him out.'

'Maybe someone should tell him.'

'What, and soil his mother's memory?'

'Difficult, eh?'

'You could say that.' Eva had something even more difficult to tell Frank, but first she needed a dash of courage. 'I've got some brandy, left over from the Christmas we never had,' she said. 'Would you like a drop to warm you up?'

'Why not?' Seated in the chair, he looked very much at home. The firelight played on his face and gave it a little boy look, and his brown eyes were filled with such pleasure at seeing her again, she felt moved.

While she bottomed the two glasses, his with brandy and hers with advocaat, he came to her and slid the most beautiful bracelet round her wrist. 'Do you like it?'

Startled, Eva looked down. The bracelet was exquisite, with a hem of tiny diamonds and a ruby clasp; she had never seen anything like it. 'It's beautiful.'

'Like you, my lovely.' Swinging her round, he told her softly, 'I wanted something really special to bring back to you.' Putting his finger beneath her chin he raised her face to his. With the greatest tenderness, he kissed her full on the mouth, and then he held her as if he would never let her go.

JOSEPHINE COX

'I don't want to be parted from you ever again,' he whispered. 'From now on, everywhere I go, I want you with me.'

'You're so good to me, Frank,' she told him gratefully. 'The way you've pampered Tommy, and kept an eye on all of us through this bad time, I don't know how to thank you.'

'Love me.'

'I do.'

'Not enough.'

'So you say.'

'Let's make love, here and now.'

'Sit down, Frank.' Drawing away she took the glasses and placed them on the coffee table between them. 'I've got something important to tell you.'

As always, he did as she asked. 'What's wrong, sweetheart?' Concerned by the serious expression on her face, he leaned forward to hold her hand. 'Is it Tommy? Is there a problem?'

'No. Tommy's fine.'

'So, what's wrong?'

She didn't really know how to begin. 'A few weeks back, when I was worried sick about Tommy and . . . everything, you and I made love.'

'I haven't forgotten. How could I?' It was the most wonderful thing that had ever happened to him, making him all the more determined to marry her. 'Are you telling me you regret it, Eva? Is that what you're trying to say?' Suddenly, he looked haggard.

Anxious, she looked him straight in the eye. 'Yesterday I went to the doctor. I'm having your child, Frank.'

For what seemed an age he sat there, stunned, his eyes staring and his hands trembling. Then he gave a shivering groan. 'Oh, Eva! Eva, that's marvellous!' Leaping out of the chair, he grabbed her to him, half laughing, half crying. 'I don't know what to say. I can't think straight.'

Eva was ashamed. She had feared he might put all the blame on her and walk away from the responsibility. She didn't trust him enough. 'I thought you'd be angry,' she said.

His eyes were filled with tears. 'Angry?' He gently shook her. 'Oh, Eva, it's what I've always wanted, you and me, and a family of our own. All these years I've gone from one relationship to another – women who had a look of you, women who I tried so hard to settle down with. But I never married, Eva, because none of them ever measured up to you.'

Eva was shocked. 'I didn't know.'

'Just now you said you loved me. Maybe not as much as I love you, that would be asking too much. But I'll always look after you.'

A shadow of regret crossed his features. 'When I got that letter, the one you left with Mother—' even now, it was painful to remember – 'I felt as though my whole world had turned upside down.'

'What letter?' Eva was puzzled.

Astonished, he stared in disbelief. 'Surely you remember?'

Eva shook her head. 'No, Frank. All I remember is that your mother wanted rid of me.'

The truth struck them simultaneously, but it was Frank who voiced it. 'My God! *She* must have written it! She gave me a letter, supposedly from you . . . you were going away, to someone else, that's what the letter said.' Groaning, he covered his face with his hands. 'I was a fool. I should have known it was her.'

'It's all in the past,' Eva told him. 'Besides, it was time for me to leave, I can't deny it. You were getting serious, and I wasn't ready for that.'

He hugged her so tightly she could hardly breathe. 'Oh, Eva, you can't know how long I've loved you.' Holding her at arm's length, he smiled into her troubled eyes. 'Say you'll marry me.'

A moment of doubt; a moment when Patsy's words ran through her brain – 'Jealousy can be a dangerous thing.' And Frank did have a jealous nature. Look how he questioned her about her every move each time he returned from a business trip.

'Eva, don't be afraid of the future. We were meant to meet again because we are made for each other. I knew it from the very first.' He kissed her softly. 'No man could love you more than I do. Marry me, Eva. Say yes.'

The doubt was growing. The child too, but gentler, warm and amazing – *Frank's* child. In her heart she knew he meant every word he said. Frank was a good man, even Patsy had admitted that. He loved her, that was no lie, and just now he had promised he would take care of her and the child.

His voice penetrated her thoughts. 'Eva, say yes. You'll never regret it.'

Torn two ways, Eva hesitated, trying to reason, trying to persuade herself that it was the best, the only way. She was coming up to thirty and life seemed to be passing her by.

Suddenly like a ghost from the past, Bill rose in her thoughts, in her heart. Bill. Always Bill. But he was gone, and she was here, carrying Frank's child. Frank, a man who had loved her from the start.

'Eva? Please.'

Anger welled up in her like a vicious tide. Anger with Bill; with life. Most of all, with herself.

In that moment, she looked into Frank's brown eyes and nodded. 'Yes, Frank. The answer is yes.'

'SOD AND BUGGER it, if he's not here, I'm going home on the next train.' Patsy had trodden the streets of London relentlessly until her feet felt like two suet puddings.

First one person sent her this way, then someone else sent her another. She'd been lost a thousand times, and now she was standing outside the King's Arms with her heart in her mouth.

'Bleedin' cold, ain't it, gal?' A toothless old woman poked her face at Patsy. 'Who're you lookin' for, dearie?'

'I'm looking for a man.'

The old woman laughed out loud. 'We're *all* lookin' for a man,' she cackled. 'Trouble is, there ain't none to be 'ad.' With that she waddled inside the pub, still chuckling as she closed the door.

Patsy had to laugh. 'Silly old cow, so she is.'

The door of the pub opened again and out came a big fat man wearing a greasy overall. He glanced at Patsy, walked away, then, curious, turned round to have another look. 'Are you lost, gal?'

This time Patsy was careful how she phrased her answer. 'I'm looking for Fred Johnson,' she said. 'His ex-landlady said I might find him here.'

'She'd be right an' all. The crafty bastard's just had me for five quid at cards.' Pointing to the doorway, he said, 'You'll find him at the bar, celebrating his ill-gotten gains.'

Delighted, Patsy thanked him.

Now that she had found him, what should she say? How could she explain her presence here? How would he feel about Tommy? How would he take it when he knew his wife was lying in the churchyard? And, more importantly, would he come back with her to Blackburn?

'Don't lose yer courage now, Patsy me girl,' she told herself.

Squaring her shoulders, she marched into the pub. 'I'm looking for a man by the name of Fred Johnson.' Her voice sailed above the chatter. Amid the ensuing silence, all eyes turned to stare at her.

One pair of eyes in particular searched her out. With his pint halfway to his mouth, the big rugged feller froze. 'Christ Almighty, it can't be. *Patsy Noonan!*'

Patsy smiled. 'Did ye think you'd seen a ghost, Fred, me old darlin'?' She laughed. 'Ah! Yer sins have caught up with ye, so they have.' Stretching out her arms, she told him tenderly, 'No more running now. Sure, we've done enough of that already.' The tears filled her eyes. 'I'm here to take ye home, so I am,' she murmured.

And he went to her like a child.

⇒•⇐

THERE WERE TWO reunions that day.

Away from prying eyes, Patsy and Fred Johnson sat in the corner. Like two star-struck lovers, they held hands and looked into each other's eyes. 'I can't believe you're here,' Fred told her, his eyes moist with emotion. 'All these years, you bugger, and you just turn up out of the blue like that.'

'All that time wasted, ye mean. But Fred, I just wasn't ready then. I was too young.'

'How did you find me?'

'With great difficulty!'

'Why are you here, gal? What made you search me out?'

Patsy told him everything; how she and Eva had come from Wales to make a new start; how fate had directed them towards the woman he married, and who was now lying in the churchyard. 'It's been a difficult time,' she admitted, 'and I've got more reason than most people to be ashamed.'

Shocked by the news that Mary had died and Tommy had been left alone, he remarked, 'It's not you who should be ashamed, Patsy, gal. It's me.' His expression became puzzled. 'Hang on a minute, how did you find out that the Johnsons were my family? It's a common enough name.'

'By accident,' she answered. 'It was a shock, so it was.'

'Tommy told you, is that it? He let out that his

old dad was in London, you heard what name I went by, and you put two and two together. You always were good at figures.'

'No, it wasn't Tommy who told me,' she confessed. 'No sooner had we arrived than he threw a fit and ran off. Eva went to look for him, and while that was going on, I went inside.' She turned scarlet. 'I've always been a nosy bugger, so I have,' she admitted. 'Well, I was prying around, and I found an envelope. Inside was a photograph of you and her – Mary, your wife.'

'I see.' He stroked her hand. 'That's nothing for you to be ashamed about, gal. It's only natural that you wanted to find out about the boy and his mam. If your friend hadn't found him, you might have had to look for information anyway. So, don't be ashamed.'

Patsy shook her head. 'Sure, ye don't understand.' Taking a deep breath, she revealed, 'I turned me back on the boy. For a long time I wouldn't talk to him. I pretended he didn't exist.'

'Why in God's name would you do that?'

'Jealousy. Like I told Eva, that's a terrible thing to be eating away at you. But it ate away at me. I saw the photograph, with you and her, smiling and holding on to each other, and I thought, "That should have been me!" The boy was your son – he was *her* son. Can't ye see, Fred? It should have been *me* standing beside you. Not her.'

'All the same, I can't believe you punished the boy for it.' He seemed to draw away, a look of disgust on his face.

Patsy's shame turned to anger. 'And what about you, eh? Where were you when the boy needed you? When he got beaten half to death by some monster of a man – where were you, tell me that!'

'What?' Curling his fists, he pushed out of his chair. 'Tommy was beat up, you say? Who did it, gal? What bastard beat him half to death? I swear to God I'll break his bloody neck.'

'Sit down, Fred. I can tell you nothing because I know nothing. Tommy claims it were gypsies, but we don't know.' Leaning towards him, she persisted, 'Why did you go, Fred? Why did you leave the boy?'

He sat down; his head bowed. 'She threw me out and pride kept me away. Not a day has gone by since when I haven't thought, "*This* is the day I'm going back for the sake of the boy."' He paused, a look of regret flooding his rugged features. 'I'm sorry she's lying in the churchyard. I wouldn't have wished that on her for the world. But it never worked out. We were wrong for each other from the start. You're right, Patsy. It *should* have been you in that picture. You should have been the one who brought Tommy into the world. But you weren't, you didn't. And all because you couldn't face up to life.'

'You wanted too much from me, and I couldn't give it.' Hopeful, she squeezed his hand. 'Not *then*, I couldn't. But it's a different story now. I love Tommy like he was my own son, and he loves me too. We could be a family, Fred – if you want it.'

'More than anything, gal.' He sighed from deep down in his boots. 'I found it hard, moving away from London. But if I've got you and the boy, wherever you are will be home.'

Rising from her chair, she took him by the hand. 'Let's go home then, before you have me crying in me beer.'

———⟫◆⟪———

TOMMY WAS INCONSOLABLE. 'Get him out! I don't want him here!' When Eva tried to restrain him, he kicked out. 'He ran off and left us. If he'd been here, me mam wouldn't have thrashed me all the time. She were frightened, that's why!' Looking up at his father, he cried, 'You didn't want me any more, did you, Dad? *Why* didn't you want me?' He could hardly talk for the sobs that racked his frame. And looking on, feeling his pain, Eva could not hold back her own tears.

'Ssh!' Pressing him to her, she whispered, 'Listen to him, Tommy. Listen to your daddy.'

'No!' Burying his face in Eva's shoulder, he said brokenly, 'I don't want him here, and I don't want Patsy, because she lied. She said she was going to Wales, and all the time she was looking for him.'

Fred stepped forward, his voice shaking as he confessed, 'You're right, son, I should never have left you. I didn't know your mammy was ill, or I swear to God I would never have gone away. We had a terrible row and she asked me to go. I thought after a time I'd come back and everything would be all right. But then I got to wondering if it wouldn't be better for the pair of you if I stayed away altogether.' Daring to reach out, he was surprised and encouraged when Tommy didn't recoil. 'I love you, son. That's God's truth. I did wrong in not coming back, and I'm sorry. But I'm back now, and I'll never go away again if you don't want me to.' Growing bolder, he slid his hand over Tommy's shoulder. 'Will you forgive me, son? You and me, and Patsy, let's all make a brand new start. Yer mustn't blame her, son. It ain't Patsy's fault.'

Tommy was listening but he made no response.

'Tommy? Please, all I'm asking is the chance to make it up to you.'

Suddenly Tommy was in his arms, the sobs taking his breath away.

'It's all right, son.' Fred held him close. 'It's gonna be all right now.'

All this time, Patsy had waited in the background, anxious but wise enough to make no move.

In that moment, Eva caught her eye and gestured that she should go to Tommy. Fred held out his arm, and she went to him.

With big wet eyes, Tommy stared up at her. 'I'm sorry,' he said, and she slid her arm round him.

Eva stood back, her soft gaze enveloping them – Patsy enclosed in one arm, Tommy in the other and, head bowed, Fred between. It was a sight to gladden her heart.

# Chapter Twelve

O N 31 MARCH 1966, Eva and Frank were married.

On the actual morning, Eva had misgivings but pushed them aside. 'You're nervous, that's all,' she told herself. 'Frank really loves you. He's transformed the house on Park Street just for you. You'll have a secure life, and a family to call your own. A child . . .' The softest of smiles lit her face. 'Oh, think of it, Eva, a new baby.' That was what had finally decided her.

She rubbed the flat of her hand over her tummy; the small rise was not noticeable beneath the cream satin dress. Late at night when she lay in bed, Eva imagined she could feel the child moving inside her. Knowing a new life was forming there was the most wonderful and satisfying thing.

Getting up from the stool where she had sat these past twenty minutes, going through every kind of emotion imaginable, she stood sideways on, observing herself in the mirror. 'No one would ever know,' she murmured, twirling round to see

331

herself from all angles. Still, what would it matter if people did know she was carrying a child? All that mattered was that her child should have a father, and that she should settle down with Frank and not crave a man she lost long ago.

Suddenly the door burst open and Patsy rushed in. 'Aren't you ready yet?' she demanded. 'The car will be here any minute and here you are, fancying yourself in the mirror.'

'I've been thinking.' Seating herself on the stool once more, Eva regarded Patsy in the mirror. 'I wonder if I'm doing the right thing.'

'Huh! It's too late for second thoughts now, me darlin'.' Down-to-earth as ever, Patsy nevertheless felt misgivings about this particular match herself, and before she discovered Eva was pregnant she had said as much to her. Now, though, she thought it wiser to keep her mouth shut. There was nothing to be gained from upsetting the apple cart at this late stage, she reasoned.

'Yes,' Eva agreed, 'it is too late.' She laughed. 'I must look a sketch. I didn't sleep much last night. Wedding nerves, I expect.'

Patsy took a long, hard look at her friend. 'You look stunning, so ye do,' she answered. With her corn-coloured hair rolled under, and only the suggestion of a fringe, Eva was the picture of loveliness; never one for too much make-up, she had touched her eyelashes with the softest brown, a smudge of eyeshadow above, and on her full generous lips the subtlest of pink lipstick.

'I was just thinking,' Eva said thoughtfully, 'whether to pin the coronet on top of my hair, or have it further back so it doesn't flatten my fringe.' Eva had chosen not to wear a veil, but instead had bought the prettiest rosebud coronet.

'Sure, it won't matter which way ye wear it, you'll be so lovely nobody will notice.'

Eva laughed at that. 'I'm not a young girl with starry eyes,' she reminded her. 'I'm thirty years of age and my belly's already beginning to swell.' Twirling once more before the mirror, she remarked, 'It's a lovely dress, isn't it, Patsy? I've never worn anything off the shoulder before, but I'm glad I took your advice. It was a good choice.'

'That's an understatement, so it is. The dress was made for you!' Patsy sighed, thinking how she could never have got away with a dress like that; she was too clumsy, too round and plump at the shoulders. 'Let me look at you.' Standing back, she took stock of Eva, and thought she would never see a more becoming sight.

Fashioned in cream figured satin, Eva's dress was discreetly off the shoulder, with a V neck and long, close-fitting sleeves. Narrowing to the waist, it then flared out into a swinging ankle-length skirt with ivory lace at the hem above pale blue satin shoes. It brought out all of Eva's best assets. Patsy smiled at her. 'You'll steal the show. They won't notice anybody else.'

'You underestimate yourself, they'll notice you,' Eva answered. Patsy looked very pretty; in the long lemon dress, and with her vivid red hair, she looked striking. 'Wait until Fred sees you. Tommy too. You'll knock 'em dead.'

'Never mind me.' Patsy picked up Eva's bouquet. 'If we don't go now, we'll be late for the church.'

'Brides are allowed to be late.' All the same, Eva quickly put the finishing touches to her make-up, took her bouquet, and followed Patsy down the stairs.

Eva was right. Fred and Tommy thought Patsy looked terrific. They were as nervous as kittens as they arrived at the church. 'Everybody's looking at us,' Tommy said.

'Ssh!' Taking charge of his son, Fred hurried to the front of the church where the two of them sat silently, eyes trained on the impeccable Frank who stood ready, shifting from foot to foot. Beside Frank stood one of his colleagues, a short, round man with a red face – probably the result of a few pints of best the night before.

Outside, Eva and Patsy waited for the organ music to start.

'It's like waiting for a hanging,' Eva declared, visibly trembling.

'Sure, that's no way to talk on your wedding day!' Patsy chided. 'All the same, I wish they'd hurry up. I'm bloody freezing, so I am!' Rubbing her arms vigorously, she peeped inside the church. 'Apart from half a dozen people, I don't know anybody.'

Suddenly the music started. Everyone turned as they came down the aisle. 'I feel like a film star,' Patsy whispered, smiling to one and all as she passed by.

Eva looked straight ahead, her heart lurching with every step. 'Am I doing right?' she murmured. Her gaze rose to the magnificent stained-glass windows above the altar, depicting the Crucifixion. 'I hope so. Dear God, I hope so.'

In that moment, Frank turned to smile on her, his love lighting his face, and reached his hand towards her.

Eva smiled back, and the bond was forged.

In an incredibly short time, it was all over.

Now, as she walked out of the church, arm in arm with her husband, Eva felt a sense of belonging which she had not felt in a very long time. It's going to be all right, she told herself as Frank, smiling, helped her into the limousine.

*She could not know how shockingly wrong she was.*

# Chapter Thirteen

E VA LOVED THE coming of summer. It reminded her of the happy days she and her mother had spent together on the farm. She said as much now to Patsy who, as always, had joined her on a trip to the Saturday market.

They always went by way of Corporation Park; here they could skirt the lawns and enjoy the early blossoms – rhododendrons and roses were already showing their colours. The lake was beautiful, with gliding swans and noisy geese, and excited children playing close by.

Corporation Park was a haven for Eva; when she felt lonely, and when life seemed to be getting her down, she would come into the park and stroll about, or sit and watch the world go by, and it never failed to gladden her heart. 'I do love this park,' she told Patsy now. 'Whenever I come here I'm always transported back to the farm and the orchard where we had such happy times.'

'I know what you mean.' Patsy had not forgotten those times either. 'We've come a long way since then, Eva. And sometimes it doesn't help to look back.'

'I still miss her, you know.' A child kicked a ball into her path; pausing, she kicked it back. 'Not so much my father. But I miss my mother every minute of every day. I always will.' Mingled with her joy in her pregnancy was a great sadness that her mother would never see her grandchild. 'She would have been so excited about the baby.'

'Ah, sure, it's only natural you feel the way you do.'

'If it's a girl, I'd like to call her Colette.' She hadn't yet mentioned it to Frank, but there was no reason why he shouldn't agree. 'You know, Patsy, I have a feeling that if it is a girl, she might look like my mother.'

'Sure, it's possible,' Patsy said. 'I mean, you look like your mother, so ye do. Like two peas in a pod, the pair of youse.'

In reflective silence, they strolled along the narrow pathway. Eva felt unusually nostalgic, but maybe, she thought, that's how all women get when they're pregnant.

The walk into Blackburn town centre usually took about half an hour but today, for some reason, they seemed to get there in no time at all.

The two of them headed straight for the linen stall. Eva needed towels, and Patsy complained that Fred had scorched another of her best tea towels. 'As fast as I replace them, he spoils the buggers.' There were green-striped ones and blue-striped. She couldn't make up her mind, so bought half a dozen of each. 'I'll swing for the bugger if he spoils these,' she declared.

The man on the stall told her she needn't worry, because she could always come back and buy another dozen.

'Cheeky sod!' she snapped, then accidentally dropped the lot into a dog puddle. 'Jaysus! If it's not one thing, it's another.'

'You're accident prone, that's your trouble, missus.' The stallholder had taken a fancy to her and offered to exchange them.

Patsy went away happy. 'He's got some hope.' Chuckling, she nudged Eva in the ribs. 'Even if Fred did spoil them, I wouldn't come here again. The man on the Thursday market sells 'em sixpence cheaper.'

The next stop was the cockle stall. 'Half a tub of winkles,' Patsy said, 'and the same for me friend.'

Eva took one scoop and was almost sick. 'There are things I can't stomach just now,' she apologised, tipping them into the nearest bin.

'Well, all I can say is, if it's a choice between having a tub of winkles or a baby, give me the winkles every time.'

They went away laughing, especially when the winkle man called out, 'If you ever change your mind, give us a shout, and I'll be happy to oblige.'

At the crockery stall, Eva bought a new teapot. Patsy paid for three eggcups. 'Tommy keeps accidentally throwing them in the dustbin with the shells,' she said. 'I've told the little sod to be more careful but will he listen? No, he will not! Honest to God, Eva, what will I do with the pair of them, eh?'

'You'll cope.' Eva knew how Patsy loved to complain.

'What will you call it if it's a boy?' Patsy asked.

'I haven't really thought too much about that but I suppose Frank might have a few ideas. He really wants a boy.'

'What do you want, Eva?'

'I don't mind, as long as it's a healthy baby.'

'I didn't mean the baby.'

'Oh? What did you mean then?'

'I'll tell you over a barm cake and a pot of tea. What do you say?'

'Lead on, that's what I say.' Eva was glad of a break. The shopping bags weighed heavy and her feet hurt. 'I'm that thirsty my tongue's stuck to the roof of my mouth.' The May sunshine was hot, and the market was packed with people searching for bargains. All in all, it was a tiring experience when you were nearly four months pregnant.

<hr />

STRUGGLING INTO KENYON'S tea shop, they chose a table in a quiet corner. Eva dropped her bags and fell gratefully into a chair.

Like a hawk, the waitress swooped.

'Two teas and two barm cakes, if ye please,' Patsy ordered. 'I feel ninety,' she said to Eva, and Eva nodded in agreement.

'D'you want your barm cakes toasted?'

When Eva answered yes, the tiny waitress scurried away scribbling into her notepad.

'Now then, what did you mean when you asked me what I wanted?' Eva asked.

Patsy looked at her. 'You know very well what I meant.'

'Oh, that.' Eva might have guessed. 'I wish I'd never told you about it now.'

'Well, you did, and now I'm worried about you, so I am.' Patsy paused while the waitress served them, but the minute she was gone, she persisted, 'Sure, it can't be any fun when he keeps on at ye all the time – where've ye been? Who've ye been with? What did you buy?'

'Not now, Patsy, please.' Eva didn't feel like going into all that. It was bad enough knowing that if

Frank found out she'd been 'wasting time' in town, he'd spend half an hour interrogating her.

'Sure, it's not fair. You're looking tired and worn, so ye are, an' no bloody wonder, being questioned every time you set foot outside the door. Does he not realise there are times when ye feel the need for an hour out in the fresh air? Or to stroll round the shops and enjoy a chinwag with yer old friend?'

'He's jealous, that's all. When I come to think about it, the signs were all there.'

'I hate to say it, Eva me darlin', but I did warn ye.'

'I haven't forgotten.'

'Sure, the way he's carrying on, you'd think ye weren't to be trusted.'

'I won't deny it gets me down sometimes,' Eva admitted. She knew Patsy wouldn't drop the subject, and in a way it was a relief to talk it through. 'The other day it seems I took too long paying the coalman – you know, old Tom with the yellow teeth and a laugh like a donkey. Anyway, when I came back to the sitting room, Frank accused me of flirting. He laughed and played it like a joke, but underneath he was serious.'

'Frank can't have much of an opinion of himself if he thinks ye fancy old Tom.'

'I know.' Eva recalled how astonished she'd been. 'Tom, of all people. Can you imagine?' She

laughed. 'It caused an awful row. Afterwards, he
was full of apologies, like always. It's beginning to
fall into a pattern – accusations, a flaming row,
apologies, and next day an expensive present.' She
sighed. 'Maybe it's my fault, Patsy. I've never really
loved him. Not in the way he expects me to. The
trouble is, if he keeps on like this, I'm afraid I'll
end up hating him.'

'Oh, Eva!' Concerned, Patsy leaned nearer.
'Has he ever got violent with ye? Tell me the
truth now.'

'Frank is not the violent type.' Then she added,
'He prefers mental torment.'

Grabbing her hand, Patsy said, 'Now you look
here, me darlin'. If it ever gets too much for ye,
the door at Albert Street is always open, ye know
that, don't ye?'

'Frank may be over-possessive, but deep down
he's a real softie. He'll be all right once the baby's
born. Oh, Patsy, I can't wait for the day when I
hold the baby in my arms.'

'Listen! Did ye hear what I said? I mean it,
Eva. If he goes too far, you're to come straight to
me, d'ye hear?'

'Thank you, Patsy, but it won't happen. Frank
would never hurt me, not in the way you mean.'
Laying her hand over Patsy's, she told her softly,
'I know you mean well, and I really am grateful,
but there's no need.'

'Do you wish you hadn't married him?'

Taken aback, Eva drew her hand away. 'Look, Patsy, it's silly to think like that. Oh, all right! If I hadn't been expecting his child, I might not have married him. But, like it or not, I'm his wife now.'

'It's not written in blood, though, is it?'

'It might as well be.' She and Patsy had different values. 'Look, Patsy. It's no good harping on about it. I've made my bed and I'll have to lie on it. It's no use thinking about what might have been. That only leads to heartache.'

'And won't it lead to heartache the way it is now?'

The question was one Eva had asked herself many times these past weeks, but she refused to look on the dark side. 'I hope not,' she answered.

Privately, she felt differently. In the early days she had made so many plans, and now they might never materialise. Nowadays she felt a deep sadness that wouldn't go away. Even the joy of this miracle growing inside her could not shake off the feeling that her marriage to Frank was starting to go horribly wrong.

They stayed awhile in the tearooms. They talked about Maggie, and how she had kept her distance since Fred had moved back into Albert Street. 'Sure, I can't blame the old cow for feeling cheated,' Patsy remarked. 'When all's said and done, the house should have been hers by rights. I'll give her her due, though, she's friendly enough when we see her in the street, and she always has a good word for Tommy. But since Fred came back she hasn't once stepped foot over the threshold.' Her mind skipped back to Tommy. 'Sure, *that* little bugger grows by the minute!'

'Given time, he'll make a strapping young man, I'm sure.' Eva had been surprised to see how Tommy was springing up in height, and filling out with it. 'How does he get on with Fred?'

'He's like a puppy dog with two tails, so he is. Every day after school he's down to the bus stop and waiting for Fred to come home from the brewery. The two of 'em come in arm in arm, talking about this and that, and I hardly ever get a word in.'

Eva didn't believe it for one minute. 'I can't see that somehow.'

'Ye cheeky bugger!'

'And how's Fred liking his job at the brewery?' A mischievous smile lifted her lovely face.

'He's not drinking the profits, if that's what you're askin'. Sure, he seems content enough to go out on a Saturday with his mates. Sometimes I go along, and we have a good time, so we do. That's when Tommy goes over to sit with Maggie. She really looks forward to it.'

'I still can't believe it – you and Fred.' When

she heard how Patsy had known him long before they came to Blackburn, Eva had been amazed. 'And you never said a word to me.' At first that had hurt her, but now she fully understood why Patsy hadn't wanted to talk about it. Sometimes there were things a woman could not bring herself to discuss, even with her best friend.

'I can't believe it myself,' Patsy replied with a grin. 'I was too young and stupid when I fell for Fred Johnson. He was big and strong, full o' the ol' blarney. He charmed me right off me feet, so he did. You know the rest, Eva. He got me pregnant; I was too young to cope and drove him away.' Her voice shook. 'I only saw the baby for a few minutes – a lovely little lad, it was. Had the look of his daddy, so he did. Me mammy made me give him away; she'd always been a hard-hearted old biddy. I pleaded with me father, but he sided with her. "It's all for the best", that's what he said. I never saw the child again.' Her expression hardened. 'God help me, Eva, but I'll never forgive them.'

'Are you sure about that, Patsy? Never is a long time.'

'Oh, I'm sure right enough, me darlin',' Patsy answered. 'All me bridges are burned. Sure, I suffered nightmares for too many years to forget or forgive. Not a day passed when I didn't wonder where the lad was, or if he was happy.' She paused. 'I'll tell ye something ye *didn't* know, shall I?'

'Not if you don't want to, Patsy.' It was obvious to Eva that the memory was very painful for her.

'I went to see him.'

'Who? The boy? Your son, you mean?'

Patsy smiled. 'I spent a whole year tracking him down. It wasn't easy, but I kept at it, asking questions, raiding me parents' private papers, following leads, and getting people to trust me. In the end, I discovered his address in Kensington. Very impressive it was too. Big posh house, fancy car and all that. I went back three times before I had the courage to knock on the door. I stood outside, looking up the drive and wondering if I might get a glimpse of him, but it never happened. I couldn't leave it at that. I *had* to see him.'

'But how?' Eva's heart went out to her.

Remembering, Patsy had to smile. 'I always fancied meself as an actress, so I did. I devised a little plan. After spending a whole week's wages on cosmetics, I put it all in a suitcase, wore a smart two-piece and knocked on the door, bold as ye please.'

'Honestly, Patsy Noonan! What then?'

'I got sent on me way, so I did! The snotty little bugger who answered the door probably thought I was a confidence trickster.'

'Why ever would she think that?'

'Ah, now, don't be so bloody cheeky, young madam!' Patsy had got the poison out of her system long ago and could now see the funny side of it. 'Anyways, like I say, I got shown the door. But I got to see the lad. Oh, but he was a bonny thing. As I went away down the drive, I heard a sound behind me – like a child laughing, you know?'

When, serious now, Eva nodded, Patsy went on, 'I went back up to the side gate that led to the garden, and there they were, all three of them. The man was a very distinguished gent, and the woman had the kindest, loveliest face.' Pausing, she regarded Eva. 'Matter of fact, I've always thought you had a look of her.' Taking a deep breath, she continued, 'The lad was playing round the woman's feet. At first I was shocked to see how much like Fred he looked. For just one awful minute I had the urge to run in and snatch him away. I tell ye, I don't know how I stopped meself.' Suddenly her voice broke and she looked away, the tears bright in her eyes.

Gently, Eva said, 'Do you want to go?'

'I want you to know how it was.' Composing herself, Patsy went on, 'I just watched for a time, hidden behind the shrubbery. Oh, Eva, they were such lovely people, and the lad was so happy with them. His new parents would always cherish him, I could see that. And it was plain to see that he would never go short of anything in his life. What could I offer him? Nothing, that's what. I was too young to look after him properly, and I had no money at all. I'd already turned my back on me parents, like they turned their backs on me and my baby. I was living in a one-bedroom flat and was already two weeks behind with the rent. Oh, I had a job, but it paid next to nothing.'

Eva could only imagine how Patsy felt. In her heart, she thought Patsy must have suffered like she had when both her parents died in that fire. 'Oh, Patsy. I'm so sorry.'

'For the first time in me life, I put someone else before meself. I knew that where the lad was he must be better off, so I walked away.'

'That must have been so hard.'

'What would you have done, Eva?'

'The same.'

'Thank you for that.'

'And you never made any attempt to see him, or your parents, ever again?'

Patsy shook her head. 'Like I said, I burned all me bridges.' Her face crinkled in a smile. 'Soon after that, I came to work for your mother, and I swear to God, Eva me darlin', I'd never been so happy as I was in that lovely place.'

'What about now, Patsy? Are you happy now?'

'Oh, I am that! But it's a different kind of happiness. I'm older now, so I am, and mebbe a bit more tolerant. I have a lot to make amends for. That night, when we arrived in Albert Street and you ran after the boy, I went inside and nosed about a bit, like I do, you know?'

Eva smiled. 'I know.' In fact, Patsy had already told her, but it seemed as if she needed to talk it through, so Eva let her go on.

'When I found the photograph upstairs in the bedside drawer, sure it was a terrible shock, I can tell ye. Tommy was Fred's son! Not mine. Oh no! *My* son was given away.' She gave a deep, withering sigh. 'Oh, Eva, I did a shocking thing, so I did. The poor boy was innocent in all of it; on top of that he'd lost his mammy, and his father had run off. But I took it out on the boy. I was jealous, d'ye see? So jealous I couldn't see straight. Now I've come to love the boy like my own. Isn't that a funny thing?'

'No, I don't think so, Patsy.' Eva had never felt closer to Patsy than she did right now. 'It's a strange world, and what do we know? You had one child taken from you, and you did the right thing in giving him every chance of a better life. And I believe with all my heart that you were given a second chance with Tommy. You're as good as his mother now, and he adores you, anyone can see that. Life has turned full circle for you, Patsy, don't you see? Fred too. You've both come back to each other, and you've got Tommy. Oh, Patsy, you can't know how happy I am to see you so content.'

'You're such a good friend to me, Eva. What would I ever do without you?'

'Will you ever tell Fred about his other son?'

'Would you?'

'I don't think any good would come of it, Patsy,' she answered honestly. 'But you're the one who has to live with whatever decision you make. Can you do that?'

'I've lived with it for so long now, it can stay between the two of us.' Quietly she added, 'I only wish to God you were as happy as I am, Eva. Ah, sure, it doesn't seem fair. You've lost so much, and ye still haven't found contentment. What are we gonna do with ye, eh?'

Not wanting to mar Patsy's new-found joy with her own troubles, Eva told her brightly, 'You can stop fretting and carrying on about me. I've been lucky. I've found a man who adores me. I've got a beautiful home and money enough never to worry about a single thing.' Her smile was incredibly beautiful as she added softly, 'And I've got the most precious gift of all to look forward to.' Tenderly caressing the growing child beneath her skirt, she told Patsy, 'In here, there's all the contentment I need.'

THEY ORDERED ANOTHER pot of tea and chatted about Eva's hospital check-ups and the knowledge that all was well.

'Don't you forget, Eva me darlin', when Frank goes away on another of them business trips, you can always come and stay with us. Or, if you'd rather, I'll come and stay with you at the big house. I don't like ye being on your own up there.'

Eva gratefully refused. 'You've got your own family to look after now,' she reminded her.

'And what are you if not family?'

'Honestly, Patsy, I'm perfectly all right on my own. Anyway, if I needed anything, there's always Olive next door. Staying at the house is better than going with Frank on his business trips.' The one and only time she'd allowed him to bully her into accompanying him to Scotland, he had asked her to charm his clients, then watched her like a hawk, and afterwards put her through sheer hell. She had seen a side to Frank that night that had shocked and frightened her. Now, nothing on God's earth would persuade her to go with him.

---

THAT EVENING, FRANK returned from London, greatly excited about a new venture. 'I think I've got a buyer for the land behind us,' he told Eva over dinner. 'Once he's seen it, I'm sure he'll sign on the dotted line.'

Anxious, Eva asked, 'What does he plan to do with the land?'

Frank shovelled food into his mouth. With his eyes on her the whole time, he chewed the mouthful for a few minutes before answering, 'Sometimes, Eva, you can be really stupid.' He said it as though he was talking to an imbecile.

'What do you mean?' Anger rose in her, of a kind that she had never felt before.

'What I mean, my sweet, is this. I'm a developer. The buyer is a developer. What the hell do you think he's going to do with it?'

Pushing her chair back, she stood up and faced him with equal contempt. 'You told me only a few days ago that you meant to keep that land. "Leave it for nature to shape," you said. "A wonderful legacy for our baby," you said. You went into great detail to explain how it would never be built on, by you or anyone else. "The house would have to be pulled down if the land was built on," you said, "because it's the only feasible access." So you can hardly blame me if I ask what this buyer means to do with it.'

'Whatever is the matter with you, Eva? You don't usually take things so much to heart.'

He was genuinely shocked that she should have taken it so badly. But then he didn't know how she felt these days. He hardly ever bothered to ask. He assumed that she was content with her lot, proud to live in this beautiful big house, with a chequebook of her own and an expensive car parked in the drive. Being the materialistic man he was, Frank could not imagine any woman being dissatisfied with what he had given his precious wife. She had his undying love; she was carrying his baby. What more could she want?

'I thought you would be delighted,' he said, looking like a boy chastised; and the pity of it was, he actually meant what he said.

Leaning across the table, Eva looked him straight in the eye. In a hard voice she said, 'And another thing, Frank, don't ever call me stupid. I may be a lot of things – too trusting maybe, badly misguided, and sometimes very, *very* wrong.' Especially in my judgement of you, she thought. 'But not stupid, Frank. Never that.'

Calmer now, she excused herself and left the room, inwardly cursing herself for ever having married him.

She had been up in the bedroom for only two minutes when he came in. 'I'm sorry,' he apologised. 'It's me that's stupid, and you're right. I did tell you the land would never be built on because that would mean pulling down the house, and yes, I had intended the valley to be our baby's legacy, but we stand to make a great deal of money. Think about it, Eva. We'd be crazy to turn it down.'

'Why does everything have to centre on *money*?'

Suddenly she felt as if all the fight had been knocked out of her. It had been a long day. The baby was kicking fitfully, and she felt overwhelmingly tired. 'Leave me be, Frank,' she said. 'Do whatever you like. It's your land. Your money. And your decision. I have other things to think about right now.' Like how I can make myself love you when you make it so bloody hard for me. Into her mind came another face. Bill's. He was the man she loved. He was the man she would *always* love; damn it!

Coming to where she sat on the edge of the bed, he slid his arm round her shoulders, either not caring or choosing not to notice how she cringed at his touch. 'Look what I've bought you, sweetheart.' Dipping into his pocket, he drew out a slender black box. 'Open it.' Placing it on the bed beside her, he waited.

To his dismay, Eva didn't even glance at it. Instead she got up and walked to the window where she leaned on the wall, staring out across the valley. This place was so beautiful, she thought, the idea of bulldozers and trucks, and all manner of habitat being ripped up, was nauseating. And so was the realisation that he had lied to her. 'How long have you been planning to sell the valley?' She couldn't even bring herself to look at him.

'I only want the best for you. That's all I've ever wanted, you know that.'

'How long, Frank?'

'I didn't exactly plan it, sweetheart. I just mentioned it to a business acquaintance and he made me a tentative offer, subject to seeing it.'

'And if I don't want it sold? What then?'

'Look, Eva, I don't want you to worry about this, and I certainly don't want us to argue.'

Swinging round, she confronted him with troubled green eyes. 'Answer me, Frank. What if I don't want it sold? What if I want us to keep it? To let nature reclaim it, like we planned? A legacy for our children, that's what you said, and behind my back you're busy making other plans. You lied to me, Frank. Why?' She felt cheated, left out, as if she didn't matter.

'Please listen to me, Eva.' He came to her. 'I would never deliberately hurt you.' His voice was persuasive, his smile full of contrition. 'I'll ring him right now and tell him the deal's off.' He kissed her on the forehead. 'I had no idea you loved this place so much. Trust me, sweetheart. I would never do anything that you didn't agree with. I should have told you, and I'm sorry. From now on, I promise I won't keep you in the dark.' Nuzzling her neck, he murmured, 'Am I forgiven?'

Eva's first instinct was to thrust him away, yet she couldn't help but wonder if she had overreacted. He seemed genuinely sorry, and he had not only apologised but offered to turn the deal on its head. It would be churlish of her to fuel the argument further. Besides, she didn't feel it would change anything, and even if it did, what would it matter?

It struck Eva that she was not in fact hitting out because he had schemed behind her back but because she didn't love him, and that angered her but it was anger with herself. The only thing Frank had ever wanted from her was her love, and she couldn't give it. Maybe it was she who should be apologising. Guilt swept through her. If Frank knew she fantasised about another man while she lay in his arms, he would be devastated.

Guilt tinged her face as she turned away. 'Leave me for a while, Frank. I don't feel like talking right now.'

'Are we friends?' Always like a puppy dog, she thought sadly.

'Of course.'

'Kiss then?' Putting his finger under her chin, he turned her to him. When she didn't resist, he grew bold, kissing her long and hard. 'Don't go quiet on me, sweetheart,' he pleaded. 'I hate it when you go quiet.'

Eva knew exactly what he meant. There were times when he might be talking to her and she would be miles away – back at her mother's farm, or on the road with Patsy. And sometimes she imagined herself in Canada with Bill at her side. That was the best, and worst, of all.

Now, when she felt Frank begin to remove her clothes, she made no effort to stop him. When he steered her to the bed, she lay there, hating his touch yet needing his love, for she had no other.

She felt him climb on her; she felt his stiff, warm member gently enter her. The rhythm of his movements made the bed dip beneath them, slow at first, then faster. She even responded.

Growing excited, he gripped her tight, and she thought of Bill. When he thrust hard, climaxed, and crumpled on top of her with a long, drawn-out sigh, she imagined it was Bill. And it wasn't at all unbearable.

——————

LATER THAT NIGHT, when Eva was sleeping, Frank slunk downstairs.

Creeping into the study like a thief, he picked up the phone and dialled.

'John, is that you? There's been a slight change of plan. Between you and me, when you come here, the reason for your stay will be the same, but when my wife is around, you are simply an old business colleague here for a social visit. She's very fond of the house, and I don't want her to know about our little agreement. Do you understand what I'm saying?'

Obviously it was understood; a broad grin spread across Frank's face. 'I knew you'd see it from my point of view. That's right, next weekend as agreed. I'm looking forward to it, and I'm sure you'll be delighted when you see the site. It's prime, I tell you.' Glancing anxiously towards the door, he lowered his voice. 'If I wasn't planning on cracking the markets abroad, you wouldn't even get a sniff at it.'

While the other man talked, Frank kept a wary eye on the door. 'Yes, I do know it could mean us moving abroad. To be honest, that's the whole idea. A fresh start will be good for both of us, what with the baby and all. No, I won't be selling my interests here, merely expanding internationally. That's where the really big opportunities are.' He smiled slyly. 'Oh, and John? I know I can trust you not to mention this to my dear wife. I want it to be a lovely surprise. She tends to get excited, you see. You're right. Women have no idea about the mechanics of big business, bless their hearts . . . Indeed, that's what I thought – keep it simple. I'm glad you understand why I won't be telling her until it's all settled.'

# Chapter Fourteen

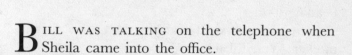

B ILL WAS TALKING on the telephone when Sheila came into the office.

Realising he was talking to his mother, she turned to leave, but Bill beckoned her to come in and close the door. When she was seated opposite him, he gestured that he would only be a minute.

'Okay, Ma,' he smiled at Sheila, 'no, don't you worry about a thing.' The smile slid away. 'Don't antagonise him. You know what a mean devil he can be. I know all about the deal – heard it on the grapevine yesterday, and no, I'm not bothered at all. If he's moving in that direction he's making a big mistake, but he'll do whatever he wants, regardless. He always has.' He listened for a while, nodding occasionally, and glancing at Sheila. 'Look, Ma, if he wants to trust Todd with that kind of responsibility, that's up to him, but he may live to regret it. It's always been the same, Todd can do no wrong in his eyes, but there's no need for you to worry. If the firm goes broke, you'll always be looked after, I can promise you that.'

Another moment of listening, and then, 'I know it's late to be at the office, but there are things I have to do. Yes, I'm almost finished for the day. No, I won't overdo it.' Raising his eyebrows at Sheila, he smiled. 'That's right, Ma. I'm about ready to close shop now – just one or two things to clear with Sheila first, then I'll be heading home.'

However busy, Bill always had time for his mother. 'Yes, I'll tell her.'

He looked at Sheila, who mouthed the words, 'Sheila sends regards to you too.'

'Okay, Ma. Look after yourself now. See you Tuesday as arranged. 'Bye now.' Replacing the receiver, he told Sheila, 'Seems like the old boy has bitten off more than he can chew this time.'

'I got the gist of the conversation,' Sheila replied. 'I can't believe he's given Todd more responsibility, especially when he lost half a million on that riverside site.'

'He's a fool.' Getting out of his chair, Bill walked round the desk, where he stood, leaning nonchalantly against the filing cabinet, his active mind going over all his mother had said. 'Apparently Dad shrugged it off. "Just bad luck", that's what he called it.'

'He must be losing his marbles.' Thoughtful, Sheila leaned back in her chair. 'Even I could have done a better deal. That riverside location was always dubious. No wonder he had to offload it at a loss.'

'If he'd done his homework, Todd would have discovered how the river spills over at that particular point.' At one time, Bill had been interested, but he soon backed off. 'And if he'd only taken the trouble to check with the authorities, he would have known there was planning approval to build industrial units right next door.'

'What's going on, Bill? Why is your father handing over more and more responsibility to Todd?'

'Who knows?' Bill had wondered himself. It was something that had happened over the past year. 'All I do know is that if Todd keeps making expensive mistakes like this, the company won't last another six months.' Turning, he took a file from the cabinet. 'I don't care what happens to that pair,' he said bitterly. 'As for Ma, she'll want for nothing while I'm able to provide for her.'

Seating himself at the desk, he scanned through the documents before him. After making a few hasty notes, he looked up. 'Right. Let's see what you've got for me. It's been a long day. Time I took you home, young lady.'

'Not so young these days,' she sighed, handing him the folder. 'I might think of retiring next year.'

Perusing the papers in the folder, he laughed.

'You've been saying that for the past four years.' Serious now, he looked her in the eye. 'You're not ill, are you?'

'Fit as a fiddle.'

Visibly relieved, he declared mischievously, 'In that case, you *can't* retire. I'd sink without trace if you left me.'

'Not you. You'll outlast them all, and die a rich old man.'

'A *lonely* old man, isn't that what you mean?'

For a time they sat, Bill signing letters and Sheila watching him. Two very dear friends, each with their own quiet thoughts.

After signing the last letter, Bill handed back the folder. 'That's it. The rest can wait until Monday. Get your coat. I'm taking you home.'

June was his favourite month. Though it was gone eight o'clock, the skies were still the most beautiful turquoise blue and, judging by the songs emanating from the trees, even the birds were reluctant to go home. 'Your carriage awaits.' Opening the door of his new Jaguar, Bill waited for her to climb in.

In the car, Sheila picked up on his remark about being 'lonely'. 'Have you decided what to do about Eva?'

Day or night, Vancouver was a busy city. With his mind on the road and a junction looming, he didn't answer straight away.

Impatient, Sheila persevered. 'Just now you said you would die a lonely man. What about Eva?'

'Not now, Sheila. Please.'

But she persisted. 'I'm glad you told me about her . . . though I know sometimes you wished you hadn't.'

'You're wrong. Who else could I turn to?'

'Then turn to me now, Bill.' Her voice softened. 'I'll ask you again . . . what about Eva?'

'What about her?'

'Some time ago, you wondered whether you should make an effort to find her.'

'I decided against it.' Easing the car to a standstill at the traffic lights, he kept his gaze straight ahead. 'I've put it right out of my mind.'

'Why would you do that?'

Shrugging his shoulders, he gave her a sideways glance. 'You know things haven't been too good between me and Joan these past years, but what with the death of our son, and then a miscarriage two months ago, she came close to a nervous breakdown, and she needs me now more than ever.'

'I understand that.' What she didn't understand was Bill's devotion to a woman who was obviously no good to anyone. 'But Joan isn't the only reason, is she?'

'Oh?' When you were afraid it was always easiest to plead ignorance. 'And what's that supposed to mean?'

'It's your pride, isn't it? Eva asked you not to find her, and you've done what she asked all these years. Now, when you really would like to find her, you're afraid.'

'Is that so?' Sometimes Sheila knew him better than he knew himself.

'You're afraid she might reject you. Afraid she won't return the love you feel for her.'

He laughed softly. 'You're a very perceptive lady.'

'I'm also your friend.' What she wanted to say was, 'I'm your mother and I haven't got long on this earth.'

Oh, how she yearned for him to be happy. And the only person who could bring him real happiness was Eva Bereton. But he would never seek her out, Sheila knew that. He was too fine and loyal a man. Bill had old-fashioned ideals and a deep belief that the marriage vows given in church were sacred. Joan's drinking had almost destroyed her, but now that she had dried out and was beginning to enjoy life again, he would never break her heart, whatever sacrifice it cost him.

---

TODD WAS NO stranger to his brother's house, or his brother's wife. 'You're a wicked tease,' he laughed. 'A woman like you could drive a man crazy.'

Naked and wanton, Joan stood before him. She was in her thirties, tall and slim, and very desirable. With her long, dark hair and beckoning eyes, she had a thirst for men, which was not easily quenched. 'How much do you want me?' Taunting, she laughed in his face, staying just out of arm's reach.

Red in the face and aching with need, Todd would have snatched her to him, but with a laugh that put murder in his heart, she moved away. 'You little bitch! I warn you. Don't torment me.'

'Now, now, it's just my little game.'

For a moment they regarded each other, he with a kind of hatred in his eyes, and she basking in her power over him. 'How much do you want me?' she asked again, leaning brazenly against the bedhead.

'Too much, and you know it.' He edged towards her once more. This time she didn't move, until he took hold of her. Fighting him off, she laughed in his face.

Together they rolled on to the floor. 'I should kill you,' he murmured, his two hands round her throat.

Her eyes bathed his face, and there was madness in her smile. 'You'd rather mate with me though, wouldn't you?' Like a thing possessed, she reached down to play with him. The hardness of his erect penis excited her. Closing her eyes, she pleaded, 'Now! Take me now!'

For one long, excruciating moment, he made her wait. 'You're crazy,' he hissed. And she was. But that was why he needed her. That was why she played on his senses like a powerful, intoxicating drug.

———⟫◦⟪———

'MIND HOW YOU go.' Sheila waved to Bill as he drove away. 'Take care, son,' she murmured.

She watched him go left at the bottom of the road, waited a while, then turned her back on the house where she had lived these many years and walked away down the street.

She wasn't in the mood for being alone. Not tonight. This morning she had seen her doctor and the news was not good. Suddenly, sunshine and birdsong were gifts to be cherished. A walk in the fresh air will blow away the cobwebs, she thought; and besides, she had some very important decisions to make.

Full of quiet thoughts, Bill made his way home. There had been something about Sheila tonight that worried him. It wasn't just the light-hearted hint about her retiring. It went deeper than that. She wasn't ill, she said, but he felt she was hiding something from him.

It was strange how she could almost read his thoughts, he mused. Especially where Eva was concerned. But then, Sheila knew the score. Eva was his dream. Joan was his reality. Joan needed him. Eva did not.

He considered that for a moment. Maybe Eva did need him. How would he know? He prayed she did, then he prayed she didn't, because it would serve no purpose. He was tied to someone else, and no doubt Eva had her own family, her own responsibilities. After all this time, he ought to be able to accept that.

But he couldn't. His love for Eva was as strong as ever.

Normally, he would leave the car outside on the drive and go in through the front door, but tonight, for no particular reason, he drove it into the garage and made his way into the house through the side door, silently cursing because he found the door unlocked. 'For God's sake, Joan,' he muttered, coming into the kitchen, 'how many times do I have to tell you, there are burglars operating in this neck of the woods.' This week the police had posted warnings everywhere.

Thinking she was in the lounge, he went through. When he saw no one was there, he thought she might have gone next door – Cath Parker was her one and only friend.

Going to the fridge he took out a carton of orange juice and poured himself a generous measure.

He was raising the glass to his lips for the second time when he heard a noise. 'What the devil's that?' Cautiously, he followed the sound through the kitchen and on up the stairs. 'Burglars?' He cursed Joan again for leaving the door unlocked.

At the top of the stairs he realised the sounds were coming from the bedroom he and Joan shared. Fists clenched, he approached the door on tiptoe. The best way to deal with a burglar was to take him by surprise, he thought. Cautiously he edged open the door and peered inside – and froze. His wife and a man were thrashing about on the bed, both naked, and so deeply entangled in each other they seemed to be one and the same.

Joan saw him at the door and began screaming that she'd been attacked. 'I couldn't stop him. Honest to God, Bill, I couldn't stop him!' For effect she started hitting her 'assailant' who by this time had turned to see Bill charging towards him, his face black as thunder.

'She's a liar!' he yelled. 'She's crazy!'

His words were lost in the crunch of Bill's fist as it landed with a sickening blow on the side of his face. '*You!*' Yanking Todd off the bed, he threw him across the room. 'You filthy bastard!' White with rage, Bill advanced on him again.

Behind him, Joan cried, 'I begged him to leave me be but he wouldn't listen.'

Like the coward he was, Todd hid behind a chair. 'I swear to God, she's lying!'

'Get up!'

'Listen to me, Bill.' Todd was crying like a child now. 'Ask her how many times we've been together. Ask her where she went when you thought she was away at a health farm – she was with me, I can prove it if you'll only give me a chance. She's cheated on you all along, Bill. First with Father, then with me. She hates you – deep down she hates you.'

Bill kicked aside the chair and drew him out. 'You're a filthy liar!' What he had just heard was too terrible to believe.

'Hit me, I don't care. It's the truth. Go on! Ask her!' The sweat was pouring down his face. 'Ask her about the baby you thought she'd miscarried. It wasn't yours, Bill! Father arranged for her to get rid of it.'

From behind them came the most terrible of screams. Bill turned, startled, to see Joan crouched at the bottom of the bed, her gaze fixed on him. Trembling from head to foot, she was sobbing uncontrollably.

In that moment, Bill knew. It was written in her eyes.

It seemed to take an age for it to register. When it did, and he realised that everything Todd had said must be the truth, Bill felt as though he had been hit with a sledgehammer. For a long, terrible moment he continued to stare at her. Behind him he could hear Todd whimpering. He looked from one to the other, and saw them for what they were.

'Please, Bill, I do love you.' Joan crawled along the bed towards him.

'My God!' His voice was like gravel, his face contorted with disgust as he stared at the two of them. 'How could I have been such a bloody fool?'

As he walked out of that place, he could hear her calling, 'Please, Bill, don't leave me.'

'Your lies won't work,' he murmured. 'Not any more.'

# Chapter Fifteen

Eva had been primed all week about their imminent guest. 'John's an old friend. I haven't seen him since our college days,' Frank lied. 'Funny how we bumped into each other after all that time.'

'How long is he staying?' Eva thought it would be nice to have another face around the house. Frank had a strong dislike of visitors, particularly when the visitors were Patsy and Tommy, who regularly came to see her, preferably when Frank was out. As yet, Fred had not found the time to visit, but he was always welcome, Eva had assured him of that.

'A few nights,' Frank answered, buttering his toast. 'He'll be gone Monday morning.'

'What's he like, this old friend of yours?' Somehow, she had never imagined Frank having a friend. He was a loner, who trusted no one, especially her.

'Much like me, I suppose. A dedicated businessman, with a certain degree of success, and aspirations to do even better.'

Eva reached for the marmalade. 'What kind of business is he in?'

Looking up, Frank smiled. 'Why do you need to know?'

Sensing suspicion behind his smile, Eva answered cautiously, 'Just curious, that's all.'

'Mmm.' Putting down his toast, then dabbing his mouth with his napkin, he answered, 'John is into all sorts. Mostly shares – gilts, that kind of thing.'

'Not property then?'

'Why do you ask that?'

Eva shrugged. 'I don't know really. I just thought you might have met up through one of your business deals.'

'Ah, well, in a way you're right, sweetheart. You remember I told you about the new company I've taken on, to refurbish the older hotels, bring them up to date, introduce conference and leisure facilities?'

'Yes, I remember.' Eva had thought it an excellent idea.

'Well, John has major interests in that particular company. That's how we came to meet up again.'

'What's he like?' Eva asked again. It was so rare to get a real conversation out of Frank, she was beginning to enjoy herself.

Frank's patience was running thin. 'I've already told you. He's a businessman, much like me.'

'No. I mean how old is he? What does he look like? Is he married? Has he got children? That kind of thing.'

Containing his anger, Frank stood up. 'You want to know a great deal, don't you?' His voice had an edge that Eva had come to recognise. Realising she had touched that jealous chord again, she wisely dropped the subject.

'You're right. What does it matter?'

He nodded approvingly. 'As long as he's fed and made welcome, that's all that matters. This visit will be a one-off. I've no doubt we will never see him again.' He had no liking for men in this house. Eva was *his* property, not to be shared or ogled. She had come to mean more to him than life itself, and however much she resisted, he must protect her from the bad things. It was his goal in life to love her with all his being and always take the utmost care of her, shower her with expensive gifts and take her twice round the world if that was what she wanted.

Rounding the table he bent over her from behind. Kissing her tenderly on the top of her head, he murmured softly, 'There's nothing for you to concern yourself about, sweetheart.' He thought it was time to tell her what he had done. 'So you don't overtax yourself while he's here, I've arranged for some help.'

In a minute Eva was on her feet. 'What? *Domestic* help, you mean?'

'That's right, and before you say anything, I'm only thinking of you.' He tapped her bulge. 'And the baby, of course.'

Eva was furious. Stepping away from him, she said, 'You had no right to do that. You know how I feel about looking after this house myself. And now you bring one visitor to see us and suddenly you think I can't manage.'

Equally determined, he took hold of her by the shoulders. 'No argument, sweetheart. It's all arranged.'

'Then, it can be *unarranged*.' This was the second time he had gone behind her back, and she didn't like it one bit. 'I mean it, Frank. I don't want to be treated as if I'm incapable. It's only a house, for God's sake, and there are only two of us. One more won't make much difference. All right, I'm pregnant, and I get a little tired now and then, but I'm not an invalid. If I can't care for three adults over a couple of days, what use am I?'

'Entertaining is not easy, any hostess will tell you that. I don't want you wearing yourself out. There are all the meals to prepare, an extra bedroom to sort out and keep tidy. In your state it's too much to burden you with.' What he really wanted was a spy in the camp.

'Of course it isn't,' Eva insisted. 'And don't forget, Frank, I did run a hotel at one time.' Well, near enough, she thought. She would not allow him to push her aside as if she couldn't cope. Nor was he going to rule her like he might a child.

Taking her two hands in his, he said, 'Sorry, sweetheart. I really didn't know you felt so strongly.'

Eva drew her hands away. 'Yes, you did! You know I've fought all along against having help here. If I didn't have this house to tend, I'd be bored out of my mind.'

'All right, sweetheart. I'll cancel it.' Kissing her on the mouth, he promised, 'In fact, I'll do it right now.' With that, he hurried away.

Eva sat in her seat, looking across the breakfast table, and wondering if she would ever come to love him. 'I don't belong here,' she sighed. 'I have nothing to occupy my mind, and Frank is hell bent on wrapping me in cotton wool.' She knew he loved her, but it was a strange kind of love that gave a woman no freedom. She was an accomplished person. There was a time when she had plans, and a life. Now, all that was sliding away, and the longer she stayed, the more hopelessly trapped she felt. 'I don't belong with a man like Frank.' Closing her eyes, she let her mind wander. 'With a man like Bill,' she whispered, 'that's where I belong.'

'All done.' Frank had come back, startling her.

'What?'

'I've cancelled the help.' Standing there, he

gazed down on her pink, guilty face. 'It's not a good idea, you know.'

'What isn't?'

'Talking to yourself.'

Before she could answer, he swept her, laughingly, into his arms. 'After John's left, I think I'll take a week or so off. We could go away – a cruise maybe. It would do us both good.'

The idea was so abhorrent to Eva that she remained silent; at the back of her mind she suspected he might have heard her say Bill's name.

Walking with her to the front door, he gave no indication that he had heard. 'Behave yourself while I'm away now. No making eyes at the postman.' He gave a small laugh, kissed her lightly, and was soon disappearing down the lane in his car.

At the bottom he turned to wave, as he always did.

Eva did not wave back. In her heart she prayed he would stay away for ever.

⟶∙◆∙⟵

FOR A LONG time after he'd gone, Eva sat in the garden, looking out across the valley. 'It's so beautiful here,' she murmured.

Grateful to Frank for ruling out the sale of this land to a developer, she felt her heart soften towards him. 'He means well,' she sighed. 'Deep down, I know he means well.' She actually laughed. 'If he had his way he'd surround me with guards and prison bars. Oh, Frank, yours is a funny kind of love.' But it was love nevertheless. He cared for her more than he cared for anything in his life, she was aware of that. And if she didn't have Frank, who else was there? Only the baby, she thought, and the baby was Frank's.

After a while, she glanced at her wristwatch and was ashamed to see how the hour had flown. 'Come on, Eva,' she chided herself. 'You've only just got through telling Frank how you're able to cope on your own, without help. And here you are, letting the dishes lie dirty, and the bed unmade. There's washing to be done and hung out, and endless little tasks to be finished before you go to Albert Street.' The thought of seeing Patsy put a smile on her face.

She tore into the work. The dishes were washed and stacked away, the washing finished and hung out on the line, a chat with Olive before going back inside. Then she ran the Hoover round and dusted. Upstairs, the bed was quickly made, the curtains tied back and Frank's robe put tidily away. A last look round, and it was time to get washed and ready.

It was eleven thirty.

A short time later Eva emerged from the bathroom to towel her long hair and comb it through. Having already sorted her clothes for the day, she got dressed. The pretty cream underwear had been bought from Marks and Spencer the week before; Patsy had bought the same, but in black. The shoes were sensible, in view of her condition. The brown trouser suit only just fitted across her middle but it was comfortable, and quite attractive. A touch of make-up, mostly round the eyes and lips; a quick comb through her hair, which was almost dry, and she was ready for the world.

Looking in the full-length mirror, she observed herself with a wry little smile. 'Not bad,' she said, cocking her head to one side. 'Considering you're past thirty, and about to be a mum.' The bulge was not too prominent, but it was there all the same, and Eva was beginning to notice it more and more by the day.

Patsy thought she looked lovely. 'Ye look like a film star, so ye do!'

Embarrassed, Eva shoved her inside the house. 'I think you need glasses,' she said. 'I'm fat and spotty, and my breasts are beginning to sag.'

Inside the sitting room, Patsy boldly regarded her. 'Whatever ye say won't alter the fact that ye look lovely.' With a giggle she added, 'Even if your breasts *are* sagging.'

Eva threw a cushion at her and the two of them collapsed with laughter. 'It's so good to see you,' Eva said. 'I feel like I've been let out of prison.'

The pattern was always the same. Eva would put the kettle on and make the tea, Patsy would get out the biscuits. When the tray was ready, they would make their way back into the sitting room and place themselves either side of the fireplace, whether winter or summer.

In winter the fire would be cheery, with the flames roaring up the chimney; in summer, like now, a pretty flowered screen stood in the hearth to hide the black grate.

Once they were settled, they would catch up on the gossip and pass on any moans, groans, or news. Today, Eva told Patsy about the scene with Frank earlier.

'Sure, the way he treats ye, anybody would think ye were helpless,' she tutted. 'He loves ye too much, that's the trouble. He's afraid you'll blow away in the wind, that's what it is.'

'So you don't think I was being ungrateful?'

'Not at all! If it had been me, I'd have knocked him aside the head with the frying pan, so I would.'

The talk went from one thing to another. 'Maggie took Tommy to the pictures last Saturday, did I tell ye that?' She hadn't, and Eva was delighted that Maggie was growing ever closer to the boy.

'I have some other news, so I have.' Looking shy, Patsy grinned from ear to ear. 'Me an' Fred were gonna tell ye when we were together, but I can't keep it to meself a minute longer.'

Seeing the sly little look on Patsy's face, Eva almost dropped her cup. 'Patsy Noonan, you're pregnant, aren't you?' Patsy nodded and threw herself into Eva's arms. The chair rocked on its feet and they laughed and cried, and couldn't believe how things had turned out.

'What happened to all our plans?' Eva laughed. 'The little business we wanted, and all that hard work to save enough money?'

'Aye, an' here you are living in a fancy house and married to a monster, an' there's me, coming up to me pension and having a bairn!' She couldn't stop giggling. Eva asked her if she'd been at the gin, and Patsy answered, 'What do you think?'

'The money we saved is still invested,' Eva reminded her. 'You can leave it there or you can take it out. I've already signed it all over to you, so it's for you to decide.'

Patsy had had no idea Eva was planning to do that. 'Why, ye little bugger! You'd no right to sign it over to me. We *both* worked for that money. I'll not have your share. Thanks all the same, but I'd feel like I were stealing it from ye.'

'Take it for your baby, Patsy. Don't refuse me. Please. You know I don't need it.'

So it was decided.

Patsy told Eva how Fred had got some time off work. 'I was going to phone and tell ye,' she said.

'First thing tomorrow morning he's taking me and Tommy to Blackpool to celebrate the new baby. Oh, and Tommy's been promised a job at the paper mill when he leaves school next year.'

'Oh, Patsy, that's wonderful!'

'I can't believe it. Everything's come right for me, and in spite of your feller being too possessive, ye seem to be taking it all in your stride, so ye do. You've always been able to handle the rough times, and now, me darlin', I'm beginning to think it will all come out in the wash. Besides, I've got a feeling you'll be happy as a pig in muck when your baby's born.'

Eva raised her cup of tea. 'To *both* our babies.'

'Aye. And now you've told me about your half of the money, that's something else to celebrate.'

When, some three hours later, Eva left for home, she felt a great deal happier than when she had arrived.

But then, she always did.

Her spirits dipped when she thought about the weekend ahead and Frank's visitor. She suspected Frank might have been lying about this John being an old college friend. But she had no real cause to doubt his word. All the same, she and Frank were going through a bad patch, and it was very worrying. Was Patsy right? she wondered. Would it all come out in the wash?

'It has to.' She found herself talking aloud as she turned the car into the drive.

She had a strange kind of feeling about this weekend. A kind of premonition that something bad was about to happen.

# Chapter Sixteen

F RIDAY EVENING ARRIVED, and got off to a
bad start.

All day Eva had worked hard, and now, just as
she was turning the joint, a knock came on the door.
'Frank!' Twice she called his name but there was
no answer. 'Damn and bugger it!' Taking off her
pinafore, she set it down on the table and rushed
to answer the door.

It was a young girl, small and trim, with big
eyes and a bold, well made-up face. 'I've come
from Delton's Domestic Agency,' she said. 'I'm
to stay the weekend and carry out general duties,
as directed by the lady of the house.' She handed
Eva a long, folded card. 'At least that's what it
says there.'

'There's been a mistake,' Eva answered, returning the card. 'The booking was cancelled.'

Frank arrived. 'What's the problem?'

'I've come from the agency,' the girl explained.
'This lady thinks the booking was cancelled, but

it couldn't have been. If it had been cancelled, I wouldn't be here, would I?'

Turning to Eva, Frank assured her he had cancelled the booking himself. 'There's obviously been some mix-up. But never mind. As long as she's here, I'm sure you could find something for her to do.'

It was obvious to Eva that he was lying. 'Sorry, Frank,' she answered stiffly, 'there is nothing at all for her to do. Everything is under control, just as I said it would be.' Addressing the young lady, she apologised. 'I'm sorry you've come unnecessarily,' she said, 'but if the booking was not cancelled before, I'm cancelling it now. If there is money to be paid, I'm sure my husband will deal with it.' With that, she excused herself and returned to the kitchen, leaving Frank to sort it out.

A few moments later he followed her into the kitchen. 'You didn't have to do that.'

'And you didn't have to lie to me. You didn't cancel the booking at all, did you?'

For a moment he toyed with the idea of lying yet again, but he knew she wouldn't believe him. 'I did it for you,' he said sheepishly. 'I don't want you overtiring yourself.'

'Oh, Frank. Why don't you let *me* be the judge of whether I'm overtiring myself? I don't need cosseting every minute of every day. I'm a grown woman. I can take care of myself.'

'Sorry, sweetheart.' When he went to kiss her, she turned away.

Bristling, he stood there a moment longer, then left without saying another word.

Eva followed him into the lounge where he was sulking. 'We're not going to have an atmosphere all weekend, are we, Frank?' she asked. 'Because if we are, you can call the agency and get the girl back. I'll go and stay with Patsy until your visitor's gone.' She knew Patsy was in Blackpool for a few days, but he didn't.

He had been standing by the fireside with his hands in his pockets. Now he turned and stared at her, his face set in a hard expression. 'Would you really do that?' He sounded hurt, like a child denied his sweets.

'Sometimes you drive me to despair.' Eva had to say what was on her mind, and the devil with the consequences. 'You lie to me. You make plans behind my back. You've cancelled the papers because you thought I was flirting with the paper boy – a lad young enough to be my son. And you did your level best to make me sell my car because you were afraid I'd be involved in an accident.'

'I'm only looking after you.'

'Oh, Frank! You smother me. I know you do it for all the best reasons. But I need space. I need to be able to breathe.'

He gave a long sigh that seemed to make him shrink. 'I love you, Eva, so very much.'

'Do you think I don't know that?'

There was a silence while he studied her, thinking how lovely she was and how he would kill, with his bare hands, anyone who tried to take her from him. 'I'm sorry, sweetheart. Really.'

Lost for words, she put out her hands in a gesture of frustration. He didn't understand what she was saying. Worse, she realised, he would never understand.

When, a few moments later, he came with her to the kitchen, asking if he could help, she found him a task in the dining room. Out of her way.

<hr>

JOHN WAS DIFFERENT from what Eva had expected. Slimmer and younger than Frank, he had a bright smile and a charming manner that put her at ease straight away. Frank introduced them. 'Eva, this is John, my old friend from college.' When he said that, he gave John a crafty wink. 'John, this is my lovely wife, Eva.'

'She's certainly lovely.' He didn't extend his hand in a greeting. Instead, to Frank's dismay he leaned forward and placed a very polite kiss on Eva's cheek. 'It's a pleasure to meet you,' he said. 'Frank is a lucky man.'

Apart from Frank's little spans of silence, the

dinner was a success. The conversation was lively, and the food cooked to perfection. Eva served homemade potato soup, followed by thick, juicy slices from a succulent joint of gammon dressed with pineapple rings, accompanied by vegetables done lightly in minted water. Dessert was strawberries laid on a bed of choux pastry and topped with fresh cream, with coffee and brandy to follow.

'That was one of the best meals I have ever tasted,' John said appreciatively. 'To get a meal like that in London would cost a small fortune.' Beaming at Frank, he said, 'She's not only lovely, she's a real gem. You'd best hold on to her, Frank. There aren't many like her out there.'

Frank merely smiled, but underneath his smile he was fuming. He had made a bad mistake bringing the fellow here, and he was frantically thinking of how he might get rid of him. Eva too was annoying him. Instead of ignoring the man's absurd praise, she seemed to be enjoying his attention – flirting with him even!

The whole thing came to a head the following evening. After a day of cat and mouse during which he and John went down to the valley, John seemed to be showing more interest in Eva than he was in the deal he was here to secure. Eva was upstairs getting changed when Frank confronted John in the drawing room. 'I want you to leave.' Frank had come to the end of his tether.

John was astonished. 'What do you mean, you want me to leave? We haven't talked the deal through yet. I like the look of it, Frank. You were right in everything you said – executive houses should go a bomb in this location. Bulldoze the house, and you've a wide, attractive access in the making. But there's more to it than that. You can't expect me to commit good money without going into all the smaller details. You know how it works, Frank. I need to see papers, deeds, outline planning and that sort of thing. You have got them, haven't you?' He stared at Frank with suspicion. 'I hope you didn't bring me down here on a wild goose chase.'

'I've changed my mind. I'm not selling after all.'

'Bugger you, Frank, you can't do that!'

'I can do what the hell I like. Now get out. You're not welcome here.'

It occurred to John that the reason for this show of temper was nothing to do with the deal, and everything to do with Eva. 'I see. Afraid she might take a fancy to me, is that it?' He laughed, but the laugh caught in his throat when Frank took hold of him by his shirt collar. 'All right! All right!' Wriggling loose, he realised that Frank was not the amiable fellow he'd thought he was. In fact, the look on his face just now had been frightening. 'I'll go, but you've wasted my time, Frank. I won't forget that in a hurry.' As he spoke he walked to the door. 'I'll get my things.'

'No.' Afraid that he might speak to Eva, Frank brushed past him. '*I'll* get your things. You wait here.' Before John could protest, he was on his way up the stairs.

Eva heard him coming. One look at his face and she knew something was wrong. 'What's happened?'

'Nothing for you to worry about. Our guest is leaving, that's all.'

'But I thought we were all going into town this evening?'

'Well, now we're not, so you can take off your glad rags.' Eva had on a straight black dress with blue trimming, and blue shoes to match. Her hair was wound back, and she looked wonderful. It only served to antagonise Frank further.

As always, he hid his anger beneath a layer of charm. 'On second thoughts, stay as you are. You look lovely, sweetheart. We'll go out if you like, just the two of us. After I've got rid of him.'

<hr />

A T THE FRONT door, he warned John, 'Remember what I said. I'll ruin you if I hear you've breathed a word of this to anyone.'

'Don't worry, I won't.' Glancing over Frank's

shoulder, John was surprised and pleased to see Eva at the top of the stairs. He raised his voice slightly, just enough for her to hear. 'I wouldn't want anyone to know how you lured me here with the promise of a deal, and once I got interested you pulled the rug from under my feet.' He laughed cynically. 'I'd look a right bloody fool, wouldn't I?'

'You know your way, down the street and turn left at the bottom. Once you get into town, there'll be signs all the way.' Frank opened the door wide. 'Now, get out.'

John lingered. 'This is a lovely place, Frank.' He looked about the spacious hallway, with the beautiful panelling and high ceilings. 'In a way I'm glad we haven't gone through with the deal. I don't know if I could bring myself to bulldoze a grand old house like this. But then, it's a case of making money, isn't it, Frank? Nothing can be allowed to stand in the way of profit, isn't that right?'

As Frank bundled him out of the door, John glanced up to see Eva's face, white with shock. He smiled, and then he was gone.

A s FRANK PEERED through the window to make sure John was on his way, Eva ran back to the bedroom where she took a suitcase from the cupboard and began packing a few basic items. She wanted nothing more.

'What the devil do you think you're doing?' Frank stood in the doorway, blocking her path.

'I'm leaving you, Frank,' she said quietly. 'I should have done it long ago.'

'What's wrong? What's upset you, sweetheart?' His face was grim. 'Is it because he's gone, is that it? I saw the way you flirted behind my back. Shameful, the pair of you!'

Eva pushed past him. 'You're mad! You're also a born liar.' At the top of the landing, she spun round. 'He's not an old friend, is he?' When he opened his mouth she put her hand out to stop him speaking. 'No, Frank, don't make it worse. I heard you downstairs just now, and I know. You brought him here to do a deal. You had every intention of going ahead with your plans to sell the valley and raze this house to the ground. It doesn't matter what I want. It never has. What sort of a marriage is that?'

He took her by the shoulders, holding her so tightly she couldn't move. 'It's a *good* marriage and you know it. We can go abroad, make a new start, you and me, and the baby. I want to get you away from everything you knew before. Patsy's a bad influence on you. She's not the kind of woman I want you mixing with. Then there's the boy, Tommy. I don't want him here. I don't want *any* of them here. I don't want them to be any part of your life, or mine. A new life. New people. That's what we need.'

'No, Frank, what you need is to keep me all to yourself. Well, that's not possible. You can't cocoon me, as if I'm a specimen in a glass case. I'm alive, with feelings and needs, just like you. You go off to work, and I stay here. I'm entitled to some sort of a life, just like you are. As for Patsy, she's more of a friend to me than you will ever understand. I won't turn my back on her or Tommy just because you think I should.'

'You don't need them.'

'That's for me to say, Frank. What I *don't* need is you trying to mould me into something I can never be.'

'Oh, but you're wrong.'

Eva could never remember what happened after that. She vaguely recalled turning away; Frank called out; there was a sharp pain in the back of her neck, and the vision of a suitcase cartwheeling down the stairs. Then darkness closed in.

A T EIGHT O'CLOCK on Sunday morning, Bill and Sheila sat down to breakfast.

'I shouldn't be imposing on you like this,' Bill said. 'I'd be quite happy in a hotel until I find a house.'

'Don't be in such a rush to move out,' Sheila pleaded. 'If you mean to buy a house, it has to be the right one for you, and that takes time. And anyway, I love having you here, you know that.'

'I know, and I'm very grateful.' Bill glanced round the homely little kitchen, at the blue ging-ham cosy over the teapot, and the colourful little pictures of fat chefs, the hanging copper pans and wicker baskets. It felt so right. 'You have a lovely home, Sheila. No wonder you've never wanted to leave here.'

'It's taken me a long time to get it together,' she replied. 'But it's never really been a home. Not without children.'

Ever since he had turned up on her doorstep after finding his brother with Joan, she had wanted to tell him, 'You're not alone. I'm your mother, and you're always welcome here.' But common sense prevailed and the secret remained.

Bill had been concerned about her these past weeks. He was concerned now. 'You're looking pale,' he observed. 'Are you sure you're all right?'

'I've had a few bad days,' she admitted, 'but I'm fine now.'

'I can't have helped, bringing my troubles to your door like this.'

'You're like family to me,' she murmured. That was the closest she could come to telling him the truth. 'I'm glad you're here. Besides, it gets very lonely on your own.'

Getting up from the table he made a suggestion. 'Look, I've got an idea. Why don't you help me find a house? You don't have to stay here on your own. You could stay with me.'

She smiled, her heart leaping with joy. 'I see. You think I'm getting old and frail, do you?'

'Of course I don't. It's just that I don't like to think of you being lonely.'

'I know someone who's even lonelier.'

'Who?'

'You.'

'I can handle that.'

'Bill, why don't you find her?'

Turning, he gazed at her, his heart in his mouth. 'Eva, you mean?'

Sheila nodded.

He looked away, his mind going back to Eva. She filled his soul like a bright, burning light. 'What if I find she's happily married, with half a dozen kids? Maybe some things are best left as they are.'

Sheila knew he was saying one thing and meaning another. 'Life is so short,' she told him. 'Find her, Bill. Find her and be sure.'

Laughing, he kissed her on the cheek. 'Why would I want to find another girl when I've got one right here?' Funny, how he could laugh and joke when his heart was aching.

'I won't be here for the next few weeks,' she told him. 'I took your advice and went to see the doctor. He thinks I need a complete rest. So, if it's all right with you, I've decided to take a holiday.'

Immediately concerned, he said, 'I knew you were doing too much, but you wouldn't have it, would you? And of course you have to do as your doctor says. Have a long rest, and if you'll just tell me where you want to go, I'll have it all arranged for you.'

'Let me worry about that. I'm not senile yet, you know.'

Later, while Bill went out house hunting, Sheila read the letter she had received this morning once more:

I'm sorry to report that the woman you asked me to trace was killed in a traffic accident some twenty years ago; she and her adoptive parent.

I've enclosed the photograph and documents you sent me, together with a copy of the death certificate, and details of where she is buried in England.

I know this information is not what you

wanted to hear. I'm sorry I wasn't able to bring you better news . . .

The rest was irrelevant.

She looked at the photograph of two babies, a boy and a girl, and cried at her loss. 'I'm sorry,' she murmured. 'It's hard to know I'll never see you again. But I found your brother, and I thank God for that.'

———◆———

THE FOLLOWING MORNING, on Bill's strict in-structions, she stayed at home. 'I'll get a temp in,' he told her. 'You're not to worry about a thing.'

She allowed an hour for him to arrive and get settled into his work, and then she rang the office. 'I've booked a holiday,' she told him. 'A few weeks, and I'll be as good as new.'

Predictably, Bill wanted to know where she was going, and how he could keep in touch.

'It's a long leisurely cruise,' she told him, 'and I don't want anyone bothering me, not even you.'

'I see. Well, promise me you'll get in touch if you need anything – anything at all.'

'There's nothing I need,' she said, 'but if some-thing should turn up, I know where you are.'

'God bless then. Get lots of rest, and take care of yourself.'

'I will.'

With a deep sigh, she replaced the receiver, then picked it up again and made another call. 'I'd like to come in this morning, if that's all right?' she said to the person who answered.

A short time later she left, carrying only a small overnight bag. It was a long drive. When she got there, the doctor greeted her like an old friend.

'I'm ready,' Sheila told him. 'It's time to make my peace.'

# Chapter Seventeen

W HEN SHE CAME to, Eva found she couldn't
move.

At first she didn't understand, but then, as her
senses slowly returned, things became clearer. The
awful cold, and the penetrating damp. The unfa-
miliar gloom, infiltrated only by the daylight coming
through the grating above. In the shaft of light she
could see small black particles dancing and sparkling
like diamonds. With a feeling of horror she realised
where she was.

'God Almighty! Frank? Frank, where are you?'
She remembered the weekend visitor, the things he'd
said at the door, and afterwards, when she and Frank
had rowed at the top of the stairs. Frank had been
behind her – *behind her*. 'Oh, my God!' She hardly
dared think it. Had Frank pushed her down the
stairs? Why was she here? What was happening?

'Frank!' Feeling weak, she began to struggle, but
it was too painful. Ropes were bound, viciously tight,
about her wrists and ankles. With every movement
she made, they sliced into her flesh.

For a time she lay there, shivering from the cold, and hurting all over. Fear for the baby was paramount. 'Please, God, don't let any harm come to my baby,' she pleaded. At the back of her mind was the knowledge that Frank had been looking forward to the baby, just as she was. He would never hurt it. She kept telling herself that, over and over. 'Frank won't harm the child.'

But then she was filled with another dread – that he could be so eaten up with hatred and jealousy that he might think the baby would steal her affections.

The door swung open to admit a beam of torchlight. She knew it was him. Instinctively, she kept very still.

'It's no good pretending, sweetheart.' His voice increased her terror. 'I heard you calling my name, and here I am.' He gave a small laugh. 'I always try to please you.' Shoving some bread into her hands, he ordered, 'Eat up now. It'll make you strong.' When she didn't respond, he snatched the bread away and replaced it on the tray. 'There's water too. See how I look after you?'

'Let me out of here, Frank,' she pleaded. 'Think of the baby.'

His voice hardened. 'What baby?'

'*Our* baby, Frank, yours and mine.'

'Oh no, you can't fool me any more.'

'What do you mean?'

'You know very well what I mean. Whose baby

is it really?' In the half-light his face took on a sinister expression. 'You can tell me because it doesn't matter any more.'

Believing her only chance was to stay calm and appease him, she asked, 'Why doesn't it matter any more, Frank?'

He shifted closer, his breath on her face. 'Because the only thing that matters is that we'll be together now, you and me. What happens to the baby is no concern of mine.'

'Please, Frank. Let me out of here.' It took all her self-control not to scream for help. 'We can talk.'

'No!'

'Don't you trust me, Frank?'

He laughed. 'I don't trust myself.'

'How long do you mean to keep me here?'

'A week, a month – for as long as it takes.' Reaching out, he took hold of her cold hand. 'You've been here three days, and in all that time I had to keep you alive. You see, we never got to have our evening out, did we?' He smiled, a childlike smile that curdled her heart. 'It's all right now, though,' he murmured, 'because now you're awake, and I can start to make plans.' He sighed, a long, weary sigh. 'You look so lovely in that dress.'

'Which restaurant are we going to, Frank?' She had to humour him. It was her only chance.

'Why *here* of course.' He stretched his arms out to encompass the cellar.

'Don't you want to show me off, like you always do?'

He grabbed at her then, his face close to hers and his mouth actually touching her lips, in his excitement coating them with a film of spittle. 'You flirted! I saw you.'

There was no use denying it, he wouldn't believe her, and anyway it would antagonise him. 'I'm sorry, Frank. I didn't mean to.'

'You're mine,' he whispered. 'I don't want other men looking at you.' Now, as he took her two hands in his, he shivered. 'You're so cold.'

'Let me come upstairs, to sit in front of the fire.'

Like a scalded animal he fell back. 'You're trying to trick me.' He scurried to the door. 'Sleep now. We'll talk in the morning.' He went out and bolted the door behind him.

Eva thought he must have pressed his mouth close to the keyhole, because when he next spoke she could hear him clearly. 'Tomorrow I'll get everything ready for our special evening. It won't be long, sweetheart. Soon, we'll be together for all time, where no one can hurt us.'

<hr />

GROANING WITH EVERY step, Patsy hobbled into breakfast. 'Will ye look at me!' When Fred pulled out a chair for her, she fell into it. 'Four days into our holiday, and me ankle's up like a balloon.'

Fred tutted. 'Well, if you don't mind me saying so, me beauty, you did ask for it. I mean, a woman of your age, riding the bleedin' ghost train.'

'Morning all.' The stout landlady had taken a liking to this down-to-earth family. 'Let me see.' She went round the table with her pencil. 'Eggs, bacon and two sausages, smothered in fried tomatoes, for the gent, scrambled eggs on toast and a pint mug of tea for the lady, and everything that's going for the boy. Is that right?'

'No food for me,' Patsy groaned. 'Just a mug of tea, and an aspirin if you've got one. Sure, I've not had a wink of sleep all night with this bloody ankle.'

'Hmh! A cold compress, that's what you want.' The landlady prided herself on knowing all about these things. 'Right. Two breakfasts then, tea all round, and an aspirin for the lady.' Softly whistling, she ambled away to the kitchen.

'I'm sorry.' Sheepishly, Patsy looked from Fred to Tommy and back again. 'We'll have to cut short the holiday, so we will.'

Fred was understanding. 'Well, it'll save us a bob or two, that's for sure. And anyway, the forecast says rain all day today.' He winked at Patsy, and she knew he was only trying to make it easier for Tommy.

Tommy saw the wink. 'It's all right,' he said. 'If my ankle was up like a balloon, I'd want to go home an' all.'

Patsy hobbled round to give him a hug. 'Ah, you're a little angel, so ye are.'

'Will I have time to get Eva's present before we go?'

'We'll make time so we will!'

And Fred promised, 'Next year, we'll come to Blackpool for two whole weeks, if you like.'

'I've always fancied going to Rome,' Patsy announced, 'and having a ride in one of them gundolis.'

'Don't you mean Venice and gondolas?' Fred said.

'Well, whatever, just so long as I get a ride with one of them pretty men on the back singing me a love song.'

'You'll not catch me going near no water, I'll tell yer!' Returning with the tray, the landlady joined in the conversation. 'I've only ever been on a boat ride once, and it were nothin' but a disaster from start to finish. I lost me best shoe in the water, and when me late husband bent down to grab it, the boat capsized. I tell you, we were bloody lucky we didn't all get drowned. That's not all neither. They made us bloody *pay*! Can you imagine that? There we were, soaked to the skin and me with only one shoe, and the buggers made us pay!' Snorting with disgust, she went off tutting, leaving the three of them cracking up with laughter.

'I think I've gone off the idea of a gundoli ride,' Patsy chuckled, and that set them all off again.

———⋙⋅◈⋅⋘———

P ATSY AND HER little family were home by late afternoon. By the time they'd unpacked and had something to eat, it was going on for eight o'clock. 'Can I take Eva's present now?' Tommy was itching to go up to the big house. 'I can't wait to show her what I've got.'

'Well, you'll have to wait,' Patsy told him. 'Your dad's got to take the car to a mate of his. The damned thing's been playing up all day. And I need you to come with me to the doctor's, but we'll not be long.'

'Then can I go to Eva's?'

'Aye, when you've seen me safely home again. And only if you promise not to tell her I hurt me ankle riding the ghost train. She thinks I'm daft enough as it is.'

'And she's right.' Fred had done all he could to persuade her not to go on it, but when Patsy made up her mind, there was no stopping her.

———⋙⋅◈⋅⋘———

A T EIGHT THIRTY, Frank returned to the cellar for a third time. 'I'm sorry I had to gag you,' he apologised, 'but I couldn't have you shouting and carrying on, now could I? I even had to turn up the volume on the television in case anyone heard you. Whatever would they have thought?'

Quite casually, and with an air of disapproval, he went on to describe how he had seen Olive next door going out. 'With a gentleman, no less. Seems she's got herself a boyfriend while the mistress's back is turned.' He rolled his eyes. 'Love is a funny thing, don't you think, sweetheart? I mean, look at us. I know you could never love me, not the way I always hoped you might. Oh, I'm not blaming you, it's just one of those things. The way I see it, there are only two options. You either love me, or you leave me, and I really think you were on the point of leaving me. I couldn't allow that, now could I?' He scratched his head, as though thinking his way through a dilemma. 'It's better this way, don't you think, sweetheart? This way we'll always have each other.'

Dressed in full evening wear, he carried a bottle of wine and two glasses. 'Now, you see, I kept my promise, didn't I?' He left the wine and glasses just out of Eva's reach, before heading back through the doorway. 'I said we'd have our romantic evening, and we will.'

A few moments later he returned with a tray, beautifully set out with sausage rolls and dainty sandwiches. Round the edge of the tray were tiny iced biscuits. 'I'm not very good at this,' he apologised, setting the tray down. 'But this is all I could find. There was a lot of food left over from the other evening, but it was all covered in fungus. I didn't think you'd want that.'

Eva stared at him, unable to say a word. She felt desperately ill. Every bone in her body was screaming, and she was so cold she couldn't stop shaking. All her efforts to reason with him had failed, and so, too, had her plans to escape. The cellar walls were two feet thick, and the only likely escape routes were the door leading into the house, and the grating above the coal chute. Even if she hadn't been trussed up the way she was, escape was impossible. The grating was heavily padlocked, and the door leading into the house had a foot-long bolt on the other side. Eva was beginning to believe she might well die in this place.

Tucking a napkin under her chin, Frank said quietly, 'I'm going to undo your gag, so you can join me in our celebration dinner. If you scream out, I'll have to kill you here and now, and that would be such a shame, especially when I've gone to so much trouble for our special evening.'

Suddenly, he laughed. 'How thoughtless of me, sweetheart. I know how much you enjoy your music.' Kissing her lovingly, he departed through the door. 'I won't be long,' he promised.

Eva heard the music, soft at first, and then very loud. It was one of her favourite songs. While it played, she closed her eyes, feeling her senses slipping away.

'Oh no!' A sharp slap on her face brought her round. 'You can't sleep. Not now.' He took the gag from her face. 'Remember what I said. If you scream out, you'll leave me no choice but to kill you now.'

In his blind madness, he couldn't see that Eva was already dying, that she had no strength to scream, no strength even to plead with him any more.

With great tenderness, he removed the gag. Taking up a sausage roll between finger and thumb, he put it to her lips. When, nauseated, she managed to turn her head away, he tutted impatiently. 'All right, you may have a drink. But if you want to dance with me, you have to eat first.'

⤜●⤛

TOMMY CONTINUED TO bang on the door. 'Eva! It's me, Tommy!' he yelled over the music. 'Bleedin' Nora, what a racket! No wonder they can't hear me.'

Curious, he peered in through a window. All the lights were on but there was no one to be seen. 'Eva!' Clenching his fist, he banged hard on the window, but it was to no avail.

Never one to give up, he went round to the back. Here, he peered in through the drawing-room window. The curtains were open, but again, there was no one in sight. 'That's funny.' A cheeky grin crossed his face. 'Happen they're upstairs and don't want to be disturbed.'

He began to tiptoe away when he saw flickering light coming from the side of the house. 'Hello, what's that?'

Softly, he approached the grating.

Sure enough, there was a light of sorts down in the cellar. Getting down on his knees, he squinted through the grating, and what he saw made him reel with shock. Trussed up and white as a ghost, with her head lolling to one side, Eva was in Frank's arms, being dragged round the floor in a weird dance to the music. Lying on the ground was a torch which sent shadows flickering up the walls every time they swept past it. 'Gawd Almighty!' It was obvious to Tommy that Eva was unconscious, and in great danger.

'What have you done to her, you bastard!' Yelling through the grating, he screamed for Frank to let him in. But Frank didn't hear him. He was smiling with pleasure, engrossed in the dancing.

Scrambling to his feet, Tommy fled next door. Banging and shouting brought no one; no one was there. The same the other side. In the garden of that house was a bicycle. Tommy stole it and, as though his own life depended on it, he raced to the police station where he poured out his story.

The constable would have ignored him, thinking he was either crazy or a mischief-maker, except for one very important factor. The boy was in tears, sobbing so hard he could barely answer his questions.

The constable put out an alert. 'It's all right, lad, you stay here. We'll need to talk to you.'

In minutes, the cars were out and racing down the street, sirens full on. Only minutes behind, Tommy followed on the stolen bike, praying they would not be too late.

# PART FOUR

---

# AUGUST 1966
# THE
# RECKONING

# Chapter Eighteen

M ONDAY MORNINGS WERE always busiest in the
offices of Dollond and Travers, the old and
well-respected firm of Bedford solicitors.

The older partners had retired long ago, and a
new generation had taken over. Leonard Dollond
was the senior partner now. 'It never rains, but it
pours,' he said, drawing his secretary's attention to
the letter he had just read. 'Take a look at that.'

The meticulously dressed young lady scanned
the letter, a two-page account of what had taken
place right here in these offices many years ago.

'That's strange,' she looked up, 'it's almost iden-
tical to the one we received last week, all about the
tragic death of that couple, and about their daughter,
Eva Bereton, who was turned out of her home by her
uncle, Peter Westerfield.'

'My father had an idea that the girl might have
been the one who burned the cottage down. I was
a junior clerk here when it all happened, and I
remember he never voiced his suspicions to anyone
except me. His sympathies were always with the girl.

415

As far as I can recall, he didn't have one good word to say about her uncle.'

'If I remember rightly, the letter last week was from a Bill Westerfield.'

'Peter's adopted son. They never got on.'

'He was looking for Eva Bereton. And now this.'

'Did you discover her whereabouts?'

'A last known address, that's all. I'm afraid the trail runs cold after that.'

'Have you replied to Bill Westerfield?'

'Not yet. It's taken me a while to locate the information. It's on my list to reply to him this week. But it's not our policy to give out private information like that.'

Taking the letter from her, he said, 'What I suggest we do is this . . .' And he outlined what he saw as a satisfactory solution.

———◈———

Eva had been in hospital for two weeks. She had severe bruising and a gash to her wrist that needed several stitches. When they brought her in, she was emaciated and shockingly weak, and they had little hope for her full recovery.

Also, the knowledge that she had lost her child took away her reason for living, and for many anxious days she gave no visible signs of rallying.

Patsy stayed by her side day and night, with Tommy running errands and saying little prayers whenever he was allowed to sit beside her. 'Come on, gal,' he'd plead. 'We all love you, so don't leave us. Don't you dare leave us.'

And, in the end, she didn't.

———❦———

T ODAY, THE DOCTOR had given her the all-clear and Patsy had come to take her home. 'You've actually got some roses in your cheeks, so ye have.'

Eva smiled, a sad little smile that betrayed her sorrow at losing the baby. 'I'm really looking forward to coming home with you,' she said. 'Are you positive it's all right with Fred?'

'Ah, sure, he's the one who's insisting. If he had his way you'd stay with us till the cows came home, so ye would.' She watched Eva putting on her stockings. 'Let me help you, me darlin'.'

'I'm okay. I'm stronger than you think.'

'Eva?'

Eva looked up.

Patsy backed down. 'Nothing. I were just thinking.'

Eva smiled knowingly. 'If it's about Frank, I already know. He's been committed to a psychiatric hospital.'

'Who told you?'

'Inspector Marshal. He was here this morning.'

'And are you all right? I mean . . .'

'I know what you mean, Patsy, and you've no

need to worry. I'm fine. I can put it behind me.'
But not for a long time, she thought. It was too
horrendous to forget in a hurry.

⇒●⇐

IT WAS STRANGE living with Patsy's family, and
both comforting and disturbing to see Patsy growing larger with child by the day. Patsy had been
advised by the doctor to encourage Eva to talk
about all her troubles. And, after just a few days, it
seemed to be working really well. Not only was Eva
beginning to sleep well at night, she was smiling more
and taking a real interest in everything that went on
around her. Tommy played cards with her, and she
always lost. 'You're a cheat,' she complained, and he
laughingly admitted it.

On her first weekend home, Eva had a visitor.
'It's an old friend,' Patsy explained.

Eva's first thought was of Olive, who apparently
had been away staying with her new boyfriend but
was home now, having given him the push. 'He's got
some very nasty habits,' she told Eva in a letter, and
it was plain to see the relationship would not last
much longer.

All day Patsy had been hopping about with
excitement, and now, when the doorbell rang, she
ushered Tommy and Fred out of the room. 'We're
off to the pub for a pint,' she told Eva. 'You'll be all
right with your friend till we get back, so ye will.'

As she answered the door, she instructed Tommy and Fred just to say hello and then to be on their way, and that was what they did, Fred with a wink and a nod and the advice, 'Go easy on her, mate. She's been to hell and back.'

Looking lean and fit in dark trousers and a pale blue shirt open at the neck, Bill promised he would take good care of her. Addressing Patsy, he asked, 'Does she know it's me who's come to see her?'

Patsy shook her head. 'I haven't told her. To be honest, when I wrote to the solicitors I never thought anything would come of it, but then when I heard from you, I knew it was meant to be.'

He looked down the passage. 'I think it's time I said hello, don't you?'

'Go on then, and God go with ye.'

With a pounding heart, he went inside and softly closed the door. As he went on hesitant footsteps towards the sitting room, he was actually trembling. He had waited so long for this moment and now that it was here, he felt desperately afraid.

Eva was in the kitchen putting the kettle on when he came into the room. 'I won't be a minute, Olive,' she called out. 'I'm just making us a pot of tea.'

The sound of her voice was like heaven to him. For one precious moment he stood quite still, eyes closed, thanking the good Lord for bringing them together again.

'Sit yourself down,' Eva was saying.

Quietly now, he went to the kitchen door, and there he stood, unobserved, watching her as she busied herself making the tea. She still looked the same, he thought wonderingly; somewhat thinner, but that was understandable after what she'd been through, but still incredibly lovely, with the same long, corn-coloured hair. As she swung round to stare at him, he saw those wonderful wide green eyes and his heart turned over.

'Hello, my love.' The tears welled in his eyes and he could hardly see her. The fear rose again. Would she want him? Would she turn away? Dear God, don't let her turn away.

Eva felt as though she'd seen a ghost. She wanted to go to him, but she couldn't. It was as if a great hand was holding her back. As she stared at him, she shook her head from side to side, the tears rolling down her face. 'Bill, oh . . . it really is you,' and in that wonderful moment he took her in his arms.

'I've loved you for so long,' he whispered, and her joy was like a great tide, washing away all the pain of those long years.

With his arms round her, she felt safe. For the first time since they had parted a lifetime ago, she felt as though, at last, she had come home.

# Chapter Nineteen

THREE MONTHS LATER, after much legal hassle, during which they justifiably secured their freedom from their respective partners, Eva and Bill were married. It was a quiet affair, in a small, local church, and attended only by Patsy's family, Olive, and Maggie.

It was a beautiful late-October day, with the sun shining, and only a light breeze blowing. Eva looked lovely in a pastel-blue two-piece. Patsy was wearing a cream dress with bolero jacket, Fred was choking in the high-necked shirt Patsy had made him wear, and Tommy looked very grown-up in his new suit.

Bill was just Bill, standing beside the woman he loved, feeling as though his every dream had come true. He could think of nothing he had wanted more in the whole of his life than this day – himself and Eva being married. God had been good to him. Eva felt the same, and even now Bill hardly dared believe it.

Eva had wanted a small, intimate reception,

and everyone had a wonderful time – except Fred who copped it in the neck from Patsy for drinking too much.

Afterwards, they said their goodbyes. 'Mind you write now, and phone me the minute you get there.' Patsy had cried all morning, but now she was full of smiles. 'Ah, sure, you'll have a wonderful life, me darlin',' she said brokenly. 'And I'm that happy for ye, so I am.'

They hugged, and for a precious moment or two, Eva and Patsy stood aside. 'I'll never forget what you did for me,' Eva told her. 'I do love you, Patsy.'

They cried, and held each other, and Eva told her she would never be far away. 'Go on with ye now,' Patsy shoved her into Bill's waiting arms, 'before you have me blubbering all over again.'

As they drove away, Eva waved out of the window. In her heart she would always carry the picture of them standing there. Patsy dabbing her face with a handkerchief; Fred looking emotional and shuffling his feet from side to side; and Tommy, that scruffy little Tommy, now tall and fine, and every inch a man in the making. She loved them all.

As she looked, Bill reached out to hold her hand. 'They'll be all right,' he promised. 'We'll look after them, my love.' And she knew he would.

'How long will it take us to get to the airport?'

'We're making a detour.'

'Oh? Where are we going?'

'You'll see. But it's a long drive, so maybe you should get some sleep.'

She looked at him, at this man who was her husband, and her heart swelled with love. Just now, when she asked where they were going, she was certain he had a quiet, secretive smile on his handsome face. 'Are you up to something?' she asked laughingly.

'I might be.'

'But you won't tell me, will you?'

'Nope.'

'I might as well get some sleep then.'

He gave her a sideways grin. 'Good idea.'

---

THEY STOPPED ON the way for refreshments and to stretch their legs. In the cafe, they sat hand in hand.

'I bet they've just got married,' said one waitress to another.

'How can you tell?'

'Don't be daft, anyone can see that,' she replied. 'I mean, they've let their teas go cold for a start!'

Eva was asleep when they got to their destination. When Bill woke her, she looked out and her heart leaped. 'It's the old farm!' she cried, scrambling out of the car. 'Oh, Bill! You didn't forget, after all.' She had mentioned to him that she would like to see the old place and visit her parents one last time before leaving the country, and here they were.

They stood for a moment, surveying the magnificent landscape. 'I've kept something to show you,' Bill said and, reaching into his wallet, took out the photograph of her mother. 'I found this on the floor of the cottage, many years ago.' He put it in her hand.

Eva caressed the photograph, and wept. 'It was me who burned the cottage down,' she confessed.

'I know.'

'What else do you know?'

'Only that I love you.'

On tiptoe she kissed him.

The sight of what remained of the house, slowly being reclaimed by nature, brought more tears. Walking to where the old range used to be, she tenderly laid her mother's charred photograph on the place. 'It belongs here,' she said, covering it over. 'She loved this place. I don't need my mother's picture to remember her. I'll always have her here.' She pointed to her heart. Then she wiped her tears and suggested brightly, 'Let's go and see the barn.'

Astonishingly, though sagging dangerously, the old barn still stood. They went inside.

'The farm is yours now, Eva. Father went broke

last year, and everything went to auction. I bought this for you, to do with as you like.'

Eva was thrilled. She went outside to look across the meadows; all around, the hills seemed to embrace and protect them. 'Let it stay just like it is now,' she said. 'Let no one ever touch it.' And so it was decided.

———➤◆◄———

HAVING BEEN TOLD by Sheila that she was going on holiday, Bill became concerned when she didn't get in touch. He found her, too late, in the hospital, where he learned to his horror that she did not have long to live. Shocked and saddened, he wanted to take her home and be with her, but she dissuaded him. Sheila had so much to confess, and what she revealed was bitter-sweet to him.

She told him he was her son, and that when his father was killed she was forced to give him and his sister up. It was a terrible thing for her to have lived with all these years . . . being so close to him yet not daring to tell him in case he turned her away. Now though, at long last, she knew how much he loved her, and her joy was complete.

Sheila died a contented soul, her hand clasped in that of her son, and her eyes shining with a mother's love.

Bill had been broken-hearted, but he consoled himself with the knowledge that at least he had known the truth, and been able to reassure her. It gave him great comfort.

Frank was never released from hospital.

Poorer but wiser, Peter Westerfield and his son returned to England. Bill's mother went with them. 'It's where I belong,' she said, but Bill kept a close eye on her all the same.

Eva and Bill made their home in the Rockies. Wherever they went in the world, they always came home to Whistler.

They lived a long and happy life, and were blessed with three children, two sons who made them proud, but first a delightful daughter who fell in love with Tommy. Despite the difference in their ages they made a perfect couple and gave Eva and Bill four beautiful grandchildren.

Patsy lost her baby, due to 'trauma and age', the doctor said. Patsy told him he was talking out of his arse. 'I'm still a young woman!' and he knew better than to argue. In truth, Patsy had always believed she was too far past her prime to be a mother. She had never learned to be patient, and a baby would have tried her to the limit.

But she enjoyed being a grandmother, and spoiled the children rotten. 'Sure, you're the apple of yer granny's eye,' she used to say, and they loved her dearly, just as they loved Eva, the quieter one; the one who told them of their great-grandmother, Colette, and of their colourful history.

Eva's wishes for the old farm were written into that history. As it passed down through the generations to follow, it was known as 'Eva's Meadow'.

Through all the years to follow, Eva Bereton was never forgotten.

Headline hopes you have enjoyed reading LOVE ME OR LEAVE ME and invites you to sample the beginning of Josephine Cox's compelling new saga, TOMORROW THE WORLD, out soon in Headline hardback . . .

# Chapter One

'Are you afraid of me?'

'Never!'

'Then trust me?'

A charming, confident fellow, Peter Doyle had the mistaken idea that every woman in the world fancied him. 'The snow's coming down heavy,' he told Bridget. 'You'll never get through on foot.' He'd had his eye on Bridget ever since she came to work at Weatherfield Grange. 'I insist on taking you home.'

'No, thank you, sir.' Wise beyond her years, Bridget always felt nervous in his presence.

'You *are* afraid of me!' His smile was wonderful, but he had a certain naughty gleam in his eye, and – judging from the way he moved his hand inside his trousers – a rising bulge that would not be contained. But then, she always did that to him and, besides, it was a long time since his wife had shown him any favours. Consequently, a man had to get his pleasures wherever he could.

As a rule he had no difficulty in persuading even the shyest of creatures into his bed. But Bridget

Mulligan was not like the others; at only twenty years of age, she was delightfully fresh and different. It was no wonder he wanted her but, as yet, he had not managed to worm his way into her affections . . . or her bed, more was the pity! Still, he promised himself slyly, there was time enough yet. And he was known to be a patient man.

'It's very kind of you, sir,' Bridget answered. 'But I don't need to put you to any trouble, because my father's collecting me any minute now.'

'Really, my dear?' Suspicious, he scrutinised her pretty features. 'I wasn't aware of that. When did you manage to get word to him?'

'It's a standing arrangement.' When needs must, Bridget lied beautifully. 'Dad's always told me that if it snows, like today, I'm to wait for him at the gate . . . and I must not accept a ride home from anyone else.' She blushed deepest pink, her face shining like a beacon, hot and aflame. 'So, I'd best be on my way . . . thanks all the same, sir.'

'Your father's right, my dear,' he grudgingly conceded. 'Not to accept a ride from anyone . . . yes, quite right!' Secretly, he thought it was downright wicked . . . especially when he could have been giving her the best 'ride' of her life.

'I'm sorry, sir. You don't mind, do you?' She was suitably apologetic, but, seeing how frustrated he was, Bridget felt the urge to giggle.

'Of course I don't mind!' Damn her eyes! he

cursed, and damn her father with her! For what seemed an age he stared at her; the smile frozen to his face like a mask, and his trousers straining to burst right open.

When she nervously returned his smile, he gave a shrug, a little laugh, then turned abruptly and was out of the room before she realised. 'Good shuts!' she giggled, relieved that he'd given up. 'Randy old bugger, I know what you're after, but you can whistle in the wind till kingdom come, for all you'll get from me.'

She was still smiling as she fought her way down the back path to the servants' gate. Once outside, though, she was shocked to see how the weather had deteriorated since midday. Now, at half past six of an evening, the wind was sharp and bitter-cold. The snow fell out of the skies with a vengeance, settling soft and thick on the ground.

Wild and spiteful, the night air cut through her clothes, like a knife through butter. 'By! It's bloody freezing!' Drawing her coat tighter about her, she glanced back to the house; warm and cosy, the lights blazed a path through the night. 'Happen I should have let him take me home after all.' Thinking of his disappointed face made her smile. In truth, she would rather run naked in a storm than let a man like Peter Doyle have his way.

Coming to the gate in a hurry, she lost her footing and slid over. 'Damn and bugger it!' Now she was wet to the bone, her boots letting the snow in, and her hooded-coat no match for the driving cold. And, to make matters worse, as she tried to struggle up she realised with a sinking heart that she had turned her ankle.

Taking stock of her situation, she realised she had two options. She could either bear the discomfort of her ankle and press ahead, or she could try and get back to the house.

A pleasant thought struck her.

If she was to go back to the house, *Harry* might be there. But, no, she remembered . . . Harry wasn't back from Manchester yet. She knew that, because she'd been watching for him all day. It was strange how she missed him whenever he was away.

Feeling ashamed, she chastised herself. 'Bridget Mulligan, shame on you! Here you are . . . thinking pleasant things of Harry, and you a married woman these past four months.' She had no right even *looking* at another man, let alone missing him. Not when she had a loving husband like Tom.

'Aw, well!' Brushing herself off, she sighed, 'I'm not going back to the house, not with the squire after me at every turn, and I don't mean to sit here and freeze to death.' Foolish though she knew it was, her mind was made up. 'There's nothing else for it,' she reluctantly decided, 'I'll have to go on.'

As she struggled on, Bridget was afraid she might fall down some deep ditch and be lost for ever. With the landmarks rapidly disappearing beneath a mountain of snow, it was becoming increasingly difficult to keep to the lane. 'The squire was right after all,' she groaned, her teeth chattering uncontrollably. 'Though I would never give him the satisfaction of telling him so.'

With the wind howling and the snow lashing down, Bridget didn't hear the cart coming up behind her.

'Woa, boy!' Catching sight of the small, forlorn figure in front, Harry Little drew back on the reins. 'Easy there . . . woa!'

A strong young man in his early twenties, Harry had no trouble bringing the horse to a halt. Dropping the reins, he leaped from the cart and hurried forward. By the time he reached her, Bridget had turned to face him, curious to see who it was that had drawn up behind her.

'Bridget!' Harry was astonished. 'What the devil are you doing out in this weather?' He was angry, but that was nothing new. Bridget had a way of making him angry; mostly because she was married to someone else.

Relieved, and utterly exhausted, Bridget fell into his arms. 'Harry! Oh, Harry, you don't know how glad I am to see you.'

'Don't you worry, sweetheart,' he told her. 'I'll get you home.'

'I know you will.' Harry had a habit of calling her sweetheart. Tom never did, and that was a shame because when Harry called her sweetheart it made her feel warm all over. But then, Harry and Tom were like chalk and cheese. Harry was twenty-two, and Tom was only four years older, but there was a world of difference between them. Harry was full of life, always smiling and happy, while Tom took life too seriously, rarely smiling, and always looking for the next problem.

Conversely, the thought of Tom was strangely reassuring. Bridget did love him, she told herself. In fact, she told herself that time and again, as though wanting to believe it. Somehow it helped her through the long, lonely days.

# Cradle of Thorns

## Josephine Cox

Nell Reece has never known her mother and her father's burden of guilt about his wife has kept him cowed for years, working as a common labourer on his sister's farm. For all her aunt's spiteful attempts to break Nell's independent spirit, she has never succeeded. But now Nell, pregnant and alone, is forced to leave behind the men in her life, believing she might never be able to return.

With little but the clothes she wears and a tatty horse and cart, she travels across the Bedfordshire countryside of 1890; a journey fraught with hazards for a vulnerable young woman. When she encounters a scruffy urchin called Kit, a ten-year-old orphan who's lived his whole life on the street, she takes him under her wing. The pair become devoted friends, never knowing where their journey will take them, but each aware that the time will come when there must be a reckoning.

'A born storyteller' *Bedfordshire Times*

'Hailed quite rightly as a gifted writer in the tradition of Catherine Cookson' *Manchester Evening News*

'Pulls at the heartstrings' *Today*

'Driven and passionate, she stirs a pot spiced with incest, wife-beating . . . and murder' *The Sunday Times*

0 7472 4957 1

**HEADLINE**

# The Devil You Know

## Josephine Cox

Sonny Fareham's lover – and also her boss – is the charismatic Tony Bridgeman, a successful and ruthless man who usually gets what he wants. But for Sonny, the affair that has promised a future of hope and happiness must end in desperate fear. Late one evening, Sonny overhears a private conversation between Tony Bridgeman and his wife. Only then does she realise she is in great danger.

Confiding in the two women she can trust, Sonny must leave home to make a new life elsewhere. Shocked and afraid, she flees to the north of England where she meets a gregarious and motherly new friend, Ellie Kenny. When the mysterious and handsome David Langham seems drawn to her, she almost dares to believe that she could be happy again. But never far away is the one person who wants to destroy everything that she now holds dear . . .

'Pulls at the heartstrings' *Today*

'Hailed quite rightly as a gifted writer in the tradition of Catherine Cookson' *Manchester Evening News*

'Driven and passionate, she stirs a pot spiced with incest, wife beating . . . and murder' *The Sunday Times*

0 7472 4940 7

**HEADLINE**

## If you enjoyed this book here is a selection of other bestselling titles from Headline

| | | | |
|---|---|---|---|
| LIVERPOOL LAMPLIGHT | Lyn Andrews | £5.99 | ☐ |
| A MERSEY DUET | Anne Baker | £5.99 | ☐ |
| THE SATURDAY GIRL | Tessa Barclay | £5.99 | ☐ |
| DOWN MILLDYKE WAY | Harry Bowling | £5.99 | ☐ |
| PORTHELLIS | Gloria Cook | £5.99 | ☐ |
| A TIME FOR US | Josephine Cox | £5.99 | ☐ |
| YESTERDAY'S FRIENDS | Pamela Evans | £5.99 | ☐ |
| RETURN TO MOONDANCE | Anne Goring | £5.99 | ☐ |
| SWEET ROSIE O'GRADY | Joan Jonker | £5.99 | ☐ |
| THE SILENT WAR | Victor Pemberton | £5.99 | ☐ |
| KITTY RAINBOW | Wendy Robertson | £5.99 | ☐ |
| ELLIE OF ELMLEIGH SQUARE | Dee Williams | £5.99 | ☐ |

Headline books are available at your local bookshop or newsagent. Alternatively, books can be ordered direct from the publisher. Just tick the titles you want and fill in the form below. Prices and availability subject to change without notice.

Buy four books from the selection above and get free postage and packaging and delivery within 48 hours. Just send a cheque or postal order made payable to Bookpoint Ltd to the value of the total cover price of the four books. Alternatively, if you wish to buy fewer than four books the following postage and packaging applies:

UK and BFPO £4.30 for one book; £6.30 for two books; £8.30 for three books.

Overseas and Eire: £4.80 for one book; £7.10 for 2 or 3 books (surface mail)

Please enclose a cheque or postal order made payable to *Bookpoint Limited*, and send to: Headline Publishing Ltd, 39 Milton Park, Abingdon, OXON OX14 4TD, UK.
Email Address: orders@bookpoint.co.uk

If you would prefer to pay by credit card, our call team would be delighted to take your order by telephone. Our direct line 01235 400 414 (lines open 9.00 am–6.00 pm Monday to Saturday 24 hour message answering service). Alternatively you can send a fax on 01235 400 454.

Name .........................................................................................

Address .....................................................................................

..................................................................................................

..................................................................................................

If you would prefer to pay by credit card, please complete:
Please debit my Visa/Access/Diner's Card/American Express (delete as applicable) card number:

| | | | | | | | | | | | | | | | | | | |
|---|---|---|---|---|---|---|---|---|---|---|---|---|---|---|---|---|---|---|
| | | | | | | | | | | | | | | | | | | |

Signature ........................................... Expiry Date..............